LEFT TO

EDWARD PRIME-STEVENSON

LEFT TO THEMSELVES

BEING

THE ORDEAL OF PHILIP AND GERALD

Edited with a new introduction and notes by
ERIC L. TRIBUNELLA

VALANCOURT BOOKS

CONTENTS

FOREWORD

This edition makes Edward Irenæus Prime-Stevenson's *Left to Themselves* widely available for the first time in over one hundred years. According to WorldCat, there are currently only eight known library copies: five in the United Kingdom and three in the United States. This edition by Valancourt Books changes that. Stevenson's 1891 text is historically significant as one of the first children's books described by its author as homosexual; Stevenson is also credited with writing the first avowedly gay American novel for adults, *Imre* (1906). *Left to Themselves* is an American boys' adventure story set in the northeast of the United States, and its main characters, two male youths, enjoy a passionate friendship as they evade a mysterious villain. It should be of interest to readers of both contemporary and historical gay fiction; to fans of nineteenth-century classics like *Ragged Dick* by Horatio Alger, whose influence is reflected in Stevenson's works for children; and to scholars and students of children's literature, gay studies, and the history of gender and sexuality. Important to literary history, Stevenson's novel provides an earnest depiction of boyhood, romance, sport, mystery, and danger. My hope is that this edition contributes to the efforts of Noel I. Garde, James Gifford, and others to reignite interest in Stevenson and his body of work.

INTRODUCTION

Edward Irenæus Prime-Stevenson and *Left to Themselves*

James Gifford describes Edward Irenæus Prime-Stevenson (1858-1942) as "the first modern American gay author" ("Stevenson" 686), and both Noel I. Garde and Byrne Fone credit him with having written the first openly gay American novel (Garde, "First" 185; Fone 194). *Imre*, published in 1906, offers an explicit representation of avowed love between homosexual men and ends happily with the two as companions, seven years before E. M. Forster would begin writing *Maurice*, which ends similarly. Stevenson, now mostly forgotten, broke other literary ground as well. Fifteen years before publishing *Imre*, an adult work, he released a children's novel titled *Left to Themselves: Being the Ordeal of Philip and Gerald* (1891), which depicts the passionate friendship between two male youths and actually concludes with a description of their lifelong companionship, as *Imre* later does. Remarkably, Stevenson identifies his writing for children as "homosexual in essence" and *Left to Themselves* in particular as a depiction of "Uranian adolescence" (*Intersexes* 368; see also Gifford, "Left to Themselves" 113).[1] The term "uranian" was a nineteenth-century word for "homosexual" derived from the writings of German homosexual rights pioneer Karl Heinrich Ulrichs,[2] so *Left to Themselves* could be described as quite possibly the first avowedly "gay" American children's book.[3]

Born in Madison, New Jersey, in 1858, Stevenson was one of seven children and the youngest of five to survive to adulthood (Livesey 92). His father, Paul Stevenson, was a Presbyterian minister and school principal who died when Edward was twelve. His mother, Cornelia Prime, came from a literary family and taught at the Mt. Pleasant Female Seminary before her marriage. She was 52 when Edward was born (Garde, "Mysterious" 94). Stevenson studied but never practiced law and instead wrote for magazines, including *Harper's Weekly* and *The Independent* in New York. Much of his journalistic writing focused on music, and he published and later lectured on opera and classical composers (Gifford, "Introduction" 22-23). Little is known about his personal life, though *Left to Themselves* is dedicated to Harry Harkness Flagler, the only son of the Florida railroad magnate Henry Flagler.[4] Gifford explains that the two men were romantically linked, but their relationship became estranged in 1893 (Gifford, "Introduction" 27) and ended with Flagler's marriage in 1894 (Gifford, *Dayneford's Library* 83). Some elements from *Left to Themselves*, such as the distant relationship between Gerald and his father, may have been inspired by Flagler.

During the 1880s and 1890s, Stevenson lived in New Jersey and New York and began publishing fiction and poetry in various periodicals, including stories for children that were published in magazines such as *Harper's Young People, Christian Union*, and *St. Nicholas*. He published these works as Edward Irenæus Stevenson or E. I. Stevenson, adding his mother's maiden name to his own only later. He published his first books during this time: *White Cockades* (1887) and *Left to Themselves* (1891)—both for children—and *Janus* (1889), a short novel for adults later reprinted as *A Matter of Temperament*. His mother died in 1896, and Gifford speculates that Stevenson may have come into an inheritance that allowed him to travel extensively ("Introduction," 23).

After the turn of the century, Stevenson eventually relocated to Europe, which was thought more permissive of homosexuality than the United States. He spent time in a number of countries, including Italy and Switzerland, and became familiar with the work of the major sexologists and homophile writers of the day.[5] He continued to write music criticism, poetry, and fiction, though he is perhaps best known now for *Imre*, which he privately published in Italy under the penname Xavier Mayne. Two years later, Stevenson released *The Intersexes: A History of Similisexualism as a Problem in Social Life* (1908), described by Byrne Fone as the first American work of nonfiction in support of homosexuality (196).[6] Among his better known works are a collection of short stories, *Her Enemy, Some Friends—And Other Personages*, published in 1913, and a collection titled *Long-Haired Iopas: Old Chapters from Twenty-Five Years of Music Criticism* published in 1927. Stevenson died in Switzerland in 1942.

In *The Intersexes*, Stevenson defines a uranian as "a human being that is more or less perfectly, even distinctively, masculine in physique; often a virile type of fine intellectual, moral, or aesthetic sensibilities; but who, through an inborn or later-developed preference feels sexual passion for the male human species" (72). Later in the same work he comments on the possibility of homosexual children's literature and offers as an example of "uranian" books for children his own *White Cockades* (1887), about a romantic friendship between Prince Charles Edward Stuart and a devoted Scottish youth named Andrew, and *Left to Themselves*, which he calls even more distinguishably homosexual. Stevenson describes *Left to Themselves* as "a romantic story in which a youth in his latter teens is irresistibly attracted to a much younger lad, and becomes, *con amore* responsible for the latter's personal safety, in a series of events that throw them together—for life" (368). Although only 125 copies of *The Intersexes* were printed, at least some of his contemporaries would have been aware of the homosexual content of *Left to Themselves* as a result of Stevenson's later writings.[7] A great many additional readers may have intuited or discerned the special nature of the relationship between Philip and Gerald, as Stevenson himself suggests in the preface to the novel.

Stevenson borrowed several elements from his 1884 short story for children "A Question of Taste" for use in *Left to Themselves*, such as character and place names and the focus on boyhood friendship. Like the later novel, "A Question of Taste" features two boys who experience various adventures, including false criminal accusations, while traveling from an Upstate New York resort called the Ossokosee House to New York City, just as Philip and Gerald do. The 1891 edition of *Left to Themselves*, subtitled *Being the Ordeal of Philip and Gerald*, was published in New York by Hunt & Eaton and in Cincinnati by Cranston & Stowe. The 1893 edition was published in London by Hodder & Stoughton with the title *Philip and Gerald: Left to Themselves*. It added four illustrations by Osman Thomas, a popular book illustrator. *Left to Themselves* has since been out of print.

Most scholarly treatments of Stevenson make brief references to his two children's books, though only Gifford provides any sustained attention to *Left to Themselves* and *White Cockades* in a short article describing them. Nevertheless, Stevenson's *Left to Themselves* offers a vitally important contribution to literary and cultural discourses on childhood and sexuality and deserves more attention. Reading Stevenson's boy books shows how same-sex love was represented to children at the end of the nineteenth century, just as homosexual identity itself was crystallizing and receiving more acknowledgment in Euro-American culture. As Matthew Jerald Livesey explains, Stevenson is important for what his work can tell us abut how turn-of-the-century homosexuals understood themselves and their experiences (76). Ultimately, what may be most indicative of the novel's status as homosexual children's literature is not its surface-level homoeroticism, which is common in nineteenth-century boys' fiction, but the ways Stevenson encodes a homosexual ethos. In *Left to Themselves*, Stevenson signifies homosexuality and the dynamics of the closet through the depiction of blackmail, secrecy, and self-disclosure, and he promotes same-sex love through the conflict between the shamelessly amorous boys and their mysterious antagonist, who is also marked as homosexual.

Boys Books and the Queer Tradition in Children's Literature

In its representation of same-sex desire, *Left to Themselves* anticipates gay children's literature of the twentieth century. Standard histories of homosexuality in children's and young adult literature understandably trace its emergence to the Stonewall era of the late 1960s. Kenneth Kidd, one of the first literary scholars to address gay children's literature critically, writes in 1998 that "explicitly themed works have appeared only in the last several decades" (114). Critics frequently cite

John Donovan's *I'll Get There. It Better Be Worth the Trip.* (1969) as the first gay American novel for children or young adults (Jenkins 180, Trites 144, Mallan 188).[8] Though *I'll Get There* includes a brief sexual relationship between two teenage boys, Davy and Altschuler, Davy ultimately rejects his feelings after being caught with Altschuler and blames the tragic death of his beloved dog on his experimentation with homosexuality. More sympathetic portrayals of gay children or adolescents who avoid tragic fates remain rare until the 1980s and 1990s, with the publication of works such as Nancy Garden's *Annie on My Mind* (1982), Francesca Lia Block's *Weetzie Bat* (1989) and *Baby Be-Bop* (1995), and the collection of stories *Am I Blue?: Coming Out of the Silence* (1994), edited by Marion Dane Bauer.

To be sure, many *homosocial* works for children, including those depicting passionate same-sex relationships, long preceded Donovan's novel. Kidd notes that "many classics of Anglo-American children's literature are fundamentally homosocial, or concerned with same-sex friendships and family bonds. In retrospect, some of these classics seem decidedly queer" (114). He cites as an example Kenneth Grahame's *The Wind in the Willows* (1908), which involves the rather moving and perhaps surprisingly intimate relationship between Mole and Rat.[9] Fifty years earlier, classic boys' school stories represented intimate friendships between boys and even alluded to homosexuality. A number of scholars such as Isabel Quigley, Beverly Lyon Clark, and Claudia Nelson have commented on the homoeroticism of boys' schools stories more generally, including those like Howard Sturgis's *Tim* (1891) and H.A. Vachell's *The Hill* (1905), in which romantic same-sex friendships are the central focus.[10] Nelson also observes that nineteenth-century boys' adventure stories similarly contain homosocial and what she calls homoemotional relationships (120), and the traces of such can be seen in boy Robinsonades such as R.M. Ballantyne's *The Coral Island* (1857), which depicts the idyllic life of three boy castaways who "embrace each other indiscriminately" and utter "incoherent rhapsodies" when reunited, just before the coy adult narrator "draw[s] a curtain" over their intimacies (214). Michael Moon persuasively argues that the boys' books of Horatio Alger, whom Gifford describes as inspiring Stevenson, reformulates "domestic fiction as a particular brand of male homoerotic romance" (88).[11]

Stevenson's life as an expatriate in Europe may explain the fact that *Left to Themselves* reflects qualities of both British and American boys' fiction, while departing from each of these national traditions. In Britain, one of the most prominent strands of nineteenth-century children's literature for boys was the school story, like those noted above. Popularized by Thomas Hughes's *Tom Brown's Schooldays* (1857) and Talbot Baines Reed's *The Fifth Form at St. Dominic's* (serialized 1881, published as a single volume in 1887), the school story was typically set in a boarding school and focused on close friendships between boys. Many of the British school stories with more overtly homosexual content, like James Welldon's *Gerald Eversley's Friendship* (1895) and A. W. Clarke's *Jaspar Tristram* (1899), are far more tortured and sentimental than Stevenson's distinctly optimistic boys' adventure. *Left to Themselves* includes the element of romantic friendship and begins in the relative isolation of a resort, like the similarly self-contained boarding school, but the scope of Stevenson's novel in terms of geography and adventure is greater than that typically found in school stories. The other most popular genre of the British boy book was the imperial adventure tale, such as the popular works of G. A. Henty, who published his first boys' novel, *Out on the Pampas; or, The Young Settlers*, in 1870. These works usually featured stories of survival or exploration in faraway lands.[12]

American boys' fiction differed in several respects from its British counterparts. In the United States, where boarding schools occupied a less prominent place in the popular imagination, school stories never overcame their "relative invisibility" (Clark 13).[13] Boys traveled overseas less frequently in American adventure stories, though *Left to Themselves* incorporates a shipwreck and castaway sub-plot reminiscent of British adventures. The most distinctly American type of boys' fiction was the "bad boy" book, a genre fully initiated by Thomas Bailey Aldrich's *The Story of a Bad Boy* in 1869.[14] Though Twain's *Adventures of Huckleberry Finn* took its protagonist on a geographically sprawling adventure, most bad boys remained firmly rooted in their neighborhoods. Philip and Gerald are too good to be considered bad boys, and their adventures move far beyond the boundaries of a neighborhood or town. However, the boys' sports story, such as Oliver Optic's *The Boat Club* (1854), was popular in the United States, and Stevenson features a rowing competition involving Philip early in the novel before they depart for Nova Scotia. Stevenson's work is most similar to that of Horatio Alger, which sometimes remained set exclusively in New York City, as in the Ragged Dick series, but sometimes took boy characters on faraway adventures involving war, kidnapping, or other capers. In Alger's *Ragged Dick* (1867), an older boy cares emotionally and physically for a younger one, much like in the later *Left to Themselves*. Of course, Alger is most associated with his tales of upward mobility, and Stevenson's orphaned Philip does rise from hotel laborer to law student, in part through the eventual patronage of Gerald's father.

Clearly, a tradition of homoeroticism and homosociality in boys' fiction predates Stevenson, and this tradition made it possible for some nineteenth-century readers to remain unaware of the homosexual dimension and content of *Left to Themselves*, as we can see in contemporary publication announcements and reviews. However, Stevenson's novel differs from other boy books, both British and American, in important ways. In most cases, the boy protagonist who becomes passionately attached to another boy must give up his childhood friend to relocate or marry, as Tom does with Arthur in Hughes's novel. In other cases, the boys are separated by death, as happens to the characters in the school stories written by Farrar, Sturgis, and Vachell. None of the authors of the works cited above claimed them as "homosexual" or "uranian," and none publicly described his having intentionally written homosexual literature for children, as Stevenson does. Kidd notes the distinction between such works and later gay writing: *"The Wind in the Willows* is not by any stretch of the imagination about the gay male subject" even if "homosocial texts are not that far removed from contemporary lesbian / gay literature" (114). While seventeen-year-old Philip and twelve-year-old Gerald do not identify themselves as homosexuals, Stevenson nonetheless understands them as such and says so publicly. *Left to Themselves* might not be an "explicitly gay" children's novel or one about the modern "gay male subject" the way Donovan's *I'll Get There* is, but neither is it merely a standard homosocial or homoerotic work. In Stevenson, homoeroticism or homoaffectionalism are not simply the accidental literary effects of the broader cultural prevalence of homosocial institutions and social practices, including the nineteenth-century permissibility of passionate same-sex friendship. Rather, he builds on this earlier tradition and begins to move toward and anticipate the self-consciously LGBT fiction of the twentieth and twenty-first centuries, bridging the two. Stevenson notes that "[f]iction for young people that has uranian hints naturally is thought the last sort circulating among British boys and girls" (*Intersexes* 366). He offers his own boys' books as defying that expectation and filling a gap in the available literature. Thus, *Left to Themselves* represents one of the earliest contributions to the tradition of homosexual or gay children's literature.

Boyhood Sexuality and *Left to Themselves* as a Gay Children's Novel

Because *Imre* is even more explicit in its depiction of same-sex desire than is *Left to Themselves*, it points to ways in which Stevenson more subtly alludes to same-sex desire in his book for boys. For instance, the language of "human nature" provides one of the key frameworks for referencing homosexuality in the two texts. Stevenson was familiar with the work of nineteenth-century sexologists, whose writings frequently theorized same-sex desire in terms of "human nature."[15] In *Imre*, Oswald indicates his knowledge of sexology and articulates his feelings for the younger soldier and his sense of difference from other men by referring repeatedly to his having a different nature. In the critical scene in which Oswald reveals his true feelings for Imre, he expresses his need to show him "[s]ides of my nature unknown to others" (80). He continues, "From the time when I was a lad, Imre, a little child, I felt myself unlike other boys

in one element of my nature. That one matter was my special sense, my passion, for the beauty, the dignity, the charm,
the—what shall I say?—the loveableness of my own sex" (82).
He describes the close friendships of his youth with boys who
failed to care for him the way he cared for them: "These incidents made me, too, shyer and shyer of showing how my whole
young nature, soul and body together, Imre, could be stirred
with a veritable adoration for some boy-friend that I elected,
an adoration with a physical yearning in it" (83). In the absence
of a widely accepted vocabulary or understanding of same-sex
desire, Oswald explains himself in terms of his different nature.

Stevenson further acknowledges childhood sexuality by
devoting a chapter of *The Intersexes* to describing the possibility of inborn homosexuality in youth. He collects case histories of men recalling boyhood instances of same-sex love (152)
and writes that a "boy or girl assumes 'the mask' with curious
precocity" (153). In his preface to *Left to Themselves*, Stevenson
similarly points to the possibility of such boy readers, ones who
may want to read books depicting same-sex desire, using the
language of human nature: "But there is always a large element
of the young reading public to whom character in fiction, and
a definite idea of human nature through fiction, and the impression of downright personality through fiction, are the main
interests—perhaps unconsciously—and work a charm and influence good or bad in a very high degree" (3). Stevenson acknowledges that even children possess complex internal lives
and "finer and more perceptive natures" than many typically
assume. Moreover, they do not always share these feelings with
adults, and they do not always recognize or understand their
own feelings, sentiments that might resonate with homosexual or potentially homosexual youth: "Jack feels more than he
says from the personal contact, feels more, may be [*sic*], than
he knows; and Jill is surely apt to be as sensitive as Jack." Here
Stevenson alludes to the child who "feels" before he "knows,"
which surely describes the experience of many gay- and
lesbian-identified men and women who recall feeling different
as children before identifying the meaning of those feelings.
This notion of feeling without knowing also acknowledges

child readers who may have appreciated Stevenson's writings
without recognizing why. Ultimately, the preface is subtler than
the novel itself, and Stevenson notably addresses it "solely for
the benefit of the adult reader." While the boy yearning for "the
personality in narrative" might be eager to read about the romantic relationship between Philip and Gerald, Stevenson is a
bit more circumspect in addressing parents and schoolteachers.

Left to Themselves opens with the young Gerald Saxton, the
son of a wealthy businessman and widower, left alone at a
resort in Upstate New York while his father travels with friends
to fish in Nova Scotia. When Gerald is attacked in the woods
by a tramp who wants to steal Gerald's watch, the orphaned
Philip, a ward of the hotel proprietor, Mr. Marcy, leaps to his defense and chases off the vagrant. The boys immediately strike
up an intimate friendship, and when Gerald's father writes for
his son to join him in Canada and charges Mr. Marcy with finding a chaperone, the attentive Marcy senses the boys' desire
for each other and allows Philip to accompany Gerald. *Left to
Themselves* is a fairly conventional boys' adventure novel in the
tradition of Alger, and so the two boys experience a number of
extraordinary events and obstacles as they travel by train and
ship to be united with Gerald's father: an overnight stay in New
York City, a shipwreck and brief time as island castaways, false
criminal accusations, and several unbelievable coincidences
linking virtually every character in the novel. The central antagonist is a mysterious and predatory man who inexplicably
pursues the boys and appears and disappears at various points
along their route. Eventually identified as a man named Winthrop Jennison, he presents himself as having a different name
each time he confronts them, and he tries to blackmail Philip
into turning the younger Gerald over to him. Thus, he tests the
honesty and commitment of the boys, and his criminality and
secrecy provide a contrast to the purity and openness of the
boys' relationship. Eventually, the novel's mysteries are solved
and Philip and Gerald remain companions for the rest of their
lives.

Left to Themselves makes numerous references to the desire
of one boy for the other, and Stevenson writes in *The Intersexes*

that when desire "springs up in us, stirred to life by a quickening sense of physical beauty in the object of our interest, then there cannot be logical [sic] question of our sentiment being mere strong friendship" (24). Stevenson describes Gerald as observing his new friend "furtively" and noticing that he possesses a "broad, well-developed chest, active legs, and a good straight way of carrying himself" (10). Gerald possesses a "curious hold" over Philip (25), and Gerald's eyes sparkle "like stars" when he looks upon the older boy (29). The boys become immediately inseparable, even sleeping in the same room, Gerald "with one hand under his yellow head and the other just touching Philip's arm" (33). Others around the boys notice the peculiarity of their "friendship": Mr. Marcy comments to Philip that "the boy seems already oddly fond of you" (34). Philip, once entrusted with Gerald's care, decides that the latter's welfare will always be his "North Star" (48). Sometimes Philip looks upon the younger boy while he sleeps: "He did not know it, but such moments when he, as it were, struck a balance between Gerald and himself, and appreciated how Gerald depended upon him for society and care, were already moments that converted the manly metal in Philip into finest steel to cleave and endure" (96). Thus, looking at the vulnerable boy with love matures and masculinizes Philip, and since desire for and care of a beloved can betoken mature manhood for male youths, this scene is suggestive of Philip's love for Gerald. Descriptions like these occur throughout the text.

Stevenson often expresses same-sex desire in the language of friendship. Initially, the boys fail to understand their relationship:

> Why each of these lads, so entirely out of his own free will, should have mutually confided details of their two histories, when each was so much a stranger, met to-day, and perhaps never sitting again within speaking distance after tomorrow, was a riddle to both of them. But the solution of it is as old as the rocks in Wooden's Ravine, perhaps older. We may keep our lives and thoughts under a lock and key as tightly as we like until the day comes when, somewhere

> along this crowded highway called Life, we all at once run
> square against some other human creature who is made by
> fate to be our best friend. (13)

We cannot assume that the use of the term "friend" here means
that Philip and Gerald's relationship is a common or platonic
one. During a key scene in *Imre*, Oswald reveals that one of his
earliest realizations of his homosexuality came when he made
friends with "a lad a year older than myself, of striking beauty of
physique and uncommon strength of character" (83). Oswald's
recollection of his first love echoes Stevenson's description of
Philip in *Left to Themselves*. Oswald describes this friendship as
characterized by a "vehement *passion* [italics in original] (I can
call it nothing else) on both sides" (83). This "intensely ardent
regard" is reciprocated by his friend, who dies after an illness. As
an adult, Oswald continues to seek the "passion of friendship"
that characterizes what he calls the "Over-Friendship, the Love-
Friendship of Hellas, which meant that between man and man
could exist the sexual-psychic love" (84). Near the conclusion
of the novel when Oswald and Imre finally commit to being together, Oswald still voices his romantic love in terms of friendship: "Imre, I will never go away from thee. Thy people shall
be mine. Thy King shall be mine. Thy country shall be mine,
thy city mine! My feet are fixed! We belong together. We have
found what we had despaired of finding, 'the friendship which
is love, the love which is friendship'" (126). Even 15 years after
the publication of *Left to Themselves* and in an adult novel, Stevenson employs the language of friendship to articulate same-
sex romantic and sexual love.

Historian Jonathan Katz notes that in the absence of a
vocabulary for describing a same-sex lover or beloved, the language of friendship was one of the only options during the
late nineteenth century: "Walt Whitman's unpublished notes
on language, written between the early 1850s and the early
1860s, reveal his profound, persistent concern about the lack
of words to express men's deep feelings for men." Katz continues, "The words Whitman did use—'friends' and 'friendship,'
'friendly sentiments' and 'passionate fondness'—were, for

him, inadequate to express the intense emotions and relations they named" (*Love Stories* 95). In Forster's *Maurice* (1971), which shares much with *Left to Themselves*, Maurice also uses the term "friend" to express his desires, saying to Scudder, "Did you ever dream you'd a friend, Alec? Nothing else but just 'my friend,' he trying to help you and you him. A friend,' he repeated, sentimental suddenly. 'Someone to last your whole life and you his' " (197). *Left to Themselves* employs this language of friendship to convey the passion of Philip and Gerald's relationship.

Another element that places this work in a different category from other homoerotic boy books of the nineteenth and early twentieth centuries, apart from its author's identification of it as homosexual, is its ending. At one point in the story, Philip and Gerald are taken in by an older husband and wife, the Probascos, who comment on the boys' friendship and their future together. Mr. Probasco tells them that he hopes they will have "a long life together," and he observes that they have "begun to make friendship the way it'd ought to be made, an' as it's grown older it'd ought to be of a kind that aint common in this part o' the world" (107). Philip responds that he hopes so as well, and the narrator continues, "Yes, and he believed it. His 'old head on young shoulders' for one moment pictured in flashing succession years to come at Gerald's side, himself his best friend ever, to companion and care for him" (107). At the conclusion of the novel the reader is permitted to glimpse their future. Both Gerald and Philip attend Columbia College in New York, with Philip's waiting back a couple of years so his time there overlaps with the younger boy's, and they remain devoted to each other for life. While the language of friendship is most often used to describe their relationship throughout the novel, it turns to that of love at the end, with the narrator's declaring "how good are friendship and love and loyal service between man and man in this rugged world of ours; and how probable it is that such things here have not their ending, since they have not their perfecting here, perfect as friendship and service sometimes seem" (161). If Philip and Gerald's relationship remains to be perfected and they already possess friendship, then that perfection must be realized in something else: the romantic, the sexual. The

narrator leaves us with the image of Philip and Gerald's "walking forward, calmly and joyfully, and in an unlessened affection
and clearly mutual understanding—into their endless lives"
(161). In *The Intersexes*, Stevenson clarifies the distinction between friendship "as that feeling is commonly understood" and
love, explaining that the latter includes the desire for physical
and psychical possession (22). The lifelong companionship of
the two boys suggests this element of mutual possession and
hence romantic love, and Stevenson's refusal to give the boys
a tragic fate or separate them from each other precedes by
almost a century the gay-affirmative children's literature of the
1980s and '90s.[16]

As I have argued elsewhere, forms and representations of
child sexuality, or the proto-erotics of youth, will often look
quite different from those of adult sexuality, and the language
of adult sexuality can prove inadequate for understanding childhood desire, pleasure, and relations, which must be understood
on their own terms (Tribunella, *Melancholia* 32-33). For instance,
genital contact and explicitly amorous language may figure less
prominently for children as expressions of desire or pleasure,
and the frameworks used to understand adult dynamics, such
as the continuum between platonic and sexual relationships,
can obscure the meaning or significance of childhood experiences. Philip and Gerald do not engage in genital sexual activity or refer to themselves as lovers, though that does not mean
their relationship can be dismissed as a conventional boyhood
friendship. As we have seen, Stevenson describes the intensity
of their attachment and longing in emotional and sometimes
physical terms, and thus as erotic, and in the sections that follow, I show how *Left to Themselves* further differs from the children's literature of romantic friendship in the ways it encodes
the inchoate dynamics of the homosexual closet still under
construction at the end of the nineteenth century.

Blackmail and the Homosexual Ethos of *Left to Themselves*

Though *Left to Themselves* appears qualitatively different from
other homoerotic boys' books of the nineteenth century in

the ways I have already described, it shares with other works of "gay" Victorian literature techniques for encoding homosexuality in covert ways. Eve Sedgwick's enormously influential *Between Men: English Literature and Male Homosocial Desire* offers ways of understanding Stevenson's depiction of homosexuality. Sedgwick examines a continuum of male homosocial desire, from men promoting the interests of men to men loving men, that underlies and structures patriarchal societies and institutions. One of Sedgwick's key points is that given the significance of male homosocial desire as a force or glue maintaining patriarchal social structures, "any ideological purchase on the male homosocial spectrum—a (perhaps necessarily arbitrary) set of discriminations for defining, controlling, and manipulating these male bonds—will be a disproportionately powerful instrument of social control" (*Between Men* 86). The control or manipulation of male bonds provides a useful access point or mechanism for power, and the terroristic unpredictability of homophobic threats functions as a way to manipulate the entire range of homosocial bonds, not just those between the boys or men who identify as homosexual or belong to a distinct homosexual subculture: "Not only must homosexual men be unable to ascertain whether they are to be the objects of 'random' homophobic violence, but no man must be able to ascertain that he is not (that his bonds are not) homosexual. In this way, a relatively small exertion of physical or legal compulsion potentially rules great reaches of behavior and filiation" (Sedgwick, *Between Men* 86). That all homosocial bonds "can look, with only a slight shift of optic, quite startlingly 'homosexual,'" creates the possibility for what Sedgwick calls the "blackmailability" of men and maleness through homophobia.

This discussion is relevant to *Left to Themselves* because the central plot, the pursuit of the boys by the mysterious Mr. Jennison, centers on his repeated attempts to blackmail Philip. Since Philip has committed no crime, Jennison's threats remain empty and inexplicable. He nonetheless uses blackmail as his chief device for tormenting the boys and attempting to kidnap Gerald; except for his final gambit, he never tries simply to steal Gerald away by physically overpowering or harming Philip.

Moreover, Jennison had gone missing before reappearing to stalk the boys after being involved in an attempt to blackmail "two old ladies" by putting "a family secret into all the newspapers" (117). The futility and peculiarity of blackmail as a strategy for kidnapping Gerald, the eroticism of the boys' relationship, the suggestively predatory nature of Jennison's pursuit of the boys, and the inconsistent motive for Jennison's wanting Gerald at all, point to blackmail as a motif for coding homosexual desire in the novel.

In *The Intersexes*, Stevenson decries the scourge of blackmail as a product of legal and moral injunctions against homosexuality: "Blackmailer!—the blackmailed!—tyrant and writhing victim! In all sorts of relations where human rashness, passion, folly, weakness, carelessness, sordid mercenariness or vengeance attack the individual, we meet this dark process. But nowhere else does blackmail operate with such terrible alertness as in the uranian world" (455). Out of all the crimes associated with homosexuality at the turn of the century, including prostitution, it is blackmail that possesses "all-important bearings on the social and legal status of the uranian intersex in so many contemporary civilizations" (455).[17] Stevenson presents numerous cases of homosexual men from Europe and the United States being blackmailed by prostitutes, lovers, or acquaintances, and he describes it as a source of constant fear for many homosexuals. His emphatic denunciation of blackmail suggests his keen awareness of its unfortunate prominence in homosexual life, and the attention Stevenson gives to it in his study supports the reading of Jennison's attempted blackmail of Philip as further hinting at the coded homosexuality of his children's novel.

Stevenson cites Oscar Wilde as a notable victim of blackmail (*The Intersexes* 481). Only four years after the publication of *Left to Themselves* blackmail would play a pivotal role in the Wilde trials, in which Wilde would testify about efforts to extort both Lord Alfred Douglas and himself over indiscreet letters Wilde had written Douglas. Indeed, Lord Queensberry's accusations that Wilde was sexually involved with several young men and Wilde's subsequent conviction for acts of "gross indecency" placed true and false accusations, acts of blackmail and claims of innocence, and the defense of same-sex love at the center of a public spectacle, which did as much as any scientific or psychological writing to intensify public visibility of and discourse on homosexuality. According to Alan Sinfield, "the dominant, twentieth-century queer identity" was constructed "out of elements that came together in the Wilde trials" (12). With blackmail so key to the trials, the association between homosexuality and blackmail would be solidified in the public mind.

However, that association long preceded Wilde. As Netta Murray Goldsmith explains, the crime of blackmail flourished from the eighteenth century on, just as homosexuality became more visible and more criminalized (21). Prior to the eighteenth century, "blackmail" referred to the "protection money exacted by raiders from farmers and others living in the Border country" (97). Goldsmith describes how in the 1770s and 1780s the judiciary expressed a growing awareness of the "mental agony endured by a man faced with the threat of being falsely proclaimed a homosexual" (99). According to Angus McLaren, "Sexual blackmail was first and foremost a symptom of heightened concern with stigmatized homosexual acts," and blackmail as we now understand it was first criminalized in the eighteenth century, he notes, to protect men from false charges of sodomy (11). In fact, McLaren cites Stevenson's *The Intersexes* for its discussion of the pervasive problem of homosexual blackmail. McLaren claims that "few writers of fiction could have been ignorant of homosexual blackmail" (18). References are made to the crime of sexual blackmail in Robert Louis Stevenson's *Strange Case of Dr Jekyll and Mr Hyde* (1886), Wilde's *The Picture of Dorian Gray* (1891), and E. M. Forster's *Maurice*. According to Laurence Senelick, "The infamous §175 of the imperial code in Germany (1871) and the Labouchère amendment in England (1885) [both further criminalizing homosexual relations] became known as blackmailers' charters and incidentally helped to define the popular notion of homosexuality" (206). Senelick finds the association between homosexuality and blackmail also prominent in turn-of-the-century theater: "So when homosexuality, as the fin-de-siècle defined it, does make its stage debut, it is hedged round with melodramatic devices and closely associated with blackmail" (204). It would have been difficult for informed nineteenth-century readers, even in the United States, not to read scenes of blackmail as invoking hints of sodomy or homosexuality.[18]

The blackmail plot emerges during the boys' second encounter with Jennison, while journeying by ship from New York City to Halifax. At this point, Philip already realizes that Jennison is following them, but he is unsure as to his motives. Philip wants to conceal their danger from Gerald so as not to alarm him, and thus he conspires to confront Jennison without the younger boy present. While Gerald sleeps in the boys' cabin, Philip searches the ship for Jennison, who demands they meet in private. The boy attempts to rebuff him, but Jennison insists on talking with Philip and threatens to go to the boys' room where Gerald can witness their discussion. This threat succeeds in eliciting Philip's consent to meet, and Jennison subsequently reveals, in the manner of pulp fiction villains, his entire plan, which involves taking possession of Gerald. He demands that Philip simply give up the boy and threatens to tell the Captain that Gerald is somehow related to him and that Philip is the boy's kidnapper (56). Philip recalls that the Captain had requested earlier to meet with him, and now he thinks that Jennison has already met the Captain, told his lie, and cast suspicion on the boy.

This accusation of kidnapping is only one component of the blackmail, and Jennison's knowledge of the criminal past of Philip's father threatens the exposure of Philip's own potentially criminal nature. In a convoluted sub-plot, we learn that Philip's father was accused of a crime, convicted, spent time in prison, and later died. His shamed family name haunts Philip, but he remains convinced of his father's innocence. For reasons that I will leave the reader to discover, Jennison possesses special knowledge of Philip's father's crime. This adds force to his blackmail of the youth, since he implies that he will re-expose Philip to public shame and that Philip's criminality will be confirmed by his father's criminal history, as though his father's presumed guilt might somehow predispose his son to crime.[19]

In McLaren's history of sexual blackmail, he observes that often it is the person making the accusation who is assumed to be the true homosexual, thus suggesting that it is Jennison himself who is marked as a potentially homosexual adult. McLaren explains that "the criminalization of blackmail was first used to deal with the specter of well-off men being plundered by so-called perverts, of the mysterious metropolis witnessing the unnatural mix of the rough and the respectable, and of the ruthless miscreants driving members of the social elite to murder or suicide" (11). Stevenson himself confirms this in *The Intersexes*: "No female blackmailer, however audacious and cruel, ever has shown herself quite so torturing in shattering nerves, happiness, fortune, courage, social quietude, and life as has the methodical, homosexual blackmailing demon proved himself, time and again, the world around" (457). Again, *Left to Themselves* anticipates these pronouncements in Stevenson's later work.

While Philip, in his forthright love for Gerald, remains noble, Jennison's pursuit and blackmail of the boy casts him as sexually predatory. The narrator introduces Jennison as "a strikingly handsome and well-dressed man of about forty years of age," and he successfully misrepresents himself to the boys as Mr. Hilliard, the bachelor friend of Mr. Marcy, with whom they are meant to stay in New York (34). Thus, he proves to be both physically and socially charming, implying his seductive and threatening sexuality. After the boys are accidentally separated from Jennison and arrive at the home of the real Hilliard, their genuine host observes keenly what the imposter likely intended, explaining to Philip, " 'He could have taken you to his quarters. . . . There he would have given you, probably, a better supper than I have, added a dose to insure your sleeping, robbed you, and found means to get rid of you, very likely without injuring you, before morning.' (Mr. Hilliard did not choose to suggest any other notion than that 'very likely without injuring you;' but he had others.)" (48). Hilliard must remain circumspect lest he reveal too much about his own insider knowledge, so while his implication is not explicitly sexual, it is suggestive. Moreover, Philip himself suspects that Jennison pursues them not for "mere robbery, but for some sinister end" (52). When Jennison actually reveals his plot to Philip, he tells him simply, "First of all, that boy has got to come at once into my hands. . . . I mean to have him, henceforth and forever, if I can!" (56). If he means to ransom Gerald, as Mr. Saxton later speculates, he would not have him "forever." The Probascos note that Jennison is unmarried and "his life an' his business seem to be matters that honest folks needn't inquire into too closely" (114). This presumably refers to his criminal activities, but the language also implies personal and therefore sexual matters as well. At the conclusion of the novel when Philip meets him a final time, he says to the youth for no particular reason, "Nice youngster that Master Saxton is! Not extraordinary that strangers should take a fancy to him, eh? Pretty boy!" (153). The cumulative impression created of Jennison is that he is a sexually deviant, maybe even pedophilic, bachelor whose mysterious designs on Gerald cannot be explained fully by the plot.

Coding the Closet in *Left to Themselves*

If Jennison's attempted crime is vaguely sexual, he is also depicted as mysterious and duplicitous, and hence shamefully closeted, in contrast to the boys and their openly romantic friendship. The novel thus gestures to and thematizes the dynamics of the closet while endorsing the value of willing self-disclosure. In *Epistemology of the Closet*, Sedgwick addresses the significance of "the closet" as a means of figuring sexuality, and homosexuality in particular:

> I want to argue that a lot of the energy of attention and demarcation that has swirled around issues of homosexuality since the end of the nineteenth century, in Europe and the United States, has been impelled by the distinctively indicative relation of homosexuality to wider mappings of secrecy and disclosure, and of the private and the public, that were and are critically problematical for the gender, sexual, and economic structures of the heterosexist culture at large, mappings whose enabling but dangerous incoher-

ence has become oppressively, durably condensed in certain figures of homosexuality. "The closet" and "coming out" ... have been the gravest and most magnetic of those figures. (71)

The motif of the closet seems especially relevant to understanding *Left to Themselves* for several reasons: Stevenson's explicitness—his literary outness—in identifying this as uranian children's literature is one feature that distinguishes *Left to Themselves* and *Imre* as milestones in gay literature, Stevenson's comments in the Preface imagine a boy reader who may or may not be "out" to himself about why he wants to read about certain kinds of characters, and Stevenson's depiction of the antagonism between avowedly romantic boy friends on the one hand and the mysterious and suspicious Jennison on the other mirrors the opposition between being out and being closeted.[20] Stevenson casts the character whose manners and actions are most suggestive of closetedness as the villain, while the boys whose affections for each other are openly displayed are the heroes. In fact, Philip's ability to triumph over Jennison by resisting the latter's efforts to blackmail him involves precisely his willingness to tell all.

Each time Philip is threatened by Jennison he refuses to submit to blackmail, which thematizes an ethos of "outness," even if the identity Philip maintains is that of an honest youth rather than that of a homosexual. Stevenson codes a kind of proto-gay pride in Philip's absolute assertion of innocence, virtue, and frankness. When Jennison threatens Philip the first time, the youth ultimately replies, "I challenge you or anyone else! Say what you like, do what you like, you have no business with Gerald Saxton" (56). This struggle continues for some time, until Philip again asserts his innocence: "And you believe you can fight the plain story that Gerald and I can tell? Do your worst! I'm not afraid to face it" (58). Jennison finally offers to compensate Philip somehow for turning Gerald over to him, and this compels Philip to demand a public hearing:

"No," he replied, determinedly, "you haven't right on your

side! You are trying to frighten me! Call up the whole ship! I
dare you to bring things to the point. I don't know," he continued, raising his head and looking up at [Jennison], "how
well you may have planned to get me in trouble; but I know
myself and Gerald, and I can soon prove all that I shall say.
Get the captain—any body [sic]! I'll answer all questions
people may ask." (59)

In the final confrontation between the two, Philip again chal-
lenges Jennison to make his charges public so that Philip's
honesty and true identity can be professed before witnesses
(140). Asserting that he is indeed the boy who survived the
shipwreck means claiming his full name and thus his father's
criminal reputation. Philip willingly does this in the name of
honesty and in the service of his role as Gerald's companion
and protector.

While Philip's refusal to submit to blackmail does not imply
that he literally identifies as a homosexual youth, it does gesture to an ethos of willing disclosure. In *The Intersexes*, Stevenson argues that the best way to respond to blackmail is to
confront it directly, encouraging homosexuals to take a "heroic
stand" (461) and to "face down the blackmailer with rudest or
calmest contempt and with counter-threats and action" (480).
Stevenson seeks to alleviate the concerns of potential victims
regarding self-incrimination when the blackmailer threatens to
expose the truth that the victim is homosexual. He writes, "If
the person necessarily incriminating himself in the complaint
against his blackmailer, when arrested and on trial on homosexual charges, can prove medically, psychichiatrically [sic], that
he is homosexual by inborn, ineradicable nature, then his case
is often materially made light or even dismissed" (482). Eve
Sedgwick also associates immunity to blackmail with being
out. She identifies those men who "are no longer susceptible to
homosexual panic" and thus to homosexual blackmail as "the
historically small group of consciously and self-acceptingly homosexual men" (*Epistemology* 186). Thus, Stevenson's depiction
of Philip predicts his later advice to homosexual men regarding blackmail, and he associates the youthful protagonist of his

boy book with the brave homosexual of his treatise. Philip's apparent immunity to blackmail further identifies him with "self-acceptingly" gay men.

The repeated references to the mystery and secrecy surrounding Jennison are further suggestive of the closet and are another way the novel codes homosexual concerns. First, Jennison assumes no fewer than three identities over the course of the novel, and we learn that he has used at least two additional aliases in his past. Philip repeatedly observes that Jennison leads a "double life," saying at one point to one of Jennison's acquaintances, Mr. Banger, "That man has been a forger and blackmailer. He leads a regular double life that you don't know any thing about. . . . I don't deny he is Mr. Jennison, but he is a bad man—he is half-a-dozen bad men, besides. He keeps his mask on for you as for the most [*sic*] of the world" (142). Stevenson also refers to the significance of masks to homosexuals in *The Intersexes*: "Ever the mask, the shuddering concealment, the anguish of hidden passion that burns his life away!" (86). He continues, "The Mask, ever the Mask! It becomes like the natural face of the wearer" (87). For Stevenson, the homosexual's having to conceal his desire for men damages him, as Jennison appears damaged by his habitual dishonesty. Mr. Banger begins to see Jennison anew, and when Jennison laughs "a loud, coarse laugh," Banger is "struck by its peculiarity, the curious hint in it of another man beneath this one" (144). When Jennison is finally exposed, it oddly comes almost as a relief to him: "His look, as much as his odd words . . . showed that he knew thoroughly that the 'double life' and the relics of such local respect as was left in this place, near the house of his ancestors, were forever shattered" (145). He then simply withdraws his accusations against Philip, confirms that Philip was telling the truth all along, wishes everyone present a good morning, and turns "with his easiest manner, to the officers in plain clothes" (145). Philip essentially outs him for what others like the Probascos and Jennison's lawyer already vaguely suspect, thus invoking the dynamics of the closet—secrecy and disclosure, the maintenance of open secrets—which Sedgwick argues are inseparable from homosexual definition. The outing of Jennison seems to benefit him, so this entire plot suggests the liberatory potential of disclosure for homosexual men.

The honesty and forthrightness of the boys contrast with Jennison's duplicity and mystery and attest to the novel's ethos of disclosure. The text repeatedly insists on the boys' public transparency and willingness "to tell." Only a few days after Philip and Gerald meet, Gerald overhears several guests of the hotel beginning to discuss the alleged crimes of the older boy's father. Gerald wants to rush away to avoid learning something Philip would not want him to, but Philip stumbles upon the scene and makes Gerald listen. Gerald is shocked that Philip insists on his staying to hear, but Philip explains, "Yes, I made you listen! I wanted you to know the story before you saw any more of me. . . . I wanted you to hear what you did. . . . I don't care for mere outsiders, who know it already and think none the worse of me for it. But other people, if I care any thing about them, why, they must know with whom they are taking up" (20). The first time Jennison attempts to blackmail Philip aboard the ship, he again exhibits this willingness to disclose all, insisting on getting the captain as an audience (56). Moreover, that everyone who witnesses the relationship between Philip and Gerald immediately observes their feelings for and devotion to one another pits their unashamed romantic friendship against the secretiveness of the man who pursues them.

These characterizations create two distinct homosexual types, a strategy Stevenson repeats in *Imre* to show that, like heterosexuals, homosexuals can be both virtuous and villainous. In *Imre*, one of the key ways Oswald understands and defends himself is by a series of contrasts between "virile" and "masculine" homosexuals like himself and the "patently depraved, noxious, flaccid, gross, womanish beings" who are "perverted and imperfect in moral nature and in even their bodily tissues!" (86). Oswald goes on to provide two contrasting lists of historical figures of each type, with men such as Socrates, Alexander the Great, Byron, and Whitman representing noble homosexuals, and men like the Marquis de Sade and Gilles de Rais, a fifteenth-century French general accused of murdering hundreds of boys, representing "the cynical debauchers of little boys"

and "pederastic perverters of clean-minded lads in their teens"
(87). As he explains in *The Intersexes*, the "better" uranians are
"Averse to Boyish Pederasty [*sic*]" (432). Stevenson first employs
this move, so central to Oswald's homosexual apology in *Imre*
and his own in *The Intersexes*, in his depiction of the antagonism
between Philip, a "clean-minded lad," and Jennison, a "pederastic" debaucher, indicating that *Left to Themselves* provided a pro-
totype for his later writings. In this key way, Stevenson's children's novel paves the way for one of the first openly gay adult
novels and nonfiction defenses of homosexuality in American
letters.

Conclusion: The Possibilities of Gay Children's Literature

By trafficking in familiar tropes of homosocial and homoerotic
boyhood friendships, *Left to Themselves* appears to be indistin-
guishable from many other nineteenth-century boys' books
while nonetheless anticipating the more explicitly gay literature
of the twentieth century. In its obsessive concern with mystery
and revelation, with intimate same-sex bonds and vaguely pedophilic predation, the novel clearly signals its concerns with
homosexuality while remaining, paradoxically, ambiguous.
Thus, what makes *Left to Themselves* a gay or proto-gay novel
are not only the relatively explicit references to same-sex friendship, love, and companionship throughout the work, but also
the structures of the closet embedded in the narrative itself. Its
status as a boys' book thereby permits *Left to Themselves* to func-
tion as a novelistic open secret, both obvious and not, revealing and yet coy. The reading practices employed by queer critics
like Sedgwick make these dynamics, perhaps only intuited by
some nineteenth-century boy readers, clearer.

That Philip and Gerald are youths and that *Left to Themselves*
is a children's or adolescent novel attach specific possibilities to
its valorization of disclosure. When Gerald first meets Philip
he finds the older boy to be "not so much boy or man, but a
confusion of both" (11). As part boy and part man, Philip is able
to claim or embody simultaneously the familiar boyhood privilege of same-sex romantic friendship and the emergent figure

of the self-identified homosexual adult. Given the centrality
of same-sex friendship to nineteenth-century boy culture and
the permissible exchange of passionate sentiments in a time
before homosexuality was widely recognized (Rotundo 75-
76), the relationship between Philip and Gerald could appear
to many readers not unlike quite common friendships between
boys or youths. As Axel Nissen writes, "A particularly striking
difference, compared with more recent times, is the extent to
which American men during most of the nineteenth century
could feel and openly express an unashamed, unselfconscious,
all-consuming love for members of their own sex" (4). Gifford
confirms the ambiguous quality of *Left to Themselves*: "Yet no
matter how 'distinguishable' the author might term its homosexual context, the inscription in my copy, to 'Frederick Clarke,
a present from the Wesleyan Reform Sunday School, 1896,'
suggests that it remained invisible to at least one, and probably most readers" (Gifford, "Left to Themselves" 115). What
Nissen describes as the celebration of same-sex friendship in
nineteenth-century America makes it possible for Stevenson's
boy books to circulate widely in ways that more explicit adult
works like his own *Imre* could not. However invested in disclosure or outness *Left to Themselves* is, it nonetheless remains ambiguous precisely because it is a boys' book.

What goes on in this boys' book dovetails remarkably with
developments in the increasingly explicit homosexual literature
for adults being written in the final decades of the nineteenth
century. *Left to Themselves* is the children's version of Wilde's
A Picture of Dorian Gray and Melville's *Billy Budd*, two seminal
"gay" novels from 1891, the same year Stevenson's book was
published.[21] Indeed, Garde refers to Jennison as a "Dorian Gray-
like character" ("Mysterious" 95). As Sedgwick explains, "The
year 1891 is a good moment to which to look for a cross-section
of the inaugural discourses of modern homo/heterosexual-
ity" (*Epistemology* 49). A comparison with *Dorian Gray* and *Billy
Budd*, two similarly positioned adult works, clarifies what Stevenson's book accomplishes as children's literature. Sedgwick
writes, "In such texts as *Billy Budd* and *Dorian Gray* and through
their influence, the subject—the thematic—of knowledge and

ignorance themselves, of innocence and initiation, of secrecy and disclosure, became not contingently but integrally infused with one particular object of cognition: no longer sexuality as a whole but even more specifically, now, the homosexual topic" (*Epistemology* 74). *Left to Themselves* clearly shares a role in constructing this system of signification by which homosexuality is coded in and through interplays of knowledge and ignorance, innocence and initiation, secrecy and disclosure, and so on.

However, it departs in important ways from these two adult novels in which the "homosexual" characters almost always meet tragic fates as a result of confession or disclosure. Stevenson's children's novel, in contrast to these adult works from the same year, offers a far more celebratory and optimistic vision of homosexual or queer potential. Whereas Philip and Gerald happily disclose all, enjoy the intimacy of their relationship, and remain together for the rest of their lives, the men coded as homosexual in *Billy Budd* and *Dorian Gray* are effectively punished either for their own same-sex desire or because they are desired by others. Sedgwick identifies John Claggart as *the* homosexual in *Billy Budd*, though she notes that "*every* impulse of *every* person in this book that could at all be called desire could be called homosexual desire, being directed by men exclusively toward men" (92). Claggart is killed by a single blow from Billy when he implies that the youthful sailor is part of a conspiracy to mutiny, and Billy is himself executed for mutiny after confessing to Claggart's murder, saying "Captain Vere tells the truth. It is just as Captain Vere says" (55). Both men, therefore, die for acts of accusation or confession, while both Jennison and Philip remain alive and free. In *Dorian Gray*, Basil Hallward, who is in love with Dorian, confesses his feelings for him and his fear that his painting of Dorian reveals too much about him to the world. He says to Dorian, "Ah! you don't know what it cost me to tell you all that I have told you. . . . It was not intended as a compliment. It was a confession" (130). Later, Dorian makes his own confession to Basil by revealing the state of his portrait, now disfigured by his selfish and debauched life. Dorian is then moved to murder Basil and eventually slashes the painting as well, killing himself in the process. Similarly, in Alan Dale's *A*

Marriage Below Zero, published in the United States just two years earlier in 1889, the young husband Arthur Ravener leaves his wife, Elsie, and runs away to Paris with his lover, an older gentleman named Jack Dillingham.[22] Elsie reads about a homosexual scandal in the newspapers and tracks her husband to a Parisian hotel, where she finds him dead from suicide following Dillingham's arrest. The framed photos of her husband and his lover hanging on the wall over Arthur's dead body confirm what she has suspected about him.

In these adult works, homosexual desire leads to misery and jealousy, and disclosure and confession lead to murder, execution, or suicide. In *Left to Themselves*, even the villain, coded as homosexual himself, avoids a truly tragic fate. Unlike the protagonists of these canonical adult works, the boys of *Left to Themselves* provide sympathetic and optimistic models for boy readers, and Stevenson's work reflects a subtly didactic trace missing in Melville and Wilde. Bayard Taylor's 1870 American novel *Joseph and His Friend* possesses the potential to end happily with the union of Joseph and his beloved friend Philip, who try to imagine a life together despite Joseph's commitment to his unhappy marriage. They wish to find "a great valley" free from the "distorted laws of men" (216). However, when Joseph's wife Julia dies, he finds himself drawing closer to Philip's sister, Madeline, and Philip resigns himself to being "vicariously happy" for them (361). It would be another 21 years before Stevenson has Philip and Gerald meet in that happy valley, showing that the boy reader can be like Philip and Gerald: happy, homosexual, and alive.

More about *Left to Themselves* remains to be investigated by scholars. For instance, adult male patrons of upwardly mobile boys, a topic addressed by Moon with regards to Alger's work, appear important in Stevenson as well. The boys rely on benevolent male benefactors, as Alger's most famous boy protagonist, Ragged Dick, does. Cross-class relations, a prominent issue in the Wilde trials and seen in *Maurice*, are also a feature of *Left to Themselves*. Gerald is repeatedly described as the son of a wealthy man, while Philip is the orphaned son of a modest bank clerk. Since both boys eventually attend law school together, their status may equalize through their companionship, suggesting a relationship between sexuality and social class and mobility.[23] It would also be worth considering further how this novel engages with a variety of genres, including Gothic literature and adventure, and how the particular choices represented by its generic conventions impinge upon its depictions of boyhood sexuality. Finally, questions of age and audience require more consideration. I have described *Left to Themselves* as quite possibly the first gay children's novel, but with a seventeen-year-old protagonist who is a "confusion" of boy and man, this work might also be described as the first gay adolescent novel and should therefore prompt a reconsideration of the standard chronology that affords such a position to *I'll Get There*. Stevenson's historically important work clearly deserves far more attention than it has received, since it encourages us to reconsider the possibilities of children's literature more broadly and to reevaluate the history of "gay" children's literature specifically.

Eric L. Tribunella
University of Southern Mississippi
November 2015

NOTES

1. According to Garde, Stevenson was partial to the theories of Karl Heinrich Ulrichs (1825-1895), who understood same-sex desire as natural and who articulated a complex taxonomy of different types of men and women based on sexual desire ("Mysterious" 97). As Simon LeVay explains, Ulrichs's term "urning" is "a reference to a passage in Plato's *Symposium*, in which Pausanius calls same-sex love the offspring of the 'heavenly Aphrodite,' daughter of Uranus" (12). For Ulrichs, urnings were "hermaphrodites of the mind." "Urning" is translated as "uranian" in English, and this is the term Stevenson uses to describe *Left to Themselves*. Ulrichs, sometimes described as the first openly homosexual writer and activist and hence founder of the first modern homosexual rights movement, differs from other early writers about homosexuality in that he was a trained lawyer and not writing as a medical scien-

tist (LeVay 12). Notably, Stevenson has Philip and Gerald attend law school at the conclusion of *Left to Themselves*.

2. Michael Matthew Kaylor strongly objects to attributing the use of the term "Uranian" to Ulrichs and claims that the men who popularized its use to refer to homosexuals, such as John Addington Symonds and Edward Carpenter, drew on their Classical training to derive it directly from Plato (Kaylor xiii n.2). However, Stevenson attributes his own use to Ulrichs (*The Intersexes* 72). Timothy d'Arch Smith used the term "Uranian" in his 1970 book *Love in Earnest: Some Notes on the Lives and Writings of English "Uranian" Poets from 1889 to 1930* to refer to late-Victorian writers such as Lord Alfred Douglas, Symonds, and others who idealized the love of boys in particular (Smith xx). In this latter context, "Uranian" refers more specifically to pederastic love, and Kaylor does mention Stevenson in his study. However, in *The Intersexes*, Stevenson seems to use "Uranian" to refer to homosexuality more generally, and the tem "pederasty" when discussing the love of adult men for male youths. He repeatedly distinguishes between uranianism of a "better type" and "pederastic homosexualism" (432). Most uranians, he writes, "prefer a decidedly mature youth, and will rather embrace and be caressed sexually by a vigorous man from twenty-two to thirty-five, than by a boy in his early teens" (432-433).

3. Jonathan Ned Katz refers in *Gay American History* (1976, revised in 1992) to *Left to Themselves* as "one of the earliest documented homosexual 'juveniles'" (659 n. 160). I use the term "gay" as the more contemporary alternative to "homosexual." Of course, using "gay" to describe an 1891 novel is anachronistic: according to George Chauncey, "gay" was not used to mean "homosexual" until the 1920s, and this usage of the term did not become widely recognizable until the 1940s (17-19). Some critics might employ the term "queer" in this instance, as Kenneth Kidd and Michelle Abate do for their collection *Over the Rainbow: Queer Children's and Young Adult Literature*, in which they note that "what we're calling 'queer children's literature' predates and may outlast the LGBTQ movement" (3). They and other critics use "queer" to refer to non-heteronormative sexualities or anti-heteronormative and anti-identitarian politics. However, I want to insist on the more specific "gay" or "homosexual" because Stevenson himself was concerned with the construction and articulation of uranian or homosexual identity, and I want to distinguish between the queer-

ness of a work like Alger's *Ragged Dick* and the subtle though distinct homosexuality of Stevenson's *Left to Themselves*.

4. Stevenson also dedicates his short story for children, "The Golden Moon," to Flagler. The story was serialized in *The Christian Union* magazine in 1885.

5. *The Intersexes* is dedicated to Richard von Krafft-Ebing, whom Stevenson credits with taking an interest in his project. Krafft-Ebing was a German physician and psychiatrist, who published a groundbreaking study of sexuality, *Psychopathia Sexualis*, in 1886. The 1892 English translation of this work was the first appearance in English of the word "homosexual."

6. Stevenson notes in the preface to *The Intersexes* that it was actually written "several years" before its publication in 1908/1909 (xi). Though *The Intersexes* bears a 1908 copyright, Gifford indicates that it was published in 1909 ("What Became" 25).

7. Curiously, *White Cockades* and *Left to Themselves* are missing from Francis Edwin Murray's *A Catalogue of Selected Books from the Private Library of a Student of Boyhood, Youth, and Comradeship*, published in 1924. Murray, an English publisher and bookseller, included titles of 454 works of poetry, drama, biography, belles-lettres, and fiction related to boyhood and youth, including Stevenson's *Imre* and other works referenced by Stevenson in *The Intersexes*.

8. Donovan's *I'll Get There. It Better Be Worth the Trip.* is routinely described as gay young adult (YA) literature, but its status as a gay novel is not unambiguous. First, neither the protagonist, Davy, nor the friend with whom he has a sexual encounter, Altschuler, identifies as gay. In fact, Davy repeatedly denies being "queer," and Altschuler never says anything definitive about his sexuality other than that he does not feel guilty for what he and Davy did together. Their one sexual encounter happens off the page and fairly late in the novel, which is as much about Davy's coping with the death of his grandmother, his relocation to New York City, and his emotionally abusive and alcoholic mother.

9. Describing Mole and Rat's relationship as queer might surprise some readers, but consider that Mole leaves home abruptly to move in with Rat and later defies his natural impulses to burrow back into his home in order to remain with Rat. This scene, in which Mole is torn between the smells of his old home and staying with Rat, is described in the most emotional of terms. Moreover, the society of *The Wind in the Willows* is entirely homosocial.

10. Though *Tim*, published the same year as *Left to Themselves*, depicts

quite explicitly the passionate love of Tim for the older Carol, the
latter becomes involved with a woman and the former falls ill, his
death intimated at the close of the novel. Stevenson cites *Tim* in
The Intersexes as a "study of 'psychic homosexuality' between two
school-lads" (367). *The Hill* details the rivalry of two boys, Verney
and Scaife, for the friendship of a third boy, Desmond. It concludes
with Desmond's death in the Second Boer War.

11. None of the authors cited above, save for Sturgis, identified as uranian or homosexual, though Alger was accused of having sexual
relations with boys and eventually devoted his life to the care of
boys in New York City (see Scharnhorst and Bales).

12. Boys' adventure stories were also popular in the United States.
Ballantyne was himself inspired by the American castaway novel
The Island Home (1851), by James F. Bowman. Oliver Optic's Army
and Navy series features boys in different branches of the service,
and the first of the series, *The Soldier Boy; or, Tom Somers in the Army*
(1865), was an early Civil War novel for boys. Another popular
adventure novel was James Otis's *Toby Tyler* (1881), the quintessen-
tial story of the boy who runs away with the circus.

13. Some American school stories were published even though they
did not achieve the same status or longevity as their British counterparts. Louisa May Alcott's *Little Men* (1871), Edward Eggleston's
The Hoosier School-Boy (1883), and Edward Stratemeyer's *The Rover
Boys at School; or, The Cadets of Putnam Hall* (1899) are among notable examples.

14. Mark Twain coined the phrase "bad boy" in his short story "The
Story of the Bad Little Boy," published in the *Californian*, a weekly
publication, in 1865.

15. For instance, Ulrichs believed that homosexual men, or urnings,
were distinguished from heterosexual men, or dionings, by their
different natures. According to LeVay, "As long as homosexuality was inborn, Ulrichs felt he could justly claim that homosexual behavior was natural for homosexual people, and therefore
should not be criminalized or viewed as sinful" (13).

16. The lifelong companionship of the boys is especially striking
given that Stevenson concludes the novel with a description of
the future domestic relations of many of the novel's characters,
including very minor ones. For instance, we learn that the clerk at
the Knoxport hotel, who barely utters a line, marries the owner's
niece (319).

17. For Stevenson, homosexual men and women are "intersexes"

who exist "between the two great major sexes that we recognize as distinctively 'man' and 'woman'" (16). A number of Stevenson's contemporaries held this view, including British poet and philosopher Edward Carpenter, whose 1908 study of homosexuality is titled *The Intermediate Sex: A Study of Some Transitional Types of Men and Women.*

18. This association between sexuality and blackmail and the sense that homosexual men are particularly susceptible to blackmail persisted well into the twentieth century in the United States and were frequently cited during the 1950s as reasons to expunge homosexual workers from government positions (Johnson 24, 67). In Britain, the 1957 Wolfenden Report recommended decriminalizing homosexuality in part because of concerns about the threat of blackmail, demonstrating how entrenched this association had become. As Quentin Crisp observes pessimistically in 1967 in response to the passage of the Sexual Offenses Act, which enacted recommendations of the Report, "To rob blackmail of its potency, it would be necessary to remove the homosexual's feelings of shame. This no power on earth can do" (203).

19. This aspect of Jennison's attempt to blackmail Philip is echoed in *The Intersexes*, where Stevenson relates a real case in which a German man is blackmailed over an alleged crime committed by his father-in-law (468).

20. The term "out," the phrase "coming out," and the notion of "the closet" were not used until the mid-twentieth century. Chauncey explains that the phrase "coming out," a reference to debutante balls, emerged in the United States in the years before World War II and that gay men came out *into* the world, not *out of* the closet (7). This latter usage did not appear until after the War. The *OED* lists the first recorded use of "out of the closet" as occurring in 1963. Nevertheless, public self-disclosure was practiced and advocated by Ulrichs a century earlier. He told his family of his love for men in 1862 (Kennedy, *Pioneer* 45), and in 1865 he founded the Uranian Union to publicly advocate on behalf of uranians, or homosexuals (Kennedy, "Karl Heinrich Ulrichs" 32). At other times, Ulrichs, like most advocates of political and scientific reform benefitting uranians or homosexuals, wrote under a pseudonym. Though the language of "coming out" was not available, men and women in the nineteenth century who loved others of the same sex wrestled with concealment and disclosure in personal, professional, and political contexts.

21. *The Picture of Dorian Gray* was serialized in *Lippincott's* magazine in 1890 and revised for publication as a novel in 1891. "Billy Budd" was discovered as an unpublished work in progress at the time of Melville's death in 1891 and not published until 1924.

22. Alan Dale was the penname for Alfred Cohen, a music and drama critic from Birmingham, England, who wrote for the New York *Evening World* (Austen 16).

23. John D'Emilio argues for a direct connection between the emergence of gay identity in the United States in the latter half of the nineteenth century and the development of economic conditions that made it possible for individuals to survive outside of family units (see D'Emilio, "Capitalism and Gay Identity").

WORKS CITED

Abate, Michelle and Kenneth Kidd, editors. *Over the Rainbow: Queer Children's and Young Adult Literature*. Ann Arbor: University of Michigan Press, 2011.

Austen, Roger. *Playing the Game: The Homosexual Novel in America*. Indianapolis: Bobbs-Merrill, 1977.

Ballantyne, R.M. *The Coral Island*. 1858. Richmond, Va.: Valancourt Books, 2015.

Clark, Beverly Lyon. *Regendering the School Story: Sassy Sissies and Tattling Tomboys*. New York: Routledge, 1996.

Crisp, Quentin. *The Naked Civil Servant*. 1968. New York: Penguin Books, 1997.

Dale, Alan. *A Marriage Below Zero*. New York: G. W. Dillingham, 1889.

D'Emilio, John. "Capitalism and Gay Identity." *The Lesbian and Gay Studies Reader*. Edited by Henry Abelove, Michèle Aina Barale, and David M. Halperin. New York: Routledge, 1990. 467-476.

Fone, Byrne R. S. *A Road to Stonewall: Male Homosexuality and Homophobia in English and American Literature, 1750-1969*. New York: Twayne Publishers, 1993.

Forster, E. M. *Maurice*. 1971. New York: W. W. Norton, 1993.

Garde, Noel I. "The First Native American 'Gay' Novel." *One Institute Quarterly of Homophile Studies* 9 (Spring 1960): 185-190.

———. "The Mysterious Father of American Homophile Literature." *One Institute Quarterly of Homophile Studies* 3 (Fall 1958): 94-98.

Gifford, James. *Dayneford's Library: American Homosexual Writing 1900-1913*. Amherst: University of Massachusetts Press, 1995.

———. Introduction. *Imre*. By Edward Prime-Stevenson. Petersborough, Ontario: Broadview Press, 2003. 13-26.

———. "Left to Themselves: The Subversive Boys Books of Edward Prime-Stevenson (1858-1942)." *Journal of American & Comparative Cultures* 24.3-4 (fall-winter 2001): 113-116.

———. "Stevenson, Edward Irenæus Prime-." *The Gay and Lesbian Literary Heritage: A Reader's Companion to the Writers and Their Works, from Antiquity to the Present*. Edited by Claude J. Summers. New York: Henry Holt, 1995. 686-687.

———. "What Became of *The Intersexes*?" *The Gay & Lesbian Review* (September-October 2011): 25-27.

Goldsmith, Netta Murray. *The Worst of Crimes: Homosexuality and the Law in Eighteenth-Century London*. Brookfield, VT: Ashgate Publishing, 1998.

Jenkins, Christine. "Heartthrobs and Heartbreaks: A Guide to Young Adult Books with Gay Themes." *Out/Look* 3.3 (Fall 1988): 82-91.

Johnson, David K. *The Lavender Scare: The Cold War Persecution of Gays and Lesbians in the Federal Government*. Chicago: University of Chicago Press, 2006.

Katz, Jonathan Ned. *Gay American History: Lesbians and Gay Men in the U.S.A.* Revised Edition. New York: Penguin, 1992.

———. *Love Stories: Sex Between Men Before Homosexuality*. Chicago: University of Chicago Press, 2003.

Kaylor, Michael Matthew. *Secreted Desires—The Major Uranians: Hopkins, Pater, and Wilde*. Brno, Czech Republic: Masaryk University, 2006.

Kennedy, Hubert. *Karl Heinrich Ulrichs: Pioneer of the Modern Gay Movement*. 1988. Concord, California: Peremptory Publications, 2005.

———. "Karl Heinrich Ulrichs, 1825-1895." *The Gay 100: A Ranking of the Most Influential Gays and Lesbians, Past and Present*. Edited by Paul Russell. New York: Kensington Publishing, 1995. 31-33.

Kidd, Kenneth. "Introduction: Lesbian/Gay Literature for Children and Young Adults." *Children's Literature Association Quarterly* 23.3 (Fall 1998): 114-119.

LeVay, Simon. *Queer Science: The Use and Abuse of Research into Homosexuality*. Cambridge: The Massachusetts Institute of Technology Press, 1997.

Livesey, Matthew Jerald. "From This Moment On: The Homosexual Origins of the Gay Novel in America." Dissertation. Madison: University of Wisconsin, 1997.

Mallan, Kerry. "Queer." *Keywords for Children's Literature*. Edited by

Philip Nel and Lissa Paul. New York: New York University Press, 2011.

McLaren, Angus. *Sexual Blackmail: A Modern History*. Cambridge: Harvard University Press, 2002.

Melville, Herman. *Billy Budd, Sailor and Other Stories*. 1891. New York: Bantam Books, 1984.

Moon, Michael. "'The Gentle Boy from the Dangerous Classes': Pederasty, Domesticity, and Capitalism in Horatio Alger." *Representations* 19 (Summer 1987): 87-110.

Nelson, Claudia. "David and Jonathan—and Saul—Revisited: Homodomestic Patterns in British Boys' Magazine Fiction, 1880-1915." *Children's Literature Association Quarterly* 23.3 (Fall 1998): 120-127.

Nissen, Axel. Introduction. *Romantic Friendship Reader: Love Stories Between Men in Victorian America*. Edited by Axel Nissen. Boston: Northeastern University Press, 2003. 3-12.

Prime-Stevenson, Edward. *Imre*. 1906. Edited by James Gifford. Petersborough, Ontario: Broadview Press, 2003.

———. [as Xavier Mayne]. *The Intersexes: A History of Similisexualism as a Problem in Social Life*. 1908. New York: Arno Press, 1975.

———. *Left to Themselves: Being the Ordeal of Philip and Gerald*. 1891. Richmond, Va.: Valancourt Books, 2016.

———. *White Cockades: An Incident of the 'Forty-Five'*. New York: Charles Scribner's Sons, 1887.

Quigly, Isabel. *The Heirs of Tom Brown: The English School Story*. London: Chatto, 1982.

Rotundo, E. Anthony. *American Manhood: Transformations in Masculinity from the Revolution to the Modern Era*. New York: Basic Books, 1993.

Sedgwick, Eve Kosofsky. *Between Men: English Literature and Male Homosocial Desire*. New York: Columbia University Press, 1985.

———. *Epistemology of the Closet*. Berkeley: University of California Press, 1990.

Senelick, Laurence. "The Homosexual as Villain and Victim in Fin-De-Siècle Drama." *Journal of the History of Sexuality* 4.2 (October 1993): 201-229.

Scharnhorst, Gary with Jack Bales. *The Lost Life of Horatio Alger, Jr.* Bloomington: Indiana University Press, 1985.

Sinfield, Alan. *The Wilde Century: Oscar Wilde, Effeminacy, and the Queer Moment*. New York: Columbia University Press, 1994.

Smith, Timothy d'Arch. *Love in Earnest: Some Notes on the Lives and Writings of English 'Uranian' Poets, 1880-1930*. London: Routledge and Kegan Paul, 1970.

Taylor, Bayard. *Joseph and His Friend: A Story of Pennsylvania*. New York: G. P. Putnam & Sons, 1870.

Tribunella, Eric L. *Melancholia and Maturation: The Use of Trauma in American Children's Literature*. Knoxville: University of Tennessee Press, 2010.

Trites, Roberta Seelinger. "Queer Discourse and the Young Adult Novel: Repression and Power in Gay Male Adolescent Literature." *Children's Literature Association Quarterly* 23.3 (Fall 1998): 143-151.

Wilde, Oscar. *The Picture of Dorian Gray*. 1891. New York: Signet, 1995.

ABOUT THE EDITOR

Eric L. Tribunella is Associate Professor of English at the University of Southern Mississippi. His research interests include children's and young adult literature, lesbian and gay literature, and gender and sexuality studies. He is the author of *Melancholia and Maturation: The Use of Trauma in American Children's Literature* (University of Tennessee Press, 2010) and the co-author of *Reading Children's Literature: A Critical Introduction* (Bedford / St. Martin's, 2013). He contributed the chapter on children's and young adult literature to the *Cambridge History of Gay and Lesbian Literature* (Cambridge University Press, 2014).

A NOTE ON THE EDITION

This text is based on the first edition of *Left to Themselves: Being the Ordeal of Philip and Gerald*, published by Hunt & Eaton (New York) in 1891 and sold for $1.00. It follows the spelling and punctuation of the first edition, but obvious printing errors have been silently corrected. The 1893 British edition of the novel, which also follows the first edition, adds a single line on page 67 of that edition: "— often the unguessed beginnings of trouble."

ACKNOWLEDGMENTS

I would like to thank Megan Norcia, who first encouraged me to pursue editing an edition of *Left to Themselves* and who suggested Valancourt Books to me as a possible publisher. If not for her, I might not have considered undertaking this project at all.

Portions of the introduction of this edition first appeared in my article "Between Boys: Edward Stevenson's *Left to Themselves* and the Birth of Gay Children's Literature," published in *Children's Literature Association Quarterly* 37.4 by the Johns Hopkins University Press and reprinted with permission. Thomas Crisp and Lance Weldy edited the special issue of the *Quarterly* in which my article on Stevenson appeared, and I appreciate their encouragement and feedback. Kate Capshaw served as editor of the *Quarterly* at that time and also provided commentary, for which I am grateful. I want to thank the Children's Literature Association for the faculty research grant that facilitated my research on Stevenson and made it possible for me to examine extant copies of *Left to Themselves*.

I am grateful to Dr. Steven Moser, former Dean of the College of Arts and Letters at the University of Southern Mississippi, for the summer research leave that allowed me to complete this project. I appreciate Monika Gehlawat's covering for me while I was away. Ellen Ruffin and the staff at the de Grummond Children's Literature Collection and McCain Library and Archives assisted with my research, and I appreciate their help.

I first learned about Stevenson by reading the work of Jim Gifford, and I thank him for responding so kindly to my inquiries about his research on Stevenson and for encouraging my own. He and Simon Stern provided extremely helpful suggestions for this edition, and I thank them for their thoughtful feedback.

Danielle Sypher-Haley provided invaluable support by helping me with the technical aspects of preparing the text file.

Many thanks to her. C.J. Yow assisted with copy-editing the introduction and notes. Jameela Lares helped me with selecting a Greek translation for the epigraph.

I very much appreciate James D. Jenkins's encouraging response to my initial inquiry and his helpful editorial guidance along the way. Finally, I want to thank my partner, Jerrid Boyette, who encouraged my interest in Stevenson and saw the merits of this project.

LEFT TO THEMSELVES

TO

H. Harkness Flagler[1]

THIS VIGNETTE OF THE BEGINNING OF AN EARLY
AND LASTING FRIENDSHIP

IS INSCRIBED

ΑΘ. τοιγὰρ κατὰ χθόν' οὖσ' ἐπικτήσει φίλους.—ÆSCHYLUS.[2]

PREFACE.

A preface to a little book of this sort is an anomaly. Consequently it should be understood the sooner that these forewords are not intended for any boys or girls that take up *Left to Themselves*. It is solely for the benefit of the adult reader led by curiosity or carefulness to open the book. The young reader will use his old privilege and skip it.

It was lately observed, with a good deal of truth, that childhood and youth in their relations to literature are modern discoveries.[3] To compare reading for the boys or girls of today with that purveyed even twenty-five years ago, in quantity and quality, is a trite superfluity.

But it has begun to look as if catering to this discovery of what young minds relish and of what they absorb has gone incautiously far. There exists a good measure of forgetfulness that children, after all is said, are little men and little women, with hearts and heads, as well as merely imaginations to be tickled. Undoubtedly these last must be stirred in the story. But there is always a large element of the young reading public to whom character in fiction, and a definite idea of human nature through fiction, and the impression of downright personality through fiction, are the main interests—perhaps unconsciously—and work a charm and influence good or bad in a very high degree. A child does not always live in and care for the eternal story, story, story, incident, incident, incident, of literature written for him. There are plenty of philosophers not yet arrived at tail-coats or long frocks. They sit in the corners of the library or school-room. They think out and feel the personality in narrative deeply. This element, apart from incident, in a story means far more to impress and hold and mold than what happens. Indeed, in the model story for young readers—one often says it, but often does not succeed in illustrating it—the clear embodiment of character is of the first importance, however stirring or however artistically treated or beneficial the incidental side. Jack feels more than he says from the personal contact, feels more, may be, than he knows; and Jill is surely apt to be as sensitive as Jack.

Has there not little by little come to be a little too much of kindly writing down to childhood and to youth? of writing down to it until we are in danger of losing its level and getting below it? Is not thoughtless youth more thoughtful than our credit extends to it? Certainly a nice sense of the balance between sugar and pill seems needed just now—admitting the need of any actual pill. Children, after the earliest period, are more serious and finer and more perceptive natures than we may have come to allowing, or for which we may have come to working. We forget the dignity of even the young heart and mind. Light-hearted youth does not necessarily mean light-headed youth.

This story—with apology for such a preamble—is written in the aim at deferring to the above ideas; and, furthermore, at including in the process one or two literary principles closely united to them. It will be found its writer hopes to embody study, as well as story, for the thoughtful moments in young lives, on whose intelligences daily clearly break the beauty and earnestness of human life, of resolute character, of unselfish friendship and affection, and of high aim. To them, and of course to all adult readers, who do not feel themselves out of sympathy with the idealizings and fair inclusions of one's early time in this world, what follows is offered.

NEW YORK CITY, *February*, 1891.

LEFT TO THEMSELVES:

BEING

THE ORDEAL OF PHILIP AND GERALD.

CHAPTER I.

MR. SIP'S APPEARANCE AND DISAPPEARANCE—
PHILIP AND GERALD BREAK ICE IN SUMMER.

Mr. Patrick Sip had seated himself by the side of the brook that purled through the deep green ravine lying about three miles back of the Ossokosee House.[4] Mr. Sip was not a guest at that new and flourishing summer resort. Mr. Sip, indeed, had hardly found himself a welcome guest anywhere within five or six years. He possessed a big, burly figure, a very unshaven and sunburnt face, and a suit of clothes once black, when upon the back of an earlier wearer, but long since faded to a dirty brown. Mr. Sip never used an umbrella nowadays, although he exercised much in the open air. Upon his unkempt hair slanted a tattered straw hat. Beside him lay a thickish walking-stick without any varnish. There was one thing which Mr. Sip had not about him, as any body would have inferred at a glance, although it is often difficult to detect by sight—a good character. In short, Mr. Sip looked the complete example of just what he was—a sturdy, veteran tramp of some thirty summers and winters, who had not found through honest labor a roof over his head or a morsel between his bristly lips since his last release from some one of the dozen work-houses that his presence had graced.[5]

"Humph!" said Mr. Sip, half aloud, as he changed his position so as to let his bare feet sink deeper in the rippling creek (Mr. Sip was laving[6] them), "I see plenty o' water around here, but there aint nothin' in sight looks like bread. Plague them turnips! Raw turnips aint no sort o' a breakfast for a gentleman's stomach. Is they, now?"

He splashed his feet about in the pure cold water, by no means to cleanse them from the dust of the highway, but simply because it was easier to drop them into the stream than to hold them out as he sat on the abrupt bank. He whistled a part of a tune and seemed to forget having put his question to the wrens and wagtails in the sassafras.

"If, now, I could jist stick out my hand and pull a ham sangwich off o' that there useless little tree," pursued Mr. Sip, complainingly; "or if you could sort o' lay here an' meditate an' presen'ly find a good-sized pan o' cold victuals a-comin' a-floatin' up."

Neither of these attractive phenomena seeming likely to occur immediately, Mr. Sip sighed as if injured, shook his head, and said with decided temper, "Ugh, natur'! They talk so much about natur' in them books an'—an' churches, an' p'lice courts, an' sich. What's there nice about natur', I'd like to know, when a man can keep company with natur' as stiddy as I do an' never git so much as his reg'lar meals out o' her one day in the week? Natur', as fur as I've found out, don't mean nothing 'cept wild blackberries in season. I don't want no more to do with natur'!" Mr. Sip concluded with an angry slap at a huge horsefly that had lighted upon his ankle, and uttered his favorite exclamation, "My name aint Sip!"—which, although he meant the phrase merely as an expletive when he was particularly put out over any matter, happened to be the case.

Just at that moment Mr. Sip looked across to the opposite bank of the creek and discovered that he and the horsefly were not alone. A boy was standing rather further up the stream with a fishing-rod in his hand observing the odd figure this wandering philosopher upon nature cut. The boy appeared to be in the neighborhood of twelve years of age. He had a trim figure and fair hair, and the sunlight on it and through a green branch of a young maple behind him made the brightest spots of color in the somber little chasm. On his young face were mingled expressions of amusement and disgust as to Mr. Sip. Across his arm was a basket. A napkin dangled out of this suggestively.

"Come here, sonny," invited Mr. Sip in an amiable tone, and with a leer of sudden good feeling—for the luncheon basket.

"What did you say?" the boy called back rather timidly, without moving toward his new acquaintance.

"I said, 'Come here,'" repeated Mr. Sip, sharply, drawing his feet out of the water and beckoning. He took a hasty glance up and down the stream. "How many nice little fishes has you and that pa o' yourn caught since morning? Ten?"

"I haven't caught any fish so far," replied the lad, "and my father isn't here. He's up in Nova Scotia, thank you."

"O," Mr. Sip responded, "Nova Scotia? I remember I heard o' his goin' there. Say, sonny," he went on, wading out to the middle of the creek with an ugly expression deepening over his red face as he realized that the bearer of the basket was alone, "What time is it?"

The boy retreated a few steps, pulling out a neat little silver watch, too polite to refuse the information. "Half past eleven," he said, in his pleasant accent.

"O, but is that there watch correck?" inquired the evil-faced gentleman, taking several steps in the water toward that margin from which the lad had drawn back prudently. "Let me come up and see it for myself, wont you? That looks like a new watch."

"I say, keep off!" cried the owner of the watch, all at once suspecting the designs of Mr. Sip and turning slightly pale. "Keep off, there, I say!" The intrepid little fellow dropped his rod and caught up a stone that lay near. "I—I don't like your looks! I'll throw this at you if you come any closer."

The boy's face was whiter at each word, although his spirit gave a ring to his threat. But Mr. Sip had invaded too many kitchens and terrified far too many helpless servant-maids to allow himself to be daunted by a boy well dressed and carrying a watch and a basket of good things. He uttered an angry oath and splashed violently toward the lad, stumbling among the sharp flints of the creek. It was open war begun by hot pursuit.

The path by which Gerald Saxton (for that happened to be the name of the solitary little fisherman) had made his way to the creek was steep and irregular. He ran up it now, panting, with Mr. Sip in stumbling chase, the latter calling out all manner of threats as he pursued. The boy was frightened greatly, but to be frightened is not to be a coward, and he knew that the path led into Farmer Wooden's open meadow.

Through the green underbrush he darted, running up along the slope of the ravine, prudent enough not to waste his wind in cries that would not be at all likely to reach the farm-house, until he should dash out in the field itself, and planting his small feet carefully.

"If he catches up to me," thought Gerald, "he will knock me over and get the watch and be off before I can help it! I *must* make the meadow!"

On hurtled Mr. Sip, floundering up the narrow path, still giving vent to exclamations that only quickened Gerald's flight. Suddenly Mr. Sip saw an opportunity for a short cut by which Gerald might yet be overtaken. He bounced into it. Just as Gerald shot forth into the long meadow the furious philosopher found himself hardly ten yards in arrear.

"*Now* I've got yer!" he called, too angry to observe that the farm-house was in sight. "You drop—that basket—an' that watch—or—" Now Gerald shouted lustily, still flying ahead.

But Mr. Sip did not finish. A new figure came into action.

"What under the canopy is that?" cried a boy who was so much older and larger than little Gerald that he might almost have been called a young man. He was standing by the well up in the Woodens's dooryard waiting for the horse he had been driving to finish drinking. In another moment he grasped the situation and was leaping swiftly and noiselessly down the long slope over the stubble.

Tramps had been plentiful lately. His voice rang out to comfort Gerald and warn Mr. Sip. Gerald looked up, but with a white, set little face ran past him. Mr. Sip, taking in the height, weight, and courage of the frightened boy's new ally, turned and began running toward the low oak trees.

A strong ash stick, thrown with excellent aim, struck Mr. Sip squarely in the small of his back. He staggered for an instant, but rallied, and, a coward to the last, vanished in the thicket with a parting curse. Within an hour he might have been seen drinking buttermilk thirstily at a cottage a mile away. The good-humored farmer's daughter gave it to him, pitying a man who was "walking all the way from Wheelborough Heights to Paterson, in Jersey, marm, to find my old boss and git a job he's promised me."[7]

And now good-bye, Mr. Sip! You have done something to-day that would surprise your lazy self immensely. You have done a stroke of work. Thanks to your being a brutal vagrant, there is just coming about an acquaintance that is of the utmost import in the carrying on of this story—without which it would never have been worth writing or reading.

"Well, upon my word!" ejaculated the newcomer, wheeling about as if disposed to waste no more pains upon a man of Mr. Sip's kidney,[8] and coming back to Gerald Saxton. "I am very glad I heard you! What did that rascal want of you? His kind have been uncommonly thick this autumn."

"Why—he was after my watch, I think," replied Gerald, sitting down on a flat rock, a smile re-appearing upon his startled face. "I was standing down at the bottom of the path in the glen when he began talking to me. First thing I knew I saw that he meant mischief. I suppose it wasn't wonderfully brave of me to run from him."

"Brave in you!" exclaimed merrily the solid-looking older lad. "As if a brute like that was not as big as six of you! You acted precisely as any sensible fellow of your size would do. 'He who fights and runs away,' you know.[9] Did he do you any harm?"

"Not a bit, thanks. He didn't get close enough to me"—this with a chuckle.

"Were you fishing down in that lonely glen? It is a very fair spot for bass."

"Yes; Mr. Wooden took me down into the ravine quite a little way above it. Do you know the place, sir?"

"O, yes, sir; I know the place very well, sir," answered Gerald's defender, with a quizzical twinkle in his eyes as he repeated those "sirs." Then they both laughed. Gerald slyly compared their respective heights. His new friend could not be so very much taller. Certainly he was not over seventeen.

"You see, I was raised here—after a fashion," went on the latter in his clear, strong voice. "You are one of the guests over at our Ossokosee House, aren't you? I think I've seen you on the piazza."

"Yes; I've been stopping there while my father is away. My name is Gerald Saxton, though almost every body calls me Gerald."

"And mine is Philip Touchtone, but every body calls me Philip, and you needn't call me 'sir,' please. I know Mr. Marcy, who keeps the Ossokosee very well. It was to deliver a message from him to the Woodens about the hotel butter that I stopped here this afternoon. But do tell me how that scamp dared run after you? The minute I saw him and you, even as far off as Mrs. Wooden's back door, I suspected that it was a tramp, and I didn't hesitate very long."

"No, you didn't," answered Gerald. And he walked along, swinging his arm manfully and fighting over again for Philip Touchtone's benefit those details of the brief skirmish between himself and Mr. Sip that had hurriedly followed one another previous to Philip's advent. He continued his furtive observation of his new friend all the time. Touchtone had gained about five feet four of his full height, with a broad, well-developed chest, active legs, and a good straight way of carrying himself that reminded one of his sharp, pleasant way of speaking. His hair was dark enough to pass for black, as would his eyes and eyebrows, although they were actually brown, and full of an honest brightness. As for his face, it was rather long, full, and not particularly tanned, though the sun was well acquainted with it. The most attractive feature of it was a mouth that expressed good humor and resolution. In short, Gerald might have easily made up his mind that Philip Touchtone was a person born to work for and get what the world held for him.

"Whew!" exclaimed he, as Gerald reminded him, "I forgot Mrs. Wooden's carpet-beater![10] I threw it after your friend down there. He got the full benefit of it."

"And I forgot my rod! I dropped it when I thought it was best to run."

"Wait a minute and I'll get both," said Philip. "I know that identical rock where you say you stood—at the foot of the path." And before Gerald could remonstrate Philip ran from his side and darted down into the glen where Mr. Sip must have still lurked in wrath. But sooner than Gerald could feel alarm for him Philip came back with rod and beater.

"We need never expect to see him again," he said, breathlessly. "But—halloa! There are Mrs. Wooden and Miss Beauchamp, who boards with her. She teaches the district school here, and it's just begun. They must be wondering what has become of me. Suppose we hurry up a trifle. You can ride back to the hotel with me, unless you care to stay and fish—for more tramps."

"No, I thank you," answered Gerald. "You would be nowhere near to help me fight them." A determined flash came into the boy's countenance, such as he had shown when he caught up the bit of rock in defiance of the ragged Sip.

"O, I beg your pardon," he went on in his odd, rather grown-up manner; "I haven't said how much obliged to you I am for coming down there."

"You are quite welcome," laughed his new friend, looking down with frank eyes upon the younger boy.

"Perfectly welcome, 'Gerald,' you were going to say," added his companion, simply, feeling as if he had known for years this winning new-comer, who seemed not so much boy or man, but a confusion of both, that made up some one with whom he could speedily be on familiar terms. "Hark! Mrs. Wooden is calling you. That horse of yours is eating an apple out of Miss Beauchamp's hand, too."

The two Woodens and their boarder, Miss Beauchamp, walked forward to meet the boys as they advanced from the lane.

"Well, Philip," was the white-headed old farmer's greeting, "where did you fly to so sudden? Neither wife, here, nor I could set eyes on you. And so you've struck up an acquaintance with Master Gerald, have you?"

"Well, yes; and struck an acquaintance of his in the middle of his back," responded Philip. "How do you do, Miss Beauchamp? Didn't you, any of you, see the fight?"

"Fight!" cried Mrs. Wooden, clapping her fat hand to her bosom and nearly dropping the wooden tray of fresh butter she held. "Why, Philip Touchtone! Who has been a-fightin'? Not you—nor you?" she added, turning to Gerald.

"We all have been fighting, I'm afraid, Mrs. Wooden," said the latter—"three of us."

After this preamble there had to be an account of the skirmish. Miss Beauchamp and Mrs. Wooden alike decided it was "shocking."

"He might have drawn a pistol on both of you!" exclaimed Miss Beauchamp, "and a great deal more might have come of it."

"Well," Gerald protested, "the only thing that's come of it is that I have met a friend of yours here."

"And you couldn't do a better thing, Gerald!" exclaimed Mrs. Wooden, beginning to stow away butter and eggs in the spring-wagon[11] from the Ossokosee House. "Mr. Philip Touchtone is a particular pet of Miss Beauchamp's and mine when he is a good boy—as he almost always is," the farmer's fat wife lightly added.

"And a capital friend," added the grave Miss Beauchamp, with a smile, "for a boy about the age and size of one I know to have on his books. You ask Mr. Marcy over at the hotel all about him, Gerald. Now, you do that for me soon."

"O, pshaw, Miss Beauchamp!" Philip interrupted, his wide-awake face rather red, and straightening himself up to endure these broad compliments, "you and Mrs. Wooden ought to remember that people who praise friends to their faces are said to be fond of slandering them behind their backs. Come, Mr. Wooden, I promised Mr. Marcy to be back as soon as I could. Jump in, Gerald."

The boy swung his slender figure up to the cushioned seat. Philip quickly followed after a few more words with the farmer. Then the wagon rattled out into the road and was soon bowling along to the Ossokosee. Philip favored the baskets and bundles in the back of the spring-wagon with a final glance, and then turned to Gerald with the manner of a person who intends asking and answering a large number of questions. And Gerald felt quite eager to do the same thing.

Why each of these lads, so entirely out of his own free will, should have mutually confided details of their two histories, when each was so much a stranger, met to-day, and perhaps never sitting again within speaking-distance after to-morrow, was a riddle to both of them. But the solution of it is as old as the rocks in Wooden's Ravine, perhaps older. We may keep our lives and thoughts under a lock and key as tightly as we like until the day comes when, somewhere along this crowded highway called Life, we all at once run square against some other human creature who is made by fate to be our best friend. Then, take my word for it, whether he is younger or older, he will find out from our own lips every thing in the bottom of our hearts that he chooses to ask about; and, what is more, we ought to find ourselves glad to trust such a person with even more than the whole stock that is there.

CHAPTER II.

MUTUAL CONFIDENCES; AND PHILIP TURNS RED IN THE FACE.

"This has been my first summer at the Ossokosee," said Gerald, as the wagon trundled on. "Papa and I live in New York, in the Stuyvesant Hotel.[12] We have always been to Shelter Island until this year."[13]

"I have lived quite a good deal in New York myself," remarked Philip. "You see, I have nobody to look after me except Mr. Marcy. My mother died several years ago. In three or four weeks from this time Mr. Marcy takes me down to the city with him when this house is shut."

"Is Mr. Marcy your uncle?"

"O, no! No relation at all. I often feel as if he was, though. He has kept watch of me and helped me with my education ever since my mother's death."

Touchtone's eyes lost their happy light an instant.

"During the summer, of course, I have no time to do any studying, and not too much in the winter. I have a great deal else to busy me, helping Mr. Marcy."[14]

"Why, what do you help him with?" inquired Gerald, with

interest, remembering Touchtone in the office and the dining-room, and indeed every-where about the Ossokosee, except the parlors.

"Well, Mr. Marcy calls me a kind of aid-de-camp to him and Mrs. Ingraham, the house-keeper, too, particularly when there is danger of the kitchen running short of supplies. Now and then, if the farmers around here fail us, I have to spend half the day driving about the country, or you might starve at supper-table all at once. O, and then I look after one or two books in the office!"

Gerald laughed.

"Papa has kept me here because he heard so much about the table; and because Mr. Marcy told him there were so few boys that I couldn't get into mischief. Papa used to be a broker,[15] but he don't do any thing now. I believe he retired, or whatever they call it, a year or so ago. He's been camping out with a party of gentlemen from the Stock Exchange ever since midsummer away up in Nova Scotia. I haven't any mother either."

"Why didn't you go with them?" inquired Philip, guiding Nebuchadnezzar[16] skillfully through an irregular series of puddles. The view of the rolling green country, dotted with farm-houses and gray or red barns, was now worth looking at as they came out on the flat hill-top.

"I should have liked to go very much; but papa said that they were all expecting to 'rough it,' and the weather might be too cold for me. He was afraid I would be sick or something, and I know I'd be a good deal of trouble to him. Hasn't it stayed hot, though? I suppose they are having a splendid time up there all by themselves hunting and fishing. He wrote me that there wasn't a house within five miles of them. In October we are to meet in New York again. School begins next week; but I'm not to hurry back this year."

Gerald spoke of the "splendid time" rather wistfully. The little fellow had been lonely in the big Ossokosee, Philip fancied.

"What school do you go to?" inquired Gerald after a moment; "that is, when you are in New York?"

"Not to any now," soberly responded Philip, with a frown

coming over his forehead. It was the secret grief of his spirit that he had not been able to advance further in a thorough education. When Gerald spoke of his holidays coming to an end; he involuntarily envied this boy. "But before I came to live so much with Mr. Marcy, and when my mother was alive, I went to the Talmage School."[17]

"Why, that's my school now!" exclaimed Gerald, smiling. "How queer! But it's a pretty old school."

And then came interrogations as to what pupils or teachers had been there in Philip's school-days.

To Gerald, who was quite wide awake to reflections upon a good many more problems than thinkers of his age often pause over, already there seemed to be something like a mystery hanging around this young Touchtone. He made up his mind that his new friend did not appear a shade out of place this morning driving around a hotel-wagon after butter and eggs from the farms. But he also decided if he should meet Philip in a tennis-suit with a group of the most "aristocratic" lads of Murray Hill, or see him marching about the floor at some crowded "reception" given by the school, why, Touchtone would look just as much in his proper surroundings—only more so.[18] While he was assenting to these ideas something else occurred to make the younger boy puzzled about the older one.

A buggy came spinning along the road to meet them. From the front leaned out a young man, ten or twelve years older than Touchtone, wearing a brown beard. He checked his horse as he approached and called out some words that Gerald at once knew were German. Philip laughed and answered them in the same language quite as fluently. The occupant of the buggy—Gerald rightly supposed him the young German doctor that lived in the village—began quite a chat with Touchtone entirely in German. Both spoke so rapidly that Gerald found his study of the language at the Talmage School did not help him to catch more than an occasional "ja" or "nein."

The young doctor rode on.

"How well you must know German," said Gerald, admiringly. "Did you learn it across the water?" the boy added, half in joke.

"Yes," responded Touchtone, to the astonishment of the other lad. "I learned it in Hanover, when I was there, before we lived near New York."

Gerald happened to glance at Philip's face. It was oddly red, and his voice sounded strangely. All this time, too, there was certainly one particular person to whom he had not so much as referred. But after Gerald had bethought himself of this omission and put his next question he would have given a great deal not to have uttered it. The regret did not come until he had asked Philip point-blank:

"I think you said that your—your father was dead, didn't you? Was that after you came back?"

Philip made no reply. A blush reddened his frank face painfully. His pleasant expression had given place to an angry look. He gave unoffending Nebuchadnezzar a sharp cut with the long whip, as if to conceal mortification in showing his feelings, whatever they arose from, to a comparative stranger. He looked away from Gerald's startled blue eyes toward the flag-crowned gables of the Ossokosee House, that now were in full sight, as the wagon turned into one of the graveled avenues leading to the kitchen.

"My father died after we came home," he said, as if he had to face himself to speak of something that he could hardly bear to think of. "I was born in Germany, and lived there until we sailed."

"I—I beg your pardon," said Gerald, blushing in his turn.

"What for?"

"Because I think I asked you something that—that there was no reason for me to be told."

"O, don't mention it," returned Touchtone. He recovered his self-possession so curiously lost. "It is just as well that you did, I rather believe. Some day, perhaps, I can explain about it to you. No harm done. Pompey! Pompey!" he called out in his pleasant voice to a tall servant walking across the back piazza of the dining-room. "Come here, please, and help take some of these things to Mrs. Ingraham's store-room. If you will wait a moment," he continued, to Gerald. "I'll walk around to the front with you. I want to see Mr. Marcy."

The contents of the wagon were disposed of among the servants. Nebuchadnezzar set out by himself for the stables, at a word of command from Philip.

On the front steps were some groups chatting, reading, writing, or watching the nearer of two games of tennis, played at a little distance, out upon the wide lawn. The Ossokosee was to close for the season within about a fortnight, and only the uncommon heat of the September weather kept it still fairly full.

"Halloa, Philip!" called Mr. Marcy from the desk. The office inclosure was a handsome addition to the hall, with its cheerful stained glass, carved railings, rows of letter and key boxes and bell signals. "Where did you light upon that young gentleman? I'm not sorry, Gerald. Your father has left you in my charge, and you're too heavy a responsibility. I think I'll turn you over to Philip there. You might make a pretty fair guardian, Philip."

"All right," returned Gerald, gayly. "I say, guardian," he continued, turning with mischievous eyes to Touchtone, "can't you come up to my room after you get through your luncheon? Harry Dexter and I are going down to the lake at four o'clock to see them practice for the regatta. But we'll have plenty of time first."

"I am going to the lake myself," said Philip. "I belong to the Ossokosee crew that rows, you know."

"O, yes; so you do. Then we can all go together. You'll come, wont you?" And he seemed so anxious that Touchtone answered, "Yes," and "Thank you," at once.

Philip turned into the office, where he began giving the gentlemen there the history of the battle at Wooden's Ravine. "Served him right, Philip!" heartily exclaimed the genial bookkeeper, Mr. Fisher, on hearing of the stick throwing," and you'll find that little fellow a youngster worth your knowing."

Meantime Gerald was running lightly up the broad, smoothly polished oak stairs and entering the room that the father had engaged for his son's use. Not being able, or thinking he was not, to have the boy with him in Nova Scotia, he had wished to make Gerald as luxuriously comfortable as a lad could be. The gay Ossokosee House had, nevertheless, a perfectly new interest to Gerald now. The little boy had been welcomed by a good many of the guests stopping there. There were a few of his own age that had been his chums, for want of others. But now that he had met Touchtone things began to look all at once more enjoyable.

And what could be the reason that so open-hearted and jolly a companion should be so alone in the world, and feel so terribly cut, and blush in that embarrassed fashion because of a simple question concerning his father?

Philip came up to Number 45 in due time that afternoon. He looked over Gerald's foreign photographs and his coin collection. And so the time sped on, and interest in the acquaintance mutually prospered.

The next day they did not meet until after supper. Mr. Marcy had only three or four letters he wished Philip to write. When these were finished he and Gerald walked out into the hotel grounds, talking of the coming regatta and feeling quite like old companions. Two crews only were to row—the Ossokosee Boat Club and the Victory Rowing Association—and much interest was attached to the race. Mr. Marcy had offered a prize of two hundred dollars to the winners, and, furthermore, the Ossokosee Club were determined not to be beaten for the fourth year. The last three regattas had resulted, one after another, in the triumph of the elated Victors. Philip was a zealous member of the Ossokosees, and found it hard work to keep in any kind of training, what with his duties at the hotel. But then the whole affair was not so "professional" as it might have been, and Touchtone's natural athletic talents and Mr. Marcy's indulgence helped him to pull his oar as skillfully and enduringly as any other of the six.

Gerald listened with all his ears to his friend's account of their last year's defeat. All at once Philip remembered a message for Mrs. Ingraham about the flowers from the conservatory.

"Please stand here by the arbor one moment?" he asked. "I'll just run to the dining-room and find her."

Now, there was a long rustic seat outside the thick growth of vines, running over the same arbor. Gerald sat down upon this bench. Some guests of the house were grouped inside, conversing together. No secrets were being told. Gerald did not feel himself an eavesdropper. In fact, he did not pay any heed to the talking going on just back of his head until he heard a slow voice that was a certain General Sawtelle's.

"O, young Touchtone, you mean? Yes, yes; a remarkably fine young fellow! Any father might be proud of such a son—and any son ashamed of such a father as he had."

Gerald started almost to his feet.

"Why, who was his father?" asked another indolent voice. "What did he do?"

Gerald was a boy of delicate honor. He was about to hurry away, eager as he was to sympathize with his attractive "guardian's" trouble. He scorned to play the eavesdropper, and he equally scorned to be told this secret until Philip would utter it. But before he could step to the soft turf, and so slip out of ear-shot, Philip Touchtone himself came up beside him. Philip had stepped with unintentional lightness to the bench where he had left his little *protégé* and caught the last clearly spoken sentences.

Gerald would have drawn him away, too; but Philip took the hand of the younger boy and made a sign to him to remain and hear what General Sawtelle would reply. He put his finger upon his lips.

"Why," responded the general, from within the arbor, "his father was Touchtone—Reginald Touchtone—who was so badly involved in the famous robbery of the Suburban Trust Company, years ago, in X——, just outside of New York."

"O," returned the other speaker, "I remember. Touchtone was the cashier."[20]

"Yes; the man that turned out to be a friend of the gang that did the business," another speaker chimed in.

"Certainly. They were sure that the scamp opened the safe for them. They made out a clear case against him. He went to the penitentiary with the rest of 'em."

Gerald was trembling, and held Philip's cold hand as the two lads stood there to hear words so humiliating to one of them. But Philip whispered, "Don't go!" and still restrained him.

"Yes, it was as plain as daylight. The fellow opened the safe for the rogues! At first the indictment against him was rather shaky. He was tried, and got off with a light sentence; only a year or so, I believe."

"Convicted, all of 'em, on State's evidence, weren't they?"

"Yes, this Touchtone included. One of the crowd decided to speak what he knew. I presume Touchtone had had his share of what they all got. But it didn't do the man much good."

"Why, what became of him?" asked another voice.

"O, he and his wife rented a little cottage up here. They left their house near New York, or in it, and came here till Touchtone died. He had consumption. Marcy was an old friend of the lad's mother, and helped them along, I understand, till this boy, Philip, was left alone by her dying, too. She was a fine woman, I've been told. Stuck to her husband and to his innocence, till the last. After that, Marcy took Phil with him. I think he expects to adopt him."

"Well, he's a nice boy, anyway," came the other voice, "and Marcy's proud of him, I can see. I guess he'll turn out a credit in spite of his father. What time is it? My watch has stopped."

"Come," said Philip, softly. He walked away with Gerald. Neither spoke.

At length Gerald said, gently, "Is that all, Philip? You *made* me listen!"

"All?" replied young Touchtone, bitterly. "Isn't it enough? Yes, I made you listen! I wanted you to know the story before you saw any more of me. There's another side to it, but that isn't the one you will find people trouble themselves over. I wanted you to hear what you did. But I couldn't tell you myself. I am the son of—of—my father. I don't care for mere outsiders, who know it already and think none the worse of me for it. But other people, if I care any thing about them, why, they must know with whom they are taking up."

It cost him a struggle to say this. Gerald was younger than he. But the manly, solitary little guest of the Ossokosee had gained in these two days a curious hold over him. Philip had never had a brother. If he had ever thought of one, the ideal conjured up would have been filled by Gerald. He felt it now as he stopped and faced the latter in the moonlight.

But Gerald looked straight up into Philip's face. He smiled and said, "Philip, I believe your father didn't do that."

Touchtone put out his hand with a quick gesture of intense surprise.

"Gerald!" he cried as their two palms met in a clasp that hurt the smaller one, "what in the world made you say that?" There was something solemn, as well as eager, in his tone.

"O, nothing particular," the heir of the Saxton impulsiveness answered, simply; "but I don't believe it, that's all! I don't!"

"He don't believe it either," Gerald heard Philip say, as if to himself, "and I don't. What a little trump you are, Gerald Saxton!" They walked a little further in silence; then Philip again spoke, in a tone from which all the sudden joy and cheerfulness were gone: "Well, Gerald, you and I may be able to prove it together some day to the people. But I don't know—I don't know!"

Certainly they were to accomplish many strange things together, whether that was to be one of them or not.

CHAPTER III.

ALL ABOUT A ROW.

The guests of the Ossokosee had the pleasure of seeing a bright, still day for the regatta. By nine o'clock the shady road leading to the lake began to echo with carriages. In the little wind that stirred flags swayed down in the village and from the staffs on the Ossokosee and the little boat-house. As for the pretentious Victors' headquarters, they were flaunting with streamers and bunting[21] to an extent that must have severely taxed the treasury.

"I don't see where so many more people than usual have come from!" exclaimed Mr. Marcy to Gerald and Mrs. and Miss Davidson as they drove along toward the starting-point. And, in truth, for a race between two crews of lads, and of such local interest, the crowd was flattering. Country wagons lined the bank, in which sat the farmers of the district, with their wives and daughters gorgeously arrayed in pink and blue and white calico gowns; and bunches of roses and dahlias were everywhere about them.

"There are Mr. Wooden and Mrs. Wooden, with Miss Beauchamp," exclaimed Gerald, nodding his head vigorously to the group.

Fashionable carriages were not few, filled with ladies in gay colors, who chatted with knickerbockered[22] young men, or asked all sorts of questions of their husbands and brothers and cousins about the two crews.

"Those must be regular parties from the other hotels about here," said Miss Davidson, "made up expressly to drive over here this morning. Well, well!"

"Yes," Mr. Marcy assented, "I never expected to see such a general turning out at one of the Ossokosee regattas. Do notice, too, how the shores over there are covered with people, walking and sitting! Bless my heart! I hope that Phil and his friends are—h'm—not going to be so badly beaten, when there are so many hundreds of eyes to see it! Never was such a fuss made over our race before, especially a race so late in the season."

Mr. Marcy jumped out. They were near the Ossokosee boathouse. After he had seen how the oarsmen who bore the name and credit of his hotel were feeling over their coming struggle he was to get into a good-sized barge with several other gentlemen, one of them being the starter and umpire.

Gerald was looking at him with the full power of his blue eyes as Mr. Marcy stood directing the driver where to station the carriage for Mrs. Davidson and her daughter. The boy's glance was so eloquent that the proprietor of the Ossokosee House exclaimed:

"Why, Gerald, what was I thinking of? You come along with me if you choose to. That boat is apt to be crowded, but you're a little fellow and wont add much to the party. I guess I can have you squeezed in."

So the delighted boy followed his elderly friend through the grass toward the boat-house and the judge's barge.

"Shall I see Philip?" he asked, as they advanced to the inclosure. A long line of stragglers hung about the gate leading down to the Ossokosees' quarters. The village constable good-naturedly kept them from entrance.

"Yes; come right along," Mr. Marcy said, taking Gerald's hand. They hurried down to the rear door together.

"Hurrah! there's Mr. Marcy," was the exclamation, as they were allowed to step in. The six boys, Philip and Davidson foremost, were already in full rig and busy over the long shell²³ just about to be easily deposited in the water by the side of the float. Mr. Marcy and a couple of his friends saw this feat accomplished safely. Others of the barge-party walked in. The excitement became general. All the oarsmen talked at once, gave opinions of the state of the water, bewildered Mr. Lorraine or Mr. Marcy with questions, and hurried about the dim little boat-house to attend to the usual last things and one.

"Well, Frank, what do you think?" inquired Gerald of Davidson, with a face of almost painful interest as he glanced first at Touchtone, then at him.

"He thinks just what I think, Gerald," interrupted Philip, pulling the crimson silk handkerchief lower across his forehead, "and that is—"

"That the Victors are bigger men with a lighter boat, and have beaten us for three years running," Davidson said, quickly; "but that the weather is perfect, that the water is as smooth as if we'd taken a flat-iron to it, and that the Victors don't pull together after the style the Ossokosees do. Look at them now out yonder as they come around the point again! See that second fellow! If he don't keep better stroke he can put the whole crew out!"

Twenty minutes later Gerald was seated out under the awning of the barge, sandwiched between Mr. Lorraine and Captain Kent. He waited in feverish impatience for the grand moment. The umpire, a Mr. Voss, from the next county, was arranging some matters between Mr. Marcy and the supporters of the Victors. There were to be three races; but, the second one being between two members of the Victors, and the last an informal affair between four of the village lads in working-boats, the special rivalry was not eclipsed. Gerald's heart beat faster and faster as the crowd along the shores cheered six figures in crimson that glided quietly to their post of departure on the east; accompanied by the second shout for the yellow-filleted[24] Victors who pulled proudly across the open water and rested, like pegs driven into its bed, opposite their rivals.

"Looks as if it would be an uncommon good race for both of 'em!" Gerald heard some one near him say. But Mr. Voss was standing up and waving his hand.

"Are you ready?"

"Ready!" from the right.

"Are you read-y?"

"Ready!" from the left.

"Go!"

Bang! And the echoes clanged over the low hills and startled Farmer Wooden's skittish colt as Mr. Voss dropped his arm with the smoking pistol. Neck and neck, with a quick, snapping leap of the oars and a splendid start with which neither crew could quarrel, the slender, shining shells shot rod after rod up the lake.

Babel began at once—cries, cheers, applause. "Victors! Victors!" "Go it, Ossokosee!" "That's it; stick to the lead!" "Ossokosee forever!"

"That aint no bad send-off for the Ossokosees!" exclaimed Farmer Wooden to his wagon-load as the swift flight of the boats made them diminish in size every few seconds.

"No," said Miss Beauchamp, with her head full of Philip and of his satisfaction if there should be any bettering of the Ossokosees' record; "but those strong-armed fellows in the Victors' boat are holding off, Mr. Wooden. Don't you see that? They're going to give a tremendous spurt after that stake-boat[25] is turned."

By this time the road that ran parallel with the course was in a whirl of wheels. Dozens of carriages dashed up after the boats, to lose no yard of the contest. The Ossokosees were, in fact, a little in advance of the Victors. But, as Miss Beauchamp had supposed, that was evidently the policy of the older champions. They darted along well to the left of their rivals and kept carefully outside of a certain long strip of eel-grass where a danger-signal had been driven, and with their rapid pulling they were already beginning to lessen the number of boat-lengths between them and their opponents. Every body having taken it for granted that the excitement of this race was not who should beat, but how honorably the hotel faction should be beaten, there arose all along the mile of skirting land a buzz and then ragged cheers as people began all at once to discover the new possibility of the Victors being dishonored for once in their proud career.

"Hi! Look at that, I tell you, Fisher!" cried Mr. Marcy, as enthusiastic as Gerald himself, when he made up his mind that up there toward that stake-boat the Victors now began to pull with might and main. "Our boys—why, our boys are working like Trojans![26] And those chaps have found it out!"

"Hurrah! They're 'round the stake-boat first, as true as I live!" said somebody else in the barge.

Gerald was standing balanced on the outermost edge of a seat, with Mr. Marcy's arm about him to keep him in any kind of equilibrium. His eyes sparkled like stars as he held up his field-glass, and his color came and went with every cry he heard. It was for Philip's sake; all for Philip! It was wonderful, by the bye, how many persons watched that race that morning, giving one thought for the Ossokosees in general and two to Philip Touchtone!

"Yes, they are!" exclaimed another. "Gracious! what ails the Victors? Pull, you sluggards, pull, I say! Those boys are gaining on you every second with that stroke. It must be nearly forty." Louder and louder rang the clamor from all sides as the stake-boat was left behind by the belated Victors, not after all so much in arrear of the Ossokosees. Every body knew that the most remarkable "finish" ever to be dreamed of for Ossokosee Lake was begun. The carriages rolled quicker and quicker back to the goal, and began to pack together in the open meadow, abreast of the judge's barge. Shouting boys and men ran frantically along the road and side-paths, waving hats. From the knots of on-lookers the crowded Victors' club-house, the private boats moored by the ledges, fluttered handkerchiefs, veils, and shawls in the hands of standing spectators; and every thing increased in intensity, of course, as the two glittering objects flashed forward nearer, nearer, until the bending backs of the six rowers in each could be seen, crimson and yellow—and the panic-struck yellow sweeping onward last!

"O-h-h-h! Victors! Victors!" rang the echoes on the left, where most of the village partisans lined the wagon. "Osso-kosees!" "Now, then, Ossokosees! Give 'em your best!" "Good for you! That's right, don't let 'em make it!" "Touchtone! O, Touchtone!" "Go it, Dater, that's the way to give it to 'em!" "One good spurt now, Victors, and you can have it your own way!" "Bravo, Ossokosee!" "Oss-o-ko-see!" And then mingled with all this voicing of favorites, began the patter, at first gentle, but strengthening, of thousands of hands clapping together in the open air, and whips and sticks pounded on wagon-bottoms, and parasols clattered with them. O, it was a great finish; and— sweep—sweep—as the now desperate Victors flew down it was clear that Philip and his friends were not yet nearly overtaken, and that with a hope that gave each arm the power of steel the Ossokosees were bound to win that race if they could hold two minutes longer their advantage.

Gerald let fall his hand. Mr. Marcy, Mr. Lorraine, Mr. Voss, and the others were leaning forward in strong hope; and, as to the friends of the Victors, in courage till the last. The stroke of the Ossokosees was weakening a trifle now, just at the unlucki-est climax. In fact, the six had never pulled so fast in their lives as something had enabled them to do today. Their flesh and blood and wind were likely to fail at any instant now, in revenge. If Davidson should faint, or McKay come within a tenth of catch-ing the smallest crab,[27] why, then the charm must break and all end in defeat.

Many times since that day Gerald Saxton has said, smiling, "Well, I shall never forget the first time I knew that praying for a thing meant that you wanted it with all your heart and being! I prayed over a boat-race once, when I was a little boy."

"Now, then, steady with that match!" called Mr. Voss to the men in charge of the salute to greet either winners and signal the race's end. "They've got it! They've got it, sure!" cried Mr. Marcy, squeezing Gerald till the little boy wondered if his ribs would stand it.

Ah, now desperate Victors, that was a splendid spurt, but it's of no use! Two and one half lengths behind instead of three; that is all you get by it, and there are six rowers in that boat ahead of you who will fall over, and overboard, before you shall pass them now. Again? Another spurt? Yes; well done, and you deserve the cheer for it that you scarcely hear in your frantic efforts. But there is a roar drowning it out already, which signals your defeat. At them! At them one last time, Dater, the Consequential! But you know how to pull. It must be the last. For, look! you can see the very scarf-pins in the bosoms of Mr. Voss and Mr. Marcy in the barge; and on it with them, in an agony of delight at your vain prowess, stands Gerald Saxton, the friend of Philip Touchtone—Philip Touchtone, whose strong stroke has helped mightily to tell against you all the way up and back. Ah, you falter a little now; nor can you save yourselves by any more spurting. The green amphitheater rings again and again with cheers and applause, but not for you. You dart two boat-lengths behind those crimson shirts, that even your warmest friends yonder must hurrah over as they shoot by the goal! The cannon booms out their welcome far and wide! You who are the Victors must call yourselves the Defeats, for the race is over and the Ossokosees have won it gloriously!

How the next half hour passed for Philip, Davidson, McKay, Rice, and all that enraptured crew, as they received in the boat-house the friends who could press their way inside to congratulate them—this the reader may imagine. Philip and his friends forgot how exhausted they were in the delight of such praises and hand-shakings. As for Gerald and Mr. Marcy, they were among the first to greet them when they were cool enough to quit their shell for a few moments. Gerald was quite unnerved with rapture.

"O, Philip," he exclaimed, "I never was so glad over any thing in my life!" And the boy spoke the exact truth.

"You deserve to be carried home on a church-steeple—a blunt one—everyone of you!" declared Mr. Marcy, adding to the patron of the Victors, who stood near him, "Mr. York, your young men have lost their laurels forever. Our boys don't intend to be beaten again." And, as a matter of fact, they never were;

for the Ossokosee Club rowed them another year and utterly routed them, and before the third season the Victors were disbanded and a new organization had grown out of their ruins.

The two other races were duly pulled. Dater came out first in that which concerned his own club. The Ossokosees were presented at the side of the barge with their prize. Mr. Voss made a little speech. The crowd gave their final cheers as Philip received it for his associates. That two hundred dollars was to be spent in improving the boat-house. Somebody had talked of buying a new shell with it; but that was not heard of again after the day's deeds with the old one. Then the crowds broke up. The carriages rolled in different directions. The excitements of the morning were over. In the evening there was to be a special reception at the Ossokosee House, given by Mr. Marcy.

"But I never went to a regular grown-up party, even," protested Gerald, in visible concern when Miss Davidson declared he must go with her and see how Philip and the rest would be lionized. "I—I'm not old enough."

"Neither am I, for that matter, Gerald," laughed Philip, with a droll glance at the amused Miss Davidson; "so you ought to go along to keep me company. I am not a ladies' man, like Davidson or McKay."

"Well, you will have to walk about the hotel dining-room with some girl; you see if you don't," declared Gerald. But Philip did not. Nearly all the evening Gerald found his friend near him, where the boy could listen to the fine speeches lavished on Touchtone and every member of that crew of Ossokosee—quite numerous enough to turn older heads than Philip's. Miss Beauchamp, who was quite old enough to be Philip's aunt, declared that she, for her part, "felt jealous of Gerald" when Philip said that he would leave the scene for a while to see the boy quickly to his bed, Gerald having become fagged out with his enjoyment.

"You had better adopt him, Touchtone," Mr. Marcy suggested as the two turned away.

"O, I will, if his father will let me," retorted Philip, laughingly.

"Humph!" said Mr. Marcy, half aloud, "I doubt if he'd mind it half as much as he ought."

The party broke up half an hour later. Early hours were the custom at the Ossokosee. Philip was to sleep in Gerald's room that the accommodation he thus vacated might be given to some particular guests. The races had filled the house.

The hotel grew quiet. Mr. Marcy had not read the evening mail through, so busy had he been kept during the regatta. He sat in the office with his night-clerk, concluding the letters hastily.

"Holloa!" he exclaimed, breaking a seal, "Nova Scotia postmark? Saxton's hand? I guess I'd better look at it before I go to bed." He glanced at the first lines. His face grew attentive. He read on and turned the page. It wasn't a long letter, but it was plainly about an important matter.

He laid it down. Then, folding his arms, he stared in consideration at the uninteresting picture of a North German Lloyds steamship over his desk.[28] Then he said, half aloud, "Certainly he'll do! He's just the person." He rose quickly. "I'll go up and read it to them at once. No! On second thoughts, they would neither of them sleep a wink if I did. Tomorrow will do."

Mr. Marcy put the letter in the desk, turned out the gas, bade Mr. Keller good-night, and walked away to his room.

In that letter were involved the fortunes of the two lads, the big and the little one, who were asleep in Number 45, Gerald with one hand under his yellow head and the other just touching Philip's arm; as if he would have him mindful, even in dreams, that their existences now had ceased to be divorced, and that a new responsibility had come to Touchtone in that fact.

CHAPTER IV.

UNDER SAILING ORDERS.

They had just finished dressing next morning. Philip was asking himself whether, after all the fun of the last few days, the idea of adding up columns of figures in the office was a pleasant one.

"Come in," was Gerald's reply to a knock.

"Good-morning," said Mr. Marcy. In his hand was the letter.

"Gerald," he began, walking up to the lounge, "your father wants you."

"Papa!" exclaimed the boy, starting up as Mr. Marcy sat down. "Where is he? When did he come? Isn't that just like him!"

"No, sit down," laughed Mr. Marcy, holding up the letter. He isn't down-stairs. He's just where he was, in Nova Scotia. Listen to this and tell me what you think of it."

He read, while Philip listened from across the room:

"CAMP HALF-DOZEN,[29] *September,* 188–.

"DEAR MARCY: Please send Gerald up to me at this place, *via* Halifax, as soon as possible. When he arrives he can go to the Waverly Hotel.[30] Somebody in our party, or myself, will meet him. We have not roughed it so much as I expected. We shall stay here; the hot weather seems to hold on too long down your way. Of course, Gerald cannot make such a journey alone. Put him in charge of an experienced servant used to traveling, or make some arrangement of the kind convenient. I inclose check. Supply whatever extra is needed.

"We are having a first-class time—lots of fishing and shooting. Our nearest civilization is miles off. Hope the Ossokosee is doing well these closing weeks. It's a late season everywhere, isn't it?   Yours, etc.,

"GERALD B. SAXTON."

"P. S.—Give my love to Gerald. Tell him to write me immediately what day he starts. Tell him to be a good boy, and not let the whales[31] have any excuse to eat him on the way."

"There!" exclaimed Mr. Marcy, as he handed Gerald this business-like letter from any father summoning his son on such a journey. "That's your father all over! Not a word to spare. Disposes of you and every body else just as if you were a package of goods to be forwarded by express."

"Yes," returned Gerald, with a queer tone in his voice, "that *is* papa to the life. But he never took me quite so much by surprise. Of course, I've wanted to go up. I was dreadfully disappointed when he said I couldn't. But it's too bad to have to break up here and leave before the rest of you do." He glanced at

Philip, who sat in a surprise not particularly pleasant looking over the letter Gerald had handed him.

"Well, I think myself you will face the hardship better if I let Philip go along to take charge of you," said Mr. Marcy, quizzically. "How does that idea strike you?"

"O, Mr. Marcy!" exclaimed Gerald, with a look of intense pleasure; "do you really mean that?"

"I surely do," returned the proprietor of the Ossokosee. "I thought of it the moment I read your father's letter. I haven't at hand just now any servant that I could spare, or, in fact, be willing to commit you to, and I have no time to write to find out if friends can arrange to look after you on the steamer. Philip needs a change. Last year," he continued, turning to Touchtone, "you had no rest at all, from Mrs. Ingraham and me." He smiled as he spoke. "So I made up my mind last night that the nicest thing I can do for both of you, and for that harum-scarum father of yours, Gerald, will be to pack you off in Philip's care. What do you say to it, Philip?"

"I'd rather do it than any thing else in the world," replied Touchtone, "if you can spare me."

"O, this rush may end any day now. Then I shall close the hotel at once. Sit down here again—and be sober. To-day is Saturday. Your father wants you to set out, Gerald, as soon as you can. I will write him to-day, with you, and say that you and Philip will leave here for New York next Tuesday to catch the Wednesday's steamer. You will get to New York on Tuesday night, and you can either go to the Windsor to spend it, and the morning of the following day (the *Old Province* usually sails at one in the afternoon), or else you can adopt another plan."[32]

"What is that?" asked both at once.

"Why, as it will be rather lonely for you in that big hotel, I thought I would drop a line to a friend at his bachelor apartments on Madison Avenue and ask him to let you put up with him instead of at the Windsor. He has plenty of room, and he will be delighted to entertain you. Don't you think you would enjoy that arrangement? His name is Hilliard. He has been in London for a year or two, or Philip there would know him better than by hearsay."

Gerald and Philip declared that great enjoyment was promised by this arrangement.

"There's one of the breakfast-bells!" Mr. Marcy exclaimed presently, hurriedly rising. "I believe I have talked over every thing with you that is necessary now. You can begin your packing as soon as you like, Gerald, though you have time enough. I never knew you so quiet over any excitement before, Philip. Are you afraid of being seasick?"

"No, he's afraid of the responsibility of looking after me!" exclaimed Gerald, quick as a flash.

Philip smiled. "Nothing of the sort," he said. "Only it's a good deal more to me to think of going away on such a long journey so very unexpectedly than it is to you. It makes me your guardian in good earnest," he concluded, with a half smile.

To Touchtone, who nowadays was accustomed to only occasional winter trips to and from New York with Mr. Marcy, and who had known little change from the summer routine of his hotel duties and pleasures, this sudden episode was, truly, a little bewildering. It had all happened in a night—like Aladdin's palace.[33] To Gerald there was only a passing surprise. Orders from that handsome, gay, idle young father of his, who seemed to think of his son very much as he did of his best horse, or brightest diamond, or any other possession that he liked because it was his own and beautiful and pleasant to have near him, or easy to leave in good hands when it was more convenient, why, to Gerald such changes were already a common story. But the boy's delight that Philip was to go with him was so keen that nearly all else was forgotten.

The next few days were rather busy ones. The telegrams and letters to Nova Scotia and New York were duly dispatched. The letters might arrive at the forest camp little sooner than the travelers, but the telegram promised more expedition. Moreover, a hospitable reply came back from Mr. Marcy's friend in New York, the aforesaid Mr. Hilliard. He would be happy to entertain the two. He added that he himself might board their train at a certain station toward noon. He expected to be out of the city "visiting a friend over Sunday."

"If I stay up there until Tuesday," he wrote, "coming back,

I will hunt the boys out. Then we can travel the rest of the day together."

Bag and trunk were packed before night, and the trunk expressed direct to the steam-ship baggage-room, that it might be "off our minds," as Gerald put it. (Afterward they were not sorry.) They drove over to bid Mrs. Wooden and Miss Beauchamp good-bye in the afternoon, and at the tea-table in the evening a good many of the guests stopped to wish a pleasant journey to the two. After Gerald was in his room and asleep Touchtone came downstairs, where Mr. Marcy sat awaiting him in the office.

"Two hundred and fifty dollars," he said, handing Philip a roll of bills. "You cannot very well want more for your tickets and incidental expenses. You will, of course, stay in Halifax until Saxton sends for Gerald. He is a man who arbitrarily consults his own convenience, especially when he's off with a set of his Wall Street cronies on a summering lark. You may be obliged to remain several days."

"Thank you, sir," said Touchtone, putting the money into his pocket. "It's a wonderfully jolly little spree for me. I needn't say again how I thank you for putting me in the way of it."

"O, pshaw, Philip," returned the hotel proprietor, lightly, as he reclosed the heavy safe door, "that's all right! I don't know how I should accomplish Saxton's wishes without you. I shall miss you. One word more. This journey, as long as it lasts, and until Gerald leaves your hands, commits this little fellow to your care. So far as anyone can be responsible for him, of course you are. I have spoken to Gerald and drawn his attention to the fact that he must now really obey you, not merely as his friend, but his 'guardian' in every sense of the word. The boy seems already oddly fond of you. I don't think you will need to use a bit of authority. He will hardly attempt to differ with you foolishly. Still, he is in your hands, and he is a valuable handful. Saxton is a careless, rattling fellow in some respects, but he's fond of his boy, after his fashion."

Philip went up-stairs soberly. He was not eighteen. Somehow the tie between himself and this young charge who seemed to stand so in need of his friendship all at once weighed on our hero's heart. He *was* Gerald's guardian indeed; and, though the journey ahead was not like a trip to Europe or California, there were probably unexpected events to happen in its course where he must act for two. Well, he would try always to "do the best he could;" and Gerald's welfare should be his North Star all the way from the Ossokosee to Halifax.

They were up bright and early next day. They ate their breakfasts hurriedly, and were driven over to the station just before the express came rolling into it. They could not reach New York before six o'clock in the evening.

CHAPTER V.

"THE UNGUESSED BEGINNINGS OF TROUBLE."

About a dozen persons occupied the parlor-car.[34] Neither Philip nor Gerald paid any attention to them; they were absorbed, first, in settling themselves, and, next, in the discovery that the station, Youngwood Manor, at which Mr. Marcy's friend Hilliard should board their train, was not to be reached till after one o'clock. They consulted the letter from him (Philip happened to have brought it in his pocket), written in a neat, precise, hand—rather an elderly sort of hand—and felt disposed to like the sender of it, in advance.

But while they talked rather loudly and eagerly, and certainly with mentioning plenty of names and places, something of much importance to them suddenly got into progress near them. Let us say it was something fate had willed that they should not observe. They did not observe it. O, these big and little decrees in the destinies of boys and men![35] In this case it was their failure to be aware of apparently a very simple matter—the conduct of another passenger.

There sat back to back with Gerald, the tall chair doing its usual office of a screen, a strikingly handsome and well-dressed man of about forty years of age, who wore eye-glasses and was running over the contents of a newspaper when they settled down. Before long this well-appointed traveler, in changing the position of his chair, happened to let his eye fall on Gerald's traveling-bag lying overturned in the aisle, and painted, as to the bottom, in large black letters with the name, "Gerald B. Saxton, Jun., New York City."

A name—only a name! But what mysterious recollections, what quick impulses, it must have stirred up to vivid life in the mind of that grave traveler sitting so close to the fair-haired owner of the satchel and his friend! A slight start, a frown showing itself between his level eyebrows, a sudden sharpness of attention to the speakers beside him, and his sinking himself, little by little, down into his chair, while at the same time he drew the *Herald* over his face as if in an after-breakfast doze— these things succeeded one another rapidly in his conduct, until whoever watched him would have inferred, if with some surprise, that this man was surely doing every thing in his power to play the spy upon the two lads near him, and to overhear whatever they might say, without their even suspecting that they had a neighbor. Leaning his head against the cushion, well toward the left, he listened and listened, motionless, without a rustle of that sheltering newspaper; and often, now, as he so curiously fixed his attention on their desultory talk and discussion, one of his firm, well-shaped lips bit the other nervously under his dark mustache, and that frown of concentration became deeper on his forehead. Strange.

Ah! A letter was lying on the carpet within reach of his hand, between his chair and Gerald's. A letter—was it the same letter, he wondered, that he had just heard them speaking about— from a Mr. Hilliard? It was, because Gerald had carelessly dropped it from his hand, and the loss was not yet noticed. It was, indeed, odd and disgracefully ill-bred that any stranger should carry his curiosity or his interest, or whatever it was that influenced him, so far as to get possession of that letter very gently by a single motion of his arm, and, then raising it noiselessly to his eyes, to read it through behind the boys' backs. But this unseen companion of theirs did so; and, more than that, he read it through so carefully that you might have supposed he was getting it by heart. At length he laid it again on the carpet, just where he had noticed it, and presently Gerald's eye caught sight of it, and with an exclamation the letter was put safely into Philip's care once more. The name "Touchtone" written on it, and overheard from Gerald's lips, "Philip Touchtone," seemed to be another singularly interesting surprise to this reserved traveler.

But all at once he made up his mind to change his position. He did more than that. He raised himself gracefully in his seat, got possession of his silk hat, umbrella, and bag, and, rising quickly, walked down the length of the car he had faced, and vanished in the one coming behind it. Neither Philip nor Gerald remarked this sudden retreat any more than they had remarked that he had sat so near them for more than an hour. They were both in a gale[36] of good humor, and, with Gerald, to laugh hard was simply to forget every thing else but the fun on hand.

Did it ever occur to you from experience, my friend, young or old, what a small place is this big world after all? We do nothing, it sometimes seems, but jog elbows with folk we know or with folk who know us. You may go to Australia or Crim Tartary to get out of the way of people; but it may not be a week before you find that neither place is a safe retreat.[37] I once knew of a man who wished to fly from the face of all humanity that he happened to be acquainted with; he being, if one must tell all the truth, very miserable because of an unlucky love-affair, and anxious not to be reminded of the persons or places that had been nearest to him before his woes came to a climax. So our friend forthwith set out for northern Africa, and he decided to cross the great Sahara country with a caravan. Lo and behold! when the party was made up that were to go with the traders over the desert, he found that two cousins of—well, the cause of his gloomy spirits were to meet the expedition at a certain station, early on the route, both men he knew being in the same heart-broken state as himself, from the same reason. That was too much for him. Like a sensible man, he went straight home to Boston, and took to business energetically, and got back his health and spirits with his friends much sooner than he could have done in the Sahara, I am pretty sure. But I am getting away from this story of Touchtone and Gerald Saxton.

"Youngwood Manor," called out the guard, suddenly, as they steamed into a tiny station. The stop was only for an instant. They had hardly time to put their heads out. Nobody was getting aboard.

"Well, I declare! He couldn't have come up from New York," said Gerald, in disappointment. "I'm sorry. It would be more fun to have him meet us on the train than for us to go and hunt him up in his own street."

"Wait a minute or so," returned Philip. "Mr. Hilliard would have jumped on the car very quickly, knowing what a short stop the train makes. If he did, he is looking through it for us this minute."

The rear door opened. A tall gentleman with a fine face stood looking along the seats, his satchel in his hand.

His look fell on the boys. He started, gave a half-smile of recognition, and came slowly toward them.

"It must be he!" exclaimed Gerald.

"No doubt of that!" replied Touchtone. "He's making straight this way. Swing round that seat, Gerald. It hasn't been taken all day, I think."

"I believe I have the pleasure of finding some travelers I was to look for," began the new arrival as he stood before them. "My name is Hilliard; and this, I presume, is Mr. Philip Touchtone, and this Gerald Saxton? I'm very happy to meet you both."

He had a wonderfully pleasant, smooth voice, and his white teeth shone under his fine mustache as he smiled.

"We were afraid that you had not come out from the city, sir," said Gerald, making room.

"O, yes," replied Mr. Hilliard, with a little laugh. "I—I really couldn't stay at home. My friend —— that I wrote of expected me."

He took the offered seat, brushing out of it as he did so a gray linen button lost from a duster,[38] along with the advertising-page of a newspaper.

"And now, pray, tell me how you left Mr. —— Marcy? His letter said he was in his usual health."

"O, yes, sir," responded Philip, "and busy as ever with the hotel."

"It has done better this season than last, I understand?"

"Much better, sir. I hated to leave for even these closing weeks."

"Ah, I dare say," replied Mr. Hilliard, sympathizingly, "and, by all accounts, I don't see how he ever gets along without you. But really this *is* a journey you are about making! To Newfoundland is quite—"

"To Halifax, you mean, sir," Gerald corrected, laughing. "Papa isn't so far off as he might be."

"Certainly, Halifax, I would say," their new companion said, quickly. "But it's a delightful trip, especially if you go by water."

"Mr. Marcy said that *Old Province* was a very handsome steamer."

"She certainly is. By the bye, your father is quite well?" he asked.

"Thank you, yes, sir," replied Gerald. "He would not let me go to the camp at first, for fear I should catch something besides fish."

"I believe you are his only son?" asked Mr. Hilliard, looking into Gerald's face, with a fine cordiality.

"I am his only son," answered Gerald, who already considered Mr. Hilliard a very agreeable man—such a rich, strong voice, and such flashing black eyes. "And he is my only father, sir," he added, laughing.

Mr. Hilliard joined in it. "I have often heard of him in the city," he continued; "in fact, I have seen him occasionally. And now, Mr. Touchtone, about these traveling arrangements. Do I understand that you want to leave the city for Halifax by tomorrow's steamer?"

Philip came out of a brown study.[39] He had been thinking, for one thing, how different Mr. Hilliard was from what he had (quite without warrant) supposed he would be.

"O, certainly," he replied. "You see, Mr. Saxton expects Gerald by Friday night, and I am taking charge of him—eh, Gerald?—until Mr. Saxton sends to the Waverly Hotel. Besides, I must return to Mr. Marcy as soon as I can."

"Ah, yes, I see," said Mr. Hilliard, musingly. "Well, we will all get to town this evening early, I hope, and have a sound sleep;

but it would be pleasant if you joined other friends on the *Old Province*."

"Perhaps," answered Gerald; "but you see Philip and I travel by ourselves, so that, if either of us is very seasick, there will be no one to laugh. I couldn't, and he wouldn't."

Philip here recollected an unpaid duty. "I want to thank you, Mr. Hilliard," he began, "for so kindly taking us in tonight."

"O, dear, not a bit of trouble," returned Mr. Hilliard, vivaciously; "but that brings me to explaining a slight dilemma. A fire broke out in our house yesterday. I am a homeless character, for the time being, myself."

"A fire!" exclaimed both the boys.

"Yes, a fire. You've no further use for my note, that I see you have there? Shall I just tear it up, then? I'm like every body else; I love to get hold of a letter I've written and put it out of the way." Glancing at the clean carpet, he dropped the pieces into his pocket. "You see this fire, luckily, wasn't in my apartment, but overhead. My rooms were a good deal upset."

"Then, of course, you mustn't try to take us," Touchtone exclaimed, wondering that Mr. Hilliard had not entered upon so important an announcement a little sooner. "We'll go to the hotel."

"Not a bit of it, not a bit of it!" protested Mr. Hilliard; "you mustn't think of such a thing. I am stopping with a cousin of mine, and he has abundance of room for us all, and expects us. It's all settled."

After considerable discussion only did Philip consent to so unexpected a change. It disturbed him. Gerald rather enjoyed the odd plan. He yielded.

"By the bye, Mr. Hilliard," he said as the train sped forward with a lengthened shadow, "you said you left New York yesterday. I thought you expected to come up to Youngwood on Saturday."

"O, so I did," returned Mr. Hilliard, in his careless manner; "but—but I decided to wait, for some business reasons. I should have been very sorry not to meet you just as I did. Perhaps, if you don't find yourselves too tired by the time we finish dinner

to-night, we will go out and look up something that will entertain us."

The proposal sounded pleasantly. They fell to talking of
sights. The acquaintance advanced rapidly.

After a little time the train paused before a small junction-
station only about thirty miles from the edge of New York
city. It did not go on. They looked out. Men were to be seen
about the locomotive. They left the car with the other travelers and walked up to the group. Something was wrong with
the engine. After some ten minutes of uncertainty a couple of
brakemen furnished the information that the train must wait
for half an hour at least. "We can get her all right again by that
time," said the engineer. If the passengers chose to do so they
could stretch their legs until the whistle called them.

"We may as well pass the time that way," laughed Mr. Hilliard. "It is provoking. We'll go over and take a look at that railroad hotel they are altering."

Gerald caught up the satchel (besides their umbrella, the
only baggage the boys carried); there was a supply of ginger-
snaps in that bag. They walked out of the hot sunshine and sat
down in the shade of the wide veranda of the railroad restaurant, which displayed a very gay sign, "Lafayette Fox, Proprietor." Mr. Hilliard gave them a spirited account of an adventure
he had met with while on a sketching tour in Cuba; and when
Gerald suggested that he might entertain himself and them by
making a pencil drawing then and there of the motionless train
and the groups of people gathered near it he assented. "I'll run
over and get my pencils and a block of paper in my bag. It'll
only take a minute." They watched him hurry away—certainly
the most obliging man in the world.

Now, the restaurant was being transformed into the glory of
a hotel. Back of the rear rooms rose the yellow-pine frame of a
large wing, intended to contain, when finished, at least seven or
eight good-sized rooms.

"Let's go along this piazza," proposed Philip, as several minutes elapsed and Mr. Hilliard did not put in his re-appearance.
(Mr. Hilliard, it may be explained, was struggling with the
tricky lock of his satchel, kneeling on the floor of the car.)

"If he comes back he will think we have got tired of his society," said Gerald. But presently Philip and he, holding each other's hands, were stepping airily from one beam to another of the unplanked floor of the new building.

"I suppose he hasn't found what he went for," conjectured Philip. "Suppose we climb up that stair yonder. It's certain to be breezier overhead. Mr. Hilliard will shout if he can't find us."

The blue sky overhead, seen through the open rafters, was an inviting background. Up the stair Gerald sped, and, once at the top, called out, "Catch me if you can!" and began scudding along a narrow line of planks resting on the joists.

"Look out, Gerald!" called Philip, half alarmed, half laughing, hurrying after. "You will break your neck! Stop that!"

"Hurrah!" was Gerald's only reply. The light-footed boy dashed on the length of the addition. A ladder, descending to the floor they had left, appeared through a square opening. He scrambled down. Philip was not much behind. The room beneath was the last of the unfinished "L." It was also floored over, except where an open trap-door gave entrance to the cellar.

"Here goes!" cried Gerald, as Philip, laughing, but with outstretched hand, and anxious to put an end to this acrobatic business, pressed hard upon him. Down jumped Gerald into the trap. Without an instant's hesitation Philip leaped after his charge. Both landed, laughing and breathless, in the dry new cellar, the only light coming through the square opening overhead.

"Dear me! Didn't that take the wind out of me, though?" exclaimed Gerald, leaning against the wall. "That's an awfully deep cellar. It must be eight or nine feet; it jarred me all over!"

At that instant, shrill and unmistakable, the locomotive whistle broke the current of their thoughts.

"The train, Gerald, the train!" Philip cried, rushing under the open trap. "It's ready to go, as sure as you live!"

They sprang for the flooring above. Each appreciated, after the first leap, that getting out of a cellar was sometimes a work quite different from getting into it.

"We can't do it!" Philip gasped out in consternation, with a vain attempt to draw up Gerald after him with one disengaged

hand. Down they came on the sand together. The whistle uttered its warning again. They heard distant shouts as of belated
passengers. They called for help, but the restaurant people were
in front of their establishment. After a moment more the hum
of the departing train greeted their ears.

"O, Gerald, Gerald, here's a ladder, all the time!" called
Philip, pulling it down from its hook, over their heads in the
deep shadow.

To dash back to the long piazza and so around to the front of
the house was a half moment's flight. But they gained the place
which they had quitted to gaze open-mouthed on an empty
track and at puffs of smoke beyond the cut. That train was gone
indeed, Mr. Hilliard aboard of it.

Two very comfortable-looking and composed people, that
could only be Mr. and Mrs. Lafayette Fox, were standing in
sight. The stout proprietor of the railway restaurant heard the
story of their predicament.

"Well, ye'll have to stay here just two hours and a half," said
Mr. Fox. "There aint a train till then. Too bad! Ye'd better telegraph to your friend that's gone on ahead of you, so as he'll
know whether to wait for you at the Jersey City depot or in the
New York one or not. I should think he'd look for a message
one place or t'other when he gets in."

"Yes, that's quite likely," replied Philip; "and he mustn't think
of waiting there. We'll go straight to his rooms when we reach
town, if ever we do."

He sent his dispatches to the two waiting-rooms. He had
better send another one still, he thought; so, not knowing the
address of the hospitable cousin who was to take Mr. Hilliard
and themselves under his roof, he wired a message to Mr. Hilliard's own apartment, where they had expected to go. Somebody would send it over. "Accidentally detained from getting
aboard again; please leave new address at old one, or at place
where this is received. Will find you as soon as possible." So ran
the dispatch.

But scarcely had they sent these three communications, in
the hope of saving their kind host perplexity and fatigue on account of the odd mishap, than Mrs. Lafayette Fox came run-

ning up to Philip, breathless. Luck was favoring them, surely.
There was a fast freight-train rumbling into the little depot. A
cousin of hers, Leander Jenks, was its conductor; and, railroad
rules or no rules, Leander Jenks should take the pair of them
aboard, and so get them to New York, not so much later than
if they had not pursued their trip by way of the cellar. In came
the fast freight. In a twinkling Jenks had consented, and, before
they fairly realized it, the boys were ejaculating their thanks
and being introduced to Leander and hustled aboard a red car,
which speedily began pounding and jolting its brisk way at
the end of a very long train, but at an excellent rate of speed,
toward New York. They were well out of their plight.

"Yes," said Philip; "and even if we should be late in reaching
the city, or fail to make our connection with Mr. Hilliard, why,
we'll just go to the Windsor for the night and straighten it all
out with him the next morning."

"I wonder what he'll say?" queried Gerald.

"Well, he might advise us to look before we leap another
time," laughed Philip.

The sun had set and fog was turning into a drizzle as they
crossed the flat, salt meadows west of Bergen Hill and left the
draw-bridges of the sinuous Hackensack behind them. It was
well that Philip had expressly warned Mr. Hilliard not to wait
for them in Jersey City, for he suddenly discovered that the
freight of the road did not go to the same terminus as the passenger trains, and that he and Gerald would land in New York
a good distance up-town. The North River was wrapped in a
thick mist as they made their sluggish passage across; the rain
fell steadily, and Touchtone was glad when they landed and
set out for Mr. Hilliard's apartment as fast as the only cab they
could find might be made to rattle. "You are pretty well used
up, aren't you?" he said to Gerald, putting his arm along the
tired boy's shoulder. "Never mind; we'll be there safe and sound
presently."

Madison Avenue reached, Philip counted the numbers
through the sash. The cab veered to the gutter. The man leaped
down and opened the door.

"Shall I wait, sir?"

"Yes," replied Philip; "we want an address."

He hurried up the step of a tall apartment-house, Gerald, in his renewed excitement, declining to stay behind.

"Will you please give me the address for to-night of Mr. Frederick Hilliard?" he inquired of the footman who answered his ring. "Has he been here in course of the evening?"

"Beg your pardon, sir," replied the man, respectfully. "What did you ask for, sir?"

"For Mr. Hilliard's address since the fire."

"I—I don't understand, sir. I think Mr. Hilliard is at home, sir. Second floor, sir. Shall I show you up?"

A door above opened and shut. A short, fat gentleman, slightly bald, of at least fifty winters, came briskly down, looking forward with a very friendly curiosity in his eyes. He began smiling cheerfully at them, and his pleasant face, with a snow-white mustache, grew pleasanter at each step. In his hand was a telegram envelope.

"Mr. Hilliard," said the man, stepping aside.

"Aha, boys!" he exclaimed, hurrying across the thick Turkish rug and presenting a fat, white hand, "here you are, I declare, safe and sound! You sent me this message here, which somebody has taken the trouble to mix up on the way, so that I can't get the hang of it, though otherwise I should have given you up. Come in, come right in!" he went on, cordially clasping a hand of each. "This is Philip Touchtone, and this Gerald, according to friend Marcy's description. You're both very welcome. My, what's the matter? O, your cab! Cripps, pay the cab—here— and, Cripps, tell Barney to call at ten to-morrow morning to take us to that Halifax boat."

Literally open-mouthed in bewilderment, Philip and Gerald allowed the hospitable little gentleman do as he pleased, and to stand pumping their hands up and down.

"Excuse me, sir," Philip began, stammering, "but—but there is certainly some mistake. You are surely not the gentleman we met on the train to-day—and—"

"Train? Of course not!" laughed the irrepressible stranger. "I've been laid up in the house with malaria since I wrote Marcy. But you're *you*, Philip Touchtone; and *you* are Gerald Saxton;

and *I* am myself, Frederick Hilliard, the only and actual, at your service. If any body has been playing me, he's some oddity—doing a poor copy of an indifferent original. My dear boy, you stare at me as if I were a ghost!"

A cloud was eddying in Philip's head. Not till afterward did he think how droll his question must have sounded. But he asked, very solemnly, "Has there—been a fire—in this building?"

"A fire? In such a hot September as this!" chuckled the merry gentleman. "Bless your heart, my dear fellow, nowhere but in the kitchen, I trust! Does the hall strike you as damp? Don't know but what it is. Bring those things up-stairs, George," he added to his own servant, who appeared from above. "Follow me, boys. My rooms are on the second floor. How did you leave Miss Beauchamp? and how are Mr. Fisher and old General Sawtelle and Mr. Lorraine?"

There was no other explanation needed just now. There were two Mr. Hilliards! One was the real one—before them. Philip felt that at once. The other had been a sham one, a somebody else—an impostor! Who was he, and what could he have wanted by so unaccountable a trick? Or was there, behind his conduct, more than a trick?

CHAPTER VI.

A RIDDLE NOT EASILY ANSWERED—THE "OLD PROVINCE."

It was nearly ten o'clock in the evening. Gerald was in bed and asleep. Mr. Hilliard was lying back in his leather arm-chair, his eyes resting thoughtfully on the ceiling.

Opposite him, looking into his face, sat Philip.

"Well," remarked his host, "here we have sat ever since dinner, going over the whole affair from beginning to end! We're not any closer to solving some knots in it than we were when we started. Still, I fancy we've guessed all that is necessary, my boy. You're tired out. So am I. What's left gets the best of me completely. We'd better go to bed."

"And what about your advertising, sir?"

"O, that must be attended to, of course; as soon as George comes, in fact. It will not likely trace the scamp or make any difference, so far as you and Gerald are concerned. It may protect me, though, if he continues to sail under *my* colors for any length of time."

"You still think, sir, that he has no special designs against you?"

"Against *me*? Certainly not! He used my name simply because he happens—I'd like to discover how!—to know enough about me to serve his turn. I don't know how long he has been acting me, I'm sure."

"He must have some way of keeping your affairs before him, sir. Surely, he knows the Ossokosee House and the people there very well indeed."

"No, that don't follow," returned Mr. Hilliard. "He must have been on the train longer than you think, and within earshot of you. Such characters are amazingly clever in making a little knowledge go a great way, and, besides, he drew more from you both with each sentence. Didn't he contrive, too, to get hold of my letter by that impudent dodge? Mark my words, those torn pieces of handwriting will bring me a fine forged check some day unless I take good care. My dear boy," Mr. Hilliard continued, less ruefully, "under the circumstances the rascal had ten chances to your one, and it's not strange you were bowled over."

"But what was it all *for*?" cried Philip once again. "What object was there for such a trick? But that brings us around just to where we started."

"My dear fellow," rejoined Mr. Hilliard, rising and leaning on the back of his great chair, "his object I don't think was any worse than the one we have decided upon. Surely, that is unfavorable enough to you, too. He is a common sharper.[40] There are hundreds of them all about the country. He was coming on from B——, where, I dare say, he had been losing money. Sitting near you he heard you discuss this trip that you are making. Every thing you said implied that you were going alone; and that meant that one or the other of you carried a couple of hundred dollars, or perhaps more—"

"We didn't say a word about money."

"But your whole look and conversation told him of your having it! Very well, then; how to get it from you was the task before him. It was simple for such a scamp, if he was lucky enough to be a little familiar with my doings and gathered your references together. There are scores of scoundrels in this big city, Philip, who make a business of becoming versed in the looks, friends, history, every thing, of respectable men on purpose to make use of their information to swindle other persons."

"I've heard that," said Philip, ruefully; "but I never expected to find out how neatly it could be tried upon me."

Mr. Hilliard laughed. Nobody expected it. "Of course, the mainspring of his fraud was my failure to get aboard the train. After he was certain that I had not kept to my plan he marched up to you. 'Nothing venture, nothing have,' is the motto of a blackleg.[41] The game was in his hands. He must have dreaded my possible turning-up all the time he devoted himself to you; but practice in such acting makes perfect. All his care after the first instance lay in seeming perfectly at ease with you. That most lucky falling into Mr. Fox's cellar separated you and cut the fraud short. He must have raged when he found that you failed to get aboard the train!"

"There were other fellows on it," said Philip. "In the crowd hurrying to it when the whistle blew he probably took another couple that we saw for Gerald and me. Otherwise, I believe, he would have jumped off."

"By the time he found out his carelessness he couldn't. However, if he had met you in New York, my lad, and prevented your coming here to me he could yet get hold of that money. Down at one or the other passenger-station I don't doubt that he hung about waiting for you. We'll find out if your telegrams were called for. George can go and ask about that for us."

"After we had met him in New York, sir, he would have robbed us?"

"Certainly, if he couldn't manage it before. He could have taken you to his quarters. (Likely they are handsome enough, as he said, and they may be not far from where we sit tonight.)

There he would have given you, probably, a better supper than I have, added a dose to insure your sleeping, robbed you, and found means to get rid of you, very likely without injuring you, before morning." (Mr. Hilliard did not choose to suggest any other notion than that "very likely without injuring you;" but he had others.) "He would contrive it so that you could never have him traced out. It's not a rare scheme, remember, though its bad enough to think about."

"Then it was just a clever plan to rob two boys?" Philip asked, tapping his fingers on the table reflectively. Was he, or was he not, quite satisfied of it?

"Positively. Nothing more romantic, I am sure," responded Mr. Hilliard. "I must say I think that sufficiently exciting to satisfy most people. You will not be likely to hear of him again; I may."

Mr. Hilliard touched his bell. George came in. "I shall want you to mail these letters at once," said his master; "and these must go by hand to the newspaper-offices addressed."

Each envelope contained a notice cautioning all persons against putting any confidence in the pseudo Hilliard, whom the advertisement briefly described, denouncing him in the usual form.

"Now for bed!" ejaculated the boys' host as George vanished. "Excitement has kept you from realizing how your journey has tired you. I am glad that Gerald was so used up. There is no need to tell all our disagreeable theories to so young a boy as he. We must try to get the thing out of his head to-morrow."

Philip said good-night and closed his door. Gerald lay sound asleep. He stood beside the bed watching the younger boy's regular breathing. He did not know it, but such moments when he, as it were, struck a balance between Gerald and himself, and appreciated how Gerald depended upon him for society and care, were already moments that converted the manly metal in Philip into finest steel to cleave and endure.

Next morning found them all up early and in great spirits. Breakfast was eaten with lively chat on indifferent topics. Gerald was successfully diverted from dwelling on yesterday's mystery. George was dispatched early to the down-town waiting-rooms,

and came back with the news that the messages Philip had telegraphed had been duly asked for by a gentleman who waited
about for a long time after he received them. Philip and Mr. Hilliard exchanged glances. So the unknown sharper had indeed
expected his victims, and finally retired to parts unknown!
"Good-bye to him," laughed Mr. Hilliard.

Ten o'clock came and the carriage. Philip had several errands to do around busy Union Square. The tickets were already attended to; but somehow time was lost. When they
hurried down-town and swung around the corner of the Bowling Green[42] they discovered that they were scarcely five minutes
from the sailing of the *Old Province.*

As they rolled out upon the pier the black hull of the Halifax
boat, built for worthy ocean service, rose before them.

"They've rung the 'all-ashore bell' long ago, gentlemen! Be
lively!" called out one of the employees. They sprang out of the
carriage and hurried forward. "Halloa, there, wait a minute!"
was shouted to the deck-hands who were preparing to cast off
the plank.

"Quick! That trunk there is for Halifax!" Mr. Hilliard called
to the baggage-men. The trunk was caught up and hustled off.
"A minute in time's as good as an hour—good-bye, good-bye!"
he gasped, helping them up. "I wanted to give you some points
about the custom-house fellows and speak a good word to the
captain for you, but I can't. I'll telegraph Marcy that I saw you
off nicely. I'm going West myself to-morrow, you know. Good-
bye, and *do* take care of yourselves!" With which Mr. Hilliard
was fairly dragged down the plank by the impatient ship's
people, talking to the very bottom of it, and unconsciously
quite a center of observation.

A moment later Philip and Gerald were waving their hands
to him as the *Old Province* slipped along from the pier. Shall it be
confessed that even Philip felt something like loneliness steal
into his breast as he finally said, "Come, Gerald, let's go and
take a look at our state-room."[43]

They made themselves comfortable outside for the afternoon. There did not appear to be any considerable number of
passengers. In fact, they heard one of the officers remarking

that "it was the shortest list they had had during the season."
A dozen not very interesting commercial travelers going back
to the Provinces; as many New Yorkers bound north on special errands; some quiet Nova Scotia people—these, with four
or five humble household groups that the boys soon classed as
emigrants, were all the travelers on the *Old Province* for that trip.
They soon ceased to pay any attention to them, and they passed
the long hazy afternoon quite by themselves. The *Old Province*
steamed onward well out at sea, with the coast a pale bluish line
in the distance.

But as the afternoon closed they began to meet the tides
that roll in brusquely upon the New England inlets. A gray
fog swept about the *Old Province,* and what with a strong swell
and a bluff wind that drove the mist thicker around them, the
steamer took to rolling quite too much for comfort. Darkness
came on. The saloon twinkled with its lights in pleasant contrast to the gloom outside. Gerald, before supper, found out
that he was—for the first time in his life—a particularly bad
sailor.

"I—I think I'd better go and lie down," he said, a good deal
ashamed of his uneasiness. "I never was sick on our yacht, and
I don't believe I shall be now; but my head feels pretty topsy-
turvy."

So Philip got him into his berth. There was soon no occasion
for Gerald to blush. Not a few of the other passengers promptly
found out the rolling of the *Old Province.* They sought the se-
clusion which their cabins granted. The fog thickened. The
steamer slackened up and plowed along at half-speed, blowing
her hoarse fog-whistle. Philip went alone to supper.

He found only two thirds of those on board, besides some
of the steamer's officers, scattered about the tables. As he sat
down the captain, hurrying by, suddenly turned toward him.

"Is your little messmate under the weather?" he asked,
abruptly, but not unkindly.

"Yes, sir."

"In his berth? Quite the best place for him! Your brother, I
suppose? No? H'm! I'll try to have a little talk with you both
later."

With which Captain Widgins walked away, leaving Touch-tone decidedly surprised at this unexpected attentiveness, which he set down to the rather public style in which he and Gerald had come aboard.

He had to concentrate all his faculties on his unsteady plate. At last he pushed back his chair and wiped away the water dashed out of his glass into his face as he tried to secure a part-ing swallow. He looked across to a remote table. Two gentle-men sat there; a pillar partially hid them. But one of them was now in full sight and staring at him.

Philip nearly let fall his napkin. Those frank eyes of his met the now impudent dark ones of the "Mr. Hilliard" of Young-wood. As he looked at the man, asking himself if he were not deceived, "Mr. Hilliard" bowed politely to him, and then went on sipping his tea.

Philip told Gerald—a long time afterward—that once he had cut in two with his scythe a black snake coiled about a nest of unfledged cat-birds in a bush, evidently making up its mind which to devour first.

"I assure you the snake and that man looked exactly alike!" was Philip's comparison.

CHAPTER VII.

OPEN WAR.

During the few instants that it took Touchtone to quit the din-ing-saloon and reach the transept into which the state-room opened, a chaos of ideas surged in his head. He afterward won-dered how he could even have thought of so many things in such a hurry. There are at least two ways of being frightened: one, clean out of all your wits, the other by having them tossed about like a whirlpool so that for a time you do not know what idea is uppermost.

He stopped in the dim passageway to "pull himself to-gether." He guessed it now—the startling truth! Since "Mr. Hilliard" was there aboard the steam-ship it was, in all probability, because he knew that they, Philip Touchtone and Gerald Saxton, were there too. And that meant that kind-hearted Mr. Hilliard, number two, the real Mr. Hilliard, had been wrong. This dogging of two defenseless lads had been for no design of mere robbery, but for some sinister end. Philip's heart throbbed violently as the surmise came that a mysterious enemy was tracking, not simply two boys out of all the summer's host of traveling ones in general, but Philip Touchtone and Gerald Saxton, in particular. The question was, why were they the objects of his plot, whatever it might be? And was the attack upon Gerald or himself?

He entered the state-room softly. Gerald raised himself on his elbow.

"Is that you, Philip?" he asked.

"Yes, my lord," Philip answered, sitting down on the edge of the berth, and trying not to let his voice or manner hint of the trouble of his mind. "How is your head? Do you want any thing?"

"My head is ever so much better," said Gerald, sinking back luxuriously. "I should like some ice-water, if you'll get it, please, before long. I'd better not try to get up to-night, except to undress. Don't you think you'd like to get to bed soon yourself?"

"Yes," replied Philip, absently, "very soon."

He was asking himself whether he would not better go at once to Captain Widgins, who had seemed so friendly to him, and confide to him his peculiar story and suspicions. But then had he not best know more of the riddle before he did? The only way to do that was to turn the state-room into a hiding-place and a castle for Gerald; and as to himself, to walk out boldly and bring events to an issue. He had courage enough for that.

"I'll get you the ice-water at once," he exclaimed, starting up, "and I'll see what sort of a night it is by this time. Then I wont have to leave you alone again."

"All right," returned Gerald, yawning. "I'm half in a doze now; I dare say I'll be asleep before you get back, but I'd rather not go to bed quite yet. It can't have cleared much. That fog-whistle is going as hard as it can."

Philip locked the state-room door as he stepped out—a precaution Gerald was too drowsy to mark. He re-entered the main saloon and walked with deliberate slowness about it, while he waited for the ice-water. There seemed to be no signs of the enemy. It was a rather vacant quarter where he found himself at last. A tall figure quickly drew near and stopped before him. Philip raised his eyes. As he expected, it was the foe.

"Good-evening, Mr. Touchtone," the man began in his smoothest voice, offering to shake hands, and directing his black eyes full into Philip's steady ones.

Philip drew himself up, and, paying no heed whatever to the hand, responded stiffly, "Good evening." He made as if he would have passed on, but then the other stepped directly in his way.

"Pray, don't be in a hurry," he said, in a lower tone, with a different note coming into it, that did not surprise Philip, "I think, considering the extraordinary way that you gave me the slip yesterday, and since I have taken passage on this steamer expressly to have the pleasure of a talk with you, I deserve a little of your valuable time, eh?"

Philip flushed at the familiarity of the man's speech. However, to lose temper would be the foolishest course. Surely this was the very opportunity he sought.

"I'm sorry, but I can give you very little time," he replied. "And you are mistaken. I hope I shall never have occasion to say any thing to you or to see you again. You certainly know why, as well as I do. Good-night."

His manner and words did what he boldly undertook. Before there could be a battle, war must be declared.

It was declared. "Mr. Hilliard" leaned forward, and retorted, "Look here, Touchtone! You'd better not make things harder for yourself. I *will* have a talk with you. It's what I'm here for. Is Saxton's boy in your state-room? Well, it makes no difference; I can go there with you, and he can hear all I have to say, for that matter."

As it happened, "Mr. Hilliard" would have most assuredly preferred not to have Gerald a listener. But he chose to give Philip another idea.

"Or else," he continued, "do you meet me aft, outside—

where the pile of stools is. You know the place. It's dark there. No one will bother us. Which suits you?"

The waiter was appearing with the ice-water.

"I will meet you outside," Philip answered. With an undaunted gaze into his foe's face he added, "I may as well know, sooner or later, what you are hunting us down for in this fashion."

The other smiled maliciously.

"I will expect you there in five minutes. If you don't come I will look you up."

The waiter who handed Philip his jug might have supposed the last sentence just a civil appointment made by one friend with another.

In the state-room, which Philip reached trembling but resolved (and especially resolved on saying nothing to the captain or any body else until after the coming interview), Gerald lay fast asleep, his face turned from the light. He did not hear Philip enter this time.

"Shall I wake him?" questioned he. He set down the water-jug. "No, I wont. The little fellow's pretty sure to stay like that until I've got to the bottom of this row and am back here, ready to make my next move. Heigho! shouldn't I like to see Mr. Marcy just this minute!"

He bent above Gerald. He was sound asleep—safe to stay so, indefinitely. Philip stole out, once more turning the key on Gerald, that no intruder should disturb his calm dreams. "Only a rascal with no good to talk about would have chosen such a place!" he could not but think as he went out from the cabin. The *Old Province* was progressing very cautiously. The opaque fog was like wool around her, although straight up overhead the moon seemed struggling to show herself in a circle of wan light. The ocean's swell was much less and the drizzle over. But the night bade fair to stay very thick and to give place to a morning like it. Coming from the lighted cabin, Philip stumbled about over the slippery deck. He caught the sound of a repeated whistle rising, falling, and trilling artistically, that was plainly intended as his guide. "Mr. Hilliard" rose from where he had been lounging along the wet rail.

"Ah," said he, "you're here, are you, Touchtone? There seem to be some dry chairs on this heap. Looks as if it was going to stay muggy, don't it?"

"I'd like to know your business with me as soon as I can," replied Philip, determined to waste no time, and declining the proffered seat. "I'm not here for my own pleasure, nor because you've frightened me into coming to listen. I have found out the trick you tried to play on us yesterday. We spent last night with Mr. Hilliard. So don't try to go on with that."

Philip was somewhat surprised at his own daring. But those were the words that came, and I have set them down just as he spoke them.

"O, indeed," said the other, throwing his cigar over the rail. "Really, I presumed you must have done that by this time. I'd no intention of 'going on' with that business, I promise you. You see, Touchtone, I've concluded that you are about as sensible and clear-headed a fellow of your age as ever lived! It will be much better for me to be honest and confidential with you than to—well, to try any such little devices as I thought advisable yesterday. To begin, my name isn't Hilliard, as you know—"

"I should think I did!" ejaculated Philip.

"So you will please call me Mr. Belmont, of New York—John Alexander Belmont, at our mutual service. And, by the bye, Touchtone, I must tell you another thing. I knew your father, Reginald Touchtone, pretty well for a good many years. Surprised, eh? Well, it's a fact. We came together in—in business, before—before he made a fool of himself by pretending to be better than other people."

At the mention of his father's name, from the lips of such a man, Philip started violently. Belmont (for such, in deference to his request, he will be called henceforth here) had forgotten for an instant his self-control in his anger over some past event. But Philip's own composure was upset by the sneer.

"How dare you speak so of my father!" he exclaimed, indignantly. "You can insult me, but you can't insult him—to my face. I don't know who you are yet, nor what you have done. But I know that my father never willingly had a word to say to such a man as you. Not he. As for that matter you hint at, he was as innocent in it as—as Gerald Saxton!"

Taken aback at the boy's honest anger and courage, Belmont uttered an exclamation. Forgetful of the likelihood of being overheard, he began, excitedly, "Gerald Saxton! Ah, yes, now you've brought me to the point! It's about him I propose to talk to you, you impudent young scamp. First of all, that boy has got to come at once into my hands."

"Your hands!" retorted Philip, astonished.

"Yes, mine! I mean to have him, henceforth and forever, if I can! Hear that, please. I'm aboard this steamer on purpose to get him, as you will find out. I shall, inside of precious few hours, let me tell you. He belongs to me."

Philip was confounded. His notions had been correct. The second of his doubts was answered. Gerald—little Gerald—was the end of some villainous conspiracy! What could it be for, and how long had it been closing about him?

"That is false, you know," he replied, facing Belmont in the moonlight. "Gerald Saxton yours? What are you talking of? He is the son of a New York gentleman. You pretended to know his father. He is on his way with me to meet him. You cannot lay a finger on him! Captain Widgins—"

"Captain Widgins!" interrupted Belmont. "Captain Widgins knows all the whole affair just as I have given it to him. So do some other people on board this ship. Captain Widgins has promised to help me whenever it's necessary. You needn't expect to cheat him!"

Touchtone's heart sank. Belmont had been before him. The captain's conduct at supper was suspicion, not kindness! Yet this man was equal to any lie that might terrify his victim. He remembered that. It gave him comfort.

"To cheat the captain? I don't believe you have dared to!" he answered. "You can no more prove any thing of the sort than you can prove that you own this boat. I challenge you or anyone else! Say what you like, do what you like, you have no business with Gerald Saxton! Do you mean to claim that he is some relation to you? that he isn't traveling on this steamer with me, by his father's direction? that I can't show how it comes to be so, and where we are going? Why," concluded Touchtone, in rising wrath, "you will accuse me next of kidnapping him."

"Exactly," replied Belmont; "and that, you know, is just what you are about. Now don't fly out so quickly again, Touchtone. It really won't clear your ideas, and you will want them clear. Come, didn't I tell you that I wished to take you into my confidence? I'll be as good as my word, if you'll only keep cool. I'll start again, with a piece of advice—give up to me like a sensible fellow. The game you've tried to play is in my hands. You can't carry it on."

"Game! I don't know of any game, unless you're playing it."

"Ah, yes; that's what you ought to say, certainly, until I make you see that it will be worth your while to change your tune. You're keen. But you know this is a bad business you've undertaken, a very bad business."

Philip was bewildered by the man's audacity. To fling into his face this charge!—to utter such impudent assertions as to Gerald! Belmont went on rapidly.

"You'd better confess yourself caught. I don't care to talk much of what you have tried to manage. But on the getting possession of that boy, for my own reasons (that I may or may not explain to you)—on that thing, I tell you, once for all, I am determined." Here his voice had a ring like metal in it. "My plan has been laid. I have consulted the proper authorities. Captain Widgins and several other gentlemen—"

"Do you suppose that they will support such a man as—"

"As they, not you, consider me," replied Belmont. "Yes, I do. Unluckily for you, my reputation happens to differ—in various quarters. I shall have no trouble. Let me repeat it, you'll save yourself much by quietly joining with me. I'll tell you all that is necessary in due time, Touchtone," he concluded, with a crowning dash of assurance, probably fancying that he had already bewildered Philip into submission. "The sum total of the affair is, I want possession of that little boy. Don't try to prevent me! Bring him off the boat to-morrow morning when we stop at Martha's Vineyard. I promise you I'll let you understand things then far more fully than I can to-night. I'll fix it all right with the captain, and I'll say we've squared our quarrel. Last, but not least, you will never come across a job that will be so well worth your while. I should think not; that is, if you care for money. And not a hair of the boy's head shall be hurt, for the world, in any case. Be sure of that."

Choking with anger at having to listen to such an astounding proposal, but gathering new certainty that his adversary's scheme must be a wonderful web of sheer rascality, Philip did not at once open his mouth. Then he asked, "And if I refuse to act as you advise me—which I think I ought to do, unless I can see more clearly what it means for me—what then?"

Belmont caught at the tone and words.

"Why, if you refuse, I shall at once charge you with this abduction. My right to take Gerald Saxton is another matter. I may or may not go into that. The claim against you is enough. Come, boy—for you are a boy and I a man, prepared to hold his ground against a hundred like you! You shall be in irons in half an hour if you try to play the hero here. Remember, I know you."

"And you will actually dare to bring such a charge against me here, and at this time of night?" cried Philip, vehemently. "And you believe you can fight the plain story that Gerald and I can tell? Do your worst! I'm not afraid to face it. In irons? That is talk out of a dime-novel, Mr. Belmont."

The boy was unnerved and terribly perplexed; but he was more sure than ever that his enemy's scheme was hollow, even if he could not tell how far Belmont would support it.

Belmont was beginning to lose his temper because Philip so stood out against any thing like buncombe.[44] His voice became suddenly so hoarse with passion that it was hard to believe that it came from the smooth-talking "Mr. Hilliard" of the express-train.

"You young rascal!" he exclaimed, above the sound of the fog-whistle, "what a fool you are making of yourself! One would think you actually were all that you have been pretending. Did Saxton commission you? How? When? Or did Marcy? Did you ever see Saxton? Do you know any thing about Saxton, except from this boy, or the hotel people? Have you so much as a single letter in your pocket to bear you out?"

This unlucky lack already had occurred to Philip. He had allowed his foe artfully to destroy the letter that indirectly might have helped him. Still, there would be the telegraph and the mail, if necessary, before long.

"Why, I'll knock your Saxton or Marcy rigmarole higher than a kite. I know what I am about. O, you are cool, Touchtone, but I am more than your master in this business, and I have right on my side all through."

Right on his side? After all, how little did Philip know of the history of these Saxtons. But he reminded himself once more of the simple statements of Mr. Marcy and of Gerald, and of the cleverness of Belmont in acting a part. Besides, had the latter not betrayed himself with that promise to make Philip's yielding "worth his while?"

"No," he replied, determinedly, "you haven't right on your side! You are trying to frighten me! Call up the whole ship! I dare you to bring things to the point. I don't know," he continued, raising his head and looking up at Belmont, "how well you may have planned to get me into trouble; but I know myself and Gerald, and I can soon prove all that I shall say. Get the captain—any body! I'll answer all questions people may ask. Shall I go inside and wait? We may as well settle it now," he added firmly, thinking again of the innocent sleeper in the state-room; "the only thing I have to ask is not to let *him* know any thing till the last minute."

Thereupon Belmont drew in his breath with an oath. He was defied! Nevertheless, he seemed to have planned his attack strongly enough after all to hold fast by it against Philip's straightforward story. Indeed, Philip even in cooler hours afterward never could decide exactly how far the man might have gone.

"As you please!" he exclaimed. "I will ask Captain Widgins and Mr. Arrowsmith, the mate, to meet us in the cabin. Stay—I give you one more choice! Make up your mind; it is your last chance. I don't know why I think enough of the fraud you are, to wait a second longer. Will you give in and go ashore with the boy and me to-morrow at Martha's Vineyard?"

Belmont may or may not have expected Philip to yield. But

Philip was not called upon to utter the resolute "No, I will not!" that was upon his lips. Just as he opened them to speak, the awful shock and thrill of what each at once realized must be some tremendous explosion, far forward on the *Old Province*, made them reel and catch at one another and the rail for support. The sound was dull and choked, as if it came from the very depths of the great steam-ship. She seemed to stagger like a huge living creature that has all at once been mortally wounded. She ceased to move. Then came outcries, the rushing of feet, and the roar of escaping steam, mingled confusedly with the desolate scream of the fog-whistle. The latter sounded now like a cry of sudden agony, sent forth into the murk and the night.

CHAPTER VIII.

IN NIGHT AND MIST.

When a couple of savage dogs or a brace of quarrelsome cats stand defying one another a bucket of cold water or a lighted fire-cracker generally gives them a perfectly new subject to think about. The argument is pretty sure to be postponed.

Something like this result came to pass when Philip and the man Belmont felt the *Old Province* shivering beneath them, after that terrific jar. It was followed, shout upon shout, by what each felt sure must be the beginning of alarm and of unexpected peril.

One instant the boy and the man remained motionless, silent, with startled faces.

"What was that? The boiler can't have burst!" exclaimed Belmont. His nerves could hardly have been in a state to endure much. He sprang to the left entrance of the saloon and disappeared. Philip turned to the right, forgetting Belmont and all his schemes and threats. He was anxious to reach Gerald's state-room and to find out what had happened. Before he had gained the middle of the cabin doors were opening. Loud exclamations came from one side and the other. He caught glimpses of semi-arrayed occupants either scrambling into their clothes or hastily appearing and looking out in terror, now this way, now that. The explosion, or whatever it was, had sounded unmistakably from the forward part and below the deck of the steamer, judging from the peculiar thickness of the sound and the dull violence of the shock. By two and three a crowd was already centering forward.

He unlocked the state-room door with trembling fingers. Gerald was sitting up on the edge of the lower berth, looking about him with an alarmed air, but plainly not at all sure that any thing in particular had waked him.

"Say—Philip," he questioned, rubbing one of his eyes rather sleepily, "did you hear any thing just now? It's awfully funny. But I waked up—with such a start, and now I can't tell what on earth could have frightened me."

"You must have heard what we all heard," answered Philip, striving to speak composedly, while his alert ear caught vague sounds from without that were not re-assuring. "There was an odd noise, an explosion of some sort, forward a minute ago. I was just going to see what made it. I'll bring you word."

"An explosion? What could it have been? You don't think it's any thing about the boat? Are we running yet?"

"No; we were going very slowly, because of the fog, when it came. Hark! the whistle had stopped; now it goes on again. It hardly seems like any thing wrong with the steam. Very likely it was only a gas-tank, or something of that sort. I'll hurry back."

"Let me go with you," exclaimed the younger boy, dragging his shoes out from under the berth.

"I don't know whether you'd better," Philip returned, in sudden perplexity. Belmont came again into his mind. He was unwilling to have Gerald quit such a fortress, little as he liked leaving the boy alone. "I'll tell you what—if you don't mind I'd rather run out alone first for a moment. Then, if it's any thing interesting, you know, or worth while, you can go forward with me. If it isn't you'll have been saved the chance of taking cold and getting mixed up in the stir. What do you say?" He was very impatient to understand the accident, and spoke loudly, so that Gerald should not hear pattering footsteps and loud voices in the saloon, where the frightened passengers were collecting.

"All right," assented Gerald. "I'll wait."

"Lock the door after me. Don't open it to *any one* till I come back. It isn't safe, for particular reasons. Don't mind the noises outside; there's always some excitement where there are ladies, you know. Suppose you stuff those things into the bag again. We might have to change our quarters. I wont be long."

Philip hurried out. The saloon was half-lighted, as it had been. Already there was great confusion among passengers and servants. He caught sight at once of the steward and a couple of officials. He ran up to them only to hear them repeating sharply, "No, ladies and gentlemen! we don't know any thing yet, except that it was something down-stairs in the freight. They're making examinations forward. Please keep cool, gentlemen! there's no danger! No, sir, don't know any thing yet. Haven't heard there's any thing serious the matter. Don't go up that way, sir—nobody's allowed outside. Be composed, ladies! if there's any thing wrong you'll be told of it presently"—and so on. But Philip hurried past them, convinced that they were nervous enough themselves, to get facts from nearer head-quarters.

But when he arrived, breathless, at the upper end of the saloon, he discovered why other people, too, were not able to get at facts from head-quarters, and that matters were not in a state yet to set any body's mind at rest. Only one light was burning. Thirty or forty passengers were huddled there, wedged together in an anxious group in front of one of the outer doors and of the stair-way leading to the regions below. They were kept from going down by some officers ranged determinedly before them. "Keep back, gentlemen!" came the sharp orders. "No persons allowed forward or below. Nothing dangerous discovered yet. We'll find out what's the disturbance directly. They're working hard below now. No, sir; you *can't* go down, I say! Please keep back, gentlemen! No, sir; I can't tell you!"

By mounting on a chair at the rear Philip found he could get a sight over the heads of those before him to the deck. There was rushing and shouting there, but up the staircase came the thud of crows[45] and axes and something like the dashing of buckets of water. Could there be a fire below, or above, on the *Old Province*? The idea made him pale. But lanterns flashing back and forth in the gray mist made the only light yet visible. There was no smell of smoke. Still, up the stairs came louder than ever the breaking open of boxes and a jargon of distant activity. It was as if the freight had to be shifted. He waited a few seconds longer, but there was no more to be learned yet; that was clear. It was better to get back to the state-room and try to keep Gerald quiet in the uncertainty. Perhaps it was no serious occurrence, after all.

He jumped from his perch and turned his heel on the excited company and the flickering lights and shadows. He could answer no questions that met even him, on all sides. Evidently there was suspense—mystery. Louder and louder roared the steam from the pipes; and the shouts from below and the thumping and rolling kept on. The steamer was motionless, except for her rocking in the chopping sea.

Gerald opened the door, holding both traveling-bags in one hand. "What is it?" he began as Philip drew the bolt and took one of the bags. "Is there any danger? They're making a great fuss outside. What has happened?"

"I'm sorry, but I can't seem to find out yet. They will tell us soon though."

"I heard somebody say that a keg of powder exploded in the hold and blew up a lot of freight. May be it was that?"

"Yes, very likely. They're overturning things pretty generally down-stairs."

"But it's not the steam?"

"No, it's not the steam. We'll have to wait till the ship's people can explain what it is. Most likely nothing much."

"Aren't the passengers frightened?"

"Some are, I think, and some not. There's no need of being so till we're hurt. One or two ladies fainted, and so on."

"Are you afraid yourself?"

"Not till I know what we've got to be afraid of."

"O, well, if you're not I'm not. But it's very queer."

"Yes, it's very queer. How did you get along with the bags?"

"O, all right. Every thing's packed up again just as it was. Hadn't we better lock the room and go outside, where we can know sooner what's going on?"

Philip liked their lonely waiting there as little as Gerald did. It seemed best, for a few minutes, at least. So he answered, "To tell the truth, I'd rather we shouldn't go out just yet. We shall know here about matters just as soon, for I'll be ready to run out when I hear any thing. I've a particular reason."

"All right," assented Gerald, uneasily, but returning the smile. "What a good thing it was that we've neither of us undressed, isn't it, in case we have to move?"

"Yes, rather. It will save time. Still, there don't seem to be any thing to hurry us if we should have to move."

"Don't you think we ran into some other boat?"

"No, that wasn't the trouble. It was something on board. It sounded like a cannon. I wish they'd hurry up and tell us all about it."

"Where were you?"

"Out on the after-deck."

"What were you doing there?"

"I—I had an errand," responded Philip. With this Gerald mercifully intermitted his catechism.[46] He put himself back in his berth. Philip's quick ear caught a new sound—the pumps were started. Surely that was a hint of very certain and evil omen.

"Wait! I'll be back directly," he said, hurrying into the passage-way. There was a great stir in the saloon. "Yes, it's true!" he heard somebody exclaim. "Don't you hear the pumps?" "Who says so?" called out another. A man hurrying past him was inquiring, "How big is it? Why don't they tell us that?" There could be no mistake. Part of the trouble was a leak.

"Don't be alarmed, ladies and gentlemen," said the mate; he was coming quickly down from the group forward, followed by a dozen clamorous passengers. "We've found a leak in the hold. A barrel of explosive stuff went off, but they're getting the best of it, all right. The engineers are working. The shock's disabled the machinery a little. It'll soon be fixed. Don't be frightened."

It was a comfort to get at some part of the mystery. But the faces around the cabin were as anxious as ever. The idea of mischief to the machinery was not a soothing addition. How inexplicable the whole accident was!

Philip hied[47] him back to Gerald. Then for a time no more information could be got. There was a leak? Yes, there was a leak, but every body could be easy. They "were getting it under control all right." The little groups at the staircases, still held in check by the captain's orders, waited anxiously. The pumps kept up steadily their clanging sound that had not stopped once; and to Philip and Gerald the pumps seemed to be going faster than ever by the time half an hour had gone by. Once when Touchtone stepped out for any more news he overheard an officer running by say something about "below the water-line," and add to the head steward, "Tell Peters to get out what I said—quick!"

As he sat in the state-room, glad that he had succeeded yet in keeping Gerald so unexcited, Belmont came to his mind. "Most likely he's in that crowd forward," he thought. "One comfort! However bad a scare it is, I fancy it's upset him and his schemes in making us trouble."

But just then began a rush in the cabin and loud words and outcries. People came running down the saloon, and there was trampling of feet up the brass steps of the staircases, and hasty orders. Gerald, terrified, leaped from his berth and ran trembling out into the passage. There the two lads stood together, wild-eyed. They heard the captain speaking and drawing nearer with each word: "Ladies and gentlemen, you are aware that an explosion down in the hold has broken a hole in the bow. We thought we could manage it; we cannot. The steamer must sink inside of an hour. Be quiet, I tell you—and keep calm! There is plenty of time. We must take to the boats in as good order and as quickly as possible. We cannot beach the ship, the engines are crippled. Please prepare yourselves and come aft."

A great cry went up from those who heard. The worst was known! Arm tightly clasped in arm, the two lads tried to grasp this news that made their hearts leap to their throats. Could it be true? But following the captain's words and the sounds of panic that rose with them came the boom—boom—of the signal-gun, the tolling of the bell, the louder scream of the whistle, and the flash of rockets and Bengal lights[48]—not likely to be of much use in that dense fog.

Yes, it was true! So swiftly, so mysteriously had they passed from safety to—what? To the need of hurrying from what had been a gallant, strong ship, now become a mere sinking mass of iron and wood; to making their way to the shore, in open boats, over an angry sea, in night and mist; in a word, to meeting together—Gerald with no friend near save Philip, and Philip with none save little Gerald, who clung to him for protection, every thing—the chances of life or death. May none of us who read this history ever have to exclaim, with a prospect of the awful thing staring us in the face, "From sudden death, good Lord, deliver us!"[49] Some of us hear it read, Sunday after Sunday, heedlessly enough. It came into Philip's thoughts now with all its appeal—"From sudden death!"

CHAPTER IX.

TWO OUT OF TWELVE.

It is not good to dwell upon such scenes and moments. To write of them does not make us more composed in them when they come. But, as it proved, things on board the *Old Province* that night were wonderfully calm after the first breaking of the news. It has been said that the steamer was far from crowded. Many of the men and women were humble. Many of them were brave. The fact that there was indeed ample time and boat room was over and over again pressed on every one's attention, with excellent effect. The preparations to leave the ship went forward swiftly, orderly. People hurried about with white and frightened faces. Now and then there were exclamations from one or another quarter, but there was no panic. Captain Widgins and his aids seemed to be in all places, cheering the timid and directing every thing. No tug came to the rescue, nor did the steady signaling bring any other help through the murk. The pumps did their duty stanchly. But the water poured through the ill-stopped, ragged hole blown out, far down in the hull; and it gained pitilessly.

Philip and Gerald had little to do. It was only slipping into their state-room and catching up the few things lying ready; some broken sentences together there, of which Philip afterward could remember nothing except his bidding the younger boy be of good heart, for a tug from the shore or a steamer *might* come to their help at any moment, before they need enter the boats. Gerald used to say that in his sudden dread and bewilderment—poor little fellow!—the cheerfulness Philip managed to keep in his voice did him more good than any of the words that might have been uttered. Philip led their way through the tumbled cabin. They pressed out into the gloom and foggy chill of the open deck and halted, bidden to do so, on the outer edge of the little crowd already huddling together there, waiting— waiting for what was to come next.

After all, there were not so many to be provided for, besides the ship's officers and crew and servants. The dazed company kept bravely in order. Except for the signals of distress, the hollow roar of the escaping steam behind them, and the bustle of the crew ahead where the boats were making ready, there was a kind of breathless stillness. Philip could hear, now and then, the breaking of the surge below. The mist, thicker than ever, drove into their faces. The lanterns made only too plain its denseness. The strain was too great for them to speak. The solemn thoughts that passed, one after another, through the spirits of each boy, the younger as well as the older, I do not intend to try to describe here. They are less our business than any thing else in this story. Be sure that in such times of sudden danger and defenselessness, no matter how short a time we may have lived in this world, where the best of us leave undone so many of the things that we ought to do and do so often the things we should not, we will have our reflections, best known then and afterward only to our own souls and to God.

Belmont was not discoverable. But one special fear again beset Philip. When the confusion of getting into the boats came might not Gerald be separated from him? That Gerald had also a great doubt and dread of it he knew from the way in which he clung to him and over and over asked, "I shall surely be put into the same boat with you, Philip, won't I, if we have to go? I don't mind any thing, if they will only let us keep together." And what prayers Philip made were confused enough, but no thought repeated itself more earnestly than that Gerald and he might indeed "keep together" through it all, even to the unknown end; and that, doing whatever he could for Gerald— fighting the very wrath of the sea itself for him—he might not fail in his guardianship, even with his uttermost stroke and his uttermost breath.

The disembarking was made into two or three boats at once. Something soon directed Captain Widgins's eye to where the two waited their turn tremblingly, patiently. He waved his hand. "Quick, my lads!—you two there—next!" he called. "Make way there, Watson!" Before Gerald could realize that the descent was begun, he and Philip found themselves side by side in the nearest of the boats. It seemed to have more packages than people aboard it; and indeed it had. Some consignments of special value were on it, under charge of the second mate, Mr. Eversham. There were ten people besides themselves; but the captain knew best what were the responsibilities on him and what was the proper thing to do. As the boys found their places he called out sharply, "Eversham, are you ready? Give way, then! Quick! Remember, Knoxport Cove! Man the cutter there, next![50] This way, ladies. You're wanted now."

But just as Eversham repeated his orders, and as the loaded boat was being cast off to give place to the great cutter, Philip heard a voice overhead that he well knew. The boat was rising and falling. Gerald held fast to his arm. But he strained his ears for each syllable.

"I say, captain! Captain Widgins!" Belmont shouted. "Stop that boat! I go in her too! My son is aboard her. Halloa, Mr. Eversham!"

The *Old Province* deck seemed very high overhead. The fog made the lights on it dim. Philip could just make out Belmont's figure and gestures.

"What boat, sir?" inquired the old captain, angrily. "Why didn't you speak sooner?"

"That boat yonder—Eversham's! Halloa, I say, bring her about a moment till I get aboard!"

Philip hastily said something to Mr. Eversham. Eversham

wished no more in the boat in any case. He called out, "His son isn't here! He's made a mistake!"

"That's a lie! He is there! I saw him. I see him now!" cried Belmont, leaning over the companion-ladder. "Let me pass, I say!" This to a sailor barring his way.

"I tell you he's not here," returned Eversham, obeying Philip's prompting willingly, "and the boat's full. The gentleman's no business here!" With this, so strong a wave rolled under them that nothing but promptness saved them from a collision with the cutter behind and with the ship's side.

"Clear away, Eversham!" shouted Captain Widgins, furious at the whole interruption. "Stand out of the way, sir! Mind your own business!" This to Belmont. "You can't go in that boat! Foolery! This is no time for disputing orders. Clear away, I say!"

The captain was obeyed. The boat passed out from the vessel. Belmont could be heard in angry altercation. But he was left behind, to Philip's intense relief.

How quickly the lights and noises aboard the *Old Province* became indistinct! It was startling. The boat rose and sank, driven further and further onward. All was darkness, except the lanterns and the pale light from overhead that revealed each anxious face and the glitter of the wave-crests. The few women crouched together. Gerald pressed close to Philip's side, but now uttered no word. They had begun the lonely and dangerous pull to Knoxport Cove, the nearest harbor. The strong arms of those who rowed conquered half mile after half mile. It was impossible to see two yards around them. Once they thought that a tug was passing somewhere beyond. That was something to be feared as well as hoped for. Under Eversham's rallying they cheered again and again. Two of the men fired their pistols. They heard nothing more, however, and the rowers settled down again to their battle. All had gone well enough, so far. If they could but know whether the other boats from the abandoned ship were making as safe a progress as theirs! At length, too, there came over the surge the chime of a bell, faint at first, but gradually more distinct, "One—two—one—two—one—two—one—two; a strange, lonely rhythm, but unmistakable.

"I take it that's the buoy on Leunggren's Rock!" exclaimed Mr. Eversham. "Our course is all right."

Every one drew an easier breath. Gerald was resting his head on Philip's shoulder, listening in almost perfect silence to whatever Philip, from time to time, said softly to keep him tranquil and even to make him think lightly of the perils of their situation. The boy sat up now and hearkened. "Yes, it's a bell, Philip; it's a bell! I hear it," he presently said. "It sounds like the church-bell at Ossokosee, don't it?" he added wearily—"just before Mr. Sprowers stops ringing it. I wonder how they will land us when we get to that place we're trying for."

But, as he spoke, a shriek, a dreadful shriek, broke from the lips of a woman opposite. She had carried a baby in her arms tightly wrapped in a shawl. Standing upright, she struggled frantically with those nearest her, who held her back from leaping over the gunwale.[51] In changing her position she had lost her balance and stumbled, and the child had fallen from her very arms into the sea!

"Sit down, I say! Sit down for your lives!" cried Eversham. "The boat will be swamped!" The packages of plate in the middle were shifting perilously, falling against each other. Too late! Lurching violently on the very crest of the roller,[52] the boat toppled, plunged, and then cast out its load—men, women, boys, oars, all—pell-mell together.

For two or three seconds—the kind that seem an eternity—Philip Touchtone, thrown sidelong, struggled in the sea, conscious of but two things. He gripped the gunwale with one hand, half his body submerged. The other was upstretched, and with the palm and each finger pressing with the strength of iron levers, as it seemed, it held back Gerald Saxton from falling out, over his shoulders. Gerald had been hurled against the gunwale, not over it. Philip pushed upward and hung on. The boat righted itself. Lightened of its load, the succeeding wave lifted it like a withered leaf. It swirled it, eddying onward into the fog, out of the reach of those other strugglers in the black water, in a twinkling. All this took place in less time than it takes to tell it.

"Philip! Philip!" came Gerald's faint cry.

"Hold on!—hold on!" Touchtone gasped. He pulled himself

a few inches higher. With a desperate effort he dragged his legs over and rolled down into the boat, dashing what little breath was left in Gerald's body out of it, as the terrified boy, who had in falling clutched a thwart,[53] raised his dripping and bruised head. Touchtone struck out his arm and caught hold of Gerald's shoulder.

They were drenched to the skin by the water shipped; but so quickly had the dreadful calamity happened that not a fourth part of what might have invaded the boat was swashing about in it. They drew themselves upward. The knowledge of their deliverance became more distinct. But they were—alone! They glanced fearfully around. The pallid, feeble light from overhead told them it again. Alone! The cries of those struggling with the sea, with exhaustion and death, pursued them. Eversham's voice—they heard it. But the despairing sounds came from a distance, rods out of their reach, in the fog. The sea was running like a mill-race.[54] Not an oar lay in the boat. The distance widened with each wave. To give help was impossible. Presently the cries ceased. All was still except the lapping of the water within the boat and without.

O, mysterious choice of heaven! Out of all the rest, they two, only, were there alive! Hand grasped hand feebly.

"Gerald?"

"Philip?"

"Is your head better where you struck it? Come closer to me." He drew the dripping boy to him. "I want to feel sure that it's you. We are safe. Don't tremble so."

"Yes, we are safe—but O, Philip, where are—the rest?" His head fell back against Philip in complete exhaustion. "Hark! hark!" he added, faintly, "don't you hear the bell—the bell on the rock—that is like the one—on the church? It sounds as if—as if we were—going home."

Philip could scarcely catch the last words. Gerald's hand grew cold within his own. The boy had swooned. With Touchtone bending over him in attempts to recover him the boat still swept along in the mist. They were left indeed to themselves, and to god.

was almost gone when picked up. Some of the bodies found, however, wore life-preservers. In some cases the bruising from the rocks along the shore was disfiguring, and it is likely that many of those from the two capsized boats had what little life was left in them literally pounded out of them in the surf along Sweetapple and Knoxport Ledges.

"One boat which contained few passengers except for Nova Scotia did not come in by itself, but was picked up by the schooner *Mary Linda Brown*, bound north. It narrowly escaped being run down by the *Mary Linda Brown* instead of being rescued. The schooner's crew heard none of the distress signals from the *Old Province*. Among those brought by the schooner were Gen. John Bry, K.C.B., Sir Hastings Halbert, and Rev. Francis Holman, of Halifax; Mr. and Mrs. George Freeborn, Mr. and Mrs. Henry Earle, and Mr. John A. Belmont. A son of the latter gentleman, on one of the boats, was drowned.

"A singularly sad history attaches to the loss of a young lad named Saxton, the son of Mr. Gerald B. Saxton, of this city. He was traveling with his tutor[59] to Nova Scotia, and, according to one story, went from the ship in the same boat with Hoyt. His body was not recovered, nor his tutor's. Young Saxton's father, who has been with a camping-party in Nova Scotia, was immediately sent for. He came on to Knoxport. The shock to him was terrible, and he was so completely prostrated that his reason has seemed endangered. He was prevailed upon to speedily quit Knoxport. He is now making an indefinite journey westward in company of his friend Mr. Jay Marcy (of the well-known Ossokosee Hotel). Mr. Marcy hopes to break up the alarming stupor of grief into which Mr. Saxton is plunged. But, indeed, the calamity abounds in such distressing particulars. It might have been far worse. It is to be hoped that another originating like it, and of as melancholy an extent, may not soon be added to the list of our sea disasters."

CHAPTER XI.

Now, all night long those two floated. For hours there was but a step between them and death; but death kept its distance. The boat, like some treacherous, living thing, whose cruelty had been appeased in that angry overturn, was pacified now, and seemed resolved to protect the remnant of its charge. It rode lightly over crest after crest. They bailed it out as well as they could, and disposed carefully the odds and ends left in it—a shawl, a bottle, a soaked bundle of clothing—poor relics, terribly eloquent. They fought away the chill and misery of their situation as well as Philip's energy could devise, and not unsuccessfully. Before long he took the tiller in the darkness, and with straining eyes and tense nerves aided the boat to weather the subsiding seas.

They could not talk much—a few sentences here and there, and then long silence. Gerald was exhausted, and besides that his shoulder had suffered a severe wrench. He lay on his back in the bottom of the boat, staring into the gloom; for the moon had gone, and only a shimmer in the atmosphere marked where she sulked, far up above. The lad set his teeth, to keep from crying out with pain and with the dreadfulness of a situation so novel to a boy reared like a hot-house plant.[60]

"I wonder if we will ever get out of this alive?" he thought every now and then. But he answered Philip's solicitous questions as to his welfare with a tone that nobly feigned ease and hope. Gulping and struggling down any thing like a sob, his prompt "Yes, Philip," or "No, Philip," was the only sound that carried any comfort to Touchtone's heart. "There is no use in asking questions," he said to himself. "Philip don't know any more about what is before us than I do, and I guess he hates to have to tell me so."

By and by the dragging daylight began to whiten the air.

The ocean gradually paled from inkiness to lead-color, and from lead-color to streaked gray, and the gray to a yeasty milk. The dashing waves had given place to a rolling swell on which the boat was lifted, but ever seemed urged forward—whither? Dawn advanced. But such a dawn and such a day! For when the latter had fairly come the fog hung closer than ever. Hour by hour passed with no reasonable gain in the light. Whether the sun was on the one side or the other, before or behind, no man could have told. They were ever surrounded by a dirty greenish haze that made their faces more wan, and that mixed sea and air into one elastic wall, which moved with them as they moved and closed about them as they slid helplessly onward into it.

With the lessening of his strength and the rolling of the boat Gerald became deathly sick. Philip could do little for that. His own arms were stiff; every now and then a chill ran down his body that boded future discomfort if they were not soon delivered from this present one. But he kept to his post. Thanks to his determination, the boat met wave and crest with less and less motion and no mishap, and he said to himself, as he glanced at Gerald's despairing face, that he "was good for a whole day's steering, if need be, and a great deal beyond that." Fortunately, it was not cold, though the stormy chilliness made the early air sharp. In silence, except for a word from Touchtone or a sigh from Gerald, who lay in the bottom of the boat with his eyes closed, they moved onward whither waves and current might shape their sluggard's course.

Suddenly, about noon, Gerald sat up and declared he felt better. He seemed to have awakened from a stupor of weariness and sickness that had been on him.

"Let me take the tiller," he pleaded. "Indeed I can, just as well as you. You must be used up."

"Used up steering nowhere, and with hardly any sea running?" returned Philip, continuing to smile, not a little relieved to see color returned into his *protégé's* face, and with something like the usual tone to his voice. "Not a bit! I'm glad if you're able to move about again, though I must say you've not much occasion to do that at present. Sit down there. See how the waves have gone down. O, we're going to get along bravely presently. You'll see!"

"But which way are we going?"

"Well, that I can't positively inform you," Philip replied, trying to treat lightly the most important worry that now pressed on him, "but no great distance from land, I'm somehow inclined to think. A steamer, or something, may pick us up any hour."

"But perhaps every hour we are slipping out to sea all the farther?"

"Let us hope not. O, no! I'm sure not such bad luck as that. I—I don't think, Gerald," he added more seriously, "that you and I have been—carried through last night—to be put in worse trouble much longer. Keep up a good heart, like the brave fellow you are! We have water and biscuit enough for the time we shall need them, I'm sure." And he remembered gratefully Captain Widgins and poor Eversham's forethought. "We're drifting along the coast somewhere; we shall know before long."

"O, it has been terrible!" exclaimed Gerald, piteously. "If we only knew any thing of the others on the steamer—or about papa, or what the people on shore think about us—or how any thing is to end for us!"

"We'll know all that in good time, depend on it."

He spoke confidently; but the uncertainty of how "any thing was to end" for them was indeed a mighty weight.

"The main thing will soon be to get word to your father as soon as we can. Newspaper accounts will make him believe— well, almost any thing. Doesn't it seem about a hundred years to you since two or three days ago?" he went on, as conversationally as he could. "That funny adventure in the train—our stopping with Mr. Hilliard—last night's excitement? We can't say we haven't had a good deal crowded in, since we bid Mr. Marcy and the Ossokosee good-bye, can we? Or that we haven't had enough of a story to tell your father when we get safe and sound to Halifax?"

"I shall be glad to find out sometime what made the explosion," said Gerald, easing his position, and already decidedly more tranquil.

"So shall I. They kept it from us as long as they could, didn't they?"

"*You* did from me, I know," Gerald answered. He gave Philip a grateful look. "You wanted to keep me from being frightened. O, I know. I sort of suspected that. How *awfully* good and—thoughtful—"

"Very, very, very," Philip replied, dryly. "I wish my goodness and my thoughtfulness together had gone as far as keeping you and me safe in New York, instead of taking the *Old Province*."

"But—then—then," said Gerald, eagerly, "we couldn't have any such story to tell people for the rest of our lives—if we get through this part of it all right. I guess we will. I'm sure we will. Philip"—he suddenly changed his tone—"what was that quarrel, just before we put off last night, between some man—a gentleman, I think—and the captain? Don't you remember? He said his son was with us. You spoke to Mr. Eversham, too."

"It was a mistake," Philip quickly responded. "I—I happened to know it, and Captain Widgins didn't want to lose an instant. So he put a stop to the man's tongue."

The afternoon glided away in much the same way as the morning. After their rations had been apportioned and eaten Gerald slept heavily. No succoring vessel, no glimpses of the sun—fog and the sea still curtaining them around. Philip took account of their provisions. There were two boxes of biscuit, but the water was low in its can. The two light satchels that had been hanging across their shoulders, by straps, at the time of the boat's overturn had not parted their company, but they contained no eatables. Philip stared out, thinking, it seemed to him, every thing that had ever happened to him in his whole life until this afternoon as far away and unreal. Now and then he read a few pages in a battered copy of Scott's Poems[61] that he had been carrying in his pocket for a week or two. Night came. With the last light their situation was unchanged, except that they seemed to be in a particular current which sped the boat along with uncommon persistency in a particular direction—north, south, east, or west, he surmised in turn.

Gerald broke down pitifully once. The strain and privation began to tell visibly on the little boy. Then he slept again. Pitch darkness once more. The sea was almost tranquil. Once Philip thought he heard breakers roaring afar on his right, but the faint sound died directly. To steer was useless. He was beaten down, by weariness, exposure, and sleeplessness, night and day. He would be on the alert for both. But he could not be. Unwillingly his senses grew dull, his head drooped. He lay back in the stern, thinking that he was resisting nature successfully, and that his ears and eyes, at least, were performing their self-sacrificing task. In a few moments he slept profoundly, so unwakably that he did not feel the edge of the stern-seat pressing into his neck, nor the occasional dash of a few drops of water over his face.

Awake once more? A cry of wonder and astonishment broke from his lips when he started up. It was a shout of delight that made Gerald, too, open his eyes and lift himself quickly upright.

Where were the night, the fog, the threatenings of the sea? It was a bright, golden, enchanting autumn morning, a little past sunrise. The air was clear as crystal, the sky the bluest of blue, the sea twinkling in the early rays. As far as their eyes could see on one side stretched the water, all its threats turned to one calm smile. A pale sail or two showed above the horizon. On one side opened out the limitless ocean; on the other, only some ten or twelve miles away, stretched the coast near to which they had been tossing ever since their helplessness to reach it had begun.

But there was far more than that of immediate promise that their perils were ended as suddenly as they had risen. There lay, in full view, perhaps two miles from the spot where they drifted, in a current carrying them straight in its direction, a low green island. They could see one or two white buildings, probably a farm-house and other structures. The crow of cocks and the low of a cow came to their ears distinctly. They made out from where they were several tilled fields, stone walls and fences, a hollow tract that possibly contained a pond of fresh water for cattle; and trees grew in an orchard behind the dwelling-house, around which were clumps and patches of deeper verdure. There was no mistake. They were not to be cast on any desolate shore, like some new Robinson Crusoes;[62] but if they could make that land they would set their feet in some one of the little water-locked farms that now and then occur along the shore of the seaboard States of New England—solitary little spots that the owners sometimes make green with every thing from corn to clover, and to the kitchen-garden of which more than one yachtsman can testify.

"Do you think we can make it?" asked Gerald. They had forgotten every thing of the stern and wearisome past, in their relief and hope.

"I should say we were going there about as straight as we could," cried Philip. "This is a wonderfully steady current. They're lazy folks there, though. No smoke from the chimneys yet, and it's a good deal after six, you say. If only we could row!"

The boat kept on its course with Philip's care. The light air blew in their faces and dashed the little waves gayly. They were going to get to shore! They were saved! They should see their friends again and tell with living lips the story of their dangers and deliverance. They almost held their breaths with hope and suspense. Still nearer and nearer they slowly drew to the island. New details and those of the farm and the farm-house—there seemed to be only one—came, bit by bit, into clearer sight. At the land's nearer edge rocks and shallows alternated and long stretches of brush or meadow sloped back. A little creek opened in view, with a rough pier built out into it, and from the rickety dock ran back a road or lane, between what appeared to be corn-fields, to the door of the house, with its high roof and two or three wings. A fence inclosed it and a garden; and some tall trees grouped themselves beside its chimney.

Thanks to friendly current and wind, they made steady progress toward their unexpected refuge. At one or two points less and less fairly in front of them the surf broke, but not to any formidable extent nor for many yards, apparently. Occasionally they did not seem to move at all. Then would come a gentle impetus, and they glided on. The sun was high in the sky, a hot autumn day was well in course before the boat drifted around and into a tiny cove quite on the landward shore of the island and back of the farm and its structures, which they must reach on foot. They grounded in a shoal. They could not secure the boat, though they were unwilling to risk its loss. At last they were compelled to do this. They attempted little carrying. Wet and panting, especially Philip, without whose assistance Gerald scarcely could have landed where they came in, they got to the firm ground.

Yes, it was not a dream! Their feet pressed earth at last. They walked slowly up the narrow, rocky beach to a stony field full of daisies and coarse grass. They turned around a buck-wheat patch, and, last, they struck a lane that apparently traversed the entire length of their unknown host's farm and premises. All was beautiful and peaceful in the sunshine of noon, though they were too exhausted and anxious to think of nature. They met nobody yet. The farm-house loomed up in the midst of its trees nearer and nearer. They plodded on wearily. Soon they came to a turn in the lane. A dog barked loudly from the edge of the garden fifty yards beyond, succeeding to a great patch of wild laurel. Philip called out a friendly "Holloa!" twice or thrice as they advanced. No one answered from right or left. Perhaps it would be well for him to go on alone for a few moments, anxious as he was to have Gerald well cared for.

"You stay here," he said, accordingly, making Gerald sit down amid the laurel in one angle of a stone wall. "I'll just walk ahead—and lecture that dog—and ring the bell and rouse the community, whatever it amounts to, and then I'll come back and carry you into it in triumph. I wont leave you a moment longer than it will take me to break the news to them that they have got a couple of shipwrecked mariners on their hands who want luncheon—or breakfast."

Gerald sat down, anxious, but nothing loath. Philip quickened his steps and went on toward the distant garden-gate and the yet silent house.

CHAPTER XII.

INVADING THE UNKNOWN.

Turning his head back to glance at Gerald, already half hid by the bushes straggling beside the path, Philip followed the weather-worn fence on his left. The garden into which he now looked seemed to be flourishing, chiefly in the way of Indian corn and tomatoes and string-beans. As he came closer to the house, and its outward structure was clearer, he noticed that it was more dignified and solid looking than most of its sort. It might almost be termed a mansion. It was built of grayish stone and white-painted wood, the second story covered by the high-pitched roof with its at least dozen dormer-windows. Both down-stairs and up-stairs many of these windows were closed.

"Family must be small, and all busy somewhere in the back, or perhaps in the garden," Philip concluded, advancing.

A harmless snake darted across the way as he at length raised the gate-latch. He called out, "Holloa, here!" in as loud a tone as his fatigue permitted. His only answer was the dog's leaping forward through the shrubbery from a nook under one of the trees. But this canine warder proved to be all bark and no bite. At the sight of Philip unlatching the gate his objections subsided to a growl, his bound ended in a trot, and his tail suddenly began wagging eagerly.

"Good fellow!" exclaimed Philip, walking up the path and holding out his hand. "Changed your mind, have you? You don't think I look like a thief, eh? I should think I did—very much."

The dog jumped on him, whining curiously. He pursued the path toward the front porch, which was shaded with roses, carefully trained. The asters and geraniums on all sides showed recent care, and on a strip of grass near the porch lay a row of clean pans; and two white aprons lay bleaching, and several fat hens were scratching comfortably together under a lilac-bush.

The front window-shutters, with the exception of the furthest one—faded gray-green affairs, all of them, with half-moons cut in their broad, wooden expanses—were shut. Touchtone rapped at the front door, letting the iron knocker do its duty smartly. No footsteps replied. The dog stared at him very intently. Impatient of delay, he hurried around the corner of the house.

A walk of cinders bordered with clam-shells and china-pinks and zinnia led him toward it, past what he presumed was the sitting-room or dining-room, and two of the windows were open. Nobody was to be seen or heard yet, outside or in. He leaned over a window and peered inside. A tall, white-covered bed, with four posts and towering pillows, and various articles of furniture that his eyes glanced at in his bold inspection, loomed out in the cool dimness.

"The spare chamber, of course," he at once concluded. "Empty—in good order for unexpected company—like Gerald and me."

He slowly passed on, turning his head to left and right. The dog preceded him, whining and making sure that Touchtone followed. A well, with its arbored trellis, was on the left. He drank and was on the point of turning back to relieve Gerald's thirst, but thought it better to go on. Upon a grass-plot more aprons and some towels were bleaching, and a row of red crocks[63] were sunned on an unpainted bench by the back door. He reached the kitchen. It was open.

"Holloa, here!" he called again before the door, peering into the cool room then and once more turning to survey the garden-beds, in which more poultry strayed.

By this time the fatigues of the past few hours were half-forgotten in a certain new excitement.

"Well, Towzer, if your people are all away and are willing to leave their house and home open and unprotected, in this free and easy sort of fashion, pirates must be out of date with a vengeance![64] I don't know what strangers coming to them for charity can do except to do what Mrs. Wooden calls 'act according to their best lights'—eh?" The dog had trotted into the kitchen behind him, and now stood wagging his tail and barking a sharp note, here and there, beside an empty platter that rested on the hearth.

"Cold? Yes, and there hasn't been a fire in that stove for hours and hours," exclaimed Philip, examining; "nor have you been fed, Towzer, I begin to suspect, within the same time, have you? That's what's the matter with you. Whoever lives here has gone off on some errand or other away from the island. What sort of errand can it be that has made the family stay so much longer than they must have expected to stay?" Vague, disagreeable feelings crossed Touchtone's mind. It was strange. "I must be certain of things in the place before I go back to Gerald. What if there should have been some plague, some awful accident on the premises?"

He began to wonder, almost to dread, what might come under his eyes any minute. Suppose that this lonely house would not prove the shelter for them at all. Various reasons for the silence and desertion of the dwelling, despite all signs of recent occupancy and peaceful daily life, came thronging.

He paused a moment, leaning against a clean kitchen-table whereon were set several pieces of china ready to be laid upon the shelves around the walls—another task mysteriously postponed. The dog he had christened Towzer now whined and fawned on him hungrily. Philip whistled loudly, once, twice, half a dozen times. Then he opened the door in front of him and proceeded deeper into the dwelling.

Its central hall was before him, lighted cheerfully by a good-sized fan-light over the front entrance. The hall was of rather uncommon width and height of ceiling, carpeted with a faded but unworn green ingrain and with several antiquated rugs. Philip looked quickly into the front chamber on his right. It was the large, well-furnished bedroom he had glanced into from the garden-walk. The bed was made. He noticed a hat-rack beside the hall entrance on which depended a huge straw hat, a woman's sun-bonnet and a straw bonnet, and two umbrellas; and a wide-open closet near by contained various water-proofs, boots and shoes, and two or three pairs of clean blue overalls. He turned the knob of the parlor door and withdrew it, murmuring,

"Locked, I declare! Regular New Englanders, whatever else they are—believe in saving the parlor for Sundays and their own funerals."[65]

The sitting-room on the other side was full of the usual simple furnishings of such living-rooms. The pictures were old revolutionary scenes, besides President Lincoln and his family and an engrossed[66] copy of the Lord's Prayer and the Ten Commandments, in photograph. Up in one corner hung two highly elaborate samplers,[67] framed in an old-fashioned, heavy style. On one of these "MARY ABIGAIL JENNISON, August, 1827," was stiffly worked under the claws of a red and yellow bird of paradise; on the other he read, "SARAH AMANDA JENNISON, August, 1827," who boasted for her finer art the alphabet and the numerals arranged in rows around a red book and a green willow-tree.

"Old, those," Philip thought. "I guess the Jennison ladies must be pretty well tired out with housekeeping if they are the heads of this establishment at present."

There were sundry photographs on the walls, that he had not time to examine closely, of elderly men and women with plain, hard-featured New England faces.

The door into the room behind the sitting-room stood open. It was quite light, each shutter turned back. This appeared considerably more of a living-room than its fellows, with a sewing-machine, a big table with stockings, hickory shirts, and coarse mending, a cracked looking-glass with a comb and brush in front of it, and a quantity of miscellaneous articles distributed about. Suddenly Philip perceived a pile of very modern-looking, paper-covered books and a heap of newspapers.

"At last!" he ejaculated. He caught up several numbers of a weekly religious magazine. On the yellow label he read, "Obed Probasco, Chantico," and the name of the State.[68] On other copies of the *Knoxport Weekly Anchor* he found scrawled by the newsdealer the same name. Some new numbers of the *Ladies' Own Monthly* were directed, "Mrs. Obed Probasco, Chantico."[69] The paper-covered novels, three or four agricultural handbooks, and half a dozen recipe-books were neatly marked in similar fashion.

A last assurance that these were at least the ruling spirits throughout this lonely island, whose nearest post-office on the main-land was, doubtless, the town of Chantico, lay between the covers of a family Bible. On the fly-leaf of this was written, in a faded ink, "To Obed Probasco and Loreta, his Wife—a Wedding-Gift from their affectionate pastor, William Day, May 17, 1850."

"So then our hosts—that are to be—are this Obed Probasco and Loreta, his wife," Touchtone decided. "Elderly people, of course. No children living with them, as far as I can guess. And they stay out here alone on this island, and either own it or farm it. Where on earth have they gone to just now? When did they expect to come home, pray?" His knees fairly were failing under him. He saw what duty and necessity directed his doing for himself and Gerald. For some hours at least this lonely, inexplicable old house was deserted, and they must make themselves at home in it. He must get Gerald up at once and provide food and drink and quarters for the night, unpermitted and unasked.

But he would better finish his hasty survey. He looked up the staircase. There might be an invalid or helpless occupant still to be consulted before he boldly took possession of the premises in the license of Gerald's and his own plight; to use them until those absent should suddenly appear. He mounted the stairs.

"Good, large, comfortable rooms, with more old-fashioned furniture, not used very much," he soliloquized, passing from one chamber to another of the second story. Every thing was clean, cheerful, and in stiff and even polished order except Mr. and Mrs. Obed Probasco's own big room, evidently in too much use for apple-pie order to be preserved. One or two doors up-stairs were locked. It was plain that to the Probascos a house was one thing, living in it was another. A huge attic, that startled Philip by the bewildering array of odds and ends crowded in it, took up the space immediately under the roof.

He descended quickly to the lower hall again, on his way back to Gerald. His head was giddy; he began to feel a great faintness, but the main question of their finding shelter and food was settled.

"I will fetch Gerald, ransack for what eatables there must be, get him to bed, and then we'll await developments and the showing up of these Probascos—how many or what sort they be. We seem to be more than ever castaways, but castaways under such a state of things as never I have read about."

The dog, with a hunger very evident to him, tried to bar his way by leaping up on him beseechingly as he hurried into the kitchen. Ah! the first objects that might well have met his eye he had not noticed before—three loaves of tempting bread set on the high shelves, a pound-cake, and a cooked ham, partly cut. But he would not stretch his hand toward them till Gerald was in that room to eat with him. He left the house and hastened back to the gate, giving loud whistle-calls for Gerald's encouragement.

He found the boy just entering the yard, impatient, faint, and anxious.

"I was afraid something had happened," he exclaimed. "Well? Will they take us in? What kind of people are they, Philip?"

"I don't know, Gerald. The fact is, I can find plenty of house and food and beds, but not a single soul to hear us say, 'By your leave,' if we help ourselves. So I've made up my mind we must just do that—help ourselves."

"What do you mean?" asked Gerald in distressed surprise.

Touchtone made his explanation as brief and cheering as he could. And really, after all, there was small wrong in this self-succoring, without the license or help of these people so unaccountably absent, who, in all probability, were to be the kind of hosts likely to rejoice that two such unfortunates should take matters in their own hands.

"So, my dear fellow, you and I will just take possession here at once, feed ourselves and this unlucky Probasco dog, too, get rested out and put our clothes in shape as well as we can, and have every thing ready to leave the place the moment any of the Probascos turn up to help us or order us to do it."

"How do you know that's the name?" asked Gerald.

Philip, explaining his warrant, to Gerald's amusement, in spite of the lad's weariness and exhaustion, got his charge and himself safely into the kitchen. The cellar revealed pan after pan of milk and cream. They made a meal more ample than was altogether prudent after such spare commons as had been theirs at sea, but fortunately with no harm to them; nor was the famishing Towzer forgotten, nor the cat that suddenly came trotting up the walk, miauling, with tail erect. Infinitely refreshed, Philip went once more over the sober, still dwelling to satisfy the curiosity of Gerald. They made no new discoveries of importance. In course of the afternoon, after resting, they also somewhat examined the garden and sheds and stables, and lo! out in an inclosed lot the cow was patiently grazing by a spring. On seeing them she began complaining so sorely at being unmilked that Philip brought back a foaming pail to store away down-stairs.

"I should say, decidedly, that there was hardly any body but Mr. and Mrs. Probasco living here," Gerald decided, in course of the afternoon. Every thing pointed, indeed, to a solitary life led by a careful, thrifty couple in this isolated spot; childless, and just now called away from their home—probably to the mainland—by some sudden and oddly detaining necessity."

"Yes; they live here alone. They have gone away in a hurry for some special reason. It's plainly that, I think. And all you and I can do is to wait for them to come back," replied Philip.

"But don't you see how their not being here puts us back from letting papa or Mr. Marcy or any body know what has happened to us? They must all be terribly anxious."

Touchtone quite realized that important dilemma. There were, indeed, the others to think of besides themselves. He had long since remembered that their friends on shore now might easily be believing the worst about them. Other boats must have landed safely from the abandoned steamer, and the list of passengers have been carefully reckoned over. What might not the newspapers be circulating that very moment? But there was nothing to be done now. One thing at a time.

"We cannot help that, Gerald, quite yet. If they are anxious they must stay so, old fellow, till we find some way of sending word. If no boat lands here to-morrow with any of the people that belong here in it, we will mount a signal of distress, of some sort."

"But it's known that people live here! Signals wont count for much unless we can manage to hit on just the proper sort of one."

"O, come, now! We're not Robinson Crusoes, remember! Before to-morrow noon, I expect, we shall have the people who live here coming up that garden-walk and staring their eyes out at you and me, when we go down to meet them. We will not be left to ourselves long, depend on it, and in a twinkling after that we can get matters all straightened out—explainings right and left, and going on with our journey, and all."

As twilight came on they remembered again the boat, and would willingly have gone to make more secure that single link at present connecting them with the rest of the world. But they had neither light nor strength for it. The boat must fare as fate should decree.

Philip got Gerald to bed in the large chamber on the first floor. He decided to occupy a wide sofa he pushed in from an adjoining room. A closet of linen supplied sheets and a blanket. Gerald fell asleep at once. Apparently he should be none the worse for his trying adventures so far.

"I guess I am used up myself till to-morrow; that's certain," he declared.

A big eight-day clock,[70] composedly keeping time from a sufficiently recent winding, struck nine. Outside the frogs and tree-toads about the lonely house croaked and chirped. The sound of the sea filled the night air. The stars were bright and the moon shone gloriously. Philip wondered once more if this novel situation was reality or dream. Excitement could keep him up and wakeful no longer. He did not lock either a door or window and so break what seemed the habit of the house. He partially threw off his clothes and stretched himself on his sofa to fall instantly into a deep slumber, whether the problematical Probascos should waken him out of it at midnight or any other time.

CHAPTER XIII.

AT HOME IN MY NEIGHBOR'S HOUSE.

Touchtone woke as the clock struck nine. The farm-house was as silent as ever. He dressed himself hurriedly and made an observation outside. The garden lay peaceful in the morning sunshine. Towzer and the large white cat that had suddenly appeared, and was on the easiest of social terms with Towzer, came about his legs on the door-sill. Sails in plenty shone in the blue sea distance, but no craft was heading for the island. He discovered a group of white dots and dashes stretching along at one remote point of the shore.

"Chantico, for sure!" he thought. "We must start for there to-morrow, at the latest. It wont do to put it off an hour longer than is necessary." Then came into his mind their weary indifference to the position of the boat. It gave him a disagreeable start. If they had only been somewhat less exhausted and impatient! But he would go down to the cove and get a look at the boat in course of an hour, at the furthest.

He lighted the kitchen fire and surveyed that appetizing stock of eatables on which they had made some inroads the night before. Audacity and a notion of a more breakfast-like meal for Gerald inspired him. He found the coffee in a caddy, and descended into the cellar to plunder its stores a little. Then, arrayed in a violently green calico apron that hung behind the entry door, he proceeded to find out if he could not concoct as decent a breakfast in a farm-house that didn't belong to him as in a forest camp that did. Mr. Marcy had often declared, "Phil, you're a born cook! When the *chef* of the Ossokosee strikes for higher wages, you'd better apply to me." So he beat an omelet vigorously and then went to call Gerald.

"H-m-m?—y-e-s—what's—what's the matter?" asked the boy, confusedly, lifting his head from the pillow and uttering a round dozen[71] of sleepy sentences before consciousness came back—a specially slow process with him.

"Breakfast is ready," laughed Touchtone. "Only ourselves to eat it. Come. It's a stunning day. How do you feel?"

"O, I'm all right."

But his flushed face and unduly bright eyes and hot hands made Touchtone uneasy. He pronounced the breakfast indeed a quite surprising masterpiece, but hardly took the practical interest in it that Philip expected. When he got up from the table, yawning, he suddenly declared that he felt "too tired to walk."

Even his concern for this remarkable situation, and his eagerness to have it changed for the better, seemed slight. He moved listlessly about the rooms and door-ways while Touchtone cleared away the table.

"I guess I'm too much used up to care about the Probascos, or the house here, or how to get word ashore, or—well—any thing," he declared apologetically. Touchtone was not surprised, nor relieved. Alone he went down to the cove, Towzer at his heels, taking a short cut that saved the long walk by the road. In dismay, he realized what he had feared—that the boat was indeed gone, drifted out to sea, likely, or along toward the coast with the turning of the tide.

"How abominably careless of me!" he exclaimed, appreciating that every thing must be at a completer stand-still because of this loss. He could not find another boat about the Probascos' dock nor stored in the one or two deposits of miscellanies, nautical and agricultural.

"We've got to wait, with a vengeance!" he said to himself. Curiosity as to his hosts gave place to angry impatience at his having taken things so for granted and at his own heedlessness; came, too, greater anxiety for Mr. Marcy's and Mr. Saxton's enlightenment. "They may have had our funerals, Towzer; given us both up for dead!" he exclaimed, addressing the attentive representative of the absent farm-house folk. Towzer seemed resolved that nothing should be done without his notice, and trotted at Touchtone's heels every-where.

He was dismayed when he crossed the threshold of the farm-house. Gerald had gone back to bed with a throbbing headache and what Philip rightly judged would prove a fever. It gained perceptibly. By noon the younger boy was tossing in a restlessness that hinted at coming delirium. Now and then, as he dreamed, he muttered to imaginary people, or, awakened again, he would ask Touchtone questions that were pitiful in their sudden intensity and unanswerableness. Philip knew that a new care and suspense had come.

"He's very ill—very! And he's likely to go on and become worse." This great fear made Philip forget every thing else that was to be worried over. What should he do? How add the knowledge and care of a doctor and a nurse to the burden already on his shoulders? "If he does get downright sick, I don't know enough to fight the thing. I'll do the best I can to keep him comfortable. But, O, if any body *could* only come! What on earth would I best begin with?" He felt his own self-dependence giving way.

He ran over various necessities. Taking advantage of an hour when Gerald all at once became perfectly quiet, in an unrestful doze, he went out and quickly collected a pile of brush and kindling-wood in the space behind the garden. By throwing some kerosene oil and then water on the blaze he started a dense smoky column that he hoped should attract notice aboard some one of the vessels that glided far out. He came to the conclusion that there must be an uncertain and dangerous chain of reefs and shoals that made it necessary for vessels to give the little place a wide berth. He distinguished a lighthouse. "To those who know any thing about these Probasco people it will seem like only the farmer burning up some litter on the place, of course. Nobody will think twice about the smoke, unless the farm-folk themselves get sight of it"—which was precisely the case.

The fire smoldering successfully, he set to rummaging in the Probascos' stock of books for one the title of which had happened to catch his eye a little earlier. He found it, a flashy-backed little volume, "presented" by a patent medicine company, giving some simple directions for taking care of the sick without a doctor. This guide-book showed its chief signs of wear and tear and agitated consultation on the pages devoted to "Rheumatism" and "Influenza," hinting in what particular emergency it had been oftenest consulted. Devoting himself to one or two dark chimney-cupboards, he unearthed a limited and dingy stock of family medicines. Bottles were half filled and empty. Luckily, one or two of them were called for by Dr. Bentley's *Ready Guide* aforesaid.[72] Gerald was too weak to refuse the dose that could be ministered. "For my sake, old fellow. It's the best I know how to do for you," Philip said, apologetically; and Gerald, half in stupor, opened his lips. Then, after he had given the younger boy the last teaspoonful prescribed, and had sat beside his pillow a long time with a heavy and more and more fear-shaken heart, he sat down beside the window.

He wrote Mr. Saxton and Mr. Marcy the dispatch and the letter that ought to be ready for any opportunity. When that might arrive, of course, he could not reckon. At any moment communication with the world might be opened to them; it might not be for hours yet, possibly for days. He had given up speculating what had called away their hosts so suddenly, ceased fancying the cause of their absolutely inexplicable delay to return to their home and to the care of house, live stock, and garden. No ordinary accident probably lay at the bottom of the riddle. Now he could think of nothing besides the fact that he and Gerald were here, shut up in this singular asylum together, waiting for its owners and a deliverance to "turn up," and that Gerald lay there in the broad bed before him lapsing into a fever, now and then into a light-headedness. That topped the list of the anxieties and sufferings of the past week. But he must just take things as they came.

"I never knew before now," he ended his letter to Mr. Marcy, "what it was to feel a hundred years older, simply because what has happened in a few days has been of a kind to make one feel so. It seems as if it has been as long as that since we were all at the hotel, as gay as larks, and I with no more to worry me than Gerald had. I don't see how there has been time for so much." And verily, the Philip Touchtone laughing, rowing races on the lake, playing tennis before the Ossokosee House piazza, and riding about in Mr. Marcy's light wagon seemed like an insignificant sort of creature who had known nothing of life.

"And to think that I would be—well—that other fellow, that *old* Philip Touchtone, this minute if Gerald had not happened to come up to the Ossokosee to spend the summer!" he reflected, as his eyes turned upon the sick boy's flushed face. "But I don't believe that there are many things in life that *happen*." And it is to be concluded that there are not.

Speculations as to Belmont were not left out of his thoughts. Truly there was something more and more malevolent in the man's conduct, however explainable. But he hoped that that chapter of their experience was ended as abruptly as it had begun.

He induced Gerald to take a light luncheon, feeding him, and coaxing down mouthful after mouthful and sip after sip with the gentleness and persistency of a hospital nurse. (That is, a hospital nurse of a certain kind. There are differences in hospital nurses, decidedly.) Gerald lay quiet for an hour or so afterward. But about three o'clock, when Philip returned from a stolen absence from his bedside (for the sake of their smoldering beacon and for a reconnoiter), he found the sick boy excited, though clear-headed, and needing any cheerfulness and distraction Philip's sitting down near him could bring.

"Nothing heard from them yet, these—Probascos?" he asked, rolling about on his pillow.

"Not yet. They may march in on us any time before tea."

"What on earth will they think? O, Philip, I'm so sorry to lie here and do nothing and have you plan and look out for every thing. But I feel too sick even to fret."

"Depend on it, they will think that we have had good common sense and certainly the best of reasons for taking the hint that this big open house of theirs gave us. O, I'm not afraid of the Probascos!" he returned, in honest unconcern. "One can see what sort of people they are. I'm only too anxious for the pleasure of their acquaintance. As for your lying there, why, there's nothing for you to do if you had six legs and could walk on all of them! And I am certainly glad if you don't 'worry.' What's the use of worrying?"

"Are those letters you spoke of written?"

"All ready; and two telegrams with them, to send by the first hand that comes along. (Fancy a hand coming along by itself! I don't think I'd care to shake it.)"

But Gerald's imagination could not be interested. He mused. Then he murmured, "Poor papa!" with another nervous turn of his body. "Give me another swallow of water, please, Philip." He drank thirstily. "Cold, isn't it? I guess papa has found out by this time that I'm rather more to him than the yacht or his new racing team."

He did not speak bitterly. It was evidently not a complaint with him that his father, and only near relative in the world, seemed to regard him so carelessly. He was used to it. He neither compared the portion of affection that fell to him in life with that given to others nor with his due.

"O, stuff!" returned Philip, shaking up the spare pillow. "He's not to find that out now, take my word for it! You've always been a great deal more to your father than you've given credit for. He's like lots of other city men. He keeps his soft side inside, a little too much, perhaps. More than the new racing team! You ought to be ashamed of yourself!"

"You don't know my father," returned Gerald.

"And you, old fellow, don't understand him. From what you tell me I'm pretty sure he's exactly one of those fathers who can't *say* half what he wants to any son. I've heard of them before."

"I suppose there is that sort," responded Gerald, "but it's—not the most—satisfactory kind to have, I think."

"You may think differently some day," Touchtone answered. "Why, I once knew a man who just about worshiped his son—a fellow, I believe, not much older than you. He was as proud as you please of him—of his looks, his cleverness, the way people took to him, every thing. But he didn't often stop to realize it himself; and when he did stop he might have been dumb for all the knack he had to tell his boy what he thought. You and your father will find each other out, so to speak, some day, depend on it. Come, now, try another nap, like a good fellow. Shall I give that pillow a shake?"

He wanted to end this or any other conversation and encourage his patient toward quiet and sleepiness. But Gerald would talk. So long as he did not increase his fever too decidedly perhaps it was just as well to humor him. Meditations on Mr. Saxton presently turned his thoughts to some of Philip's early experiences. The conversation in the summer-house at the Ossokosee, the overhearing of which had so brought them together, came back to him, as it often had.

"Philip," he asked, languidly, "do you remember what you said that night at the hotel about some day being able to prove that—that *your* father wasn't what—he was believed to be?"

"And didn't do what it was decided by the most of people that he did?" answered Touchtone, in the peculiar sort of tone that always came with any reference to or even thought of his life's disgrace and of his life's hope. "Certainly. What of it?"

"What did you mean by our being able to prove it together?"

"I meant that I'm in a hurry to grow up to be a man able to take care of myself. When I can turn over—well, two or three stones that haven't been touched, I think I'll find my father's good name, all right, under one of them."

He paused a moment. Belmont's taunt came into his head. Ah! he had a new link, possibly, if he met him again—alone. "And by the time I can start into this job you, may be, can lend a hand at it too. That's all."

"If I ever can I will. Be certain of that," the younger boy rejoined, earnestly.

He turned so as to look Philip in the face affectionately. Philip saw nothing but wakefulness in it; but it was a clear and not too excited look, after all.

"You see," Touchtone continued, "the men—some of them —who did the burglary are probably living. They might be willing to tell more truth about it now than then. Or they might not. There always was more to get at; I know that." There was a pause. "Did I ever tell you about the night my father died?" he asked, solemnly.

"No. Go on, please."

"I was only a little fellow like you at the time. But father meant I should remember, and I have remembered perfectly. It had been an awfully cold day in January. My poor mother was almost worn out with anxiety, for father all at once sank terribly fast about nine o'clock, though the doctor had no idea that he wouldn't last till morning. Did I ever drive you around by that cottage that we rented of Mr. Marcy, where we lived those years after we came? I dare say not; I'm not fond of the road. Well, father had mother bring me into the room where he was. I sat by the bed, just as I sit by yours this minute, letting him hold my hand and one of mother's. Mr. Marcy was in New York. O, how tired and hollow-eyed and *dying* he looked. But he smiled a little at seeing us two there together beside him.

" 'That's right,' he said softly; 'always keep with your mother, Philip, and remember, Hilda, nothing ought to separate you two but death. Philip,' he went on, 'you're going to grow up to be a man, I hope and expect. I suppose that the best thing I can wish for you is that you may never hear the people you will meet talk of me, nor even read my name in a newspaper. But I want to say to you to-night (for I'm afraid I sha'n't have many words to spare by morning) that I, your father, under the stain to-day of a crime, and believed by almost everybody I ever knew in the world, or that you may know, to be a felon—am as innocent as you of what's laid to my charge. Remember, I say this to you on what I believe is my dying-bed, and going before the great God who judges all the world, and who is sometimes the only Knower of what is the right and what the wrong of things, great or small.'

"I began to cry. My mother pressed my hand and said, firmly, 'No; listen carefully to father, Philip! You will be glad of doing so some day.' So I bit my lips and swallowed my sobs as well as I could, and kept my eyes on his in spite of the tears.

"'It's hard to have to ask such a young lad as you to go through a scene like this, Phil' (he often called me Phil, and that's the reason I never want anybody to do it nowadays), 'and to stuff your head with such unhappy thoughts as may come. But it's best. You're my boy, and my name, good or bad, is yours. I was discharged and traduced and convicted almost altogether on the evidence of two men. One was Laverack, the ringleader of the thieves; the other, the watchman of the bank, Samuel Sixmith. Will you remember that—Laverack and Samuel Sixmith?'

"I nodded my head. Father went on: 'Some day you can read all the falsehoods that Laverack and Sixmith swore to. Never mind them now. Only do not forget that I give to you, my son, once more, my dying word of honor that they were false-hoods; and that, besides Laverack's having a reason of revenge to attack me as he did, there must have been some conspiracy between himself and the watchman, Sixmith. Possibly you may light on it before you die. I commit it to you and to God. If you do, you will clear my character before the world; and although it might come so late that the world will have little interest in it, still do it, if God opens the way, Phil. I believe that it will be opened by and by. I hope for your sake and your mother's that it may not be long shut.' "

It is to be feared that Touchtone had forgotten Gerald's fever and almost every thing else, in his story. The younger boy lay there looking at Philip in admiration and sympathy; and if his hot pulse could not but run higher at such a bit of his friend's history, compassion and regret may have kept mere physical and mental excitement within a certain check.

"He talked a little more to me," continued Philip, "and bade me recollect always that my mother and I would have a friend in Mr. Marcy. Then we all said the Lord's Prayer together, and my father kissed me on the forehead and told mother to take me into the next room. She left me with our servant. Poor old Biddy Farrelly! I wonder if she's alive now? She'd been crying as if her heart would break. I guess she'd been listening at the door a bit. Mother went back to father, and I was told to go to bed. I was too excited to sleep much in the first part of the night, and I lay there thinking over all that father had said. I haven't forgotten a word of it, names or any thing, Gerald, and I never shall. Besides, mother and I often talked it all over quietly together; and she told me more that she knew about my father's trial. I didn't see him again. He died in the night, and wouldn't allow me to be called. 'I have bidden Phil good-bye,' he said, 'and I do not want him to forget what I said to him through any other farewell now.' Poor father!"

There was a pause. The clock struck four. It was almost a home-like sound to them now. This solemn story of the past had unconsciously blunted the sharpness of present troubles.

"Laverack and the watchman, Sixmith," repeated Gerald, slowly. "Those two. What became of them? Have you ever seen them or had any chance to speak with them?"

"No," answered Touchtone. "Laverack served his term with the other four, and I dare say has had dozens of other names since, if he still lives in this country or anywhere. Sixmith was discharged from the bank at once, I believe, but father never heard what became of him."

"Did Mr. Marcy ever try to clear up the matter any further, for your mother's sake and yours?" asked Gerald.

Touchtone blushed and replied, awkwardly, "Yes—that is, no. He couldn't try much. There was so little ground to start from," he added, in apology for his protector; "and Mr. Marcy has done so much for us without it. He seldom speaks of *that*."

"But he believes, as you do, that your father wasn't guilty?" persisted Gerald, raising himself on one elbow and staring hard at Touchtone.

"Yes—yes," Philip returned slowly, and then more slowly still, "but not so much, I'm afraid, as I do. I tell you, we very seldom talk about it. I—I—don't know."

That answer told a plain story. Gerald did not pursue the inquiry.

"Well, if we get out of here and see papa you must tell him every thing. He's a first-class one to help any body in any thing. You can take my word for it. Between us all we may bring the truth to light—for every body, Mr. Marcy included. I can't tell you how I thank you for letting me hear all about this. I believed as you do from the first, you know."

"Yes, I know you did," said Touchtone. "It seemed so odd and unexpected. I was glad. But come, we wont talk any more now. You must try to get to sleep. I've been awfully thoughtless. Does your head ache as hard as it did?"

"Not nearly; and instead of being as hot and as miserable as I was I believe I'm better." His hands and temples were cooler, and after a few moments of silence Philip thankfully noticed that he dozed. The doze became a slumber.

Philip made the room less light. He was thinking of the patient cow and wondering whether he could safely go to her. Suddenly the sound of the dog's barking came into the windows. It did not waken the sick boy. Noiselessly he hurried from the room into the kitchen and around the corner of the house, where Towzer appeared to be standing in some sudden fit of vigilance.

A man and a woman were coming up from the dock, where a large cat-boat[73] was moored. They were looking toward the farm-house and at the smoke in the garden in evident perturbation. At the sight of his own figure hastening toward the gate to meet and admit them their haste and surprise doubled. On they came. They were loaded with a couple of large carpet-bags and innumerable bundles. They were middle-aged people. The man was low-statured, smooth-faced, and a little stout; the woman tall and angular. Their shrewd, puzzled faces were kindly and the man waved an unknown reply to Philip's gesture of recognition. He could hear them exchanging ejaculations and queries.

"The Probascos, for certain—at last!" he exclaimed. Advancing toward the couple outside the gate, bareheaded, he bowed and repeated the name interrogatively, "Mr. and Mrs. Obed Probasco, of this place, I believe?" as they came up.

The farmer dropped his belongings and answered in a bewilderment that had nothing of ill-nature, "The same, sir, at your service, sartin[74] sure. An' who might I have the pleasure of addressin'?"

CHAPTER XIV.

ALLIES.

The question concluding the preceding chapter of this history took more than a moment or so to answer, as the reader may suppose. Open-mouthed, as well as open-eared, with their packages, one by one, dropped heedlessly in the grassy path that led up from the little dock, "Obed Probasco and Loreta his wife" halted before Philip, still ejaculating, questioning, and with their astonishment of one kind giving place to that of another as Philip proceeded with his story. He leaned against the fence and, talking now with one, now the other, related his strange experience. The amazed New England couple turned and looked into each other's eyes at every few sentences, with many a "My gracious me!" "Did ever any body hear the like?" "You don't mean that you"—did so and so; and by Obed's frequent "Well, this beats all creation, fur as I know it!" Even Touchtone's anxiety and their curiosity as to Gerald could not retard their eagerness to learn all the facts.

The couple bore every appearance of homely thrift and

simplicity of character; of being, in short, precisely the kind of people Touchtone had hoped. It is, perhaps, needless to say that Philip's narrative was only of the circumstances since the hour of departure from the *Old Province*. Mr. Belmont and his persecution he left till a more convenient season.

"An' you mean to tell me that that poor boy an' you have been shut up here two days? No other soul about the place? An' he sick on your hands half the time?" gasped the distressed Mrs. Obed.

"That's just what I mean," replied Touchtone.

"Never heard such an astonishin' story in my life," repeated Probasco. "What would you 'a' done, though, if you hadn't brought up here? Well, it stumps me; that's all."

"The hand of the Lord's in it, no mistake!" declared Mrs. Obed. "I can't say how welcome you've been to any thing an' to every thing of ours that the old house there's got inside it. You couldn't 'a' better pleased me an' my husband here, Mr. Tombstone—I mean Mr. Touchtone—I b'lieve you said that was your name, didn't you?—than by just makin' free of every blessed corner of it. But dear, dear! If I'd only been to home."

"Yes, it's queer luck! Wife an' I've both been over on shore. We had to go across to Chantico to the funeral of a nephew of ours, that died very sudden. We stuck fast there by my bein' sick. The very time that such a thing as this came straight up to our doors!"

"Queer luck?" repeated the farmer's wife. "You'd better just say queer Providence, Obed! It's been awful unhandy for you, Mr. Touchtone—made things so much harder for you an' the little boy. But I guess if Providence could save you both bein' dashed overboard with those poor souls in that boat, he could help you to get along with a lot o' my stale stuff to eat, an' not a hand to help you to any thing better. Our house wide open, was it? Well, I don't know where you'd 'a' got in if 't been us left it last! But," she continued, turning in sudden vexation to her husband, "that's the very identical good-bye time old Murtagh'll play us such a trick! After all his straight up an' down promises that he'd never leave the place one minute! An' the cow, too!"

"Yes, I've had enough of Murtagh," assented the farmer,

sharply, "an' I guess we'll find the obligations on our side, sir. Murtagh's a man we've had on the place to help us, an' he don't appear to have no more responsibleness than a grasshopper, let alone his drinking. Wife an' I've been in a worry the hull time we was obliged to stay across the strait. But we didn't look for his acting this way."

It appeared that the derelict Murtagh had indeed been left in charge by his master; and that that neglectful hireling of the household must have scarcely waited for his employers' backs to be turned than he had betaken himself to his own little skiff and gone off shoreward, too. "Most likely, on one of his regular high old sprees!" surmised the exasperated farmer. "This is the end of Pat Murtagh's working for me!"

"Well, come, come, don't let's stand another minute here," said Mrs. Probasco, realizing that the necessary explanations on both sides were finished; "that boy you've got with you mustn't be left alone. Perhaps he's not so sick as you think. I hope he's been asleep while we've been puttin' you through such a long catechism. Let's all hurry, to make up for it. Obed, don't you rattle that gate; an' do you take off your boots before you get to the kitchen door. Thanky, Mr. Touchtone, let them things lay just where they be; there's nobody to steal 'em, you know. Come along, quick, both of you."

Leaving Obed to deprive his feet of their squeaky new coverings, Philip and Mrs. Probasco stepped lightly toward the kitchen and on tiptoe drew near the bedroom door.

Sure enough, Gerald's slumber was profound. The kindhearted woman followed Touchtone to the bedside in curiosity and pity. She beheld the face of this other of her two uninvited guests with a great stir in her motherly heart and a quick admiration of Gerald's strange and just now singularly pathetic beauty. With a woman's soft fingers she ventured to touch his skin, and with intent ear she listened to the sleeper's breathing.

"He's better than he was, I guess," she said in a hushed voice to Philip. "His skin's damp, an' he breathes in a good deal healthier way than I expected. Fever's gone down as soon as it came up, I dare say. How han'some he is!—a reg'lar picture. From New York, did you say?"

Obed looked in at the door in anxious interest. "You stay here with him while I fly around and get things sort o' settled and more ready for whatever's best for us to do." She glided out, closing the door after her. Smothered sounds, that now and then came from behind it, hinted to Philip as he sat that the flying around had begun to some purpose.

Excellent Mrs. Probasco! Whatever may have been the sentiments of your housekeeper's heart at such a delayed home-coming and such a finding of your entire domestic establishment taken possession of by boys, and not only an asylum, but a hospital, all at once on your hands—whatever the amusement or vexation at the general upsetting of order on each side, you kept it all to yourself! She darted softly about. "Time enough for talk, by and by," she said, sharply, to Obed, who was accustomed to act pretty much as she commanded. "Then we'll talk. We know plenty to start right at. We must just take care of these boys as well as we can, till they're ready to leave us an' go ahead on their journey. An', by the way, Mr. Touchtone says they'd ought to get some sort of word to their friends right away, just as soon as we see how that boy is when he wakes. Of course they'd ought! So I advise you, after you been over the place, an' done up all those chores old Murtagh's kindly left for you, to get the boat ready for early to-morrow morning, when you can hurry over to Chantico."

Obed hastened off, his Sunday go-to-meeting clothes exchanged for his every-day array, and disappeared down the garden with the chickens trooping after him in joyful expectancy; Mrs. Probasco kept at work, now and then slipping in to consult Touchtone or calling him to her.

Daylight began to wane. Gerald slept on, occasionally appearing to be just on the point of awakening, but always drifting back into sounder sleep again. Numerous, and with many hurried and whispered paragraphs of further explanation and questions and answers, were the interviews between Philip and his bustling hostess during the remnant of time before candle-light. With its windows and doors wide open, and the smell of supper coming appetizingly from the kitchen, and with a general sense of human occupation about it, the old dwelling was already like a different place from its former mysterious self. The dog ("You *will* call him Towzer, but his real name's Jock," Mrs. Probasco protested) trotted about. Upper rooms were unsealed, and Touchtone stared about them, meeting nothing to excite his curiosity except one or two quaint and battered pieces of furniture that seemed in keeping with the old house rather than with any modern inmates.

And before long came history, bit by bit, from Mrs. Probasco or Obed. As Philip had expected, the farm and premises on Chantico Island were not owned, but rented, by them—had been so for many years, through an agent.

The dignified, isolated old dwelling, half farm-house, half mansion, still belonged in a family line once distinguished in the county for wealth and social position—the Jennisons. Other people might live in it, but it was always haunted by the atmosphere of stately earlier days and aristocratic occupants.

Who were, or had been, the Jennisons? Great had they been once, in that part of the State. Early Jennisons had bought the island and named it "Jennison's Island," in Revolutionary days. One famous grandfather had built the mansion and fitted it with fine old-fashioned furnishings, and loved it, and lived and died in it. In his day this ancient roof had sheltered many a guest of famous name. Under it gay levees[75] had come off, and sumptuous dinners and country merry-makings, and lively weddings and solemn funerals. Two of the belles in the family line had been the very "Mary Abigail" and "Sarah Amanda" who had stitched those yellowed samplers on the wall. They had died, grandmothers both, long ago. And of all the Jennison estate was left to-day only this single lonely corner of it, the island, its very name changed on the government maps by some State maneuver. Furthermore, to bear the family name and own the scattered remnants of this world's goods left to its credit, there was now only a single representative, one Wentworth Jennison,[76] according to Mrs. Probasco's reserved account, an erratic and wandering man, who seldom set his foot near the home of his ancestors—once or twice a year, perhaps; then not again for another two or three seasons. He allowed an old lawyer at Chantico to lease island, farm, and house to the Probascos.

They paid their modest rent and kept the mansion from destruction. They had long been its tenants.

Of course, the connection between these details became clearer in his later talks with the good farmer's wife; but Philip gathered enough in her scraps of explanation that afternoon and evening to interest his boyish love of romance and novelty and to fill his heart with gratitude for this hospitable situation.

Just before supper-time Gerald awoke.

"Philip," he called, "Philip! where have you gone?"

Touchtone hastened in from the kitchen. A few sentences with the sick boy gave him a delightful sense of relief. It was quite confirmed during the next half hour. Gerald's fever had almost departed. He was told the good news of the Probascos' return. On the first sight of his sympathetic hostess he "took to her" (so she expressed it), "as if we'd never done nothing but spend our hull lives in this same old house." Obed was permitted by his vigilant spouse to come in and hold the boy's slender hand in his for a few moments and speak his few kindly words of welcome and help. The invalid's appetite that had developed was rewarded with a dainty supper, and he was made comfortable in fresh sheets. "O, I guess he's all right, an' doing splendidly, Mr. Touchtone," Mrs. Probasco declared. "We won't give him a chance to get real sick, between us."

"What kind people they are!" Gerald said, softly, to Touchtone, just as he was dropping off into a fresh doze, with the clink of Mrs. Probasco's dishes and the murmur of her conference with Obed making a homely lullaby from the adjoining room.

"Yes, the kindest sort," assented Touchtone. "Go to sleep, old man, and dream about them and every thing else that is pleasant. I'll add a postscript to these letters, to bring them down to the latest minute."

"O, yes, now you can. Did you write papa?"

"I have written papa and every body. Mr. Probasco is going to get up early to-morrow morning, and either take me over with these to Chantico or else carry them alone. So, you see, we are fairly started forward getting back to civilization and our friends again. The suspense all around will soon be over."

"We've been through a good deal together, haven't we? And in such a little while."

"We certainly have," said Touchtone, half seriously, half smiling.

Gerald slept. Philip added a few lines to his letters, and, now that their situation was so happily determined, his anxiety for their being dispatched came upon him with double force. Not an hour longer must needlessly intervene.

It was impossible for him to guess what conclusion Mr. Marcy and Gerald's father could have or could not have arrived at by this. According to Probasco's account there had been plenty in all the newspapers about the steamer—"Folks had done nothing else but read an' talk about it"—although Obed's "plaguey turn o' the wust sort o' rheumatism" had kept himself, his wife, and their Chantico relatives in too much excitement for reading news, to say nothing of the funeral at the house. In his last writing Philip told Mr. Marcy and Mr. Saxton that within as few hours as possible for Gerald and himself to leave the Probascos they would go to Chantico, and thence down to Knoxport. There they would wait for instructions from one or the other gentleman. In view of the absolute ignorance of affairs it seemed to Philip unwise to hurry straight back to New York by railroad, and much less advisable to think of continuing their Halifax journey, of course. There was a chance, too, that at this very minute Mr. Saxton, Mr. Marcy, or both, were lingering in Knoxport, hoping for news from some quarter, unwilling to quit the point nearest to the late accident.

Fortunately, he did not know that a body declared to be his own, drowned and disfigured, had been duly "identified" days before by a coroner's jury, and that the fate of the boat had been decided by every opinion brought to bear on it, and that, while he sat there writing, Mr. Marcy, with as heavy a heart as a man can ever bear in his breast, was packing his own and Mr. Saxton's valises and preparing to fairly drag away the distracted father from the Knoxport House on the journey that he hoped might quiet his friend's nerves, and for which Marcy had generously suspended all his own affairs.

The letters sealed, Philip felt more at rest. As the evening wore on, more excited than tired, he and Mrs. Probasco and Obed sat within ear-shot of the sick-room. In low voices they went into new particulars on both sides, discussed his plans for himself and Gerald together, and weighed this and that. Hospitable, shrewd, warm-hearted folk! Could you and your charge, Philip, have fallen into more tender or more willing hands? How interested they became in the life at the Ossokosee that had made this friendship begin, and in the thousand little or greater incidents which had perfected it and so suddenly laid such responsibilities on Touchtone's shoulders! How carefully both, the man by silence, the good woman by tactful turns of the conversation, avoided intruding on matters that they surely would have relished understanding better, but into which they would not pry!

It seemed beautiful to Mrs. Probasco's inmost heart, which one already will have divined was nothing like as unromantic as her features, this friendship between these two lads, this devotion of the elder lad to the younger.

"There never was any thing prettier than the way you an' him have been keeping together," she ventured once to remark, ungrammatically but earnestly. "It's like a book."

"But there never was any body else like Gerald—in or out of a book," Touchtone answered, simply, blushing. For if facts were on his lips his inner sentiments, as a general thing, were not.

"Well, I only hope that you'll have a long life together without no kind of quarrels between you, nor troubles after these, my lad," said Obed, stroking the dog's head as Towzer lay beside his chair. "You've begun to make friendship the way it'd ought to be made, an' as it's grown older it'd ought to be of a kind that aint common in this part o' the world, so far as I've had opportunity to jedge."

"I hope so, too," responded Touchtone, soberly. Yes, and he believed it. His "old head on young shoulders" for one moment pictured in flashing succession years to come at Gerald's side, himself his best friend ever, to companion and care for him. Or, would the future bring differences, quarrels, a breaking apart for them, and only thorns from this now newly planted vineyard, as happened to so many other pairs of friends in this strange world? Only fate knew, and only time could decide.

Bed-hour came. Philip proposed to hold to his lounge; so it was more comfortably made up for rest, under Mrs. Probasco's care, than before. Obed was to start for Chantico after the early breakfast. At first Philip decided that it was best he should go with him; but he concluded to curb his impatience and not be absent all day from Gerald. The letters and telegrams lay ready to be forwarded; Obed understood precisely what he was to do.

They said good-night. Philip lay awake a half hour or so. He was restless. Uncertainty after uncertainty and step by step of the unsolved equation of Gerald's and his situation filled his brain. He thought and planned, and heard the wind that had all at once risen blow furiously about the house. His final thought was that it had begun to rain pretty hard.

But his dismay and that of the Probascos when they met the next morning cannot briefly be described. A great gale was raging. The sea was a wild, mad, terrible creature, heaving itself in black tumult in the drenching and cold storm. The channel between the island and vanished coast was a raging body of water that no ordinary boat could safely hope to traverse. It was not a storm, but an equinoctial[77] tempest.

Obed, with as much regret as honesty, declared he could not think of attempting a passage to Chantico. Letters, telegrams, every sort of communication, must wait until the elements were lulled.

"Another day lost!" cried Philip to himself, impatiently. He walked up and down Gerald's room in chafing, impotent anxiety. Gerald was so much better that Mrs. Probasco declared danger of further illness ended. He roved languidly about the house with the farmer's wife, in more contentment than Philip had hoped the boy could be kept in. But it made his own concern come home to him heavily. Obed and he counseled and watched the sea and storm. There was nothing else to do. The gale's fury increased in the afternoon, and, worse still, the coming of the early and deep darkness of the evening found it undiminished in violence.

CHAPTER XV.

Files of newspapers, already yellowed, can give the reader, who cares for details of such events, long accounts of the famous gale that suddenly lashed the western Atlantic to a fury of destruction in the autumn of 188–.[78] It swept the rocky coasts of New England with a power that recent tempests have seldom equaled. Fishing-smacks, merchant craft of stalwart build, and yachts, belated in their return home, were dashed by dozens on the reefs of the Middle and Eastern States, swallowed up by the terrific sea that ran at its highest for days together, or, like empty soap-boxes in surf, were driven to shore. The death-list of seamen and others, unfortunate enough to be at the gale's mercy or mercilessness ran well up into the hundreds. Nor was that all. For scores of miles inland travel was interrupted by wash-outs and cavings-in, on highways and railroads. The telegraph and mail-service were suspended in a dozen directions. Bridges were flooded or swept away as if by spring freshets. In the harbors and straits such tides swelled as made the oldest inhabitants of the villages along them shake in their shoes to hear measured and compared. For four days sheets of rain descended about Chantico with only brief pauses, and when the down-pouring from overhead lightened and at last ceased the wind and ocean were things to send dread into the spirits of even cool-headed skippers and spectators.

With every thing in the way of communicating with their friends brought to a stand-still, paralyzed, Philip and Gerald waited on Chantico Island, in company with the Probascos, and watched the whirling and seething clouds and sea. Obed, however, was not able to be with them very often after the second morning. His rheumatism awoke when he did, and it kept the poor man much in his bed and in pain enough to put other dilemmas out of his sympathy. Mrs. Probasco nursed him; "ran" the house; sat for half hours with Touchtone and Gerald, chatting cheerfully and telling long stories of her and Obed's younger days, when they had lived on their parents' farms, some miles back of Chantico. She kept a watchful eye on Gerald's convalescence, and generally was like Cæsar in having "to do all things at one time," and, like the mighty Julius, she did not complain of the situation.[79]

The resources of the farm-house, except for Mrs. Obed's lively talk, were modest in such an emergency. One could not put his head out of the door except the wind nearly blew it off. But any thing must needs have been of a wonderfully distracting sort to beguile, for Philip Touchtone, at least, hours that he knew must be costing their friends great suspense or deep grief. There was a backgammon-board, with the legend "History of England" on the back, deceiving nobody.[80] Gerald found amusement in another quite astonishing pastime, entitled, as to its large and gaudy label, "The Chequered Game of Life: A Moral and Instructive Amusement for Youth of Both Sexes. By a Friend to Them."[81]

"I wonder if it is meant for us?" Gerald asked when he unearthed this ancient treasure. "I never heard of 'youth of both sexes' before.[82] I thought people had to be either boys or girls."

Philip partly spent one morning in teaching the solemn cat sundry tricks (much against patient pussy's will), which afternoon showed she had not given herself the slightest trouble to remember. With Gerald at his elbow, to add accuracy to his notes, he "wrote up" his diary, which had been abiding safely in his traveling-satchel. The partial changes of linen and the convenient odds and ends that their satchels contained were of truly unexpected value now that their trunk was in the bottom of the sea, with the rest of the *Old Province*'s baggage. Mrs. Probasco took the opportunity to put their limited clothing into thorough order.

"Next time I come away on a short voyage I think I'll pack all the things in my closet into a hand-bag!" Gerald exclaimed, ruefully, taking stock of their resources.

"Or send the trunk by land?" laughed Touchtone, grimly. "I'm glad, though, that there was nothing of downright value in the trunk that we couldn't replace. When we get to Knox-port we can get a wardrobe together directly there, or wherever Mr. Marcy and your father advise. How lucky you didn't put that daguerreotype[83] of your mother in!—the one that is to be copied."

"Yes," answered the boy, seriously; "it was lucky. Papa would have felt as badly as I if that had been lost. It's the only one we like."

Touchtone could see that this prolonged separation of the boy from his father, in more than one sense, would bring them nearer to each other than they ever had been before. "And a precious good thing," he soliloquized. "The best way to keep some fellows chums seems to have somebody give them both a sound shaking now and then. Perhaps this sort of thing for Gerald and Mr. Saxton amounts to that." In spite of the resolute silence of Gerald, for the sake of his friend, on the great topic of his father's or Mr. Marcy's whereabouts and conclusions, Philip (who certainly did not try to introduce it) knew that most of the time Mr. Saxton was in Gerald's mind.

"Do you know what I think?" he said abruptly, once, looking up from the backgammon-board, after having thrown his dice and placed his men abstractedly during several turns. "I don't believe that I've appreciated papa very much, nor that he has appreciated me very much—till now."

Obed Probasco's hobbling entrance for supper and a new study of the weather saved Touchtone's answer to a statement that it struck him came peculiarly near to the truth, and to a very common state of matters between near relatives.

They rambled over the old farm-house, the wind roaring and the rain dashing about the eaves and windows. Philip possesses to-day a substantial reminder of this exploring, in the shape of a bright copper warming-pan, one of two that had belonged to "Grandmother Probasco," which now hangs in restored glory in a place far from that dusky nook it occupied for so many years. The discovery of a rat in the wainscot of the kitchen, within convenient range of the dresser where Mrs. Probasco was accustomed to stand her hot bread and pies, gave occupa-tion to all the household, including Towzer ("You *will* call that dog Towzer when you *know* his real name's Jock," frequently remonstrated Mrs. Probasco) for a while the second afternoon. In the evening Obed took to telling tales of a certain uncle of his who had been "a seafaring man of oncommon eddication," and that chronicle whiled away the hours till bed-time, and sent them to bed sleepy into the bargain; the history recounted being of a mild and long-winded sort, and chiefly connected with the efforts of the nautical ancestor to induce "a widow that lived on Cape Ann"[84] to exchange a little piece of ground she owned for a big fishing-smack[85] that she didn't want, a wedding being part of the proposed transaction. They became, by hearsay, quite familiar with the quaint Chantico people and their characters and ways. For, although Mr. and Mrs. Probasco were so aloof from the little port, several of their kith and kin lived thereabouts, and household supplies and queer chapters of gossip came thence to the island. Philip remembers in these after years, as one sometimes does things heard in a dream, the anecdotes and homely annals that he listened to (or rather half-listened to) during those days. Sometimes a curious name that happens to be read or mentioned will bring back the scenes of that week, and even the wearisome, hoarse noise of sea and storm from hour to hour.

By mutual consent, all questions of how far their detention from Chantico might affect their plans were pushed aside, unless Gerald was out of ear-shot. And, in any case, what could they determine?

But it does not seldom occur in this conversational world that when every subject seems exhausted people hit upon one that is to turn out the most important. This experience of "talking against time," as it might be called, with the friendly Probascos gave Touchtone an instance of the fact which he has always thought satisfactory enough. It was Gerald Saxton who, in the evening of the last day of the gale, unintentionally set the ball in motion by a careless remark.

Obed happened to be out of the room for the sake of his efficacious bottle of "lineament."[86] They had been speaking of the island-farm—how fertile it was, how easily cultivated by Obed and by the extra help he employed at certain times of the year;

of the commodious old dwelling that the couple had so long occupied that it was only at the days of rent-paying that they realized themselves still tenants and not owners.

"You see," said Mrs. Obed, holding up her darning-needle to re-thread it (making a very wry face in the process), "we'd 'a' bought the island long ago, Obed and me—though there's a pretty steep price for it, disadvantages considered—but there's incumbrances as to the title; an', besides, when Gran'f'ther Probasco dies (that's my gran'f'ther over to Peanut Point—he's feeble, *very* feeble—Obed an' me'll have to take his farm and live there. It's a real sightly place, an' the land's splendid. But it'll be a hard pull for us to leave the island after spendin' so much of our lives here."

"I should think so," assented Gerald. "I don't see why that Mr. Jennison you speak of—the one who partly owns the old place still—don't come over to take a look at it now and then, in the summers. I should think he would like to."

The face of the farmer's wife changed.

"Mr. Jennison isn't the sort of man to care about that," she replied. "He does come—sometimes. As it happens, husband kind o' expected him this very month, on some errand he wrote about last July. There's a hull roomful of his things up-stairs."

"A roomful of his things!" ejaculated Philip, remembering the locked door.

"Yes; when he was a young man an' used to visit oftener, we got in the way of keepin' a chamber up-stairs that wasn't no use to the family of us, as a kind o' store-room for him. There's quite a good many old articles o' furniture an' trunks and papers. He says they aint o' any use, though they belonged in the family. He asked us to let 'em stay till he settled somewhere. He aint settled yet."

"Doesn't he live anywhere?"

Mrs. Probasco gave a cough. "I guess you might best say he lives every-where. He's a roving gentleman, by his own account."

"Then, I suppose, he's generally in New York, and makes that his head-quarters," suggested Gerald. "My father says people who live out of New York most of the time always say that. Is he a broker?"

"I don't know just what his business is," returned Mrs. Pro-basco. Philip surmised that interesting facts as to Mr. Jennison lurked about. He decided not to interrupt Gerald's thoughtless catechism. "Sometimes his business seems to be one thing, and sometimes another," the farmer's wife concluded.

"I'd like to see him."

"I don't think you'd be specially taken with him," dryly returned Mrs. Obed. "But he might happen here before you get off. He goes all over the country in long journeys. Sometimes Mr. Clagg—that's the lawyer over to Chantico—don't know his address for weeks."

"And he's really the last of the Jennisons, you say? What a pity he don't live in this old place himself, and keep it up, for the sake of the family."

Mrs. Probasco examined a stocking carefully.

"Yes, it's a pity. But I don't much think he could. Mr. Jennison isn't married, an' he isn't rich, you see, nor—"

Just then Obed's strong voice came from the door-way where he had been pausing. "Look here, Loreta," he exclaimed, banteringly, "I should think you'd feel ashamed of yourself to sit there an' try to pull the wool over their eyes! Where's the use? I know you've a considerable loyal feelin' to the Jennisons, but you needn't carry it so far. The fact is, boys," he continued, sitting down in his arm-chair with some difficulty—"the fact is Loreta an' I have come to the conclusion that our Mr. Win-throp Jennison's grown to be a pretty shady and suspicious sort of character. His life an' his business seem to be matters that honest folks needn't inquire into too closely. There, Loreta!"

"Now, Obed!" retorted Mrs. Probasco, in great annoyance, "you oughtn't to say that! You don't know, for certain, any more than I do."

"May be I don't know so much. May be I know more—more even than I've let on, my dear! For one thing, I haven't ever yet given you the particulars of what Clagg told me that last af-ternoon I went over to pay the rent an' learn if Mr. Jennison'd come from Boston."

"Mr. Clagg? What did Mr. Clagg say, Obed?" asked the wife, her work and the boys forgotten in her sudden anxiety.

Evidently the mysterious Mr. Jennison was a standing topic of debate between the pair. "How *could* you keep so still about it?"

"Well, I'll let you hear now," Obed replied, good-naturedly, with a wink at Philip, and in some enjoyment of the situation; "but wait. Before I do I'm going to tell the boys here what you know already. Then they'll understand the rest of my story better. You see, Mr. Touchtone," he began, "Mr. Winthrop Jennison grew up without father or mother, an' he was first sent to one boarding-school, then to another, by his uncle, for whom he was named—who owned this place till he died. Mr. Winthrop was a wild kind of a boy, from the first. I guess he wasn't so downright bad, but he was wild, an' easy led into bad scrapes. There was two or three we heard of, before his eddication an' his law studies was done. Then his uncle, that was his guardian, died; an' Mr. Winthrop was sent to Europe. He'd used to come here quite often in the summers before that. Wife an' I thought a good deal o' him, an' wanted to keep up his interest in the place. But in France and Germany he altered a good deal, an' spent most of his money, an' when he got back to New York he hadn't much. He couldn't well sell this place, or he wouldn't, so he always said. At any rate, that wouldn't have been o' much use. At last, Mr. Clagg found out he gambled bad, an' that he'd got into a set of men in the city that was shady enough to turn him into a real blackguard if he didn't look out! Mr. Clagg talked a lot to him an' straightened out his money-matters for him, and then he come away from New York and started into practicin' law in Boston."

Touchtone listened with interest quite as much as Gerald, to whom this was an exciting sketch from real life, which, as later he would find, alas! has so many like it. But the next paragraph of Mr. Winthrop Jennison's discreditable history made Philip's attention suddenly sharp, and a flush of color came into his face.

"We heard these things an' lots more about him, better or worse, mostly worse. Wife and I wondered at 'em and was sorry. But whenever he come over here, no matter what he might be further inside, Mr. Winthrop was always a perfect gentleman, not a bit dissipated-lookin', exceptin' his bein' generally very

pale; and we rather liked his visits. He seemed pretty well tired
out when he was here. He'd shut himself up in his room, or
take a boat an' go fishin'. Wife an' I think he's stuck so to the
place as a kind of a refuge an' restin'-place for him when things
don't suit him. He's a nice-lookin', pleasant-spoken man, of, I
dare say, forty, only he don't look his age. Well, after he'd been
in Boston a while he broke loose again with a hull set of his
worst chums. The papers said there was a forgery he and they
was all mixed up in together. And when he come here, the same
summer that Mr. Clagg knew about, then we found out that
he'd got as many as a half dozen names and two or three post-
office addresses.[87]

"But there was worse to come. One afternoon, in September, he and some o' the evilest-faced and best-dressed fellows I
ever see come to the island from off a yacht. They all sat down
there by the Point talkin' and wranglin' till sundown. Then Mr.
Jennison went off with them in the boat, only comin' up here a
minute to say how-d'-do to Loreta here. Loreta was more afraid
of him than glad to see him, for all the soft spot in her heart."

"I wasn't afraid of him, Obed, but I wasn't glad to see him,"
protested Mrs. Probasco. "I was sure that no man could keep
that kind o' company and seem on such good terms with 'em,
and be any longer a credit to his stock."

"A credit to his stock!" mocked Obed. "That's your usual
mild way o' puttin' it. She'll take the man's part, more or less,
till she dies, boys, mark my words! Well, the very week after
he and his party landed here, that afternoon, there came a
big noise about a robbery of a bank in New York, that all the
papers was full of; an' the parties that managed it planned the
hull affair in' a yacht they'd hired, an' they'd expected to get off
safe in it when the thing was over. 'Twas a little before your day,
Mr. Philip—the Suburban Bank robbery at a place close to New
York—"

The Suburban Bank robbery! Touchtone caught his breath
excitedly. Gerald nearly betrayed his friend by his unguarded
look at Philip. But it was dark now, and the storm was boister-
ous. Obed pursued his tale, unobserving and quite forgetful of
any names that he might have read long ago. "Mr. Clagg said

that the description given durin' the trial of those bank-scamps
fitted some of Mr. Jennison's friends ashore that day to a T. I'd
taken some good looks at 'em from behind my salt haystacks.
Well, after that, wife, here, she kind o' give up about Mr. Jennison. You felt terrible bad, didn't you?"

"Yes, I did," Loreta assented, soberly, "though we couldn't
never make up our minds that he was actually any nearer mixed
up in the thing. You'd ought to say that," she added.

"You've said it for me," Obed returned. "That's enough."

His regret and shame at such disgrace to the blood of the
Jennisons was as strong as his wife's, slightly as he expressed it.
He continued his story rapidly:

"Well, the very week the bank was broken into he arrived
here one mornin' suddenly, an' he stayed here a couple o' days.
We remembered that letter, in the trial; an' from here he went
off to Canada. Next thing Mr. Clagg knew he'd given up all his
law business, whatever it amounted to, an' was doing something, or nothing, in New York again. We scarcely saw him after
that. He's come less and less often, as wife may have told you
—once a year, once in two years. He was last over here in the
spring. An' now I come to what Clagg was a-letting on to me
the other day, Loreta."

"I hope, I hope, Obed, that it's nothing worse than what's
come already?" interrupted Mrs. Probasco.

In spite of any new and unexpected interest in Obed's account of the black sheep of the Jennison line, Philip felt a touch
of sympathy for her kindly grief.

"No, it aint so bad. Yet, it's a trifle wuss, in one way," Obed
answered, philosophically. "There's more ways o' earnin' a dis-
honest livin' than there is for an honest one, I sometimes think.
But give me, please, a square an' fair villain! Clagg says that last
year there was a bad case, a most amazin' one, of blackmail in
New York. Do you know what that is, wife? These boys do, I
reckon. Well, this was a special, scandalous thing, so Mr. Clagg
thinks; an attempt on the part of a couple of rascals to put a
family secret into all the newspapers unless the two old ladies
they threatened would pay 'em well on to twenty-five thousand
dollars to keep quiet. They didn't succeed. The police took the

matter up. The rogues were frightened an' got out of town as quick as they could, and they haint been heard of since. Clagg says he knows to a certainty that Winthrop Jennison was one of 'em! So that's his last piece of wickedness, and he's sunk low enough for that!"

"Clagg may be wrong," replied Mrs. Probasco, sadly.

"Clagg isn't often wrong, and this time he's certain of what he believes," replied Probasco, solemnly. "Now you can understand why I feel less than I ever did before like shuttin' that rascal out from under this roof, whether his grandfathers owned it or not. Now you know why, as I told Mr. Clagg, I'd like him to take away himself an' every belongin' he's got under it. I'm through with him. A blackguard and coward, besides all the rest of his wickedness! If he does turn up here in the course of the next few days or weeks I sha'n't tell him just that; but I'm going to remind him that this island's mine, if I pay my rent, an' henceforth he can stay away. What do you think about that, Loreta?"

"I—I reckon you're about right, Obed," responded Loreta, meekly. Apparently she realized there was no use a-wasting interest in so worthless and unsafe a direction.

"A great story, isn't it, Mr. Philip?" Probasco demanded, as his wife rose to set supper on, but stood looking out of the window sadly.

"Yes—yes—a pretty bad one," assented Touchtone.

He was about to add in as cool and indifferent a tone as he could command, "I wish you could just describe this Mr. Jennison a little more closely for me. Is he light or dark?" He cut short the question unuttered. Gerald was present. But, lo and behold! Mrs. Loreta nearly spoiled his generous precaution. She turned from the window abruptly.

"I've got a photograph of Mr. Jennison. Would you care to see it?"

"A photograph!" replied Gerald, "yes; ever so much! I'd be glad to see what such a bad man looks like."

"Like a very good-looking man," returned Mrs. Probasco from behind the supper-table. "I'll get it just as soon as I pour this milk out."

The light shone on Philip's face. Gerald was looking at the cat rubbing herself against Towzer. Philip quickly shook his head at Mrs. Probasco and laid his finger on his lips. She nodded, surprised, but obedient. Smash on the floor fell the large yellow bowl she carried. Obed and Gerald and Philip started. Gerald ran around the table to see what the calamity amounted to.

" 'Taint of the least consequence," she said; "not a bit. I aint often so unhandy. Just hand me that broom there, an' we'll get the pieces together."

Philip gave her a grateful and amused look at her clever device, and, passing near her, said, "Don't talk any more about that story. Don't let him see the picture! I'll explain later."

Mrs. Probasco not only heeded his words, but found a chance to put them into Obed's ear. Obed looked at Touchtone curiously, as he took the hurried hint.

"Odd!" he thought to himself. "Dare say he don't like the little boy to get such a story clearer in his mind. It aint such a pleasant one."

Supper passed off, the Jennison topic avoided. They had an ever-ready substitute for it in the weather. The storm was at last ceasing. The rain was less, the wind shifting. Next morning might be fairly clear. Obed's rheumatism, however, made it unlikely that they could leave so soon. The farmer was as anxious as they, generous-hearted fellow! but no risks must be run. They were too many miles from the coast. The morning would decide for them.

Gerald was disappointed of the photograph after supper. Mrs. Probasco absented herself some time from the room to try and lay her hands on it, "wherever she'd put it last," but returned without it. Philip thanked her again by an expressive look. She was a discreet woman.

Gerald was decoyed away to bed. He was wakeful and tried to engage Philip in a murmured discussion of Obed's story, and the possibility of there being any thing of private importance to Touchtone in it. But that Touchtone could not at once determine this he soon perceived; and inferring that not much could be properly expected of it the boy ceased talking and fell asleep.

Philip walked into the other room. He was a good deal more excited than he seemed.

"May I see that photograph you spoke of now, Mrs. Probasco?" he asked. "I've had a very special reason for keeping it from Gerald. I'm so much obliged to you both for helping me."

Mrs. Probasco opened the book in which she had slipped it.

"There it is. He left it in the house by accident, last spring."

She eyed Philip sharply. He bent over it in the candle-light. It was an imperial photograph[88] from a leading New York studio. It is probable that there never was taken a more unmistakable and perfectly satisfactory likeness of the calm, handsome countenance of—Mr. "John A. Belmont."

Philip was prepared for this certainty. But what was best to be done? Gerald and he, storm-stayed and sheltered under the roof of their enemy and persecutor—liable to be found there by him! They must indeed hurry from this house at the earliest instant. If only Philip had not been so reserved with Mr. and Mrs. Probasco as to the strange and dramatic interference of Belmont in their plans. If he had but given them so much as a hint at the adventure, then there would not now be so much to disclose and explain! Nevertheless, he felt sure he had acted prudently. Many courses occurred to him as he looked at the photograph with his host and hostess on either side of him.

"Have you ever seen him, Mr. Touchtone, down to New York, do you think?" asked Obed, certainly little expecting an affirmative reply.

Philip laid down the picture and turned to the couple, resolved.

"Yes, I have. I began to think so when you were finishing your story, and that's why I wanted it broken off and this picture kept back. I am sorry to say it, but that man there is an enemy of mine and of Gerald Saxton, or, perhaps, of Gerald's father. He has given us, unexpectedly, a great deal of trouble since Gerald and I left the Ossokosee. He would be glad, I am sure, to do more if he possibly gets the chance. We met him first as a Mr. Hilliard; and last, he told me to call him Mr. John A. Belmont, of New York. I—I—am a good deal afraid of him."

Obed and Loreta Probasco stared at Touchtone, and then at each other, in astonishment too deep for more than the shortest of their favorite exclamations.

"I can tell you the whole story presently. You will see. Gerald has known but very little about it; I don't intend he shall know much more. But, as to the main point, if Mr. Jennison should find us here, I don't know what might happen. He must not find us. We are in a queer pickle, without any worse troubles. His landing here before we can get away, or his learning that Gerald and I have spent this time in the house with you, would make our fix far worse, I know. We must get to Chantico and Knoxport to-morrow, if the weather will let us even try it. And if this Mr. Belmont—Jennison, I mean—comes here before you hear from me, you must not let him know we were with you or in this neighborhood. After we once meet Gerald's people it can't make any difference. More still, after that, it may be, I'd like to have a chance to talk to him myself, bad as he is. But, for the present, he must not hear our names breathed."

"Well, this is sudden!" Obed ejaculated. "But—"

"Hush," exclaimed Mrs. Probasco, going softly to the hall. "I thought I heard Gerald speaking. No, he's all right," she returned, quickly.

"I was goin' to say that wife an' me had best know more about this right away, Mr. Touchtone," said Obed, slowly. "It's pretty queer. If we're to do you any good, or, rather, not hurt your plans, you *might* post us a little further."

"Exactly," Philip replied. "You shall know whatever I can tell you as quickly as I can tell it."

So, for two hours, while Gerald was in dreamland, the "posting" continued. Philip told his story, but not that part of his family history that was hard to narrate to new friends. He answered frankly the many questions that their sympathy prompted. Once clear in their minds, neither Obed nor Mrs. Probasco doubted the story's truth.

"You needn't say more, to-night at least, Mr. Touchtone," said Obed, at last; "we've heard enough—haint we, Loreta? Your story an' mine run about as close as stories could—more's the pity. The weather's likely to be rough to-morrow, an' my rheumatics may keep me from getting across till next day. I shall be terrible sorry if I'm not better. I wish I wasn't alone. I'm pretty sure you're fairly safe from the chance of Jennison's coming to the farm this week; but I aint fully sure."

"Well, if he does we can hide you both snug as a bug in a rug," declared Mrs. Loreta, stoutly.

"Precisely," continued Obed. "Anyway, inside of forty-eight hours you'll be in Knoxport an' getting word to your friends— an' from 'em, I hope. Make your mind easy."

"Yes, we'll help you all we can to straighten every thing out right," said his wife. "Nothing will happen to you here but we'll know about it an' be ready to go through it with you and that dear boy there that's left in your charge. The good Lord bless him and you!"

The conversation ended. Philip went to bed, but not to sleep for a good hour or so. He speculated and planned. The Probascos talked together in their room assiduously enough.

The next day the sky was, to say the least, threatening, and the sea terrifically rough for small craft. Probasco's rheumatism was worse—one shoulder quite crippled. Philip was not used to navigation of the kind called for. Another day's delay seemed unwise and unendurable, though he gave up every thing at last. But toward evening it was decided that the next morning, if the weather was even a trifle improved, he and Gerald should leave, with Obed's help, or without, there being one or two obliging fishermen in Chantico who would bring back the cat-boat.

Accordingly, the next morning saw the two embarking, alone. Obed could not budge. Philip promised to exercise every kind of care, and he would communicate with Obed, by way of Chantico, within a few days. They bid these true, if new, friends good-bye. Philip shook Obed's rough hand as the farmer lay in bed suffering severely, and any thing but patient at so untimely a set-back.

"I—I'd rather have lost a small fortune than that things should come this way," he declared; "an' I'll be in as much of a fever as Loreta till we get word from you. I'm sure I wish you could stay a month."

A rough and not particularly direct passage brought them safely to Chantico about noon. It was a bright, cold day. A stage-coach ran to Knoxport. They had exactly time to catch this. By the middle of the afternoon they were trundling along the main business street of Knoxport. They were set down at the door of the Kossuth House, the largest of the few inns the town possessed.

"At last! Here at last, Gerald," exclaimed Touchtone, in deep relief, as they hurried into the office.

CHAPTER XVI.

SUSPENSE.

An elderly man, short-statured and with his grave countenance surmounted by a pair of spectacles, glanced at them from behind the desk of the neat little hotel as they approached it. Philip drew forward the register and took up the pen proffered him. Then he checked himself.

"No! It wont do to register—at least to register our own names; and I don't like to put down others."

During the instant's hesitation came an exclamation from Gerald.

"Look! look!" he whispered in joyful surprise. "There they are—both of them!"

Sure enough, sprawled in a familiar fist,[89] could be read "Jay Marcy" and "Gerald B. Saxton," under a stated date.

Philip turned quickly to the man. "Are Mr. Marcy and Mr. Saxton still with you? I'm very anxious to meet them, sir."

"Two gentlemen from New York? at least one of them? No; they went from here several days ago."

The disappointment was as sudden as the hope.

"Do you know what place they left for?" asked Philip, eagerly —"their addresses? We want to get a message forwarded to them as soon as possible."

The man consulted a memorandum-book.

"I don't know where they were going to. H'm! Letters to

be sent to the Epoch Club, New York, and to the Ossokosee Hotel.[90] That's Mr. Marcy's address. He's the proprietor."

"Papa belongs to the Epoch," whispered Gerald.

"You are sure they did not expect to return here at present?"

"I don't know. They said nothing about that; and there are those addresses. The gentlemen came on because of the loss of the steamer. Mr. Saxton's son was drowned, with a clerk of Mr. Marcy's, I believe, at the same time."

The lads turned and looked at each other in astonishment. So they were really not supposed to be in the land of the living? Philip had feared it.

"Mr. Saxton's son—and the clerk?" he replied. "How was it known?"

"O, they were both upset in a boat, overturned in making for the shore. A sailor was picked up who had been in it; he told how it happened. Nobody else escaped—out of that boat. Their bodies weren't recovered."

"Mr. Marcy and Mr. Saxton—came on?"

"Yes; got here the day after. Mr. Saxton was almost distracted, I believe. I didn't see much of either of 'em. They only stayed until the folks on the steamer that came off safe were all in. Mr. Saxton's boy was a little fellow—about as big as you," he added, pointing to Gerald. "It's been a bad thing for his father, I understand—broke him all up."

Philip laid a hand on Gerald's trembling arm to warn him not to give way to the emotions almost ready to burst out. Gerald bit his lips and looked down at the register.

"Guess you must 'a' been camping somewhere that the newspapers don't get to very quick," the elderly man said, smiling.

"We haven't seen the papers," assented Touchtone, simply. "One minute, please!"

He read down the page, recognizing several names of passengers on board the *Old Province*. He found what he expected— "John A. Belmont, N.Y.C.," and, lo and behold! beneath it, in the same hand, "W. Jennison, N.Y.C." A rogue's device, truly!

"Is this Mr. Belmont—or is Mr. Jennison in the house?" He put the question nervously.

"Neither of 'em. Mr. Jennison I know quite well. I didn't see the other gentleman with him. They had adjoining rooms. They left the day Mr. Marcy and Mr. Saxton got here. The room was vacant. I put Mr. Marcy in it, I remember."

"Can you give me their addresses, sir?" Philip inquired, more courageously.

"H'm! Mr. Belmont's left no directions, nor Mr. Jennison either. I don't find any." He laid the memorandum-book down; he was becoming impatient.

"I'd like to see the proprietor of the hotel," said Philip. "My friend and I must make some plans about stopping here or going to New York."

"I am the proprietor," returned the elderly man. "My name is Banger. What can I do for you?"

"I'd like to talk a little while with you, somewhere else than here—where we won't be overheard, please. It won't take long."

Mr. Banger suspected some confession of a school-boy lark or a runaway, shortness of funds for hotel bills, or some appeal to his kindness of that sort. He had had boys make them before. But he called to a young man coming into the office, "Here, Joe; I've business with these gentlemen. Look after things till I get through," and led Philip toward a little room across the hall. Gerald would have accompanied them, but Touchtone prevented it. It might interfere with what details he must disclose. Gerald sat down in the office with his back to Joe, and stared at the wall with eyes full of tears, and with a heavy heart that Touchtone hoped he could soon lighten.

Some persons have a faculty of not being surprised. Mr. Banger generally believed he had. But it is improbable that any Knoxport citizen was ever quite so astonished as he was by the first sentence of Philip's account. During the process of mastering the details that came after it he fairly reveled in such a story as it unfolded. He could hardly be kept from calling Joe and all Knoxport to draw near and partake of such a feast.

"I do, I *do* congratulate you with all my heart!" he declared over and over. "Your escape has been a miracle. And to think they have been mourning and lamenting and giving you both quite up," he continued. "But the mourning is nothing to make light of when it's a father's for his son, or such a kind of grief as Mr. Marcy's. I'm glad I didn't say more before that little fellow. Never did I see a man so cut to the heart in all my life as his father. Marcy had to keep with him every minute of the little time they were in town."

"The thing is, then, to get word to them both just as soon as can be. Unless they went straight back to town or to the Ossokosee—"

"Somehow I doubt if they did. I think I heard to the contrary. We'll wire at once. Will you stay here with young Saxton till you get answers to your telegrams?"

"I guess that's the best thing for us."

"I'll see to it you're comfortable. And, look here, do you know what I'd do next—the very minute you've got through your dispatch?"

"No; what, sir?"

"I'd go down to the office of the *Knoxport Anchor* and ask for Benny Fillmore, the editor. Fillmore sends all the news from this part of the country to some of the New York and Boston papers. He'll telegraph your whole story to two or three, tonight. It'll be in print to-morrow, and that's a way of telling all your friends that you're alive and waiting to hear from them that likely will beat any other."

"That *is* a good idea," Philip replied, struck with it. "It's doubtful how soon we can get direct word."

But as he spoke he remembered a reason why Mr. Banger's last suggestion was not a good one, after all. No, better not adopt it.

"I'll just step to the desk and register for you, or let you do it for yourselves. Eh? What's that?"

"I think it would be better for us not to register," Philip said, slowly, "if you don't mind; and, on second thoughts, perhaps we hadn't better be telegraphed about—to the papers."

"Why not, for pity's sake? You can keep as much to yourselves while you are here as you like. You needn't be pestered by visitors out of curiosity, if that's what you're thinking of."

"No, not that. The fact is, there is—a person who might give us a great deal of trouble and upset all our plans badly if he happened to know that we were here alone—if this person could get here before Mr. Marcy or Mr. Saxton."

Mr. Banger was nonplused. He deprecated keeping from all the rest of Knoxport and of creation this romantic return of the dead to life. Good could be done by it; and besides his own name and his hotel's would attain the glory of New York print. What foolishness was this?

"I don't understand," he said. "What kind of a person? How could you be annoyed? I'll look after you."

There was no helping it. Philip had to explain as much of the Hilliard-Belmont persecution as made its outlines clear. He hurried it over. But of the names, and especially of his discovery that the man Belmont and Mr. Winthrop Jennison were the same person, he uttered not a syllable. "Where's the use?" he thought. "I ought not to give you the name," he repeated, firmly—"at least not now."

Mr. Banger looked at him and then at the ceiling, and nodded his head slowly to show that he was considering, or would let this or that point pass for the present. Then he asked sundry questions. Philip answered them with an uncomfortable feeling that after piling Ossa on Pelion in this way he might be—doubted.[91] But he fought off that notion.

"Well," said Mr. Banger, "I don't see that you'd best let Fillmore go without his news. If this man comes, as you say he might, I will see that you get rid of him. It's a great mistake, it's downright cruel, not to use the newspapers."

"I think we'd better not," Philip said, firmly.

"It may save hours and days. Those men may have gone where letters will be slower than print."

"I know it; but I can't have that man bothering us again. If I were alone I shouldn't care."

"But you are not alone," persisted Mr. Banger. "I tell you, I'll be here to look after him, if he makes new trouble."

Touchtone held to his point. There was to be no publicity of their affairs—even in Knoxport. So Mr. Banger gave in, without the best grace. The matter was not being adjusted as he thought proper. Nevertheless both returned in good humor to

Gerald, whose quiet distress had given place to restlessness at the prolonged absence of Philip.

They were put down on the register as "Mr. Philip and brother." Their room was assigned them. Newspapers sent up were read eagerly, with the accounts of the steamer's fate. The two hurried down the street to the station where was the telegraph-office. All idea of leaving Knoxport until word came was abandoned.

"I am going to send to the Ossokosee—just that—for addresses, and to Mr. Hilliard in New York. They will be glad to hear about us, I know, and perhaps the news will reach your father or Mr. Marcy sooner."

"Mr. Hilliard said he was to leave town that day for the West."

"So he did! But here goes!"

The operator took the dispatches leisurely.

"Of course you know these may not get off this evening; perhaps they will, sometime to-night."

"Why not?" Philip asked, in dismay.

"The storm has broken our connections. They've been working on the line all day. It may be running as usual any hour now, or not until to-morrow."

Another set-back!

"Please do the best you can with them," he replied. "I will come down from the hotel after supper, to inquire."

They turned toward the post-office and sent the letters, and a card to the Probascos. There was some shopping that was absolutely necessary. That mild distraction was good for both of them. They bought whatever they needed, including a small trunk.

"Well, there's one good thing—we've money enough to get through quite a siege, Gerald. Mr. Marcy allowed us a wide margin over traveling expenses. We can wait and wait, here or elsewhere, without danger of being on the town."

"But how long must we wait, I wonder?" replied Gerald, tremulously. "O, Philip, it seems to me every thing gets into a worse muddle each minute. You're trying to hide it from me. When *will* they get word from us?"

"By to-morrow we shall hear from them, depend on it.

Perhaps in the forenoon. I don't know what you can think I'm hiding, you lost Gerald Saxton, you! It's all a queer jumble."

His effort at cheerfulness failed.

"I'm sick of it all! so sick!" exclaimed Gerald. "We're in a fix, a regular fix! I believe it will get worse instead of better. What did you and Mr. Banger have to say that took so terribly long—without me?"

"Well, I had to explain all our story to him, you know. I was sorry to leave you alone. Come, now, don't be down-hearted! There's nothing for you to be afraid of. I think the adventure is very funny, take it all in all. It's a little tiresome now, but we shall laugh over it next week—you and your father and Mr. Marcy and I. Don't you think Halifax⁹² is a small sort of a country city?" And he pointed, laughing, at Knoxport's main street and tiny green square, with its black-painted anchors and chains.

"Yes," Gerald answered, without a smile. "Poor papa!" he went on, presently. "How strange it will seem to him! He will be so glad to hear!"

Touchtone thought this opportunity not bad for bringing truth home.

"Glad? In spite of all the nonsense that you've talked now and then about his being so cool and careless toward you? Now you can't help seeing what stuff that's been, and I hope you wont ever think it again. Why, he'll be the happiest man in the world when he gets that message."

"I shall be the happiest boy to get his."

They did not see much of Mr. Banger on their return to the Kossuth House. He was engaged with some business matters, and merely called out, "Did you send them off all right?" to Philip, as they walked through the office. They had supper. Philip was anxious to escape unnecessary observation. There were not many guests; but two or three, as well as some of the towns-people, tried to engage him in chat without success.

The telegrams left Knoxport at nine o'clock, not before. It was with a sigh of relief that Philip received this news. He and Gerald, on whom it had a decidedly good effect, came up slowly from the station. Of course there was no chance of any word before some time in the next day. In fact, how fast the different dispatches were likely to go was a subject Touchtone would not let Gerald discuss. The storm had played havoc far and wide. Three or four connections between this little place and New York! And as many, perhaps, before at last the click of the instrument in the office at the Ossokosee would begin to be heard!

More than that, it was late in the season. Was the Ossokosee open yet? "It must be!" he exclaimed to himself. "Or, rather, Mr. Marcy must have gone back there to wind up the accounts and close the house, probably taking Mr. Saxton with him." But the more he thought of this, and felt that confusion of mind which is apt to occur when one worries over details, the more he came to the conclusion that he had made a mistake in not adopting Mr. Banger's suggestion as to Fillmore, the newspaper corre-spondent.

"I've a good mind to do it. What harm can come of it, espe-cially as Mr. Banger is here to help me any minute? It's ten to one that that rascal don't meddle with us."

Mr. Banger was still talking in the office.

"I believe I'll step down to the newspaper you spoke of and find that Mr. Fillmore and let him send his account," he said.

"This gentleman is Mr. Fillmore—just dropped in here," returned the hotel proprietor, pushing his neighbor, a red-faced young man with hair to match his complexion.

It would not be kind to cast any doubts on Mr. Banger's honor or on his ability to hold his tongue about even a remark-able secret; but it seemed to Philip that the editor had already numerous ideas of the story that he hastily dashed down in his note-book, and certainly Mr. Banger had been in close confab with him for an hour. Perhaps that paragraph on the escape of Philip and Gerald, and their waiting at Knoxport for word from their friends, would have appeared, without Philip's leave, in *The Tribune* and *The Herald* and *The World* and *The Advertiser* of the following morning exactly as it did—not to speak of the longer statements which graced the next day's *Anchor's* col-umns.[93] But this cannot be decided by the present chronicler. Certain it is that Mr. Fillmore seemed reasonably astonished. He hurried away with his notes to the telegraph office, where, the wires being now in order, it was promised that his news should be "rushed through;" and it really was.

The next day, from the hour that they rose until dinner, and from dinner until supper, was simply—expectation, and expectation without reward. Nothing came! They hung about the hotel, Philip abandoning even his intentions of making Gerald look about the town and its pretty suburb. The suspense gathered and increased. The fact was they were both, the older boy as well as his friend, reaching its severest limits. Touchtone had counted on some word before noon. When afternoon became a confirmed blank, his excitement increased, till he had all he could do to be reasonably tranquil—for two. What could it mean? The distance—the storm inland—some carelessness?

"There is a dead-lock—a dead-lock somewhere!" Touchtone exclaimed to himself over and over. Some of the telegrams had been duplicated. Two other persons at Ossokosee—Farmer Wooden one of them—were added. They had no available New York acquaintances. Further dispatches were useless. If the enigma had a simple answer it was as effective as one in which lay a tragedy. The silence might any moment explain itself as a calamity or a burlesque.[94] Must they wait another day for a solution—or for none?

"We wont do that, I think, Gerald," he said. "No. If this delay keeps on we will leave here to-morrow and start for home, the Ossokosee. Even if we find the doors shut in our faces we'll find people glad to take us in, forlorn creatures that we are." There was not much mirth in his laugh.

"I—I think we'd better go home," said Gerald; and this prospect brightened him a little.

Mr. Banger was on jury duty all that day, and, much to his disgust, he was locked up for the night with eleven other good and true men. He sent word to his viceroy, Joe, that he "couldn't tell when Wilson Miller (the town undertaker) would know black wasn't white, and let them all get home to their business—it was all his pig-headedness!" But about ten o'clock Mr. Banger was released and made his way back, quite put out with life and with the ways of administering justice in these United States. He had not thought of Philip and Gerald and of their mysterious detention. But it surprised him to now infer, from what Joe said, that they had not yet been able to get replies from their friends.

"Things must be decidedly out of order somewhere," he exclaimed to Joe, as they were sitting together in the office, chatting about the day's affairs. From the bar-room came the sound of a few voices, and the hotel was settling down for the night.

"Does that young fellow seem to have as much money about him as he'd ought to—by what he said to me?"

"I don't know," Joe replied. "You told me not to bother 'em."

"I wonder if his story is all made out of cloth that will wash?[95] To look at either of the two would make one suppose so. But I've been sold[96] before now by people, old and young."

As he spoke Philip walked in sight. He had left a package in the office, and came down-stairs for it. He looked pale and anxious.

"Nothing turned up yet?" queried Mr. Banger. "Odd! I should think you'd feel quite nonplused."

"I do," replied Philip, pausing. "It is—rather curious." He did not wish to seem uncomfortable. "I think we shall hear something to-morrow. Good-night, sir." And he went up-stairs again, too weary and dejected to talk over his worry with any comparative stranger.

Just as he closed his bed-room door, and as sounds from below were shut out, wheels came crackling up to the front piazza. Mr. Banger walked to the door. Somebody was standing beside his vehicle. "In half an hour," he was saying; "and rub him down well before you bring him back."

Mr. Banger recognized the voice.

"Ah, Mr. Jennison!" he exclaimed, as that gentleman came up the steps leisurely, "where do you hail from at this time of the evening?"

"When most decent people are going to sleep, ourselves the bright exceptions?" Mr. Winthrop Jennison returned.

"When most decent people are thinking about going to sleep," the landlord answered humorously.

"Well," returned Mr. Jennison, looking back solicitously after the horse, "I've been near Morse's Farms for several days.

I found I must drive over here to-night on some business. So on I came, Mr. Banger."

"You'll stop here, sir, till morning? I thought I heard you say—"

"Unfortunately, I can only rest here a half an hour, as you might have heard. I have promised to—to—give a friend of mine on the Point some important papers before to-morrow. He is expecting me. My horse is so blown that I find I must get there a little later than I like."

"The Point Road! That's six miles, at least! and you've driven twelve since you started, and in a hurry, too!"

"I know it. But it's a special matter, and I must get to that house some time this evening. My friend will sit up for me. Can you give me a good cigar, Mr. Banger? Sorry I can't stop."

Joe bustled off to the bar-room to fetch a box. Mr. Jennison glanced at the hotel register with an air of indifference.

"Are those young fellows that were on the steamer—the two that were thought drowned—still with you? I read about the thing a while ago in the paper."

"Yes; I disguised the names on the register there to oblige them. 'Mr. Philip and brother.' Odd circumstance. They haven't heard from their folks yet. Queerer still."

"They haven't?" asked Mr. Jennison. He twisted his mustache and pored over the book. Suddenly he looked up as Joe brought the cigars for his selection, and said, " 'Mr. Philip and brother.' I think I have some recollection about that name. I wonder if—" He stopped, and cut and lighted the cigar deliberately.

"By the bye, one of them, the elder, inquired after you and your friend Mr. Belmont. I forgot it, I declare!"

"Inquired after me? After that Mr. Belmont who happened to be with me? I hardly know Belmont. That's singular. But they may have heard my name. Describe them to me, if you please, Mr. Banger."

Whatever in this dialogue was acting would have done credit to any player on the boards.[97] The tones of voice, the looks, gestures, were alike highly artistic.

Mr. Banger described. He had not talked with Mr. Jennison often; but he had respect for that gentleman's supposed knowledge of the world, though he was inclined to suspect that it took in a peculiarly shady side of it. He liked Mr. Jennison; but he did not altogether understand him.

"Really, they might—they might be a pair of young impostors after all," laughed Mr. Jennison. "It's one way to get half a week's board out of you, you see, unless you've got your money or unless their story is backed."

Mr. Banger fidgeted.

"That has occurred to me, sir. This uncommon delay—"

"Well, I hope not. I'll be coming back from my friend's to-morrow morning, and you can tell me if any thing turns up then. It may be they are not what they profess in this sensation story; and they may give you the slip. I certainly do recall something about that name, Philip, and about such a pair of lads. Don't say any thing, though. Remember that, please."

The horse came up shortly. Mr. Jennison drove off. Perhaps it is as well to say whither. He did not go forward, to reward the patience of any weary householder waiting for "important papers." He rode to the junction of the Point Road with a cross-track, turned down the latter, and made his way in the moon-light to a certain deserted saw-mill, standing back among some poplars. He tied his horse, whistled, and presently was met by two men who seemed thoroughly glad to see him.

"Well, I couldn't get here sooner," he explained, tartly. "That little affair of my own, that I spoke of, has come up again and detained me."

The three disappeared in the dark building. They talked there almost until the red and yellow dawn began to shimmer between the poplar-tops.

CHAPTER XVII.

IN THE ARBOR.

Back of the Kossuth House was a good-sized garden, reaching through to a partially built-up street in the rear. Kitchen vegetables monopolized one half of it. In the other beds of phlox and petunias and hollyhocks gayly inclosed a broad, open grass-plot. A path divided it, and at the lower end of this, not far from the back street, was a roomy grape-arbor. It was a remote, quiet nook.

It was especially quiet about two hours after breakfast that sunny morning. Gerald sat alone in it, waiting for Touchtone to return from an errand in the town. It was decided. They would leave Knoxport for New York and Ossokosee at four o'clock, unless news came to them that explained their predicament and altered their plans. This seemed unlikely. Nothing had yet been heard. Touchtone was confounded and desperate.

A conversation with Mr. Banger added a new uneasiness. He perceived that his host of the Kossuth was really inclined to doubt the genuineness of their story and the identity of himself and Gerald. His manner, at least, was, all at once, cold and unpleasant. Besides that, the amount of money they possessed was not so great, after all, certainly not inexhaustible. Every day's moderate expenses lessened it. Their return journey was before them, besides.

"I can't stand it, Philip; I can't any longer! Papa is dead, or something dreadful has happened to him and Mr. Marcy. Let us get out of this place." After breakfast Gerald spoke thus.

"But we may just be running off from the thing we are waiting for. Perhaps this very afternoon, if we should go—"

"O, Philip, please, let us go! I can't stay shut up here, where we shall never find out any thing! It's telling on you as much as on me, for all you try to explain things away! Not another night here! Do say yes, Philip."

"Well—yes," replied Touchtone, gravely. "I think it will be best. Whatever this delay comes out of, it may last indefinitely. We'll be ready for the four o'clock train."

Mr. Banger received this decision in silence.

"Joe will bring up your bill before dinner," he said, dryly.

"It will be paid when Joe does bring it," returned Touchtone, with equal dryness. Then with a few words to Gerald, who preferred staying alone in the inn to allowing any possible telegram to wait in the absence of both, Philip passed out into the street.

Gerald went up-stairs. Not relishing solitude or companionship, he soon came down. Then it was that Mr. Banger made a sudden, tactless attempt at friendliness—and an unexpected catechism. Gerald quietly resisted. He did not fancy Mr. Banger. The boy strayed out along the garden-path and sat a while, in lonely despondency, in the thick-shaded arbor.

The book he had brought fell from his hand. He leaned his head on his arm, the sunlight between the leaves falling upon his bright hair as he looked over the sunny old garden. The caw of a crow, flying high above some neighboring field, and the click of builders' trowels, mingled with sounds from the lower end of the town. A footstep came lightly up to the arbor-path. He turned around, much astonished. He beheld Mr. Hilliard-Belmont-Jennison (known to him still by only the first borrowed name), scarcely thought of by the little boy, save as a vanished mystery, since the ride on the train from Ossokosee.

"Ah!" the new-comer exclaimed, in his former smooth voice, "I'm delighted to find you here, Gerald. Mr. Banger told me you were. How are you?" He extended his hand, smiling. "You remember me, don't you?" he asked, standing between the boy and the arbor's entrance.

Gerald stared at him in bewildered surprise. He would have been more terrified had not so much to cause fear long been spared him.

"I—I do. Yes, sir," he replied, with wide-open eyes and a pale face. "I—I hope you are well."

"Quite well, I thank you," laughed the other. "And *I* hope you and Mr. Touchtone have forgiven that silly trick, which I never, never meant to let go so far, that I drifted into in the train that afternoon. You remember?"

"Yes. We didn't know what to make of it. Mr. Hilliard—Mr. Hilliard said—"

"O, I saw Mr. Hilliard next evening and made it all right with him for taking his name in vain, in my little joke. I expected to clear it all up before we got to town that night. Our being separated prevented me. I would have written you and Mr. Touchtone again—"

"Again? We didn't get any letter from you!"

"What! None? Then my long apology went astray. Too bad!

But never mind now. I have better things to tell you, my boy. What do you think I came out here for?"

Whatever it was, his manner had an underlying nervousness. He looked to the right and left, toward the house and the street, especially the rear of the garden. A gate was cut in the tall fence. A horse whinnied outside of it.

"Have you any news for us? A telegram? You have heard from papa?—from Mr. Marcy?"

The lad had forgot vague perplexities and vague distrusts in hope.

"Yes, I have. Mr. Banger's just told me your trouble. Your father and Mr. Marcy are all right, my boy. I've been sent to tell you so, and to take you straight to them. Hurrah!"

The little boy uttered a cry of joy.

"O, please do! And please tell me every thing, right away! What has been the trouble? We've been so dreadfully frightened. Philip will be back in a little while. I'm so glad I stayed!"

He sat down on one of the rustic benches in intense relief and excitement.

"Well, it's too long a story for me to go through now," laughed Jennison. But the laugh was a very short one. Again he looked sharply out into the empty garden.

"There was a grand mess about every thing—telegrams, letters, and so on. You'll hear all that from your father himself, and from Marcy. The best of my news is that they are both at a farmhouse, not three miles from here! I have a horse and buggy out there this minute"—he pointed to the rear gate of the garden, over which, sure enough, rose the black top of a vehicle—"to take you over to them. We needn't lose a minute."

The strain released brought its shock. The boy's heart beat violently, with an inexpressible sense of returning comfort and joy.

"How good, how very good you are, sir!" he answered, innocently, casting aside all the mysterious "joke" of the railroad train. "It will make Philip feel like a new creature. But why didn't papa come with you? or Mr. Marcy?"

"Your father's been very ill since the report of your being drowned. He's not well over it yet, and Mr. Marcy is with him.

Don't be frightened; the shock's all past, but he's not strong. So don't lose a moment, please. You can come back in a few hours for your things."

"But you don't want me to go—without Philip. You don't mean that we must start this minute, do you?" The boy looked up in timid surprise, though the brightness of his face, since the news, would have been a pleasure for anyone to notice except a man who seemed as absorbed and hurried as was the bringer of these tidings. "I can't."

"O, nonsense! You mustn't stop for anything now. Time is precious, and it's cruel in you to waste a second before you satisfy your father that you are really alive. He doubts it yet. You don't know how ill he has been. We'll just slip right out of this gate here to the buggy."

"But Philip—"

"I've made it all right for Philip with Mr. Banger. Philip's to follow us the moment he gets back. He may be some time."

"No, no. Let us wait. We must stay till he comes. He won't be long, I'm sure. I'd rather keep papa—any body—waiting just a little longer than do that. O, how sudden, how strange it all is!"

"Yes, wonderfully strange. But, I tell you, my dear boy, I was specially asked not to lose minutes in bringing you when I found you. Mr. Marcy urged me. They thought Philip might be elsewhere. He's to come right after us."

Just then voices were heard in the back room of the hotel.

"Philip! Philip!" called out Gerald, joyfully and clearly, fancying that, even at that distance, he recognized him.

"Stop that! Keep still! Don't call that way! It'll only make a fuss! He's not there!" Jennison exclaimed, angrily.

"Philip!" called Gerald, determinedly, "Philip!"

Jennison sprang forward. He made an effort to seize the lad by the arm or the shoulder. At the same time came a strangely suspicious whirl of the heavy Mackintosh cloak[98] he had carried on one arm. It caught on the table.

Deception and danger! The idea of a shameful lie, and the meaning of the gate and buggy flashed before the boy. He cried out, "Let me go!" to the man, who he now divined was a false and malicious foe, preparing absolutely to abduct him and carry him, heaven knew where, by force! "I wont go," he cried, sharply.

Jennison attempted to catch his arm again.

"Hold on there!" came a call.

Philip Touchtone dashed into the arbor. He faced the enemy. He pushed Gerald aside and stood between them. Once more, as a while ago, at that encounter with the tramp down in Wooden's Ravine, he was on hand in time to help Gerald fight a physical battle against untoward odds.

"How dare you! Don't you touch him again! Where did you come from? What are you doing?" he asked Jennison, pale with anger and astonishment.

"I'm doing what I tried before—to take that boy to his father!" answered the other, angrily. "Again *you* interfere!" with an oath.

"Again you track him for mischief—track him to steal him! Stand over there, Gerald! Touch him, if you dare!"

Philip was of good size and weight for his age, as has been said, and all the old and new resolution and protection revealed itself in his manly, defiant attitude and upraised walking-stick.

"I *will* touch him! You spoil my plans again, do you? You shall rue it, Mr. Philip Touchtone."

He made a step forward; but fine villainy means often physical cowardice, and Philip looked no trifling adversary.

"He says he comes from papa—and Mr. Marcy," said Gerald. "He says—"

"Never mind what he says! It isn't true! He is trying to hurt us both. Aren't you ashamed of yourself to lie to that little fellow, Mr. Winthrop Jennison?" he demanded.

Of his own muscle he was not altogether sure, if an actual wrestle over Gerald came. He wished by loud talking to attract any kind of attention over in the hotel.

"You—spoil my plans—again!" repeated Jennison, regarding him indecisively, but with a look of such malignant anger, especially at the sound of that name, that it has remained in Philip's memory all his life, in his mental photograph gallery of looks.

"Yes, Mr.—Jennison. And I hope to spoil them for good and all now. I wondered whether I'd seen the last of you. I mean to, soon! What have you got to say about this new trick? Not what you've been trying to make *him* believe, Mr. Jennison."

Jennison was silent for an instant. He was, truly, on the last trial to carry forward that daring scheme which had suggested itself so suddenly, been abandoned, then taken up again, as circumstances seemed to throw in his way the chance to complete it. It was characteristic of the man and of his hap-hazard recklessness, as well as of his sense of the desperateness of his position, that he cast aside one attempt for another, and changed one position for another, each of sheer audacity, during the rest of the scene. His judgment, if bold and masterful, was ill-balanced. But he must have cowed and driven many an opponent to whatever wall seemed hardest to escape over, or he would not have changed falsehoods and purposes so swiftly as he now did. He knew his perils! Standing before the door of the summer-house, he eyed Philip. With that quick turn from force to a kind of blustering wheedle[99] which he had resorted to on the altercation on the *Old Province,* he said, disregarding Gerald's presence altogether

"See here, now, Touchtone, keep cool! We're not overheard yet, and there's no reason why we should be. I wont hurt you—"

"Hurt me!"

"No. Do you remember the last thing I said to you that night we talked? What I promised you? It's not too late now for you to ask me to keep my promise, and—once more—to save us both lots of trouble."

"You mean for me to second you in your plans, whatever they are? And if I do I'm to be rewarded? Eh?"

The other nodded and gnawed his lip.

"If I don't I'm to be made to suffer, I believe? Even if you can't gain what you're after?"

"You'll do that, depend on it."

"I told you then that I knew, I *knew,* that you could not bluff me nor cheat other people long enough to hurt Gerald or me! I tell you so again. I've no more to say. If you want to talk further here, I don't. Come up to the hotel and do it out loud. I believe I dared you to try that once before, too."

Jennison smiled savagely.

"I will, you young—hound!" he exclaimed, losing his self-control. "You seem to think you can have things all your own way."

I do not know what sincerity lay in this assent. Just then Mr. Banger came strolling around the walk. The last loud words reached his ears. He looked toward the arbor and turned toward the disputants.

"Do you mean to say that you will play a part before him," cried Philip, pointing to Mr. Banger, "as you threatened to do before Captain Widgins?"

Jennison's only answer was to look at his watch. Then he called out, "Mr. Banger! Mr. Banger! Will you step here?"

Mr. Banger regarded the scene in astonished disapproval. The anger in Philip's face, Jennison scowling darkly, Gerald, very white, tearful, trembling visibly with fear. But Gerald was the first of the three to accost the newcomer.

"Mr. Banger, that man is trying—he wants to—"

Without any regard to Gerald's voice Jennison began in a hard but reasonably controlled manner:

"Mr. Banger, I think it is as I told you. I have been telling that young man there that you and I have suspected his imposture, and the help he has taught this little scamp here to give him. I've begged him to make a clean breast of it. He has confessed, under my promise to intercede for them both with you and others. His name is Samuel Peters, and he has run away from a Boston orphan asylum with this younger lad. They are both very sorry that they have tried to play the parts of those unfortunate boys mentioned in the papers, but—"

Touchtone was aghast at this astonishing statement. Yet if his foe chose to resort to new falsehoods he would ignore them for the truth.

"That is a lie!" he burst forth. "Do you know who that man is, Mr. Banger? He is Winthrop Jennison, who owns the island opposite Chantico, and—"

"You young fool! Do you think I don't know that?" asked Banger. "I think so, and I thought so, Mr. Jennison! Scape-graces that you both are—"

"And *he* is Mr. 'Hilliard,' or 'Mr. John Belmont,' too; and he has tried to steal Gerald Saxton from his father, and from me—and—"

"You are crazy," interrupted Mr. Banger, coolly. "Mr. Winthrop, I guess we'd better—"

"I guess you'd better not be so sure you know him, nor be so ready to think I am a cheat," Philip continued, impetuously. "That man has been a forger and a blackmailer. He leads a regular double life that you don't know any thing about. Give me time, Mr. Banger! Please wait! I promise you—I give you my solemn word of honor—I can prove every thing I say. If you refuse to listen you will surely be sorry."

Mr. Banger looked angrily from Touchtone to Jennison.

"The boy has lost his senses because his trick's burst up," he said, in an undertone. Then to Philip: "Be silent, sir! Follow me, both of you, to the house this minute! The more you say the more you expose yourself. We will see what is best to do about you in a few moments."

"If you don't believe me, send to Chantico Island and bring Mr. and Mrs. Probasco to stand up for us. Or get Mr. Clagg, the lawyer, to tell you what he knows about him. I don't deny he is Mr. Jennison. But he is a bad man—he is half-a-dozen bad men, besides. He keeps his mask on for you as for the most of the world. Look at him. Can't you see he knows I am speaking the truth?"

"A constable will quiet your tongue, my boy, soon enough," exclaimed Jennison in haughty wrath. But Philip's acquaintance with some facts and names last mentioned must have astonished and confused him somewhat. "You are a young blackguard of the first water,[100] and shall be put in a place you ought to have been familiar with long ago. Will you hold your tongue and follow Mr. Banger?"

"A constable is a thing I've no fear of! Let me be put where anyone likes. The truth will get me out of it soon enough. Mr. Banger, that man tried to *steal* Gerald the day we left the Ossokosee. He tried to get me to give him up to him on the *Old Province*. He is a kidnaper."

"Peters," began Mr. Banger, "I warn you—"

"I am not Samuel Peters. I am Philip Touchtone. Ask all Ossokosee County."

His eyes flashed, and he threw back the false name with infinite disdain.

"You choose a fine *alias*—that of an unconvicted felon, a burglar's cat's-paw.[101] Banger, I knew a man of that name once."

"Ah!" cried Touchtone, "a man—that you knew! The man that you yourself told me you knew! I believe you did! and that you could clear the stain on his memory to-day by something you have always known, too, about that miserable charge. Mr. Banger, my father was Reginald Touchtone, who was accused of—"

Mr. Banger interrupted him sharply.

"I want no more of this farrago,[102] sir, about yourself or any one else. If you are, indeed, a criminal's son, your asylum's authorities did well to change your name. Once for all, will you come back to the house with me, and perhaps to leave it, as—as—your conduct and—and candor shall allow me to decide, or shall I have you dragged off my premises by force?"

Touchtone checked himself.

"Gerald, we will go with them to the house," he said, in a firm tone, looking down at the younger boy with profound sorrow in his eyes at realizing all at once what an experience was this for Gerald to be obliged to endure. "You and I are not afraid of this man nor of anyone, are we? It'll all be set right soon. Try not to cry."

He took Gerald's cold hand tightly in his own.

"We will go with you," said he, turning to Mr. Banger. "It's only a question of time to make you learn the truth. All right, Gerald; you'll be with me, you know, whatever happens."

"You are a cool young adventurer!" exclaimed Banger. "You'll make your mark in the world before you die, at this rate. Come, Mr. Jennison, I shall want your help"—(this last in an undertone.)

"Will you really need it?" inquired Jennison.

He again had been looking at the white gate. The horse was fidgeting. "The fact is, that—I—well, after all, I'd rather not help to make a stir in town, if you don't wish it."

"Eh? What's that, sir?" asked Mr. Banger, turning on the threshold of the summer-house. "I *not* wish to make a stir? I do! Pray don't hesitate. I need you, certainly! These lads' confessions—"

"Of course, of course! I'll join you in a moment, then. I left my horse yonder. I'll drive him around the corner to the front." He addressed himself nervously, menacingly, to Philip: "Are you going with the landlord? Don't take all day about it. You are at his mercy."

Now, with this impudent demand an idea must have struck him, or else it had been suggesting itself within a half minute (Philip never has decided this point).

"Take Peters with you," he said, in a quick, low voice to the landlord; "he may bolt. I'll bring the little fellow around in my buggy."

But Gerald overheard.

"No, no, no!" he cried in fear, defiance, and resistance. "I will not go with him! He shall not touch me! He—he will run away with me! I will not leave Philip! Philip, Philip! don't let them take us apart!"

Jennison burst into a loud, coarse laugh. Even Mr. Banger was struck with its peculiarity, the curious hint in it of another man beneath this one, masquerading as an aid of justice.

"Young fool! how much trouble you've given me!" Jennison exclaimed, in open fury, stamping his foot.

Truer words he never spoke. They contained all the history of a rash wickedness and of its defeat; for they were almost his last on the topic. He stepped down into the path, saying to Banger, "Don't wait. I'll be with you immediately."

But the white gate had opened. Two strangers came down the walk, hurrying, and straight toward them. Jennison glanced about him once more, but with a wildness suddenly flashing out in his eyes and a low exclamation as if he forgot himself and feared something. Ah, that hasty, searching glance! The men came directly up to him. One of them, a thick-set personage, nodded hastily to the others. He struck his hand on Jennison's shoulder.

"Mr. Winthrop Jennison? I arrest you, sir," he said, sharply.

"Arrest me?" demanded Jennison, as white as his collar. "Arrest *me*?"

Mr. Banger stood with his mouth open, most unmannerly.

"Yes," retorted the red-haired man; "here's the writ—'Winthrop Jennison, otherwise called John A. Belmont, otherwise called Murray Nicoll, otherwise called Gray Hurd. Forgery in Boston. You know, I guess. The others in it have all been looked after. No trouble, *please*. Billy!"

What did Mr. Jennison-Belmont-Nicoll-Hurd do? He held out his wrists mechanically. They were suitably embellished. Then he turned to Mr. Banger, Gerald, and Touchtone. His look, as much as his odd words (which were the beginning of that day's memorable disconcertment of the luckless proprietor of the Kossuth House), showed that he knew thoroughly that the "double life" and the relics of such local respect as was left in this place, near the house of his ancestors, were forever shattered.

"I bid you good-day, Mr. Banger," he said, smiling with all his fine teeth. "I shall leave Mr. Touchtone to tell his story again. It is, likely, a perfectly true one. At least, I withdraw mine as being—substantially incorrect. Please remember that, Mr. Touchtone. You have beaten in this fight. *I shall not trouble you again.* Good-morning."

He turned, with his easiest manner, to the officers in plain clothes, muttering something.

If an evil spirit had suddenly risen before Mr. Banger—or, for that matter, before the two lads still facing him, Gerald holding Philip's arm in a desperate grip—Mr. Banger could not have been more frightened and mute. He gasped. Then he ejaculated, with difficulty, "Mr. Jennison! You don't—" But as the Jennison party moved away Gerald leaned forward and uttered a cry.

"Philip! They're coming yonder! Look at them! Papa! Papa! Mr. Marcy! Both of them!"

And then, as those two gentlemen, in flesh and blood indeed, came running from the hotel up the path toward them, Marcy hurrahing and waving his hat, Saxton calling out, "Gerald, Gerald! my son!" and when Philip found himself seized in a mighty hug by Mr. Marcy, with a general turmoil and uproar and hand-shaking and questioning beginning in a most deafening and delightful manner—then he did something that he never did afterward. He staggered to the arbor-steps, holding Mr. Marcy's big hand, and exclaiming with something like a laugh, "Well, here you are—at last! We'd nearly—given you up! We're—not left to ourselves any more!" Then the stress of responsibility was over, and he dropped on the step, unconscious.

CHAPTER XVIII.

EXPLANATIONS; AND MR. JENNISON SENDS A REQUEST.

"Well, it's ended, at any rate. A most astonishing business it certainly has been! And nobody to blame for part of it."

Mr. Marcy made this declaration for the five-and-twentieth time at least as they were sitting up-stairs an hour after supper on that eventful day. The four were talking almost as fast as ever, each one interrupting the other with a question or a statement, this explanation or problem jumping out of that one. The subject for their consideration was quite unlikely to be exhausted as soon as themselves. What a hubbub they kept up still!

"I can't hear myself think, Philip," Mr. Marcy protested. "Saxton, beg pardon! What's that you asked? No, Gerald, we didn't get worried. How could we when we didn't know there was any thing to worry over? What's that?" So it had gone on for the two hours they had sat in the summer-house. Then they had adjourned to have dinner by themselves in the boys' room. All the little hotel, and, for that matter, all the town, was in a buzz of curiosity and interest. As for Mr. Banger, it is proper to say here that he saw that their dinner was handsomely and bountifully served, and that when later he found opportunity for a brief interview with Mr. Marcy and Mr. Saxton he did not do much except apologize and call himself a fool. He did both with a much better grace than might have been expected.

He expressed himself in just the same curt fashion to Philip as he shook his hand cordially. The latter could not resist a little revenge.

"O, no," he laughed, "I don't think you are a fool at all, Mr. Banger; but I think you had a chance to be one, and—you made something of it."

Mr. Banger in reply only smiled severely and nodded.

And now the laughter and the loud, earnest hum of conversation reached the mortified landlord as he passed their door.

Gerald sat by his father smiling, but saying less than any of the party. Philip remarked again and again the close likeness between the two. There was the same grace of figure and stature, the same shapely head and clear-cut, regular features. But the dashing, happy-go-lucky manner of the gay young broker and typical man-about-town was gone. Mr. Saxton laughed and talked as loud as Marcy or Philip. But the latter noticed how pale he was, and how deep were the circles of a great and unexpected grief under his fine eyes. He kept his arm along the back of his son's chair. From that time forth there existed a new understanding between them; and, as Gerald grows up, it has never been lessened.

What an explanation it all was, even at the best, and so far as outlines went! Need one give more than those here? Indeed, there would hardly be room. Storm-driven to a little village, without railroad or telegraph connections, and storm-and-sickness-stayed when once there, Mr. Marcy and his friend (or rather his patient nurse, for Mr. Saxton was in a dangerously morbid state of mind and body) had known literally nothing, suspected nothing, heard nothing, shut away from all rest of the world as they were. The letters and duplicated telegrams were probably all safely lodged at this minute in the town they had expected to reach days earlier, whither they had ordered the mail to be sent from the Ossokosee. At first Mr. Marcy had hoped to go straight back to his hotel, taking the unnerved father. So he set that address. But Saxton languidly prolonged their journey southward, and his moodiness kept it variable and slow.

"I was tempted lots of times," said Mr. Marcy, "to telegraph to Knoxport and elsewhere, to alter the forwarding of our mail; but I was every day less certain of what route Saxton here would urge, and I knew business was done up for the season. So I said, 'Let it go as it is, for once.' I'll never be able again to think that such a shiftless thing will make no difference. Probably it wont again, though."

"And it was the newspaper, after all, that brought you the news?"

"The newspaper? I should say so. A peddler came up to the Fork with a fresh Boston paper in his pocket and I bought it. Do you know how Saxton here behaved when I read the paragraph to him? He did just what you did, Philip, this morning—fainted."

"And do you know what Mr. Marcy did, Touchtone?" asked Mr. Saxton, flushing. "He dropped the paper and sobbed like a boy—and never tried to bring me to!"

"Come, now, shut up, Saxton!" exclaimed Mr. Marcy, turning red, and giving Philip a slap on the shoulder. "These little retaliations aren't gentlemanly, really."

But he gave Philip a glance that was eloquent of the affection he had for him and of the grief which his loss would have brought to him, during all his busy life. They had had several moments by themselves during the day.

"Well, that rascal was right, you see, after all," resumed Marcy. "We were stuck fast in a most particularly out-of-the-way place. And Gerald's father, here, was any thing but a well man. His was a good guess, even with his having read the papers in which the steamer's sinking was written up."

Saxton laughed.

"I thought we should sink ourselves, in the rattle-trap we had to trust ourselves to, Gerald, to get to the railroad connection. The track was almost dangerous on account of the rain. You were on that island, you say, all through the storm?"

"With the Probascos? Yes; it was funny."

"Funny! They are angels who live in an atmosphere of humor, then. I propose to go over there to-morrow—we'll all go—and we'll thank them as never they were thanked before. Shall we, Marcy?"

"Obed must be in bed still, and pretty sick," Gerald said, "or we'd have heard from or seen them."

"But why—why didn't somebody send us word of some sort from the Ossokosee? There was the message to the hotel—"

"Which is shut, I tell you!"

"Mr. and Mrs. Wooden ought to have got theirs! If the house was shut, where was Mr. Fisher or whoever was about the place superintending the winding-up for you."

"Ah, well, that I can't altogether explain, I admit," replied Mr. Marcy. "Of course, there ought to have been people on hand, and I should suppose they would know enough to repeat the message or answer it. We shall find out soon."

They did, but not until later. Afterward came the story of the complete stoppage of telegraphing in the county (brought about by the wide-spread tempest which had broken wires far and wide in their devious mountain courses); of a new operator, who was a sadly easy-going, inefficient, and unacquainted employee; of a most confused garbling of the messages themselves, in course of their slow progress. When they learned these matters, they all declared it was a wonder that dispatches could endure such persecution and keep their syntax even at the expense of swiftness. Two of these precious communications finally returned from a Knoxport in a western State.[103] But the next morning a reply came in from Mr. Fisher, still at the Ossokosee House, and just after that another from jolly, kind-hearted Mr. Hilliard, dated from a mining-camp in Montana, and its sender direfully distressed at what he inferred must be some bad predicament of Philip and Gerald.

"Of course," Mr. Marcy observed, "your awkward fix could not have lasted long. But for the life of me, under all the circumstances, I cannot make up my mind on the amount of time it would probably have endured. Certainly we should have learned the news and come flying to you apace. But your trouble was becoming serious, with a vengeance! You were threatened with arrest on false suspicion, or at least with finding yourselves homeless and wronged! We can't try to determine what length or end affairs might have attained."

"It's not pleasant," Philip said.

"In any case, it showed the stuff in you, Touchtone," added Mr. Marcy, quietly. "I guess we understand what that is now. We might—well—we might have had to guess at it, otherwise." He laughed. His "guessing" would have been perceptive. He was proud of such an experience for the boy.

"Now as to that villain Jennison, or Belmont, or whatever his name is," began Mr. Saxton, "I don't know what is best to do. I remember him perfectly. I did some business for him on the Street.[104] He lost largely before he was through with the stock. It went all to pieces. I was as much sold by it as were the other brokers. Jennison acted like a madman in my office."

"How long ago was that, sir?" asked Philip.

"As much as ten years, I fancy," returned the broker, reflectively. "It must have cleaned him out at the time. I knew nothing of him, of course."

"Then it was revenge that started him on this scheme about Gerald?"

"Certainly—and blackmail. I'd have had to come down roundly for you, Gerald," he added, laughing, taking his son's hand.[105] "Perhaps I'd have had to sell that new black team you're so jealous of.[106] You needn't be any longer, I think."

"He's a smart one for putting two and two together, that fellow."

"Of course. Each man possesses a talent of its kind."

"But what risks he ran! Even at the last, when he must have known there was a sharp possibility of his being overtaken that minute by the detectives, on account of the Wheelwright forgery, he wanted to carry Gerald off with him."[107]

Mr. Marcy came into the topic. "Yes; and the plan nearly proved successful. If you will think, you will see how much he had in his favor. Audacious criminals of his type are close calculators."

"Where could he have meant to go, with Gerald, too?" inquired Saxton.

"He knew what he was about. I fancy he expected to rejoin those fellows first, at the mill they tell us of. Beyond that I can't judge. He believed he had enough time, and that all was going right."

"O, he's a wonder, and no mistake!" exclaimed Philip.

"Not at all," returned Mr. Saxton. "He is just exactly his sort of rascal, as Hilliard told you. But his race is run, I fancy, especially since Knoxport and Chantico are no longer resorts for him. Let us hope another scamp is to be shut away from New York and elsewhere for some years of his life, at least, by what I heard of this Wheelwright affair." He was silent a moment, reflecting on Jennison and Gerald. Then looking up at Philip, with an expression in his eyes and voice that is not easily described, he said, "Touchtone, I can't say now—any more than I have been able to say it before what I feel about you—how I thank you! Gerald's coming back has saved my happiness, and you have saved Gerald—from I know not what. In every thing and every moment I can see—not by what you say about yourself—you have been a sort of a hero. You don't like praise to your face? I sha'n't bore you with it. But if I can only keep you with Gerald here for the rest of your life and his, and find him growing up just like such a friend as you, that is all I want now. I'll talk of *that* with you, though, later."

They kept on sitting there together, in the light of the new rising moon and the gentle glow of the wood fire until there came a knock at the door. Philip went out into the hall.

"If you please, sir," asked the man standing there, "are you young Mr. Touchtone?"

"I am."

"You don't recognize me. I am one of the officers in charge of that man Jennison down at the court-house."

"Yes; what of it?"

"He wants to see you very much, sir. We must take him off by the morning train, and there's really not much time, unless you care to come down with me to-night."

"*He* wants to see me? To-night?" repeated Philip in astonishment, but with a sudden guess at the possible relationships of such an interview. Those strange hints the man had once or twice thrown out, and which he had not mentioned to Mr. Marcy! "Very well. I'll go with you. Wait a moment."

He called Mr. Marcy aside. "Most extraordinary!" exclaimed the latter. "You really think it worth while to go?"

"Yes, I do. I want to go, decidedly."

"What for? He'll try to wheedle or harm you. Let me step down with you, if you wish to go."

"He won't do either, I think; and the man says he particularly wishes me to come without any of you. Some one will be in the room, though, all the time."

Mr. Marcy hesitated. At last, "Very well, my dear fellow, do as you please. I'll say nothing about your errand till you return and give me an account."

Philip excused himself from Mr. Saxton and Gerald, and left the Kossuth House with the officer.

CHAPTER XIX.

AFTER MANY DAYS.

The basement of the Knoxport courthouse, a small, smart affair, was used as the county bridewell.[108] The room in which Jennison sat, with an official writing in a farther corner, was a good-sized, half-furnished place.

Jennison did not rise as Touchtone came in, followed by his guide. The latter stepped away to his companion's side and seemed to pay no attention to them.

"Good-evening; I'm obliged to you for coming down," Jennison began. He looked a trifle disheveled and haggard, and had that peculiar air of a criminal expecting the now inevitable course of justice. "Take a seat."

"The officer told me you wished to see me, and, particularly, alone," answered Philip, in mingled curiosity and disgust, as he found himself once more in the presence of so bold and adroit a foe. There came vividly back to him the scene of the attack on board the steamer; the recognition of the handsome face, with its lurking treachery, in the portrait Mrs. Probasco had handed him on the island, and that last leap into the Knoxport arbor to re-enforce Gerald, at this man's mercy. "What do you want of me?"

Jennison smiled. "I don't suppose you can guess," he replied, shifting his position. "Not to talk over the occurrences of the past fortnight or so with you, nor this end of them. You can be sure of that. You've won the game, Touchtone, as I told you; won it pluckily and fairly. You are a remarkable young fellow! A good rogue was spoiled in you, perhaps."

"I think not; and I do not wish to talk of that or of affairs that are over with, any more than you do. If you have any thing particular to say I should like to hear it, and go back to the hotel."

"All happy and serene up there, I suppose?" inquired the other, coolly. "Nice youngster that Master Gerald is! Not extraordinary that strangers should take a fancy to him, eh? Pretty boy!" he laughed, ironically.

Philip made no reply except another word about the expediency of soon hearing what he was brought down for. He did not propose to go away without asking some very particular questions, if necessary. Jennison saved him the trouble. He lowered his voice and began hurriedly:

"Enough of that. What I want to say to you—you alone—is about—your father. You have heard me say I knew him."

"Yes."

"I did; though he didn't know me, since he supposed me to be an honest man and in business down-town. I was pretty well acquainted with all the circumstances of that robbery of the bank which cost him his character. I was making my living even then, you see, in what seemed the easiest way. He died of a broken heart, I heard."

"He did," Touchtone responded, inwardly more and more agitated. "What is that to you?"

"Nothing; but I might be something to it, or to his name, to-day. Stop! Don't interrupt. I knew Dan Laverack and his crowd well; and as I hadn't lost my own position in the upper world yet, and was a gentleman by education (as the other men knew), I was useful to them and I made a good thing out of them myself."

"Yes," Philip said, staring hard at the man in the flickering light and curbing his impatience.

"I sounded your father as agent for them, Touchtone—for Laverack and the others. We thought we could bribe your father. I lived in the place months—for it. But I found before I'd gone far enough to make him suspect my game that he couldn't be bought in. So I gave it up. Do you know I've seen you plenty of times when you were a little fellow? I'd never have recognized you, of course. I remember your mother pretty well, too."

"Don't talk of her," said Philip, sharply; "my time is short, and yours, too, if you leave here to-night."

"Quite true," replied Jennison, coolly. "I must get along in what I have to say. Touchtone, your father was innocent as a child of any share in that bank business—"

"Do you think I don't know that? Do you think any body who really knew him could believe any thing else?"

"O, plenty of people—all the world, pretty much! You know that. Even your mother's old friend, Mr. Marcy, never liked to talk much about the question, eh?" The blood rose in Philip's face. "But no matter. All the world who *do* think he had a hand in it have been wrong; and now you and I will just set them right forever—if you say so."

"What do you mean? How can you or I? Tell me what you are keeping back."

The lad forgot his aversion in a passionate curiosity. He leaned forward eagerly.

"Touchtone, your father had an enemy in the bank. I dare say he knew it afterward; possibly he told you so. His name was Sixmith."

"Sixmith, the janitor. Yes; go on."

"Sixmith kept his feelings to himself. He was a sly creature, Touchtone, and he had what some people will tell you I have—a black heart. Only I haven't, according to some black hearts I've met. Well, he was bent on revenge and on doing your father a bad turn. I forget what 'twas all for; I believe your father had interfered in his family to protect his wife. He drank. Well, Sixmith came in with Laverack. I managed it, and, in fact, I was so much in with that whole job, Touchtone, that if it hadn't been that the man who turned State's evidence was really a sworn friend to me I'd have had to stand out with the rest and suffer. Sixmith gave them the times and hours, and so on; it was all arranged. I did some work at imitating your father's handwriting as to a letter or two we needed. Sixmith insisted on the plan. He was to be paid besides, as you know—"

"You forged my father's hand, to help to ruin him," interrupted Philip, in loathing and anguish.

"I did, certainly," replied Jennison, calmly. "I am sorry. I didn't expect to be, I confess; but I am. Well, the bank was broken into, in such a way, as you know, that your father was considered to have a hand in it, even if the bank officers could not bring on him what they thought full justice; and that would have been harder injustice than he had to endure for the rest of his life. He escaped that. Sixmith was disappointed. But he had become rather afraid, after all, of what we had undertaken to help him with. We partly knew, partly suspected, that revenge was nearest his heart at the beginning. He weakened, and was pretty glad to find that he had not brought worse on your father than he did."

"Worse than he did? How could he? Did he not cost him his honest reputation and shorten his life? Did he not break my mother's heart? Did he not make me grow up with a stain on my name because I was—my father's son?"

"Perhaps you are right. But, any rate, the thing ended as it did. And Sixmith—well, he thought more and more about his job, I suppose, when he was shut up, and as time went on, Touchtone, he grew more and more ashamed of it. At last, about seven years ago, he died—down in New York. Laverack died before that. I'd met Sixmith again, and I was with him when he died. It was one of my winters in New York. He told me everything. We talked the bank affair all over. At last he said he wanted me to write down a kind of confession, or at least a statement, in which he gave his own account of what he had managed to do for your father, swearing in it, up and down, to your father's innocence."

He paused. Touchtone sat facing him statue-like. He was beyond words. Would Jennison ever finish?

"Your father was dead, but I was to use it as I thought best as soon as I liked. I meant to do as he asked; but, upon my word, I have waited to get on the track of your mother or you. The bank officials had an idea you were both dead. I didn't care much to press the matter, but I should have done what I promised, and used this before"—and he took from the table a paper lying there—"if the very day that brought me to you on that train hadn't brought Saxton's little boy with you. Seeing him started me on a scheme to get square with Saxton, on account of an old grudge I'd got against him, and to make something, perhaps, at the same time—professionally."

He gave his malicious, slow smile with the last word.

Touchtone mechanically took the paper Sixmith had signed, and, half in a stupor, ran over it. The donor eyed him keenly. Then, as its significance came home to Philip's heart, he realized that a seemingly vain dream was fulfilled; that what was meant to be a great purpose of his life was all at once, through this strange agent, accomplished; that a wrong was righted, and that his dead father and he, his son, were set free from an odious if nearly forgotten injustice. He had hard work to master his strong exultation and joy; but he did. This was no place for it. The officials were standing regarding them both, as in duty bound, attentive, if discreet, listeners.

"Thank you," he said; "I—I thank you for this, with all my heart." He could not find more words except in the way of questions. Jennison seemed not to expect more from him, and did most of the talking himself. He must also have realized that this act of simple justice he had done was one thing, the hand aiding in it another. His frankness was appreciated; himself, its instrumentality, was despised. They exchanged a few more sentences, however, and Philip managed to repeat his thanks for his rights, and for a rascal's not being more a knave than he was! Jennison bowed coldly.

The officers accosted them: "Our time is up. Please get ready for the train, sir."

Touchtone turned to go.

"Look here," said Jennison, buttoning his light overcoat and polishing his hat with his arm, "I—I don't know how I shall get through with this business in Boston that I am going (with these excellent gentlemen) to transact. You will probably know as soon as I do. Mr. Clagg, my lawyer, will follow me to assist me. By the bye, I am glad to infer that you have met my old friends, the Probascos, of Chantico Island. My regards to them, please, when you see them next; and any thing else you may think it best to say to them. And," he continued, buttoning his gloves nervously, "I wish you and your friend, Mr. Marcy, and Mr. Saxton and his son to understand that, no matter what may be my circumstances in the future, it is the last time they or you will ever—have any trouble with me. I promise you that. I say—would you—will you shake hands? You're a plucky fellow, Touchtone. I'd a little rather not think of you as going through life with a grudge against me. Haven't I wiped it out? Live and let live, eh?"

The strange request made Philip blush. He hesitated, stammered, was half inclined to take the outstretched gloved hand. But no—not—that! He kept back his honest palm, from the one that had forged his father's name, to the blasting of his honor, all these years—from the hand that had seized Gerald's arm in a brutal scheme worthy of a Greek bandit![109] He did not raise his own hand—not feeling quite sure whether he was doing what was really the right thing, but unable to extend it.

"Good-night, Mr. Jennison," he said, bowing gravely. "I—I—shall not forget you."

"That is precisely the thing I should urge you most to do," answered Jennison, laughing. Without the least resentment at the slight, he bent his head to finish buttoning his glove, and he did not look up until Philip had left the building.

Jennison kept his word. He managed to slip away from his captors that night on the train; but our friends never heard of him again.

When Philip reached the Kossuth House Mr. Saxton and Gerald had gone to bed. He had a long interview with Mr. Marcy; Samuel Sixmith's statement and exoneration (it was practically ready for publication, in any way) lying between them.

"I've done your father and you a great wrong, Philip," said Mr. Marcy. "It's always been a sore spot between us, hasn't it? And it might have become more than that as you grew older. I don't know exactly how far I've carried my doubts. I never liked

to define them. I'm a creature of prejudices—too much so.
But," he continued, solemnly, "I ask your father's pardon, and
yours." Philip shook his hand heartily for reply.

CHAPTER XX.

PRESENT AND FUTURE.

Friendly reader, were you at a Columbia College[110] commence-
ment, in which Philip Touchtone and Gerald Saxton graduated,
amid a great waving of pocket-handkerchiefs and a rattle of applause as the class took their places on the stage for their diplo-
mas? No, I am quite sure you were not. For Philip and Gerald
happen not to have graduated yet, though they will soon.
Touchtone is a senior this year, and Gerald a sophomore; tall,
wide-awake young fellows, both of them well up in their work
and their athletics, devoted to their college life and (though they
do not say any thing about that) to each other, as well. For Mr.
Saxton and Mr. Marcy came to a quiet agreement over some
discussed questions before that winter found the four of them
settled in the same hotel in New York.

"Gerald and I owe the lad every thing," insisted Mr. Saxton.
"We can't take him from you, but you must let him be as much
with us as is possible. I want you, for one thing, to let me be responsible, henceforth, for his education and for his professional
starting-out, whatever he chooses it to be. No more hotel for
him, please! I shall just count him another son of mine, with or
without your consent, my friend."

So it was agreed. Philip stayed out of college an extra winter
or two, that he need not precede Gerald too much, and after the
foreign *wanderjahr*[111] now before them, when their graduation
is over, they are to go into the law-school together.

Together (that word which means so much to all friends)
they have been again up the coast, and this time the trip extended to Halifax, without let or hinderance, unlike that memorable first attempt. Knoxport and Chantico are places that
alter little with years. Time runs slowly there, as of old. They

found Mr. Banger at his desk in the Kossuth, a little stouter and more business-like looking than ever. Mr. Banger received them with great unction and much admiration. They walked out into the garden and sat down in the arbor, and smiled, and then grew grave as they recalled the suspense that they had felt, that ended in the dramatic scene under its green roof. Joe has an interest in the hotel now, and he has married a niece of Mr. Banger, into the bargain.

Once upon a time there was a great day for the Probascos— when the two arrived at Chantico Island. Expecting them had kept the couple at the farm, almost with the inclusion of the sagacious Towzer ("His real name's Jock, you know"), in excitement, for a week before.

"Well, well, it's good to see you both, if you have changed everlastingly!" reiterated Mrs. Probasco. "You're—well, you're real *sights* to comfort one's eyes, both of you!" she added impartially. They spent an evening in the quaint kitchen and a night in the old room, where Gerald had tossed in his sickness, Philip watching him in lonely anxiety. Obed's rheumatics seem over. He talks more than he did. Philip vows that on this occasion Obed began to tell them again the story of the nautical ancestor and the wary "widow that lived on Cape Ann"—promptly interrupted by Mrs. Probasco, who said that "the boys hadn't come all the way from New York to listen to that old yarn." Mrs. Probasco's grandfather is still "feeble, very feeble." But he survives and bids fair to do so for an indefinite time; and so the little island will probably not soon lose its satisfied tenants from its wave-bound circuit.

The Ossokosee flourishes, enlarged, and well-kept as ever. Philip and Gerald and Mr. Saxton join Mr. Marcy there each summer, and then there are great doings in a highly private and quiet way. I don't think the two friends ever walk up one particular path in the evening without Gerald's recalling (though he may not speak of it) the night when, so much younger, he listened with Philip to those words of General Sawtelle within the embowered Summer-house.

The hope and resolve of that evening were indeed granted. To-day in the little cemetery near the hotel is a marble monument in place of a simpler stone, formerly there. One reads that it is—"To the Memory of Reginald Touchtone—Cleared of the Stain of a False Charge upon his Honor—After Many Days—Erected by his Son, Philip Touchtone, and by Jay Marcy and Gerald B. Saxton, Jr."

Farmer Wooden and his wife lead the same plodding, healthful, simple lives as ever. They likewise continue to send butter and eggs in unlimited quantity to the Ossokosee, and they delight to talk with Philip of the days when he used to be the purveyor thereof. They laugh merrily over those commissary experiences, and are sincere friends, as says Mrs. Wooden. "You see, you haven't no right to forget us, Mr. Philip. Not that I expect you ever will. You ain't that kind. But 'twas down there in the ravine, you know, you first met young Mr. Saxton. You recollect the tramp, that day?" Yes, Philip perfectly recollects both "that day" and Mr. Sip.

Mr. Hilliard—jolly, fat, good-tempered Mr. Hilliard—who has always been afraid ever since that year "of some clever vagabond borrowing my name, sir," but never has been favored with that little accident again—he is another regular guest at the Ossokosee. There are signs (so some knowing observers say) that Mr. Hilliard contemplates matrimony. He encountered dignified Miss Beauchamp, a year or so ago, at the Ossokosee, and it is known that she receives very long letters from him; and that he has lately bought a house not far from his Madison Avenue flat. I think that Philip and Gerald are sure of much pleasure in that house next season.

Well! And is this all? Have we really come to the end of this story?—which is, perhaps, a truer one than the imagination of a writer of such things as stories, or even his heart, would fain make him believe? I fear we have indeed reached the last of it, for even by bright forecast, unnecessary, I think, here, a story had best not be lengthened if truly it is all told.

But—if one yields to the temptation to be among the prophets, and closes his eyes, there come, chiefly, pleasant thoughts of how good are friendship and love and loyal service between man and man in this rugged world of ours; and how probable it is that such things here have not their ending, since they have not their perfecting here, perfect as friendship and the service sometimes seem. Therewith the inditer[112] of this chronicle sees Philip and Gerald walking forward, calmly and joyfully, and in an unlessened affection and clearer mutual understanding— into their endless lives.

And so, Philip and Gerald, as says Brutus in the play, "give me your hands all over, one by one."[113] I am loath to let you go, but I must. Good-bye.

THE END.

NOTES

1 Henry "Harry" Harkness Flagler was the son of the wealthy Florida hotelier and railroad magnate Henry M. Flagler. Harry Flagler and Stevenson met at some point in the early to mid-1880s in
New York. In 1885, Stevenson dedicated to Flagler a short story for
children titled "The Golden Moon." Flagler, born in 1870, would
have been 14 at the time. The two eventually became romantically
involved, though by March of 1893 the relationship had ended. In
1894, Flagler married Annie Louise Lamont (see Appendix E of
Gifford's edition of *Imre*).

2 This line from Æschylus's play *The Eumenides*, also known as *The
Furies*, is translated by John F. Davies as follows: "Athena: Then
bless with spells the friends whom you will gain" (173). E.D.A.
Morshead translates the line as "Then in the land's heart shalt
thou win thee friends" (124). Athena speaks these lines to the
Furies, who had sought justice for the murder of Clytemnestra
by her son, Orestes. Athena participates in acquitting Orestes but
manages to appease the Furies, who are otherwise perceived as
terrifying, by giving them a place of honor and respect in Athens.
Æschylus. *The Eumenides of Aeschylus: A Critical Edition, with Met-
rical English Translation*. Edited and translated by John F. Davies.
Dublin: Hodges, Figgis, and Company, 1885. Æschylus. *The
House of Atreus: Being the Agamemnon, Libation-Bearers, and Furies
of Æschylus*. Translated by E.D.A. Morshead. London: C. Kegan
Paul, and Company, 1881.

3 In an 1888 article titled "The History of Children's Books," published in *The Atlantic Monthly*, C.M. Hewins begins by referring to
children's books as "a late growth of literature," though she goes
on to dispute this traditional account of its brief history (112). She
also quotes an 1869 article by Charlotte Yonge that had described
children's literature as a "recent production" of the Georgian era,
which may have further disseminated the notion that children's
literature was still relatively new in the nineteenth century. Traditional histories of children's literature, defined as works primarily
designed to be pleasurable rather than instructive, date it to the
mid-eighteenth century, though that chronology can be disputed.
C. M. Hewins. "The History of Children's Books." *The Atlantic
Monthly*. Volume 61, Number 363 (January 1, 1888): 112-126. Miss

Yonge, "Children's Literature of the Last Century." *Every Saturday*. Volume 8, Number 187 (July 31, 1869): 156-160.

4 Possibly invented as a homophonic pun that sounds like "oh so cozy," the name Ossokosee House first appears in Stevenson's short story "A Question of Taste," published in the August 1884 issue of *The Christian Union*.

5 Workhouses, more commonly referred to as poorhouses in the United States. As David Wagner explains, "The workhouse was meant as a correctional institution in which actual discipline (cells, bread and water, instruments of punishment such as the ball and chain and later the treadmill) was to be imposed on the 'unworthy poor,' usually men of working age, who were vagrants, beggars, 'indolent,' petty criminals, or intemperate. They would be housed only on condition of hard work" (4-5). David Wagner, *The Poorhouse: America's Forgotten Institution*. Lanham, Md.: Rowan and Littlefield, 2005.

6 Washing.

7 Paterson, New Jersey, is located about 20 miles northeast of New York City. No record of a Wheelborough Heights, Wheelbarrow Heights, or similar geographic name can be located. However, Mr. Sip could be misspeaking. A Willingboro is located about 80 miles from Paterson, and Woodbury Heights about 100 miles.

8 *The Oxford English Dictionary* (*OED*) defines "kidney" used in this way to mean "Temperament, nature, constitution, disposition; hence, kind, sort, class, stamp."

9 "He who fights and runs away, lives to fight another day." The earliest known version of the proverb is attributed to Demosthenes (~384 B.C.E. to 322 B.C.E.).

10 A tool used to beat, and thus clean, a carpet.

11 A type of wagon with a carriage suspended by springs.

12 *King's Photographic Views of New York*, published in 1895, includes a photograph of the "Stuyvesant Hotel" at Eighth Street and St. Mark's Place, but this is the only locatable reference to a hotel of that name in New York City during the period of the novel's setting and composition and may not be the basis for the Saxtons' residence. Another possibility is the Stuyvesant Flats, or Stuyvesant Apartments, on 18th Street. Built in 1869, the Stuyvesant is often described as the first middle-class apartment building in New York. Residents shared communal living spaces; however, each private flat had a kitchen, and according to Elizabeth Collins Cromley, "Families were expected to employ their own live-in ser-

vants" (117). Elizabeth Collins Cromley, *Alone Together: A History of New York's Early Apartments*. Ithaca: Cornell University Press, 1990.

13 Shelter Island is located off of the northern shore of the east end of Long Island and was a popular resort destination in the 1870s.

14 New York State's compulsory education law was passed in 1874 and required children "between the ages of 8 and 14 to attend school for fourteen weeks a year, at least eight of which were to be consecutive" (Urban and Wagoner 155). However, according to Wayne J. Urban and Jennings L. Wagoner, Jr., the law was not widely or consistently enforced until passage of child labor laws later in the century. Wayne J. Urban and Jennings L. Wagoner, Jr., *American Education: A History*. Third Edition. New York: Routledge, 2014.

15 A stockbroker.

16 The second ruler of that name was the king of the Babylonian empire who lived from 634 B.C.E. to 562 B.C.E. He figures in the biblical book of Daniel, in which the prophet interprets one of Nebuchadnezzar's dreams as meaning that the king will go insane and live like an animal for seven years. Thus, his name is an appropriate one for an animal.

17 No record of a Talmage School in New York City is locatable. At the time Stevenson was writing *Left to Themselves*, Thomas DeWitt Talmage remained a popular evangelical preacher in New York, and he was known for lamenting both the moral decay of the city and the vice of reading impure literature. Edwin G. Burrows and Mike Wallace explain that Talmage "had been touring the nighttime metropolis ever since he had read Charles Loring Brace's *Dangerous Classes* [1872] and decided that 'I, as a minister of religion, felt I had *a divine commission to explore the iniquities of our cities.*' Talmage had policemen pilot him around brothels and saloons. He then recounted his findings in vivid (and racy) talks that drew as many as five thousand to the vast Brooklyn Tabernacle. These sensational sermons were then reprinted in newspapers and collected in books like *The Night Sides of City Life* (1878) and *The Masque Torn Off* (1880)" [1168, italics in original]. If Stevenson was alluding to Talmage, he surely must have been doing so ironically, given his own commitment to homosexual causes and literature. Edwin G. Burrows and Mike Wallace, *Gotham: A History of New York City to 1898*. New York: Oxford University Press, 2000.

18 Murray Hill is an eastside Manhattan neighborhood bordered by

23rd or 34th St. to the south, 42nd St. to the north, Madison Ave. or Fifth Ave. to the west, and the East River to the east. According to Gale Harris, "Residents of the district during the 1850s and the early 1860s tended to be affluent members of the middle-class" (4). The neighborhood became increasingly upscale in the 1870s and 1880s. See Gale Harris and Donald G. Presa's "Murray Hill Historic District Designation Report" for the New York Landmarks Preservation Commission, 2002.

20 The Suburban Trust Company appears to be a fictitious bank, but the *New York Times* reported on several bank robberies involving complicit cashiers during the 1880s. In 1882, the First National Bank of Kewanee, Illinois, was robbed with the help of the Assistant Cashier, a man named Pratt, and one of the robbers was later arrested in McDonough, New York. On September 22, 1889, the *Times* reported on the robbery of the Hurley depository in Hurley, Wisconsin. The robbers were aided by Assistant Cashier Leonard Perrin, who provided the combination for the vault. Perrin was eventually convicted of complicity in the crime and sent to prison. "A Western Town's Sensation. New Developments in the Kewanee Bank Robbery Case—Fresh Arrests." *The New York Times*. 30 August 1882. "A Bold Bank Robbery. The Thieves Capture Nearly Forty Thousand Dollars." *The New York Times*. 22 September 1889. "Banker Perrin to Go to Jail." *The New York Times*. 16 January 1891.

21 Flags.

22 Clothed in knickerbockers: knee-length pants.

23 A long, narrow rowboat.

24 Wearing a decorative ribbon, string, or band on the head.

25 An anchored boat used "as a starting-point or mark for racing boats" (*OED*).

26 A reference to the inhabitants of the ancient Greek city of Troy; used here to mean a "brave or plucky fellow; a person of great energy or endurance" (*OED*).

27 "To catch a crab" means "to make a faulty stroke in rowing whereby the oar becomes jammed under water. The resistance of the water against the blade drives the handle against the rower's body with sufficient force (if the boat be in rapid motion) to throw him back out of his seat, and to endanger the capsizing of the boat" (*OED*).

28 North German Lloyd was a German steamship company founded in 1857 to transport passengers and cargo. It was one of the largest

shipping companies in the Atlantic during the mid- to late nineteenth century.

29 Camp Half-Dozen may be fictitious, but Canadian fishing and hunting camps were popular vacation destinations. An 1884 article on salmon fishing in Canada, including in Nova Scotia where Mr. Saxton was visiting, describes a typical camp: "A well-equipped fishing-camp forms almost a small village, with its comfortable frame house, surrounded by sheds, ice-houses, cooks' quarters, etc." A.F.S., "Salmon-fishing." *Outing and the Wheelman: An Illustrated Monthly Magazine of Recreation*. Volume 4, Number 2 (May 1884): 83-92.

30 The Waverly Hotel, at times called the Waverly Inn or Waverly House, is located in Halifax; during the period of the novel it was run by two sisters, the "Misses Romans."

31 A reference to the biblical story of Jonah, the prophet who is swallowed by a whale or large fish after defying god and being thrown into the sea by sailors trying to rid themselves of the cursed man.

32 The Windsor Hotel opened in 1873 and was advertised as costing $2.5 million. Located on Fifth Ave. at 46th St., it was described in one guidebook as "the most elegant, costly, and perfect hotel in the world . . . situated in the very heart of the finest and most exclusive portion of New York City." The Flagler family lived at the Windsor for a time when Harry Flagler was a boy (Chandler 88). David Leon Chandler, *Henry Flagler: The Astonishing Life and Times of the Visionary Robber Baron Who Founded Florida*. New York: Macmillan, 1986. *The Englishman's Illustrated Guide Book to the United States and Canada*. London: Longmans, Green, Reader, and Dyer, 1874.

33 In the traditional folktale "Aladdin and the Wonderful Lamp," the genie erects a magnificent palace for Aladdin overnight.

34 Parlor-cars comprised more expensive, spacious, and luxurious seating for wealthier patrons on trains (White 287). John H. White, *The American Railroad Passenger Car*. Baltimore: Johns Hopkins University Press, 1978.

35 The 1893 edition of *Left to Themselves* adds the line "—often the unguessed beginnings of trouble." This phrase is cited in the chapter title, so its omission from the first edition must have been an error.

36 A figurative American expression for a "state of excitement or hilarity" (*OED*).

37 "Crim Tartary" was the English name commonly used for the Crimean peninsula in the eighteenth and nineteenth centuries.

The name is derived from the Tatars or Tartars, an ethnic group inhabiting Crimea. Both Australia and Crim Tartary are used here to refer to very remote locations.

38 A coat used to keep dust off one's clothes.

39 A daydream or deep reverie.

40 A "cheat, swindler, rogue; one who lives by his wits and by taking fraudulent advantage of the simplicity of others; esp. a fraudulent gamester" (OED).

41 A swindler.

42 The oldest park in New York City, Bowling Green is located in downtown Manhattan near the southernmost tip of the island.

43 A state-room aboard a ship is a first-class cabin.

44 "Empty clap-trap oratory; 'tall talk'; humbug" (OED).

45 A tool, usually with a hooked end for prying; a crow-bar.

46 Usually a method for teaching religious doctrine using a series of questions and answers; here used to refer to the act of posing questions.

47 "To hasten, speed, go quickly" (OED).

48 A type of signal flare.

49 From the Anglican Book of Common Prayer: "From lightning and tempest; from plague, pestilence, and famine; from battle and murder, and from sudden death, Good Lord, deliver us."

50 A small boat "fitted for rowing and sailing, and used for carrying light stores, passengers, etc." (OED).

51 The side of a boat.

52 A large wave.

53 A bench.

54 "A swift current of water that drives a mill-wheel" (OED).

55 The New-York Tribune was founded in 1841 by Horace Greeley (Lee 242) and was published as the New York Herald Tribune between 1924 and 1966. It had one of the largest circulations in the country at its peak in the mid-nineteenth century (Endres 139). Kathleen L Endres, "Civil War Press (North)." History of the Mass Media in the United States. Edited by Margaret A. Blanchard. New York: Routledge, 1998. 139-142. Alfred McClung Lee, The Daily Newspaper in America, Volume I: American Journalism, 1690-1940. [1937]. New York: Routledge, 2000.

56 This newspaper story and the names O'Reilly, Hand, and Heffernan appear to be fictitious. However, Stevenson may have read similar accounts of Irish nationalists attempting to transport bombs, or "infernal machines," by steamer from the United

States. An attempt of this sort was discovered in July 1881 and linked to a man named O'Donovan Rossa ("Infernal Machines"). The account of the bomb from the real article matches Stevenson's description of the device that accidentally explodes in the novel: "Although the machines are all charged with the explosive substance, there is tolerably conclusive evidence that there was no intention on the part of the senders that they should explode in the hold of the steamer while in transit from Boston to Liverpool. . . . The machine is inclosed in an oblong case of zinc. . . . The presumption is that the machines were intended to be used for the destruction of the public buildings throughout the country in accordance with the avowed Fenian programme" ("Anglo-Irish Affairs"). John Boyle O'Reilly was a real Fenian who was convicted of conspiracy in the United Kingdom and escaped to the United States from a penal colony in Australia. However, he was not involved with transporting explosives, so the use of the name is perhaps coincidental. "Anglo-Irish Affairs. More Light on the Infernal Machines—A Land Bill Contest." *The New-York Tribune.* 28 July 1881. "Infernal Machines Found." *The New-York Tribune.* 25 July 1881.

57 Founded in Ireland in October 1879, the Irish National Land League, or Irish Land League, advocated extending opportunities for land ownership in Ireland and lowering the exorbitant rents paid to landowners by Irish tenant farmers (Comerford 35). Several years of poor harvests in the late 1870s led to widespread evictions and starvation, precipitating the formation of the Land League (Dolan 190-191). In 1880, an American branch was formed in New York whereby Irish immigrants in the United States could organize aid for those remaining in Ireland (Dolan 193). The Land Leagues were not known to be violent. It was the Fenian Brotherhood and later the Clan na Gael, organizations devoted to fighting for Irish independence from the United Kingdom, that were associated with violence in U.S. papers, especially after failed attempts by the Fenian Brotherhood to overthrow British rule in Canada in 1866 and 1870 (Dolan 186-187). R.V. Comerford, "The Land War and the Politics of Distress, 1877-1882." *A New History of Ireland, Volume VI: Ireland Under the Union, 1870-1921.* Edited by W.E. Vaughan. Oxford: Oxford University Press, 1989. 26-52. Jay P. Dolan, *The Irish Americans: A History.* New York: Bloomsbury Press, 2008.

58 Harry Flagler's father owned a yacht that was named *Alicia* after

the elder Flagler's second wife, Ida Alice. The *Alicia* was launched in 1890, and at 160 feet in length, it was "the finest yacht the Flaglers ever owned" (Chandler 106, 299). David Leon Chandler, *Henry Flagler: The Astonishing Life and Times of the Visionary Robber Baron Who Founded Florida*. New York: Macmillan, 1986.

59 Chaperone.

60 A plant grown in a greenhouse. The suggestion is that Gerald has been sheltered.

61 This could refer to any number of editions of the poems of Sir Walter Scott, but the English School-Classics editions were published specifically under the title *Scott's Poems* in the 1870s and 1880s and were heavily annotated for boy readers. Each volume in the series was devoted to a different long poem by Scott. Stevenson does not specify which volume Gerald is carrying.

62 Daniel Defoe's *Robinson Crusoe* was a fictional narrative about a castaway who spends about 30 years on a tropical island following a shipwreck. Although not written specifically for children, the book was popular with young readers, especially after Jean-Jacques Rousseau recommended it as suitable for children in his educational treatise *Emile* (1762). Defoe's novel inspired a genre of castaway stories for children called Robinsonades, which were popular in Europe and the United States in the nineteenth century.

63 A pot, as in a crock-pot.

64 According to the *OED*, "Towser" or "Towzer" was a "common name for a large dog" dating to the seventeenth century.

65 It was common through the early decades of the twentieth century to lay out deceased loved ones in private homes, especially in the parlor or main sitting room.

66 A copy carefully written in large script.

67 Embroidered wall hangings.

68 The town of Chantico is fictitious. The name "Chantico" refers to a Mesoamerican god "of the fireplace and the home" who is "changed into a dog for having made an offering to deities after eating a roasted fish, that is, without observing the norm of fasting" (van't Hooft 268). In one account, this act of disrespect results in the destruction of the world by flood (Brinton 161). Daniel Garrison Brinton, *The Myths of the New World: A Treatise on the Symbolism and Mythology of the Red Race of America*. Third Edition Revised. Philadelphia: Sherman & Company, 1896. Anuschka van't Hooft, *The Ways of the Water: A Reconstruction of Huastecan Nahua Society*

Through Its Oral Tradition. Leiden, Netherlands: Leiden University Press, 2007.

69 Knoxport appears to be a fictitious town, making the *Knoxport Daily Anchor* fictitious as well. A periodical titled *Ladies' Own Magazine* was published between 1869 and 1874 (Mott 95-96), but none titled *Ladies' Own Monthly*, which is perhaps a pun on monthly magazines and menstruation. Frank L. Mott, *A History of American Magazines, 1865-1885*. Cambridge: Harvard University Press, 1938.

70 A "clock that goes for eight days without winding up" (*OED*).

71 Exactly one dozen.

72 A home remedy guide with this exact title has not been located. However, Woodruff, Bentley, and Co. was a patent medicine company co-founded by William Bentley, who was originally from New York State. The business was continued by William's nephew, Lewis Bentley, after the elder's death in 1860. It is possible that the company produced a guidebook like the one Philip finds in the Probascos' home.

73 A "sailing-boat having the mast placed very forward and rigged with one sail" (*OED*).

74 Certain.

75 A reception, party, or gathering of visitors.

76 Every other reference is to Winthrop Jennison, not Wentworth.

77 "Happening at or near to the time of the equinox; said *esp.* of the 'gales' prevailing about the time of the autumnal equinox" (*OED*).

78 The storm described in *Left to Themselves* could be based on several major storms hitting New England in late September (Saxton's telegram to Marcy calling for Gerald is dated September) and early October during the 1880s. The storm that struck the region on September 23, 1882, was described by the *New York Times* as the "heaviest and most drenching rain-storm which visited this City and neighborhood within the memory of man" ("A Very Heavy Rain-Storm"). News accounts from 1888 look back to the 1882 storm as the most recent one of such great severity, suggesting that the next storms to affect the region dramatically did not occur until 1888 ("'Twas a Summer Blizzard"). In late September of 1888, a hurricane traveled up the east coast of the United States and was described as "the most severe that has visited the New-England coast for several years" ("New-England's Big Storm"). The storm toppled trees and telegraph lines and caused flooding throughout the region. Another major storm struck New England on Octo-

ber 14, 1889, and was described as a "severe storm...attended by some serious disaster" ("Storms in New-England"). " 'Twas as a Summer Blizzard: The Severest Storm We Have Had for Years." *The New York Times*. 23 August 1888. "A Very Heavy Rain-Storm: Over Six Inches of Water Falls in One Day." *The New York Times*. 24 September 1882. "New-England's Big Storm." *The New York Times*. 27 September 1888. "Storms in New-England: A Severe Gale Along the Coast and Vessels Driven Ashore." *The New York Times*. 15 October 1889.

79 This line is taken from Book II of Julius Cæsar's *The Gallic War*, written between 58 and 50 B.C.E. (Hammond xxxii). The book has frequently been used for teaching Latin to schoolchildren (see Brown xii), and the line quoted by Stevenson sometimes appeared in Latin textbooks, such as W. M. Bingham's *A Grammar of the Latin Language for the Use of Schools, with Exercises and Vocabularies* (1867). John Mason Brown, Preface. *The Gallic War by Julius Caesar*. [1955]. Translated by John Warrington. Norwalk, Conn.: The Easton Press, 1993. Carolyn Hammond, Introduction. *The Gallic War by Julius Caesar*. Translated by Carolyn Hammond. New York: Oxford University Press, 1996.

80 Some editions of backgammon were designed to fold up and to appear like a book with the title "The History of England" printed on the cover or spine. This design could serve to disguise the game or to allow it to blend in with books on a bookshelf when not in use.

81 Stevenson may have conflated the titles of three nineteenth-century board games: John Harris's "The New Game of Emulation Designed for the Amusement of Youth of Both Sexes with an Abhorrence of Vice and a Love of Virtue" (1804), Anne Abbott's "The Mansion of Happiness: An Instructive Moral and Entertaining Amusement" (1843), and Milton Bradley's "The Checkered Game of Life" (1860). Abbott's is frequently considered the first American board game, and Bradley's was one of the top-selling games of the mid-nineteenth century (Hofer 21, 78). Margaret Hofer, *The Games We Played: The Golden Age of Board & Table Games*. New York: Princeton Architectural Press, 2003.

82 Stevenson is alluding to the popular turn-of-the-century view of the homosexual as a third sex that combines qualities of both sexes: the bodies of one and the psyche or desires of the other. This view was sometimes referred to as the intersex model, after which Stevenson titles his 1908 study of sexuality, *The Intersexes*.

83 A photograph produced by the daguerreotype process invented by Louis Daguerre in the late 1830s.

84 Cape Ann is located about 40 miles north of Boston in Massachusetts.

85 A fishing boat.

86 "Liniment": an ointment or lotion, in this case one applied to the skin to relieve pain.

87 Stevenson's description of Jennison is reminiscent of George Leonidas Leslie, one of the most famous bank robbers of the nineteenth century. According to Herbert Asbury, Leslie maintained several aliases, and he and his gang "were responsible for eighty percent of the bank thefts in America from the time of Leslie's first appearance in the East, about 1865, until he was murdered in 1884" (185-186). J. North Conway describes Leslie as handsome and charming, like Jennison: "George Leslie was a tall, handsome man—lean, fit, and muscular. Some might have called him rugged were it not for his exquisite taste in clothes. . . . He was clean-shaven, with a cleft in his chin. His complexion was clear and genial, his wide brown eyes, sincere and bright. With his dashing good looks and dress, impeccable manners, and outgoing personality, Leslie had little trouble ingratiating himself with New York's social elite" (7).

88 A large photograph, a term especially "designating a portrait photograph of approximately life size" (OED).

89 Handwriting.

90 The Epoch Club may have been fictitious, but gentlemen's clubs were popular with upper-middle-class and upper-class men in the nineteenth century, especially in large cities. Private, single-sex institutions, gentlemen's clubs provided men with a place away from home and family to eat, drink, smoke, play cards or billiards, and enjoy the company of other men (Snyder 44). Katherine V. Snyder, Bachelors, Manhood, and the Novel, 1850-1925. New York: Cambridge University Press, 1999.

91 "Piling or heaping Ossa on Pelion" or "Pelion on Ossa" alludes to "the attempt of the giants to scale heaven by piling Mount Ossa upon Mount Pelion." It means "adding difficulty to difficulty; fruitless efforts," from Virgil's Georgics, 29 B.C.E. (Brewer 925). E. Cobham Brewer, Dictionary of Phrase and Fable, Giving the Derivation, Source, or Origin of Common Phrases, Allusions, and Words that Have a Tale to Tell, Volume 2. New Edition Revised, Corrected, and Enlarged. London: Casell, 1895.

92 The boys are actually in Knoxport. Either the reference to Halifax is an error, which is more likely, or Philip is suggesting that Mr. Saxton has not yet gotten word because Halifax is a small, country city.

93 These were all common names for newspapers in the mid-nineteenth century. The *New-York Tribune*, the *New York Herald*, the *New York World*, and the *New York Commercial Advertiser* were all major daily newspapers operating in the 1880s, though Stevenson could have been referring to newspapers with similar names from other cities in the region. The *Anchor*, as noted earlier, is fictitious.

94 "That species of literary composition, or of dramatic representation, which aims at exciting laughter by caricature of the manner or spirit of serious works, or by ludicrous treatment of their subjects" (*OED*).

95 "To bear trial or investigation, stand the test, find acceptance, prove to be genuine, reliable" (*OED*).

96 Cheated, deceived.

97 A player is an actor, and "boards" refers to a stage.

98 A waterproof coat popular in the nineteenth century.

99 "An act or instance of wheedling; a piece of insinuating flattery or cajolery" (*OED*).

100 Originally meaning finest grade of diamond; "of the finest quality" (*OED*).

101 "A person used as a tool by another to accomplish a purpose" (*OED*).

102 Confusion.

103 A town of Knoxport, either in New England or in a western state, cannot be located and may have been fictitious.

104 Wall Street.

105 Pay a large ransom.

106 Horses. Earlier in the novel, the narrator says Gerald wonders whether his father thinks more about his best horse than his son.

107 Stevenson refers to Jennison's crime in Boston as the "Wheelwright forgery," which could allude to the John Wheelwright deed of 1629. Wheelwright was an English clergyman who first came to New England in 1636 and later settled there. A deed dated 1629 recorded the transmission of land in New Hampshire from four Indian chiefs to five Englishmen, including Wheelwright. The deed was later determined to be a forgery when evidence was discovered that Wheelwright was still in England in 1629. Charles

H. Bell, *John Wheelwright*. [1876]. Boston: The Prince Society, 1891[?].

108 A jail or cell.

109 Banditry was thought endemic to rural Greece in the nineteenth century (Pemble 32-33). The murder of three British travelers by Greek bandits in 1870 made headlines around the world. John Pemble, *The Mediterranean Passion: Victorians and Edwardians in the South*. Oxford: Oxford University Press, 1987.

110 What is now Columbia University, located in New York City. Founded in 1754 as King's College, it was renamed Columbia College in 1784 and operated under that name until 1896, when it became Columbia University. Robert A. McCaughey, *Stand Columbia: A History of Columbia University in the City of New York, 1754-2004*. New York: Columbia University Press, 2004. 77-78.

111 German for "wander year," meaning time taken for travel, often used in reference to the travels of youth.

112 "One who composes or dictates a literary work, speech, or letter; an author, writer, composer" (*OED*).

113 Line spoken by Brutus in Shakespeare's play *The Tragedy of Julius Caesar* (1599). Brutus shakes the hands of his co-conspirators rather than swearing an oath as they depart following their decision to kill Caesar.

APPENDICES

Appendix I: Publication Notices and Contemporary Reviews for *Left to Themselves*

Most brief publication notices and contemporary reviews of *Left to Themselves* simply provide basic plot elements, but several of them refer to the edifying or "religious" nature of the story and highlight the centrality of boyhood friendship to the novel.

From *The Annual American Catalogue 1891*. New York: Office of the Publishers Weekly, 1892. 180.

> Stevenson, E.: Irenæus. Left to themselves: being the ordeal of Philip and Gerald. N.Y., Hunt & Eaton, 1891. c. 323 p. D. cl., $1.
>
> Philip Touchstone [*sic*], a self-educated, energetic lad of seventeen rescues Gerald Saxton from the attack of a tramp, and "left to themselves" they become fast friends. On a voyage to Nova Scotia they are wrecked, and among the rescued is a man who clears up a mystery which had brought disgrace upon the father of young Touchstone [*sic*].

From *The Publisher's Weekly*. Number 1009 (May 30, 1891): 762.

> LEFT TO THEMSELVES. Being the ordeal of Philip and Gerald. By Edward Irenæus Stevenson. 12mo, cloth, $1.00.
> An exceptional story for young people, in its simple, dramatic force and decisive religious undertone.

From *The Book Buyer: A Summary of American and Foreign Literature*, Vol. VIII. New York: Charles Scribner's Sons, February 1891. 17.

> "Left to Themselves; or, the Ordeal of Philip and Gerald," is the title of a new story by Edward Irenæus Stevenson. The scene is a lonely island and later an isolated town, both near the New England coast, and the motive is described as a "romance of early friendship." It will be published by Hunt & Eaton.

From *The Literary World*. Volume XXI. Boston: E.H. Hames and Co., December 1890. 499.

> *Left to Themselves; or, the Ordeal of Philip and Gerald*, a new book by Edward Irenæus Stevenson, written primarily for young people, but also with a particular aim of meeting sympathetic interest from adults, will be published in February by Hunt & Eaton.

From *Sunday School Journal for Preachers*. Volume 23, Number 6 (June 1891): 334.

> *Left to Themselves; or, The Ordeal of Philip and Gerald*. By Edward Irenæus Stevenson. New York: Hunt & Eaton. Cincinnati: Cranston & Stowe. Size, 5x7½ inches. Cloth. 323 pages. Price, $1. Philip and Gerald, accidentally severed from their friends for a few days, shipwreck in Long Island Sound, and followed by an unscrupulous man, show of what stuff they are made. There is no preaching in the book, but Philip Touchtone's character preaches a sermon which should have many listeners among American boys.

From *The Book Buyer: A Monthly Review of American and Foreign Literature*. Volume 9. New York: Charles Scribner and Sons, March 1892. 66-67.

Left to Themselves, a story for boys, by Edward Irenæus Stevenson, is the record of a youthful friendship. Gerald Saxton, a boy of twelve, left by his father at a country hotel during a summer, meets an older boy, Philip Touchtone, and between them arises a friendship which affects the future lives of both to an important degree. The book was written on the principle that the clear embodiment of character is of the first importance in a story for young readers, and in the belief that young people are quite capable of appreciating character analysis and character development, that "light-hearted youth does not necessarily mean light-headed youth." While embodying these ideas in tracing the careers and adventures of his two young heroes, the author has presented a narrative so lively and entertaining that it can hardly fail to interest the youngest reader. A thrilling boat race, an attempted kidnapping, a steamer explosion and wreck, and life on a lonely, almost deserted island, constitute the main features of interest. After passing through numerous exciting adventures, the heroes at length reach home and safety, and the story ends with every one perfectly happy, except the evil-doer, which is always a cause of satisfaction to boy readers. [Hunt & Eaton, 12mo, $1.00]

From *The Atlantic Monthly: A Magazine of Literature, Science, Art, and Politics*. Boston: Houghton, Mifflin and Company, February 1892. 280.

Left to Themselves, being the Ordeal of Philip and Gerald, by Edward Irenæus Stevenson (Hunt & Eaton, New York.) Mr. Stevenson, in a brief preface, pleads for a closer attention to character in books for the young. The preface reads a little oddly when taken in connection with a story which appeals almost wholly to love of excitement. A boat race, an attempt at kidnapping, a steamboat explosion, a shipwreck, life on an apparently deserted island, the discovery of a forger,—these and incidents like these do not preclude appeals to the reason and to students of character, but we are bound to say that we do not believe the young readers of this book will be set to thinking because of it. It will stir them, as an involved story of adventure easily may stir them, but the hero will appear as the stuff of which heroes in such adventures usually are made.

From *Zion's Herald*. Boston. June 3, 1891. 171.

Left to themselves. By Edward Irenæus Stevenson. (New York: Hunt & Eaton. $1.) A simple story, which is strong in the purpose to unfold the real excellence of character as they are intended to mold and influence the young and growing mind and heart. The incidents recounted are not of any great or very interesting moment. The narrative, if read, will do good.

From *The Chautauquan: A Weekly Newsmagazine*. August 1891. 686.

"Left to Themselves" is a story for boys to read on a forbidding rainy day which makes necessary a long quiet time indoors just when they feel restlessly inclined. It is not calm reading, and the boys will feel their blood tingle as if from a race, while their credulity will need special care after such vigorous exercise. Two boys, Philip and Gerald, are thrown together, become firm friends, are shipwrecked, and reap enough troubles for a harvest of wrinkles, but an average amount of native practical intelligence ripens their woes into joys, and at last they become men honorable and respectable if not widely noted.

Appendix II: *The Intersexes* (1908), by Xavier Mayne [Edward Prime-Stevenson]. Italy: privately printed. 153-154, 158-160, 170, 182, 366-367, 455-457, 460-461, 480.

Stevenson's *The Intersexes* is described by James Gifford as "the first great defense of homosexuality in English," and certainly it was one of the earliest comprehensive and affirmative studies of homosexual life and culture by an American (Gifford, "What Became of the Intersexes?" 25). Groundbreaking in many ways, *The Intersexes* includes a section on "Uranian" children, who are defined by a distinctly homosexual nature, as opposed simply to young people who happen to engage in homosexual activities or experience transitory same-sex desires. Stevenson also includes sections on homosexual children's literature and on the prominence of blackmail in the lives of homosexuals, subjects directly relevant to our understanding of *Left to Themselves*.

From *The Intersexes*

[*On homosexual boys and youth*]

Unless the parent has clear ideas of similisexual[1] traits and habits, the sharpest eye can fail to notice them in a child. A boy or girl assumes "the mask" with curious precocity. Children are loyal to each other, as they are secretive, in sex-secrets. Similisexual practices among little boys and girls, to say nothing of larger ones, are concealed by instinct. Fathers and mothers should not wish to be spies and martinets. As for the parent's duty, the school-teacher, governess, tutor or housemaster, whether in the family or at a boarding-school, he or she is even more hampered. One of the most mischievous skeletons in the family-closet and boarding-school dormitory, is the similisexual one. The pederastic tutor himself may be the enemy in camp.

Two types of Uranian boyhood prevail. The child being in this the father of the man, as in other foreshadowings. One is

1 Homosexual.

the physically delicate youth, graceful, spiritual, and dreamy, highly impressionable. To this type also belong often detail of uncertain health, of shunning the ruder of sports of lads, of indifference or dislike to the society of noisy male playmates; along with a proportionate relish for playing with girls, dressing in girls' clothing, and a natural ease of comporting oneself in it. A boy should never be permitted to "dress up" in female apparel, nor a girl allowed to travesty herself as a boy. To such a delicate boy-type, pertains, the love of quiet, of solitude, tastes for reading and for arts, admiration for what is beautiful rather than what is rudely grand and heroic, and of intellect, not action. Above all, in such young Uranians occurs vivid appreciation of adult male beauty, the charm of mature male society, when the man concerned is gentle of temperament and gifted. These latter traits are more or less recurrent in heterosexual youths. But they arrive at a proper proportion in normal lads as virile maturity advances and they do not have the sentimental tinge in normal boys that they possess in the young Uranian. This Uranian frequently matures to "passive" sexuality.

The second type of young Uranian has nothing feminine in his tastes. He is, on the contrary, averse to girlish interests in life. He, indeed, passionately attaches himself to friends. He perhaps is wholly careless of other relationships. Often he is noticed as concentrating his sentimental nature, so far as it is revealed, on one or another intimacy with a boy, no matter what be the masculinity of his general equipment. At least, this is frequently a trait in him. But in his case, as in that of the relatively feminine youth, there is the superseding sense of the beauty of the male physique and male character, indifference to girlish charms, and inner responsiveness to what is manly attractiveness. Perhaps it is all hid; reserved by the lad with great pains. Naturally, this type is far less easy to separate from the normal-natured lad growing up into a quite distinct nature. But often it is strong "active" Uranianism, under a vigorously boyish veil.

Some years ago, appeared in England a little tale "Tim" (anonymous) gracefully written, giving subtly a minute study of psychic Uranianism between two school-lads of these diverse types.[1]

Indeed the general categories of schools for lads of all ages, including impressionable aesthetic natures of tender years, are the seedling-houses of uranistic impulses. The types of young Uranians mentioned above concentrate themselves on the school friendships of this time. These become real passions. The sexual relations that spring out of them are not merely misdirected boyish impulses, as one is so often told. They are unities rooted in the elementary temperaments of many of the lads. As the boy grows up, the instinct may keep him a pederastic homosexualist for all of his life, or he may experience its mutations toward mere idealism. But, first and last, it is likely to be the same aesthetic passion for masculine beauty of body, in preference over the feminine; a sense of the psychic superiority of the male, a "drawing" toward him, as the expression of sexual desirableness; of personal charm, trustworthiness, and "completeness". From the first days that the lad looks into the world, distinguishes a man from a woman, a boy from a girl, the youthful Uranian makes his choice instinctively. He knows where his heart leads. . . .

Inborn Uranianism in a youth, and real and inborn Uraniadism in a girl (the latter's outlook less decisively) cannot be "cured". If genuine, it defies "remedial" processes. Acquired similisexualism of a superficial quality frequently passes away in women under matrimonial influences, maternal emotions and other alterants. The parent, the tutor, the mature friend of an Uranian boy can help the lad to grow up with his similisexual instincts in reasonable physical and moral restraint. Intelligence and tact can define the course to prevent the boy from becoming as a homosexual man, what so many grow up to be—degenerates, criminals and victims. But beyond such solicitous, tactful help to a lad no results can be achieved, in nine cases in ten,—except illusions and failures.

1 H. O. Sturgis's *Tim: A Story of Eton* (1891) was published the same year as *Left to Themselves*. Like Stevenson, Sturgis was an American living in Europe, and his novel concerns the love of a boy for a slightly older youth. Unlike Stevenson's novel, *Tim* was not published expressly for children.

[On homosexual children's literature]

Fiction for young people that has uranian hints is thought the last sort for circulating among British boys and girls. A pathetic story "Tim" I mentioned in the seventh chapter of this book—a direct and specialistic study of psychic homosexuality in two school lads one of them wholly intersexual in type—is nevertheless to be classed in the library for young Britons. The authorship of this little tale remains anonymous. Another juvenile, "The French Prisoners" by Edward Bertz, better-known by his active career in belles-lettres, has a subtle note of the psychologic kind in question, in its emotional development. A recent story of Harrow school-life, "The Hill", by Horace Vachell (a book exceptional in its crowded field for its vividness of characterizations, manly moral uplift and charm of style) offers even more than "Tim" the ingredient of an absolutely absorbing "passion of friendship", a self-forgetting devotion and intense admiration on the part of one lad for another—the "god of his idolatry." A kind of mystic struggle of which jealousy is a factor, against the evil charm of a third schoolmate—the beautiful and conscienceless "Demon", as he is nick-named— enters into the story. It has no hint (in fact a passing incident is particularly to the contrary) of physical emotionalism. But almost first and last it is suggestive of the key of sub-conscious youthful uranianism. No other emotional factor in the book is on the same plan of elaboration and import. Also in "White Cockades", a little tale of the flight of the Young Pretender, by E.I. Stevenson, issued in Edinburgh some years ago, passionate devotion from a rustic youth toward the Prince, and its recognition are half-hinted as homosexual in essence. The sentiment of uranian adolescence is more distinguishable in another book for lads, "Philip and Gerald", by the same hand; a romantic story in which a youth in his latter teens is irresistibly attracted to a much younger lad; and becomes, *con amore*, responsible for the latter's personal safety, in a series of unexpected events that throw them together—for life.

[*On blackmail*]

Blackmailer!—the blackmailed!—tyrant and writhing victim! In all sorts of relations where human rashness, passion, folly, weakness, carelessness, sordid mercenariness or vengeance attack the individual, we meet this dark process. But nowhere else does blackmail operate with such terrible alertness as in the uranian world. We have reserved it as the concluding portion of this survey of homosexual decadence and criminality, because of its all-important bearings on the social and legal status of the uranian intersex in so many contemporary civilizations.

Blackmail is of course the essence of espionage; of vicious leverage against the individual's peace, against his social protection. It is often the most impudent of attacks. For success it requires some cleverness, some moral (or immoral) boldness, and not seldom physical courage; especially if the blackmailer must arrive at not only extortion but at robbery and murder, as finale. It is the constant resource—the sharp Sword of Democles that the average homosexual prostitute points against his client, wherever the country's laws invite it. No arm is so powerful, so silent, so safe. No female blackmailer, however audacious and cruel, ever has shown herself quite so torturing in shattering nerves, happiness, fortune, courage, social quietude and life as has the methodical, homosexual, blackmailing demon proved himself, time and again, the world round.

The police-annals of all countries witness these melancholy episodes. Broken careers, shipwrecked lives, disappearances, interrupted marriages, inexplicable money-embarrassments, murders, suicides by hundreds are to be so explained. The incessant examples of "unaccountable affairs" too often mean that some intersexual victim, persecuted by a grasping enemy, threatened with exposure as an Uranian, can hold out no longer. Perhaps early in the attack he has seen no way out. Suicide especially will cheat the blackmailer of his blood-tax, or hide from the world the motive to drive the unfortunate into the tomb. Or else murder will be a deliverance, and flight a hope.

What can the average victim *do* to escape? Despairing, fearing social disgrace and a prison's cell, perhaps already mulcted[1] for more money than he can afford and dreading the next demand—how can he win out? Possibly a single hour, nay, a few minutes of homosexual passion, or even no approach to it at all, will cost his peace of mind, his income, his home, his future! The blackmailer, who seemed so friendly an uranian type, has plundered him; has exiled him, if the unfortunate man is able to fly; or flight has been impossible or a vain expedient. Few Uranians in the hundred can afford to fly from the legal or social zone of their persecutor. The blackmailed may be married, a father of a family, at the head of a business that is his all; or otherwise not free footed.

The attacked can (and he *should*) courageously seek the police-authorities, to reveal the situation. At the price of more or less suspicion on himself, perhaps of his semi-confession, he can have his tormentor arrested and nearly always fully punished. Blackmailing is *per se* an offense of which modern Codes take severe notice. That is the best rescue, the safest escape, the only legal method, *coûte que coûte!*[2] Unluckily the victim has not always the knowledge, the courage, or evidence enough for this heroic stand. So he submits. Sometimes he resolves to kill the blackmailer. He often has done so, and has suffered death for it. But, as last and too-usual resort of the victim in half of Europe (particularly in Germanic Europe and often in America) he "gets out of it all" by—suicide. The motive of his self-murder may transpire; but usually it does not. At least, it escapes general notice. . . .

Manifestly the blackmailer relies primarily upon fear on the part of the victim. To terrorize is the first necessity. A man otherwise brave too often cannot cow such an assailant by bold demeanor or by calm ridicule. He fears more than the attack the "talk" over the remedy! True is it that a good kicking from one's doors is generally enough to send a common type of *Erpresser*[3] flying, for good. But Uranians are too often not muscular or

1 "To extract money from" (*OED*).

2 Cost what it may.

3 Blackmailer.

valorous. The victim's ignorance of the legal dispositions for his aid is general in the countries where he needs most such aid. Physical strength, moral resolution, legal knowledge, are defenses not too universally practised in any troublesome affairs. The victim is likely to be unaware that he has the rascal. Unless he be examined by pedants of morality, the victim has enough chances to avoid direct compromises by his own recital; at least that is now a tendency, in many countries. But the social whispers that will inevitably fly about hold the victim back. People will comment; they will believe more or less, will be scandalized, even if the Uranian predicament be all a tissue of persecution. Hence the struggle against some vampire, or pack of vampires, can go on for years! Immediate recourse to legal help, to betake oneself to the nearest police-court to call the nearest police-officer, to face down the blackmailer with rudest or calmest contempt and with counter-threats and action—these are not only the first defense but often perfectly efficient ones.

Appendix III: *Imre* (1906), by Xavier Mayne [Edward Prime-Stevenson]. Naples: The English Book-Press, 106-109.

Stevenson's novel *Imre* is considered one of the first explicitly gay American novels. It describes the romance between an Englishman and a Hungarian soldier as the two attempt to articulate their feelings and identities as homosexuals and the future possibilities for a life together at the turn of the century. Oswald's recollection of his childhood offers a portrait of what Stevenson describes in *The Intersexes* as "Uranian boyhood" and provides a context for our understanding of the relationship between Philip and Gerald in *Left to Themselves*.

From *Imre*, "Chapter II: Masks and—A Face"

"From the time when I was a lad, Imre ... a little child ... I felt myself unlike other boys in one element of my nature. That one matter was my special sense, my passion, for the beauty, the dignity, the charm ... the, ... what shall I say? ... the loveableness of my own sex. I hid it, at least so far as, little by little, I came to realize its force. For, I soon perceived that most other lads had no such passional sentiment, in any important measure of their natures, even when they were fine-strung, impressionable youths. There was nothing unmanly about me; nothing really unlike the rest of my friends in school, or in town-life. Though I was not a strong-built, or rough-spirited lad, I had plenty of pluck and muscle, and was as lively on the playground, and fully as indefatigable, as my chums. I had a good many friends; close ones, who liked me well. But I felt sure, more and more, from one year to another even of that boyhood time, that no lad of them all ever could or would care for me as much as I could and did care for one or another of them! Two or three episodes made that clear to me. These incidents made me, too, shyer and shyer of showing how my whole young nature, soul and body together, Imre—could be stirred with a veritable adoration for some boy-friend that I elected ... an adoration with physical yearning in it—how intense was the appeal of bodily beauty, in a lad, or in a man of mature years."

"And yet, with that beauty, I looked for manliness, poise, will-power, dignity and strength in him. For, somehow I demanded those traits, always and clearly, whatever else I sought along with them. I say 'sought.' I can say, too, won—won often to nearness. But this other, more romantic, emotion in me . . . so strongly physical, sexual, as well as spiritual . . . it met with a really like and equal and full response once only. Just as my school-life was closing, with my sixteenth year (nearly my seventeenth) came a friendship with a newcomer into my classes, a lad of a year older than myself, of striking beauty of physique and uncommon strength of character. This early relation embodied the same precocious, absolutely vehement *passion* (I can call it nothing else) on both sides. I had found my ideal! I had realized for the first time, completely, a type; a type which had haunted me from first consciousness of my mortal existence, Imre; one that is to haunt me till my last moment of it. All my immature but intensely ardent regard was returned. And then, after a few months together, my schoolmate, all at once, became ill during an epidemic in the town, was taken to his home, and died. I never saw him after he left me."

"It was my first great misery, Imre. It was literally unspeakable! For, I could not tell to anyone, I did not know how to explain even to myself, the manner in which my nature had gone out to my young mate, nor how his being spontaneously so had blent itself with mine. I was not seventeen years old, as I said. But I knew clearly now what it was to *love* thus, so as to forget oneself in another's life and death! But also I knew better than to talk of such things. So I never spoke of my dead mate." [Ellipses in original.]

Appendix IV: *Studies in the Psychology of Sex: Sexual Inversion* [1897], Second Edition, by Havelock Ellis and John Addington Symonds. Philadelphia: F. A. Davis Company, 1901. 44-50, 214.

Havelock Ellis and John Addington Symonds's *Sexual Inversion* is considered the first major scientific, book-length study of homosexuality in English. Whereas Stevenson stresses cultural and historical approaches to homosexuality in *The Intersexes*, Ellis and Symonds's study was published as a medical textbook and emphasized case studies that provided documentary evidence as a basis for scientific understanding. Ellis and Symonds do address some subjects later taken up by Stevenson, including homosexual activity in youth and the prominence of blackmail in the lives of homosexuals.

from *Sexual Inversion*

[*On homosexuality in youth*]

When the sexual instinct first appears in early youth, it seems to be much less specialized than normally it becomes later. Not only is it, at the outset, less definitely directed to a specific sexual end, but even the sex of its object is sometimes uncertain. This has always been so well recognized that those in authority over young men have sometimes forced women upon them to avoid the risk of possible unnatural offenses.

The institution which presents these phenomena to us in the most marked and the most important manner is, naturally, the school, in England especially the public school.[1] In France, where the same phenomena are noted, Tarde has called attention to these relationships, "most usually Platonic in the primitive meaning of the word, which indicate a simple indecision of frontier between friendship and love, still undifferentiated in the dawn of the awakening heart," and he regrets that no one has yet studied them. In England we are very familiar with vague allusions to the vices of public schools. From time

1 The term "public school" in the United Kingdom refers to a group of elite private schools such as Eton, Harrow, and Rugby.

to time we read letters in the newspapers denouncing public schools as "hot-beds of vice," and one anonymous writer remarks that "some of our public schools almost provoke the punishment of the cities of the Plain." But, so far as I have been able to gather, these allegations have not been submitted to accurate investigation. The physicians and others connected with public schools who are in a position to study the matter possess no psychological training, and appear to view homosexuality with too much disgust to care to pay any careful attention to it. What knowledge they possess they keep to themselves, for it is considered to be in the interests of public schools that these things should be hushed up. When anything very scandalous occurs one or two lads are expelled, to their own grave and, perhaps, life-long injury, and without benefit to those who remain, whose awaking sexual life rarely receives intelligent sympathy.

For some interesting details regarding homosexuality in German schools I may refer to Dr. A. Hoche, *Zur Frage der forensischen Beurtheiling sexueller Vergeher.*[1] Putting together communications received from various medical men regarding their own youthful experiences at school, he finds relationships of the kind very common, usually between boys of different ages and school-classes. According to one observer, the feminine, or passive, part was always played by a boy of girlish form and complexion, and the relationships were somewhat like those of normal lovers, with kissing, poems, love-letters, scenes of jealousy, sometimes visits to each other in bed, but without masturbation, pederasty, or other grossly physical manifestation. From his own youthful experience Hoche records precisely similar observations, and remarks that the lovers were by no means recruited from the vicious elements in the school. (The elder scholars, of 21 or 22 years of age, formed regular sexual relationships with the servant-girls in the house.) It is probably that the homosexual relationships in English schools are, as a rule, not more vicious than those described by Hoche, but that the concealment in which they are wrapped leads to exaggeration. No doubt, in exceptional cases, the critics of the school have justice on their side.

1 "The Question of the Forensic Assessment of Sexual Offenses."

Max Dessoir, in a study of the psychology of the sexual life which displays remarkable acumen, comes to the conclusion that "an undifferentiated sexual feeling is normal, on the average, during the first years of puberty,—i.e., from 13 to 15 in boys and from 12 to 14 in girls,—while in latter years it must be regarded as pathological." He adds very truly that in this early period the sexual emotion has not become centered in the sexual organs. This latter fact is certainly far too often forgotten by grown-up persons who suspect the idealized passion of boys and girls of a physical side which children have often no suspicion of, and would view with repulsion and horror. How far the sexual instinct may be said to be undifferentiated in early puberty as regards sex is a little doubtful to me; I should not like to go further than to say that it is comparatively undifferentiated. That it is absolutely undifferentiated, except in a few cases, I can by no means admit. However this may be, it is certain that school-life plays a certain part in developing (it would be incautious to say originating) sexual inversion.

These school-boy affections and passions arise, to a large extent, spontaneously with the evolution of the sexual emotions, though the method of manifestation may be a matter of example or suggestion. As the sexual instincts become stronger, and as the lad leaves school or college to mix with men and women in the world, the instinct usually turns into the normal channel, in which channel the instincts of the majority of boys have been directed from the earliest appearance of puberty, if not earlier. But a certain proportion remain insensitive to the influence of women, and these may be regarded as true sexual inverts. Some of them are probably individuals of somewhat undeveloped sexual instincts. The members of this group are of some interest psychologically, although from the comparative quiescence of their sexual emotions they have received little attention. The following communication which I have received from a well-accredited source is noteworthy from this point of view:—

"The following facts may possibly be of interest to you, though my statement of them is necessarily general and vague. I happen to know intimately three cases of men whose affections have chiefly been directed exclusively to persons of their own sex. The first, having practiced masturbation as a boy, and then for some ten years ceased to practice it (to such an extent that he even inhibited his erotic dreams) has since recurred to it deliberately (at about fortnightly intervals) as a substitute for copulation, for which he has never felt the least desire. But occasionally, when sleeping with a male friend, he has emissions in the act of embracing. The second is constantly and to an abnormal extent (I should say) troubled with erotic dreams and emissions and takes drugs, by doctor's advice, to reduce this activity. He has recently developed a sexual interest in women, but for ethical and other reasons does not copulate with them. Of the third I can say little, as he has not talked to me on the subject; but I know that he has never had intercourse with women, and has always had a natural and instinctive repulsion to the idea. In all these, I imagine, the physical impulse of sex is less imperative than in the average man. The emotional impulse, on the other hand, is very strong. It has given birth to friendships of which I find no adequate description anywhere but in the dialogues of Plato; and, beyond a certain feeling of strangeness at the gradual discovery of a temperament apparently different to that of most men, it has provoked no kind of self-reproach or shame. On the contrary, the feeling has been rather one of elation in the consciousness of a capacity of affection which appears to be finer and more spiritual than that which commonly subsists between persons of different sexes. These men are all of intellectual capacity above the average; and one is actively engaged in the world, where he is both respected for his capacity and admired for his character. I mention this particularly, because it appears to be the habit, in books upon this subject, to regard the relation in question as pathological, and to select cases where those who are concerned in it are tormented with shame and remorse. In the cases to which I am referring nothing of the kind subsists.

"In all these cases a physical sexual attraction is recognized as the basis of the relation, but as a matter of feeling, and partly also of theory, the ascetic ideal is adopted.

"These are the only cases with which I am personally and

intimately acquainted. But no one can have passed through a public-school and college life without constantly observing indications of the phenomenon in question. It is clear to me that in a large number of instances there is no fixed line between what is called distinctively 'friendship' and love; and it is probably the influence of custom and public opinion that in most cases finally specializes the physical passion in the direction of the opposite sex."

[*On blackmail*]

But, while the law has had no more influence in repressing abnormal sexuality, than, wherever it has tried to do so, it has had in repressing the normal sexual instinct, it has served to foster another offense. What is called blackmailing in England, *chantage* in France, and *Erpressung* in Germany—in other words, the extortion of money by threats of exposing some real or fictitious offense—finds its chief field of activity in connection with homosexuality. No doubt the removal of the penalty against simple homosexuality does not abolish blackmailing, as the existence of this kind of *chantage* in France shows, but it renders its success less probable.

Appendix V: "A Question of Taste" by Edward Irenæus Stevenson, *The Christian Union*, Volume 30, Number 8 (August 21, 1884): 180-181.

Stevenson's 1884 short story "A Question of Taste," published in the "Our Young Folks" section of the *Christian Union* magazine, features several elements that later appear in *Left to Themselves*: the Ossokosee House, a character named Mr. Hilliard, cross-country travel, false accusations, and boyhood friendship. Although the relationship between protagonists Will and Bart lacks the overt romantic quality of Philip and Gerald's, the two boys squabble like domestic partners about how to get from the Ossokosee House to New York City and ultimately spend a "jolly week" alone together. The realistic disagreement between long-time friends in "A Question of Taste" presents a contrast to the idealized depiction of the early days of Philip and Gerald's relationship in *Left to Themselves*.

"A Question of Taste"

WHAT occurred to them was the result of a decided difference of opinion, and, added to that, a queer coincidence. It did no harm, however; and it has given William Bunt and the friend who paid him a long visit this summer a capital story to tell for years to come. Barton Wilde came up to William's in August, and took a breezy room at the Ossokosee House, where William's father rented a cottage. The two lads bathed and fished and rowed, sailed or played tennis, without a wave of dissension rolling across their peaceful breasts until the question of how the pair should make the return journey to New York came into discussion. It was then discovered that William and Barton had a strong diversity of taste.

There were exactly two routes: the Millbridge and Deep Bay, and the celebrated Pumpkin Island Air Line.

"Now, Bart, for goodness' sake, don't say 'Pumpkin Island' to me again!" protested Will. "Didn't I come that way? and you know how long and dull it is!"

"Long and dull!" said Barton. "I don't think it that, Will; and surely anything is better than arriving in New York at midnight, as you must by the Millbridge and Deep Bay."

"On the Pumpkin Island the trains run so slow that a fellow can crack nuts under the car-wheels for his dinner; and the road winds so that the train is on both tracks at once half the time."

"Humph!" ejaculated Barton. "Talk about enterprise! Why, mother and father came up by your dear M. and D. B. last year. There were only two cars pretty much all the way; finally these were reduced to one. Toward noon they were pulled up very suddenly at a little side station, without any reason given for it, until in walked an official in gilt buttons. 'Very sorry to disturb you, ladies and gentlemen,' says he, 'but will you very kindly vacate the car and promenade the depot platform outside for awhile until we wash the floor here and clean the windows?' So they did; and then the passengers marched back and took their seats meekly, and the train proceeded. That's the kind of a railroad the Millbridge and Deep Bay is!" concluded Bart, triumphantly.

William could not help laughing. "Well," he said, at last, "it shows that the superintendent has an idea of getting the best of dirt. Really, Bart, I don't want to be disagreeable, but I must say that I had rather go back alone than roast myself on the Pumpkin Island." And he gave Barton a look which was quizzical, but had a good deal of determination in its brightness.

"And I am afraid, my dear William, that I shall have to deprive myself of the pleasure of your company unless you say that you won't enforce the Millbridge and Deep Bay affliction on me. Honestly, I could not stand that, you know!" Will's expression was just as pleasantly resolute as Barton's.

There were two or three such arguments. Neither friend lost his temper; but as the fortnight advanced neither gave up the point. It was very foolish in the two boys to show so much stubbornness; but then most of the discussion was carried on with laughing and banter, and each expected the opposite party to give way. At length the serious state of affairs was recognized, and William's uncle got wind of it.

"Why don't you walk fifty miles across to Lancaster, you

two, and there you can take the new Lancaster line that is just running, and so go to Grand Junction and New York," he said, after an interview with each boy, in which he was surprised to discover how absurdly stanch each one was. In fact, the contest had been metamorphosed into one of pride; nor was it the first occasion. "You are both excellent hands for long tramps—excellent legs, I mean. You can allow four days to cover the ground—enough, I should say. The mountain roads are capital, the scenery just of a sort to be seen on foot, and the weather perfect for such an expedition. I guess, after the first stage is over, you two will find all the stubbornness in you limbered up, and you will enjoy the railroad conclusion of your experiment amazingly."

Half in joke, half in earnest, this elaborate adjustment of the vexed little point was adopted. Both boys had made short pedestrian tours together half a dozen times, some not much shorter than the one at present before them. Mr. and Mrs. Bunt, however, thought that either the contestant for the Pumpkin Island road would yield at the last moment, or the upholder of the Millbridge "take water." So far from that, both William and Bart became so absorbed in contemplating the walk, in studying the county map and preparing to set out, that they forgot the scheme's originating in what Uncle McKay defined "a dumb fight" (which it had been). Each boy protested that now neither railroad should seduce him from that fifty-mile tramp, if it offered him a special train of Pullman coaches.

So it came to pass that one Tuesday the elder Brunts, Uncle McKay, and a dozen friends at the Ossokosee House waved farewell from the piazza to William and Bart.

Attired in knickerbockers, with short staves and light knapsacks, the pair struck into the mountain road at a swinging pace. Their path mounted. Before noon William and Bart were enjoying the luncheon the hotel *chef* had furnished them, as they sat under a ruined shed, built to shelter the excursion teams that crossed the summit of Mount Ossokosee. The smell of the thick woods was in the air. A partridge fluttered from her nest close by. North and west stretched out a majestic view, which almost included the smoke overhanging Lancaster.

"Rather better, this, than the Pumpkin Island line?" said Will, with his mouth not so entirely full of apple that he could not grin slyly.

"Possibly," returned Barton, with smiling dignity, as he salted his hard-boiled egg; "but certainly a great improvement on that two-mile-an-hour express that the Millbridge and Deep Bay Company advertise."

Steadfast blue eyes met answering hazel; but the inevitable laugh from both pairs of lungs revealed the easy phase of the situation. When the luncheon was over, the boys walked on, going down the side of gigantic old Ossokosee toward Drentford. All of a sudden Bart stopped short and looked into the gully beside the path.

"Halloa! What's that?" he said, pointing. Something bright glimmered in the bushes across the ditch.

"Looks like a bicycle wheel," replied Will. "Let's wait and see if it's anybody we know from the hotel."

They did so for quite a quarter of an hour. In response to whoops and calls no errant wheelman appeared. The boys leaped the gully, scrambled into the wild cedar and young maples, and, lo! not one, but two superb machines, new, apparently, and duly labeled "— & Co., Coventry."

Naturally, neither Will nor Bart for some time conceived the idea that they had made any actual "find." William expected each five minutes to hear a shout and behold the owners of the steel steeds standing to give an account of themselves and extract as much from Barton and Will. Further examination on the part of the latter tended to convince them that neither machine had been used for riding more than once, if that. Possibly this was a christening journey.

"See here, Bart," ejaculated Will in new excitement; "look at the rust here, and here—where these leaves have touched the metal! And just notice how the moss yonder is all pressed down by the tires. These machines have been left here for days, at least."

"If they have been used on this road to-day or yesterday, Will, we are certain to find the tracks up there in the road. It has not rained in this whole region for a week."

Our friends sprang again up the gully, and scanned the highway carefully. Not a wheel-track of any kind was discernible. In clambering back across the gully to the bicycles Barton set his foot upon an insecure fragment of granite. He fell heavily, straining the tendons of his ankle slightly.

"Upon my word, Will," he confessed, after one or two ineffectual efforts to walk. "I don't know how I shall even get down to Drentford village, at the foot of the mountain, let alone walking to-morrow fifteen miles. What extraordinary bad luck!"

"No so bad, my dear fellow, as it might be," returned William. "Just listen to me. These bicycles have been abandoned here, I strongly believe, by some thief who gave up trying to hawk them for sale. Or, maybe, they were taken from some one who lives not far from here. It is growing late. We should have some slight work to reach Drentford before sunset had you not lamed yourself."

"Well, what do you advise our doing?" queried Barton.

"We will wait here one half-hour longer. Then, if no owner to these appears we will just consider them treasure-trove, leave some kind of a notice behind us as to our appropriating them, and let them carry us to Drentford, or as much further as the future permits. It seems to me an out-and-out 'find,' Barton, and until we can trace the owners of these mysteries we will just use them as readily and as carefully as if they were yours and my own, that are this minute in the stables at home. You can manage with your game foot, of course."

The plan was adopted. The chances were entirely in favor of the boys having saved, either for their use or the benefit of an unknown owner, a valuable and beautiful possession, certain of ruin if left so unprotected much longer. Once arrived in the limits of civilization, Bart and Will could unravel the puzzle. The half-hour passed. Then a note was written and fastened so that only persons who had been party to the hiding of the bicycles should at once see it. The note set forth Will's and Bart's frank explanation of their course, signed with their names and addresses, and outlining their route afoot for the coming few days. Just as the sun was drawing near the summit of the rugged mountain the two boys glided easily down the smoothly graded road toward Drentford.

Barton soon grew accustomed to his awkward method of propulsion. His foot had swollen not a little, and a longer walk would have been out of the question. As it was, the whole discovery and its application had been so novel and enjoyable that the two friends were in excited spirits. They reached the foot of Mount Ossokosee without mishap (that "coasting" was not indulged in need not be said); and, in spite of a rather ominous creaking in both machines, which urged an immediate application of missing oil-flasks, Bart and Will rolled into Drentford at twilight, with a fair degree of speed, and much of the look of a pair of friends who had set out upon an autumn tour some days earlier.

"This has been still better than the Millbridge and Deep Bay route," dryly observed Barton, as Will helped him to alight in the dooryard of the "Ethan Allan Inn: Entertainment for Man and Beast"—bicycles not being particularized.

"Oh, anything is preferable to the Pumpk—" but again resounded the inevitable laugh. "Well, it was as near to a row as ever we have had," admitted he, as they walked toward the door.

"But I'm not sorry it occurred," replied Barton, limping beside him, with his hand in Will's arm. "We have had fun enough already—not including my ankle, though."

Those bicycles appeared to attract a very good deal of attention at the inn stables. In their comfortable knickerbockers the boys seemed to be unique strangers. At supper the landlady, a fat, comfortable individual, asked them various questions. The hostler and his friend, the blacksmith, strolled close to the little dining-room window, and coolly surveyed Will and Barton as they ate. Presently the landlady, with a resolute, red face, again became visible in the doorway.

From behind her ample back advanced the stout constable of Drentford, and the hostler, and both at once laid hands upon our two terrified lads, with a lusty—"My pris'ners, young gen'l'men, if you please. We have been expecting you a week."

"What in the world is the matter with you?" cried Will,

angrily springing up, and overturning his coffee-cup into the omelette. "We are—"

"Oh, we know!" retorted the official and his help. "If you think we don't, you'd better read your own visitin' kyards that was sent afore you come. There's one of 'em."

Directly opposite, on the wall, was tacked a placard. Its contents were as follows:

"STOLEN! From the B— Freight Depot, September 20th, two new Bicycles, manufactured by —, of Coventry. Supposed to be in the Possession of the Thieves (who were seen loitering about the Depot the Night of the Robbery), two Young Men, aged each about fifteen; one fair, the other dark; the taller one lame, as if from a sprain, and when last seen dressed in dark corduroy knickerbockers. Have probably gone south toward Boston, via Drentford, Lancaster, and Penthurst."

Some other details of this startlingly suggestive publication, and the signature of a well-known Augusta gentleman, completed it.

The boys were thunderstruck. There would be no way of escape at present from the disgraceful imputation. They were supposed to be the thieves of those treacherous bicycles that had trundled them so pleasantly straight into their trap!

If Bart or Will had only been prompter to mention how they came by them, to the first persons met within the precincts of the Ethan Allen! Unluckily, Will had wished to get Barton to the door of the inn without further pain, and the few words he had given the hostler hinted only at ownership.

"We haven't got time to waste in arguing with such as you," said the constable, breaking short the boys' vehement denials and explanations.

"Well, what do you propose to do about it?" inquired Barton, forgetting that the least sensible thing one can do is to lose temper in a dispute with an official. "You say we are the thieves who stole those machines. We say we are not. We have told you all about ourselves. Now prove, please, what you—"

In less than five minutes after this speech, Will and Barton proved to their own certainty that they were marching along the village street, with a disorderly crowd of urchins at their heels. The police justice was out of town for the night. Arrests were rare in quiet Drentford. The affair was now no joke to Will and Barton. They were weary, humiliated, and more outraged at each moment.

"Well, I don't propose to run no risk, asserted Constable Bluebuck, sharply, as he marched the boys away from the Justice's door. "Into the lock-up you both goes, for to-night, I assure *you!*"

That climax of the evening's bewilderment was reached within five minutes. Constable Bluebuck had suffered much from the Drentford lads, who made sport of him and his office. He considered this a good chance to teach his public a solemn lesson, through these very suspicious strangers, of what the law could do to young persons who offended constables.

The little bridewell was new and clean. There were no other prisoners. The boys sat down in the dim little cell and looked into one another's faces.

"Really, Bart, I begin to wish that we had taken that morning train on the Pumpkin Island Railway," said Will, with a smile that was not wonderfully cheerful.

"And I almost think I prefer that two-miles-an-hour express on the Millbridge, that I spoke of," replied Barton, with no smile at all.

On the way to the jail the boys had telegraphed to the Ossokosee House a statement of their uncomfortable case, and begged that Mr. Bunt or Uncle McKay would come to help and identify them. They passed a decidedly poor night, although before morning they were able to laugh a little over the affair and the suspicious mind of Constable Bluebuck.

Hour after hour of daylight passed. Instead of Mr. Bunt or Uncle McKay appearing to scatter the cloud of trouble, a message came from Mr. Hilliard, the hotel proprietor: "Your friends left this evening on a short excursion. Have forwarded telegram. They or I will come at once." Bread and water was a new breakfast menu to Will and Bart. Nor were they released in the morning. It was not until noon that Constable Bluebuck appeared. Strong as ever in the consciousness that he was doing justice splendid service, that worthy man escorted the unlucky friends, holding tight an arm of each, to the Justice's office.

The moment this functionary saw the boys, he supposed that there had been somewhere a very serious mistake. Hardly had he begun his questions, which he did quite politely, when there was a bustle without the door of the crowded little room. Mr. Bunt, Mr. McKay, and a gentleman from the Ossokosee hurried in. Fifteen minutes later the whole unfortunate affair was exploded. Barton and Will were unwilling to have the doughty Bluebuck pay the penalty for his rash vigilance. They left him in a truly pitiable state of mortification, with all the youngsters in the village academy calling to him over the fence of the play ground—for it was recess as the charge was dismissed—"Oh, Jehiel! O-h-h, Jehiel! Locked up two fellows that didn't do anythin'! O-h-h Jehiel!"

That afternoon, Mr. Brunt and Mr. McKay hired a strong team and a man, and drove the rescued ones as far as Penthurst. It was a magnificent day. Will and Bart could now think over their adventure as a joke, and the older gentlemen made all manner of fun of it. The bicycles, by the way, were left in charge of the Justice, after Will had written a letter to the advertisers. The party spent the night at Penthurst, and then rolled on, the whole of the following day, reaching Lancaster safely that evening. Mr. Brunt had been anxious to give the boys this carriage-trip as a little compensation for the unpleasing outsetting upon foot; and Barton was in no condition to walk long distances.

Of course, all the way it had been good-humoredly said, time and again, that the boys' failure to agree upon the two railroads was visited upon their heads. But a most amusing final stroke awaited them. The first thing Mr. McKay did on arrival in Lancaster was to find the new depot, in order to inquire about the next morning's train for Will and Barton. There stood the new station, shining with fresh paint, glittering tiles, and stained windows. But it was shut. "Back to the hotel!" was the unanimous cry.

"The railroad?" said the proprietor, laughing, "Oh! You see, it's marked on the maps as running, and the advertisements are out because we expected it would be doing so three weeks ago. But it isn't; and I suppose the company haven't published the fact about much, because it's only a matter of a week longer. There's been a mistake in the passenger coaches ordered, and the company's had to send all four of 'em back."

"What in the world are people to do who come here to take the cars for Grand Junction?" demanded William, in dismay.

"Oh, we send a stage twice a day to Danielstown, where folks can take the Pumpkin Island line; and there's another the railroad people keep running, till they're ready, to Green Cliff. The Millbridge and Deep Bay comes around through that, you know. What makes you boys look so queer?"

He never knew the cause of the gale of merriment that followed. It was hard to decide which looked more sheepish; but Will and Barton clasped hands, crying, "Whichever you say now, Bart!"—"Just as you like, Will!" But the end of that "dumb quarrel" was that Mr. Bunt and Mr. McKay left them in Lancaster to spend a jolly week together, and go home by the new line to New York, where they found a most polite letter and a checque from the bicycles' owner. So everything did "turn out" to their advantage in the end, and it is doubtful if they ever have a question so obstinately at issue again.

Jehiel Bluebuck is flourishing.